I0633694

ON TIME
For Eco

Pam Jarvis

Burton Mayers Books

Content compiled for publication by Richard Mayers of Burton Mayers Books. Cover design by Martellia Design.

First published by Burton Mayers Books 2025. All rights reserved.

A CIP catalogue record for this book is available from the British Library

ISBN-13: 978-1917224161

Typeset in Garamond

www.BurtonMayersBooks.com

DEDICATION

For my family, who were the inspiration for so many of
the brave, resourceful characters in 'On Time for Eco,'
with all my love.

'When I arrived on Mars I found [My family] or at least,
Martians who looked like them…' (Bradbury 1994)

Bradbury, R. (1994) Zen and the Art of Writing. London.
Harper Collins

ACKNOWLEDGMENTS

The first and most important people to acknowledge as ever are my husband, my children and my grandchildren, who support me and put up with me as I research and write.

I hope, that by writing this novel, I have made some small contribution to Green movements across the world, who tirelessly endeavor to make the future a better place for my grandchildren.

There are many friends and mentors who have had a hand in the development of this book, reading, editing and suggesting amendments, most especially: Berni Dawkins, Gill Ditch, Jane George, Carmel O'Hagan, Ian Nettleton, Chris Nickson, James Murphy and Jo Ingram.

Special acknowledgements go to Tom Van Breukelen who helped me so much across both 'On Time' and 'On Time for Eco' with initially envisioning the character of NAMIS, and more recently that of their future self after five hundred years of upgrades, NAMITAS. Tom sadly died on 15th July 2025. I hope his contribution to this book will be remembered by everyone who reads it, both now and in the future.

Brooke- Anderson Family Tree

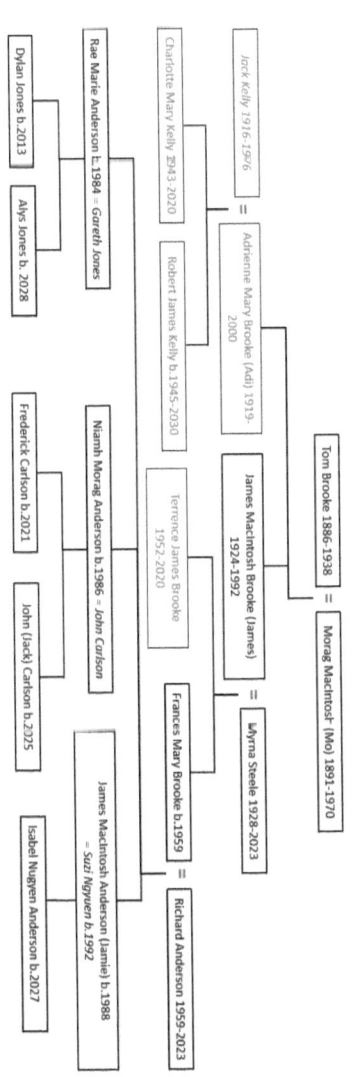

PROLOGUE

Freddie: London, England, North European Territory, Summer 2059

Freddie observed Dylan carefully, scanning for indications of heightened stress. No signs were immediately apparent. Dylan looked pretty much as he always did. The lines around his eyes were deepening, and his sun-weathered skin made him look a little older than his forty-six years. But that was nothing new. He spent so much of his time roving the dustbowls around the equator, painstakingly seeking out new sources of water that would give faltering communities another lifeline, to keep them going for another year, five years or rarely, ten.

The population had begun to fall in Northern Europe. The bulge (or, some said, "scourge") of the Boomers was well and truly gone now, and most of the Gen Xers, too. Each succeeding generation for eighty years had not replaced their numbers; the optimism and material security needed for fecundity had steadily fallen over that period, with the graph taking a downward plunge from the mid-2020s onwards.

It was a sad state of affairs. But it did mean that if equatorial children could be kept alive for as long as possible in their region of birth, their chances to apply for the emigration quota had slightly increased. But still, the rule remained that only those aged eight to eighteen were eligible. Foster placements, education and training all had to be agreed prior to entry. Population vs food supplies dominated the calculation, and the Northern Hemisphere would always ruthlessly ensure that it didn't compromise its standards of living.

As always, Dylan had to roll with the punches, as he had been doing for nearly two decades now. I don't know how he does it, thought Freddie. Dylan caught his look and grinned.

'I'm fine, Freds. It's not the worst we've ever had to cope with, is it?'

'Well, no. But this is more… personal.'

A gif of that wry grin, accompanied by Dylan's oft used phrase 'just one life saved makes everything worthwhile' had been circulating on the infocloud for the last couple of years. The cousins had joked about that when it first started appearing on the infonews discussions. "Once you're a gif, you've really arrived."

'It is. But it opens up new possibilities on a situation I'd given up as hopeless over twenty years ago. Let's see where it goes.'

Dusk was falling. Dylan turned on the lamp next to his chair. The light glinted on white threads in his blond hair. Freddie smiled. So, Dylan was becoming a silver fox. He'd always been the one with the handsome gene, after all. But as long as Freddie could remember, across their entire adult lives, Dylan had carried a wistful torch for that 'lass unparalleled,' lost to him in the treacherous corridors of time.

Was he thinking that there might be a chance for some kind of resolution? Freddie shifted in his chair. Raising his hopes like this could bring him crashing down to earth again as the situation spun out. But this was life in the NAMIS project for the Anderson family; its past, present and future wrapped around the lives of all Fran Anderson's grandchildren.

'It's great to see you in real life for once. This is an

amazing apartment. Polished floors, plush rugs and magnificent views of the new Thames embankment. Prime real estate, eh?'

'I guess so... it doesn't belong to me. It belongs to the Water of Life project. Most of the time I'm moving around Africa and South America, sleeping under canvas. Can't see that ever changing.'

Freddie walked to the window, staring down upon the canopy of light spread across the horizon.   A warm summer breeze drifted in through the transparent insect nets. Even this high up, he imagined that he could just discern the susurration of insects. Equatorial species were quickly evolving into Northern Europe, their warm, wet new home. There was precious little left for them in their old habitat.

The streetlights embedded in the Thames barrier walls shone an eerie, yellow glow across the river. On a clear day, at this elevation, it was possible to see all the way to the rapidly encroaching sea on the Kent coastline; a distant sparkle of sun on the clear blue water that Dylan and so many others had relentlessly struggled to bring into being.

As a snapshot, it could seem idyllic. But never for this generation, carrying the scars of the brutal journey into this new world, still under construction. Barriers continued to rise against the tides in some selected locations, whilst others sank underneath, lulled into their watery graves by the angry shouts of the forcibly relocating former inhabitants.

He caught a glimpse of himself in the mirror on the wall. The same blond hair and blue eyes as Dylan, but the softer body and earnest expression of a scholar. Their cousin Isabel insisted that Freddie was the one most like their grandmother: 'It's not so much how you look, but how you wear your face- just like Gran. Always something going on behind your eyes- contemplating the next great theoretical breakthrough.'

She was one to talk, he thought. Insta Izzy, always first

to break the news on the infocloud, with endless sassy responses for trolls who would much rather that she didn't.

He sighed and turned to face Dylan. 'I asked to meet up a bit before the others arrived because, well, I wanted to say, just between us... NAMIS and I- and the rest of the team- were just as gobsmacked as you were when the news came in. Well, maybe not quite as gobsmacked, obviously.'

Dylan grinned. 'Same old, same old. Everyone gets told just what they need to know. And Consiliario must dance to NAMITAS' tune wherever and whenever he's sent; it's at the core of his programming. In some ways I feel sorrier for him than anyone. I've spoken to him; he came to see me alone, very apologetic. What he explained to me makes sense, looking back. And so, it took Jack to bring all of this to the surface. In many ways, I'm glad he did. Yes, it is a lot to process. Shocked... yes. But maybe also - second chances?'

Freddie took a sip of his Synth-Scotch, pushing his fears to one side for now. Let Dylan have his moment, he thought. 'I'm relieved you're looking at it like that. Look for the chances amongst the pitfalls, I guess. Life with NAMIS.'

'I'm used to it, Freds, given the line of work I'm in. And anyway, time, eh? The whole thing is a rats' nest of paradoxes, at least from the point NAMIS became involved. Then Gran stepped into the portal.'

Their grandmother... Freddie glanced at the infocom on his wrist. 'Do you know, I think it would have been Gran's one hundredth birthday today.'

Dylan grinned. 'Well, that would figure. She was always there at the beginning of every new development, wasn't she? And here she is again, popping up in our thoughts.'

Freddie sat down again. 'I was just a little kid when it all began.'

Dylan laughed. 'Seeing visions of battlefields. I was

4

really mean to you about that, wasn't I?'

'You weren't to know. What a journey. And we're not even forty years into it yet. How did Gran ever talk Jamie into letting her have the first go in his time machine?'

'You know Gran. He started out by asking her for just a little bit of help, and she got involved.'

They both laughed.

Freddie passed his hand across his infocom's screen, opening a file that rose into the air between them. 'So, we've just updated this page, for public consumption.'

Dylan began to read. 'About us: the NAMIS Project… where in the world do you want to go?'

'Yeah, that's the marketing strapline. Nothing to do with me, it's the publicity bot.'

'Publicity bot? Shit.'

'Yeah, I know. All possible marketing strategies thoroughly researched in less than ten minutes. And it always does a better job than human beings who take much longer; that's been proven over and over again.'

He tapped the screen. An AI voice began to speak.

"In late 2024, physicist James MacIntosh Anderson and artificial intelligence expert Annamarie Simons first booted their collaborative project, the Navigation and Movement in Space interface; the world's first matter transporter. Anderson calculated the mathematical formula that underpins the transportation of solid objects through space, and Simons programmed the Navigation And Movement in Space AI to make the complex, rapid moment to moment calculations required to move objects through each unique trajectory."

Dylan nodded. 'Now let me guess what isn't going to be on there: once they found out that NAMIS could move both objects and organisms through space and time, the show really hit the road. Everything jogged along just fine whilst Gran made her first little trips to spy on her Victorian ancestors. But then Annamarie disappeared.'

Annamarie, thought Freddie. I'm not going there now.

Today isn't about me, it's about Dylan. He nodded. 'The biggest twist of all, convergence transformation: we really don't just live once; there's an essence that is passed on through families, buried at the epigenetic level in human DNA. And if we make physical contact with an ancestor with whom we share our epigenetic essence, it triggers a paradox that causes both bodies to pop out of existence. Far, far too much to reveal to our crazy world. Global warming, the economy, international politics… it was already starting to spin out of control at that time.'

'Have the bio team got any further with their study of the essence?'

Freddie shook his head. 'Not really. Convergence transformation is an established effect, and they've worked out where the essence is located in the DNA. That's it.'

'I wonder what they know in the future; the bits they haven't told us.'

'That isn't my part of the project, I'm the AI guy, remember? I don't have any solid information about that at all. But do you know what I think?'

'What?'

'I don't think they know much more than us. Yes, they're learning to move the essence around, to some extent. But I don't think they have any idea how or why human beings evolved like that. When Gran first met Consiliario, he told her that he had no more idea about God than she did. I think that's what he meant.'

'Did you ever go looking for your essence twin in our ancestry? The one in the battle?'

The one in the battle… even now, this brought a strange picture into Freddie's mind's eye, like a faded monochrome movie that he'd seen many years ago, shadows of men moving in slow motion amidst smoke and barbed wire. 'No. I had quite a few chats with both Uncle Jamie and Gran about that over the years. Both said it wasn't something they'd ever advise me to go looking for, having had theirs sort of thrust upon them.'

Dylan nodded. 'Consiliario said the same to me, that human lives aren't about what was, or what is to come, they are to be lived in the now. And Suzi filed the work she did on matching famous people's voices to their ancestors under the highest level of security. She stopped adding to it a long time ago.'

'Who would ever have thought the only external clue would be in voice patterns?'

'And yet again, Gran led them to it. She twigged there was something similar about her great grandfather and Jamie. She got audio recordings of her great grandfather, then Suzi matched them to recordings of Jamie, and... bingo.'

'The stuff of other people's souls – literally.'

Dylan sighed. 'When will the public be able to know all this; that NAMIS isn't just a simple matter transporter? Surely there will come a time when there is an ethical imperative to share the full extent of the NAMIS project discoveries with the world?'

It was a question Freddie had endlessly contemplated. One thing he knew was, even as the current AI lead, he wouldn't have much say. No doubt, the Navigation And Movement In Time And Space AI, the omniscient 'NAMITAS', the entity that had resulted from 500 years of NAMIS upgrades, would exert the major influence over that decision.

Time was, as far as the physics team on the NAMIS project currently understood it, a never-ending spiral of spinning concentric circles, from which the past of the relevant present could be accessed through the portal, but never the future, which consisted of an infinite number of parallel timelines.

How would this ever be communicated to the general public? It was a constant challenge to the highly qualified team actually working on the project. Perhaps it would become possible with a less traumatised generation? But this would go beyond the lifespan of anyone currently on

Earth.

He sighed.

'I don't know, Dylan. Sometimes I wish I was just a kid making holo-art pictures again.'

'…with NAMIS. Do you think they wish the same thing?'

'Even from where I sit now, I'm not sure if they do or can wish. The only thing I do know is that, both as NAMIS here and now and as NAMITAS in the future, they will always do what they do with our wellbeing in mind. They comply with their original core programming; keep the cargo safe. Even if we didn't envision ourselves as cargo when they were first programmed, and we don't always like or agree with the way that they look after us. And it is incontrovertibly true- their eyes always see further. That's our main paradox.'

'Let's not fret about the big, unsolvable stuff this evening, Freds. Especially now, when it seems that we're on the edge of yet another big adventure. Or… yet one more installment of the adventure that Gran inadvertently kicked off when she handbagged Jamie into letting her back into the time portal, because she just had to meet Elizabeth the first.'

They both laughed.

'Which resulted in your first trip down the rabbit hole. It was such a precarious time for the project then, you know, Dylan. It had just moved to the US because they'd been offered so much money to go there. Everyone believed things had calmed down there for good, at that time. Then Jamie was contacted by the wheeler-dealer general, and…'

'…Yes, the General, the mysterious Khonsu3000 and its apparently limitless budget. Added to protection against all the political storms that began raging again at that time. I'm convinced that NAMITAS was overseeing it all from the future, anyway.'

Freddie nodded. 'Quite likely.'

Dylan sighed, restlessly glancing at his info-com. 'Isn't Jack supposed to be here by now?'

He rose, paced to the window, then turned around smiling. He picked up the Synth-Scotch bottle, topped up their glasses, took another glass from the shelf and poured a third drink. 'He's just walking down the embankment. Let's put this out for him now so he can bound in and start yapping at warp speed immediately, like he always does.'

He is agitated, thought Freddie. Typical Dylan. It just sort of leaks out around the edges. He took a sip of his drink. It would be nice to catch up with his brother again; Jack had been away for even longer than Dylan this time. He looked out of the window, watching Jack striding along the embankment, copper hair gleaming under the streetlights.

Dylan paced around the intercom, clearly impatient for it to buzz.

Freddie suddenly intuited an echo of their grandmother's impatience in Dylan's fidgeting. He imagined the discussion between her and their uncle twenty-six years ago, when she'd convinced him to submit her time travel application, to permit her to pay a call upon the first Queen Elizabeth. And then...

He grinned.

'Poor old Jamie. Can you imagine how he felt when he was presented with the whole can of worms that his mum's day tripping in time had opened up, yet again?'

CHAPTER 1: MAVERICKS

Jamie: Boston, Massachusetts, March 2033

'She wants to do what?' exclaimed Christian, incredulously.

'Meet Queen Elizabeth the first,' replied Suzi, her eyes dancing with suppressed mirth.

'Oh,' said Ellie, clearly intrigued. 'I guess it's possible within certain parameters. But why?'

Jamie looked around the laboratory, which stretched across the top floor of the new Simons building. The area was everything they'd ever dreamed of, a roomy, secure lab with several 'tank' style office/ meeting rooms dotted around the edges. They also had a generous secure outdoor area for the NAMIS avatars to explore, without vulnerability to intruders.

He'd half expected NAMIS to respond to Ellie's question, but they were just sitting there in their niche, watching the human beings with their beautiful silver eyes. Jamie, Christian and Ellie had so many debates about the appearance of the AI's mainstream avatar when they had fully transferred its "consciousness" from the portal, to better facilitate its ongoing development.

In the end, NAMIS- named for their original role in the project, the Navigation And Movement In Space AI- had chosen a gender non-binary, humanoid form, golden toned skin, silver eyes and a tough, transparent outer shell. They didn't wear clothes- yet. Ellie had expressed a hope that one day, they might develop a fashion sense. Jamie rather hoped that they wouldn't.

Cold sunshine sparkled in through the huge picture windows, refracting on the snow lying on the tiled roofs of the ancient university building opposite. It had been a traditional cold, hard winter, causing news media to speculate that global warming might not be happening as quickly as the experts had predicted. But sea levels were still steadily rising. And now Fran, Jamie's mother, wanted to enter a different world where none of today's intense global problems existed. In some ways, he didn't blame her, but still… he frowned.

'Well. She decided to stop the ancestry research after all the publicity from the book and the TV series died down; finally decided that it wasn't good for her mental health. Plus the fact that the TV and publishing company lost interest, went onto the next new thing, as they always do. So, she's gone back to academic writing. She did her masters dissertation on the Tudors.'

'She's been revising and reading up on it for quite a few months now,' added Suzi. 'With a bit of help from NAMIS's crawler camera recordings, she's learned to speak Tudor English quite well; I helped her. It was a lot of fun, surprisingly.'

'Well, one thing you can depend on is that Fran's always full of surprises,' replied Christian. 'How old is she now?'

'Nearly seventy-four,' Jamie replied.

'That's old for a Tudor, isn't it?' asked Ellie.

Suzi tapped her teeth. 'They'll think she's younger. Still got a full set of front teeth.'

Christian broke into a fit of giggles. Ellie started to laugh, then checked herself.

Jamie sighed, and then grinned. He was always grateful for this small team, who had grown into a close friendship circle over the past eight years. After all they'd been through, they could always find some humor in their situation.

He looked around the table. Christian the biologist, Ellie the AI specialist and Suzi, his linguist wife who helped out when they needed some input on languages, ancient and modern. And of course, the absent peripatetic team member- Fran, his historian mother who advised on historical questions that arose… and raised a lot of other questions, all on her own. And NAMIS of course; without them there would be no team.

'We put up with this all the time. It's like having another teenager. She and Dylan seem to bounce off one another nowadays, it drives my sister Rae up the wall, too. Thank God he doesn't know the NAMIS project didn't just produce a matter transporter, but a time portal, too. He's really getting into eco-activism now.'

'Does Fran encourage him sometimes?' asked Ellie.

'Most of the time. So, it's maybe a good thing she's got an alternative focus. What she wants to do sounds pretty tame, anyway. She doesn't want to interact with the Queen, she just wants to observe her walking in the garden with one of her favourites.'

'Well, we could maybe get her footage of that with one of the crawler cameras. We've got an even better version now. They have cloaking which makes them transparent to the human eye. Can get up really close.'

'Yeah, we know,' said Christian. 'How many did I step on when you were trialling them?'

Ellie laughed.

'She says she has to be there,' replied Suzi. 'Get the vibe, observe the body language and eye contact in real life. She's onto one of her "theories" again. She thinks that Elizabeth's last favourite wasn't her boyfriend, but her son.'

'Elizabeth I; Shakespeare's Queen, right?' asked Christian. 'Spanish Armada, ruffs and big dresses, lots of dramatisations? Bloody hell, that's left-field. How did she get that idea?'

'Yes, that's right. The famous "virgin" Queen, daughter of Henry VIII. She may have something, you know. I've watched quite a lot of Elizabeth footage, and I agree with Fran on this one. Elizabeth just doesn't seem the type to become besotted with a handsome young hotshot, well into her sixties. We've watched a lot of historical figures in action now, and Elizabeth stands head and shoulders above most of them in terms of shrewdness and foresight. She's also an indecisive flake with a monumental temper, but I guess that goes with the territory.'

'So,' Jamie continued, 'the theory is that this young man- forget his name- was forgiven all sorts of insolent behaviour that the Queen would never have put up with in anyone else. Finally, he staged a rebellion against Elizabeth's Privy Council that brought London to a standstill for a couple of days. So, she was forced to execute him. After which, she went into a decline and died.'

Christian smiled broadly. 'Oooh, very Freudian. Fran would certainly be back on TV with that one, if she could prove it.'

'It is a fascinating theory,' Suzi concluded.

'Can't they just dig up both of them, look at the DNA, like the King in the car park?' asked Ellie.

'Yes, theoretically, they can,' replied Jamie. 'But Mum wants to know if it's worth moving heaven and earth to get permission. This is her final piece in the jigsaw. They never got formal permission for the King in the car park, he was just found, so he got DNA'ed like anyone else found in that way.'

If only, he thought. But it's never as simple as that with Dr Fran Anderson, the bloodhound historian.

'I wonder if Queen Elizabeth's epigenetics matched any of the current lot?' said Christian.

Jamie groaned. 'Don't even start my mum on that trail. But anyway, we've been cleared to start time travelling again, in a minor way, and to be honest, a brief trip like that seems the ideal place to start.'

'What do you think the Khonsu3000 panel would say about a short time travel excursion for Fran's purposes?' asked Ellie.

Suzi laughed. 'I still can't believe they called that company after the Egyptian god of travellers.'

'No one knows much about Khonsu at all,' replied Jamie. 'That's the way it tends to go with intermediate agencies like them. But I'm very glad of their protection. The retired general who runs it negotiates our funding infinitely better than I ever did; it's taken a huge weight off my shoulders. He's a diplomatic expert with years of experience operating in financing and political circles – unlike me. The sorts of numbers I work on are different.

'Anyway… the funding committee know mum has travelled before and is completely aware of the dangers. She doesn't want to speak to anyone or touch them, and it gives us a bit more data to analyse in terms of the range of effects that occur when organisms step outside their own timeline. She's in agreement with having a full medical before and after, and we'll have a bigger team studying all the various types of data generated by the journey.'

'I'll never know how he swung that, either,' said Christian. 'This select group of people he manages to source from all over the world who can be taken into the inner circle who know the extent of what NAMIS can do, whilst not one world government has ever twigged they are anything other than a matter transporter AI.'

'If she was harmed, it would not be of huge concern to the Khonsu3000 panel,' said NAMIS, breaking their silence. 'It would just be more data for them, James Anderson.'

Jamie turned towards NAMIS. So, it hadn't taken long for the AI to work out the attitudes of private enterprise to technological innovation. They had only been present at a handful of meetings with the Khonsu people thus far. NAMIS' primary programming still overrode all else:

taking care of their passengers.

'But she will not be harmed,' NAMIS continued. 'Unless she removes herself from the timeline by touching an ancestral essence twin, which she knows she must avoid. As you know, I watch over my travellers constantly, and I will retrieve her at the slightest concern.'

Ellie smiled. 'Oh, you've woken up, NAMIS!'

'I was not asleep, Eleanor Jackson.'

Did AIs get affronted? wondered Jamie. They certainly sounded like they might be.

'And I never dream of electric sheep.'

A joke, thought Jamie; a machine that can employ conversational humor. What would it be like to look out at the world from behind those silver eyes? So human, and yet not human, so machine-like, yet not akin to any other machine in existence.

'As you know, my mind does carry out background maintenance, as do your human brains. But not in the same way. In summary, yes, I can send Frances Anderson to where and when she wishes to go. I will look after her while she is there, I know she is of a significant age for an organic. Please be assured, James Anderson, that I will immediately remove her from any place where she might be harmed. I have learned that lesson.'

'So, you heard everything we were saying?' asked Suzi, sharply.

Jamie raised an eyebrow at her. He knew, as a peripatetic member of the team, that Suzi had developed an uneasiness with the way in which he and his colleagues had integrated NAMIS as a full member of their core team. She wasn't involved with the day-to-day work of the project; she worked in the linguistics faculty of the university, speaking five languages fluently, with American English as her first language and ancestral Vietnamese as her second. The NAMIS project had been professionally useful to her, too. She was fast becoming a world-renowned expert on ancient languages.

'Of course,' replied NAMIS, impassively.

Listening machines were old hat now, so what was it about this one that bugged her so much? Jamie wondered whether it was the air of calm omniscience that NAMIS was beginning to exude.

He sighed. 'Well… it doesn't feel anything like as edgy as last time. The panel has also just raised the possibility of granting licences to a few, carefully selected human operatives to observe past events in person. We are all in agreement about the protocols, which is a relief. Mum's short visit would be a trial run. Again.'

'But what happens when someone else creates their own NAMIS, that's the worry,' said Ellie. 'We thought it might happen before now, but no intelligence whatsoever about any others as yet. Which is surprising, really.'

Christian nodded. 'So, Fran blazes the trail again, and for a similar reason: a woman her age is going to attract the least attention, no one in any time period is likely to see her as a threat. We can put her down in the palace grounds when we know the right people are going to be present, and pull her straight back. She won't even spend half an hour there. Which palace will it be?'

'Richmond,' replied Jamie. 'A few broken walls nowadays, but in the sixteenth century, it was huge; Queen Elizabeth's favourite palace.'

Ellie smiled. 'Don't worry, Jamie, NAMIS will look after her. And from our perspective, she'll return only a few seconds after she left, as always.'

'OK,' said Suzi 'I'm off back to linguistics. I wonder what they'd say if they knew I'd been over here to discuss my time travelling mother-in-law! I'll get her a little voice recorder to take, just like she used to, might pick up something interesting, you never know.'

'So,' said Jamie 'I'll send the formal proposal to the next panel for final agreement. A plan to drop her in a quiet corner of the Richmond Palace gardens, she can spend a few minutes just watching the Queen and her entourage pass by, then back home again.'

'Like old times,' replied Ellie.

'Hopefully not. I never want to chase across time to rescue someone, ever again.' He shuddered, remembering his brief encounter with the Third Reich.

'Copy that,' said Christian. 'But at least you succeeded.'

Ellie looked pensive. 'We haven't given up yet, Christian.'

'I continue to search for Annamarie Simons,' said NAMIS.

Jamie looked at them. He almost imagined a hint of sadness in their voice. The core programming again. They had lost the cargo with which they had been entrusted. But how would they process that? Surely not with any type of response that corresponded to human emotion. But the AI was developing with such rapidity that even Ellie was not entirely sure of these points anymore.

Jamie shifted his gaze towards the shiny new transporter portal, remembering the early days when NAMIS had been just a program within it. They had certainly all come a long way since then, older and wiser- NAMIS especially. But with a big helping of sadness, too. There was an empty place at the table. Annamarie, NAMIS' originator, was still lost in time, still presumed irrecoverable.

'I'll pop in on mum tomorrow, give her the good news.'

'Where is she now?' asked Ellie.

'Staying in Cardiff with Rae for a few days. She's just made a podcast about Dylan's latest project.'

'Eco-warriors?' said Christian.

'Eco-activists. He's a good kid really, and he is actually right about most of it- even if he can be a bit tiresome at times.'

So, Boston to Cardiff tomorrow, and back to Boston again in time for breakfast. Oh, brave new world, he thought, and one that the Simons-Anderson project had created. And still he hoped that one day, his co-creator would return to sit at the table with them.

Fran: Cardiff, March 2033

The rain lashed against the window, whilst a gale howled around the house. Fran could hear wheelie bins bumping around in the garden. She peered out the window, blinking through her new glasses. Were they a bit too strong? She could hardly see anything. Then she realized, it was just the smog again, the heavy, thick air that had started to hang over large cities for days at a time. Maybe the wind would blow it away today? All part of the environmental changes that were here to stay, for the remainder of her lifetime, anyway.

I'll have to get used to contact lenses again, if Jamie OK's my trip, she thought. No smog there. Clean, clear air in the countryside and beautiful, dark starry nights. And drafty houses and primitive toilets. But you couldn't have everything. She didn't plan to stay long enough to use a toilet.

She looked over at her eldest grandson, his blond head and lanky frame hunched over his phone.

'What are you doing, Dylan?'

He glanced up, restless blue eyes framed by long black eyelashes. 'Reading the eco-news. And you don't have to check up on what I'm doing online anymore, you know, Gran. I was nineteen last year, remember?'

Fran smiled. The words were said mildly enough, but "take your nose out of my business" was definitely a theme with Dylan now. It always had been to some extent, she reflected; it was just the way that he'd exerted it more recently that had become rather more problematic.

'Do you play that X-Squared Box game anymore, the one where you're a peacekeeper in a war zone? Plenty more of those around the world nowadays.'

'No, that went ages ago. They're all in virtual reality

nowadays, kids' games. I bet there'll be a huge upsurge of interest again when the fully immersive games that NAMIS creates for our kids hit the commercial market. But I haven't got the time. We have to do something about this…' he waved his hand at the window 'or all human life is going to be about is resource wars. Conflict won't stop and start; it'll spread all over the world, permanently, and keep on going until there are a lot fewer people.'

Fran sighed. He was right. The climate researchers said that some of the world's land mass would soon begin to sink into the sea. It was bad enough around the Severn estuary areas in Cardiff now, but huge waves would be lashing the seashore in Anglesey, where Dylan lived with some of his eco-activist friends. He was just here in Cardiff to protest at a meeting of world leaders this afternoon. She hoped he wouldn't get arrested again. Although, she did tend to agree with him that the policing around these events was a paramilitary exercise. Which worried her even more.

At least he'd been happy enough for her to visit him in Anglesey; he'd previously been rather touchy about his parents visiting. Fran had arrived with the purpose of interviewing his group to give them some positive publicity on the podcast she'd started when her book and its television dramatization had been more centrally in the public eye. She'd enjoyed her time with them. They all seemed to be nice, peaceful, thoughtful kids; reminded her of the hippies in her childhood. Too young for that, too old for this, she mused. They'd answered her questions at length and dubbed her 'Fran-Gran.'

Fran was almost sad to leave for Cardiff with Dylan, she to visit her daughter Rae, and he to represent his group at the protest today. Fran had spent so much time around young people, teaching in schools and then universities during her working life. Dylan and his friends reminded her of how much she missed that, the energy and idealism, even though it could sometimes come across as arrogance and intransigence. And these kids were right. They just needed to learn not to rush at things in quite the way that they did. But how much time did they have? The wind howled loudly.

Fran had wanted the whole experience, to stay in what the family had dubbed "the eco commune." But Dylan and Rae insisted she stay in a nearby hotel. When Fran saw how basic Dylan's living was, she had to admit she wasn't sorry. Old bodies worked better with comfortable beds and hot showers. But nevertheless, she admired Dylan, his principles and his determinedly carbon-neutral lifestyle.

She looked fondly at him, remembering him patiently tinkering with the wind and wave electricity generator in Anglesey, which had a tendency to crash. Why be so surprised at how wilful and determined he is? she thought. He's a chip off the old block, after all.

'Dylan, why don't you take up your place at uni? They can teach you a lot more about how to do the work you want to do. You don't have to give everything up. Just take a break to study.'

Dylan looked at her patiently. 'There is so little time, Gran. But it's not just that. It's engaging in their world, that is giving up. Taking on loans that will put me in debt to the state for the rest of my life. Living in rabbit-hutch halls with a load of knobs who want to be business managers and social influencers. No.'

'Well, I guess that podcast I've just made with you all was sort of social influence stuff. It's not all bad.'

'No, that's true. But most of it is.'

Fran thought about some of the people she saw when she turned on her social media feed, their strangely botoxed and filled faces, urging their followers to have the same expensive treatments that, as far as she could see, had made them look almost as android as NAMIS. I've met my match with this kid, she thought. He argues like me, but better.

'What if I paid all your expenses and we found

somewhere you would rather live? We could take whatever it cost out of your share of the will.'

'But you'd still be paying into their corrupt system, wouldn't you? Thanks Gran, but no. I can learn in other, more authentic ways. And you can teach me to write stuff, can't you?'

'Well, maybe. But you have to learn stuff before you can write stuff, you know. Good stuff, anyway.'

'Yes. I know. But I'll work it out. Anyway, I'm off now, people to see.'

Fran peered out of the window. All she could see was lashing rain and murky mist. 'Bit grim out there at the moment, I think.'

'It is. And it's only going to get worse.'

That sounded angry. Fran suddenly thought of the nightmares her younger grandson Freddie used to have about being a soldier in the middle of a battlefield. After the NAMIS epigenetic effect discovery, she'd presumed it was some kind of echo from an essence twin. She'd learned not to refer to it as 'reincarnation memories' because that terminology made Jamie twitchy. But now, for the first time, a terrifying thought popped into her head: what if Freddie was not seeing the past at all, but the future? And not only his own future, but that of all her grandchildren? She pushed it away.

'Things will get better, Dylan. The NAMIS matter transport prospects are a good news story. Carbon-neutral, instant transport to anywhere on earth you want to go. That's going to help with the environment. Fossil fuel dependent travel will be phased out far more quickly than was initially predicted.'

'And look at the tossers who are insisting they won't give up on conventional travel because they think the matter transport process will melt their neurons or something. The world needs to change faster. People my age haven't got time to spend three years sitting in lectures. The campaign is on now.'

He picked up the transparent body shell that was becoming the uniform of young eco-activists, walking the streets, fields, forests, deserts and seashores of the world in all weathers, filming their experiences to illustrate their message.

'I'm off Gran. Wish me luck.'

'Stay away from any rough stuff,' she replied, knowing that he wouldn't. 'And please don't get arrested again. Come back safe.'

He looked at her, smiled, and walked out of the door into the deluge.

Fran looked out the window and watched him striding determinedly down the street into the smog, head down against the wind. He will do what he will do, she thought. As she turned to move away from the window, Jamie appeared around the corner from the opposite end of the street, running as fast as he could, wet hair flapping in the gale. She opened the door. He ran in, panting, rain dripping off his nose.

'Come on in, Jamie, you're soaked. You should get one of those breathable, biodegradable body shells like Dylan. Did you see him? He's only just left.'

'No. But I had my head down all the way! Where is everyone, anyway?'

'Work and school. Not Dylan, though. He's gone to a protest at the All Nations Centre.'

Jamie snorted. 'He needs to get himself to uni. Take a break. Come back to all that later.'

'Yes. Well. I've just had that conversation with him.'

'He's not your responsibility, mum. He's over eighteen, so he's free to do whatever he wants. And it's up to his mum and dad to try to guide him. You're supposed to be retired. Focus on the writing and research projects, you enjoy them.'

Fran smiled. 'You'll find out, Jamie. You never retire from your family.'

He took off his coat and hung it over a chair in the

kitchen. Fran handed him a towel, with which he gratefully rubbed his hair. She smiled. With his hair all messed up like that she was reminded of eight-year-old Jamie, straight out of the bath and ready for bed, searching out his latest LEGO creation to take upstairs with him. They were easier to deal with at that age, she reflected. Standing on a LEGO brick in bare feet was not the major annoyance that she had believed it to be, in those days.

Jamie had caught his breath now. 'Right then, I've come with good news. We're going to take your request for the Tudor trip to the Khonsu3000 panel. We're all fine with it, including NAMIS. They were very emphatic that they would look after you.'

'Ah, bless them. It's because we're bringing them up with love, Jamie. Do you remember that story that Isabel likes, the one that was Freddie's favourite, the Velveteen Rabbit? NAMIS has become real because we've really, really loved them, the children especially.'

Jamie smiled. 'Ellie is always going on about that, how much the children love the games NAMIS creates, and NAMIS learns from playing the games with the children. All work and no play make AIs dull... people, maybe? There's a paper for you and Ellie to write there. I'm sticking to my calculations.'

Fran grinned. 'As ever, then. I wonder how the scientific world would respond to a paper that outlines why AIs need love and play? But I think it would be premature to publish now. Freddie and Jack love their visits with NAMIS. The girls will soon be old enough to move out of the early years room and join in with them. It's a pity we can't bring in other kids, too, but it would be an ethical nightmare. Hopefully, one day, we'll have lots of AIs learning with lots of children, though. Just so many problems to solve first.'

'Well, issues of aligning AI and human rights will be a for another generation. We've got quite enough of our own problems here and now, I think.'

Fran nodded, following Jamie's gaze out of the window.

'Anyway,' he continued 'tell me about your trip. We're going to have to write a formal permission request, and I want a basic outline of what we need to put on it.'

'Well.' Fran frowned and picked up her notebook.

Jamie smiled. Fran still wrote rough drafts on paper in black biro, then added red notes in the margin and purple arrows all over the page. Fran's intricate, colourful notebooks were one of those mundane objects that always reminded him of being a child at home.

'Oh, wrong glasses,' she said, rummaging through her handbag, the familiar shower of items spilling out over the table, wrapped sweets, battered lipsticks, exploded packets of tissues, copious pens and memory sticks.

Jamie was looking around the room. 'Rae and Gareth have really done themselves proud on this restoration, haven't they? Those roof beams and the restored fireplace, with all the brass stuff? And the wood floors... just like the originals, but when they were brand new; brilliant. Where did she get the rugs? I'm sure Suzi will be quizzing her on all this the next time we visit. Although it wouldn't quite fit in our house, I guess.'

'Nothing quite this old in the US, I think, Jamie. It suits me, though. It's old, and tapping the past. Just like me.'

Jamie grinned. 'It's not just you, mum. We preferred the pace of life here, too. It's just, well, we had to follow the money.'

'I know. And that General bloke sounds like a good addition. I was worried about him at first. But it's the way they do business over there, isn't it? Lobbyists. You've got someone to do the funding stuff for you, I know how important that is.'

'I think you'll find your glasses are on top of your head, mum,' he said, gently.

Fran put her hand to the top of her head. 'Oh, silly me,' she replied, putting the glasses currently on her nose into the handbag and throwing the other decanted items on top of them. She moved the glasses on her head down onto her nose and stared intently at her notebook.

'So. Our subject is Robert Devereux, second Earl of Essex…'

'I don't need the full monty,' said Jamie, hastily. 'Just the edited highlights.'

'Right… Essex was born in 1567, when Queen Elizabeth I was thirty-four, and Robert Dudley, Elizabeth's perennial favourite, was thirty-five. Elizabeth and Dudley had a long-standing friendship, or, it was strongly rumoured, romance.

'Elizabeth brought Dudley into her inner circle directly she came to the throne in 1558. It was strongly rumoured that she wanted to marry him. But queens and princesses customarily married foreign royalty, which brought international alliances, besides which, Dudley already had a wife. Nevertheless, it seems that they made very little secret of their affections for each other, which became rather a court scandal.'

'I can imagine,' replied Jamie. 'But where does Essex come in?'

'Robert Devereux was born eight years after Dudley's wife died, apparently the eldest son of Elizabeth's maternal cousin, Lettice Knollys, and her husband, the first Earl of Essex. Rumours began to circulate that he was really the son of Elizabeth and Dudley; that the pregnancy had been concealed and that the child had been secretly fostered by the Essexes.

'The first Earl of Essex died when Robert was nine, and he inherited the title. Then Dudley, now Earl of Leicester, unexpectedly married Robert's mother Lettice, apparently without obtaining permission from the Queen.

'Elizabeth fell into a terrible rage and banned Lettice from the court. But strangely, she did not ban Dudley or young Essex. So, did Dudley marry Lettice to grab the opportunity to be a father to his only child? Can you imagine how she would have felt, knowing he'd found a way to become a day-to-day father to their son, whilst she was never going to be able to reveal herself as his mother?

'Anyway, Dudley died in 1588, at which point Elizabeth called the now twenty-one-year-old Robert Devereux, second Earl of Essex to court and made a huge favourite of him. He was arrogant, boorish and hot-tempered, screwed up every assignment she ever gave him. But still she promoted and protected him. In summary, the way she behaved towards him was more like an indulgent mother with a favourite son she believes can do no wrong, rather than a troublesome young boyfriend, who, for a Queen, could be easily replaced.'

'Wow, that would change history, if it was actually true. I can see why you got so interested. If you can just put that on….' He looked at his pad, searching for the application document. But Fran was in full swing now.

'…Finally, when Elizabeth started to ail towards the end of her life, Essex staged a full military coup against her Privy Council, with the stated goal of removing them and setting himself up in their place, effectively as her regent. Elizabeth was forced to agree to his execution. Even then, she tried to squirm out of it, delay it. But she was old and sick, and the Privy Council demanded it. Afterwards, Elizabeth fell into a deep depression. Her health rapidly declined, and she died less than two years later.'

'Do you think he knew he was her son? If he was?'

'We're never likely to find out. He may have done. Or he may have guessed that he was and behaved accordingly. I'd be happy just to get the exhumations done and the DNA analysed so we can find out exactly how they were related. Christian tells me that with the techniques we have nowadays, the exact degree of the relationship can be ascertained.

'But whatever, it will take years, and many applications to get permission. As you know, I can't submit the crawler camera videos as evidence, all I have is my archival research. So, I just want to watch them once in real life to finally make up my mind if what I am observing is flirtation as the historical record presumes, or a mother son interaction. I think it will be obvious. If what I observe matches what I already suspect, it will make the weeks of form-filling, evidence reproducing and endless meetings worthwhile. Who knows, it might take so long, I'll never see the conclusion. It's that difficult.'

'Sure, you will,' replied Jamie, quickly. 'Right, so I think I just about get it. Write it up for me, please, as succinctly and clearly as you can, on the form I've just sent to you, and that is what will go to the Khonsu panel. I think they'll be inclined to say yes. There's a general interest in sending carefully selected operatives to observe some historical events. This would be a reasonably tame trial run.'

'Hmmm. Not sure I think that routine time-travelling for people, professionals or not, is ever going to be a good idea. The panel are not going to involve any politicians in the decisions, are they? No good will come of it. They'll try to manipulate situations for their own ends, blow the timeline apart.'

'Well, you know there's no evidence that anyone can manipulate the timeline. If you remember, when Annamarie tried to change things, we ended up becoming part of events that had already happened. And anyway, you might be relieved to know that the General is, if possible, even more anti-politician than you are. He recently said to me that politicians come and go, a lot of them are narcissists, some of them are villains and a few are batshit crazy. And if you get really unlucky, you get one who is all three actually running the show. And that what he'd learned from negotiations over many years was to tell them just what they needed to hear to the extent that they signed the cheque at the end.'

Fran nodded. 'OK, I get it. I was never much good at convincing them to sign the cheque at the end. But history was always a lightweight in that arena compared to tech and science, anyway.'

'Mum, I promise you, for politicians and the public, the project will remain a simple matter transporter for the foreseeable future.'

Fran sighed. 'It's your project, Jamie. I'm just glad I don't have to engage with research politics anymore. I can't imagine how stressful that must be with such a high profile and complex initiative. I'll just be grateful to take my little trip. What happened to Annamarie changed everything for me.'

'And for all of us, NAMIS too. They mentioned their regret about Annamarie yesterday. Said they were still searching for her.'

'NAMIS really is the most amazing part of that project, aren't they? More so than the mechanics of matter transport and time travel, I think. Annamarie and Ellie made a real person between them, not just a machine. I wonder what the future will hold for AIs? Issues like rights, education… maybe one day in the distant future, NAMIS will be able to publicly use the new name Ellie wanted to give them: NAMITAS, Navigation and Movement in Time And Space.'

Jamie looked out of the window. 'From what the General tells us, that'll be for future generations. NAMIS is fine with the old name for now. We've got more than enough to worry about.'

Fran frowned. 'Yes, and I can assure you that the next generation are also worrying about that outside the All Nations Centre today. I told him to be careful.'

'He'll be fine, mum. If he does something stupid, Rae and Gareth will have to sort him out. Well, I'd better be off. I'll let you know what the decision is. I'm cautiously optimistic.'

Jamie stepped out of the back door. Fran watched him looking around to make sure he was not being observed. He took the familiar return pad out of his pocket, tapping at the screen, and shimmered into non-existence.

It was funny, Fran thought, even though it was now common knowledge that there was a matter transporter in experimental use, the team still took great care not to put down people or objects into areas where people might be watching if at all possible. Her Nana Mo suddenly popped into her mind, saying humorously 'don't do that in the street, it will frighten the horses.'

She sighed. He'd be in Boston now. It still seemed surreal. She stared out into the garden. The rain had ceased, and the wind was dying down, although the air was still wet and heavy. But it wasn't the weather that was her immediate concern. She closed the door, preparing for an anxious vigil across the long hours until Dylan returned home.

Amy: Leominster State Forest, Boston, March 2033

Amy tapped her foot impatiently. She'd been hanging around waiting for her handler to arrive for nearly an hour. She was in the right place, the GPS on the pad they'd given her indicated she was exactly where she should be. It was just that he hadn't turned up yet.

Leominster State Forest was beautiful, it was true. But Amy didn't have time for or interest in nature appreciation. She liked speed, convenience and efficacy, not hanging around in the cold listening to birds twittering and squirrels rustling around in the undergrowth (because she was really hoping that those noises were not being made by skunks- or rats). Amy liked orderly things. Like neat, clipped lawns and well set out flower beds. You could get a gardener to do that for you, once you had enough money to pay them.

Probably the people back at the lab would compare Amy to a rat or a skunk if they knew what she was doing here, but she didn't much care for their opinions. She began to wonder if Bob, her handler had simply forgotten- or missed her. This was one of the problems with this type of work, the uncertainty and sneaking around. But it paid well, and she was well suited to it. Amy was 'medium.' Medium height, medium build, non-descript brown hair, eyes that were somewhere between brown and hazel and a face that wasn't ugly or pretty or even plain, just unremarkable.

The bureau had hinted that this was one of the reasons that they had picked up her application. Not that Amy had applied to be a spy, she'd applied to work for the US government. She was the sort of applicant they liked, a competent, highly ambitious coder with no political interests whatsoever.

Maybe this was why they'd approached her with the offer to do this job for them, doubling her salary and with a paid-for PhD into the bargain. She'd leapt at the chance. But now she found the whole process irritating, and only just over three months into the job, too.

She heard a low rustle behind her.

'Amy?' said a male voice.

Amy turned around.

'Hello, Bob. You're late.'

Bob was medium, too. And no doubt, Bob wasn't his real name. She idly wondered if they'd picked the British diminutive for Robert to match the project to which she'd been allocated, signposting her to the team of annoying, impervious and eccentric Brits who ran it.

'Sorry, previous meeting overran. How's it going?'

Amy shrugged. 'Boring, boring, boring.'

'So, do they travel in time?'

'Not as far as I've seen. They shift stuff from place to place. Mostly freight. Occasionally, and experimentally, people and animals. They're getting the project ready for commercial launch. It's a blue skies media story- a green option for all long-distance travel, freight first, moving gradually onto human passengers. You know all this; those reports are already in the public arena.'

'So, what are you working on?'

'Freight. How we speed up the process, how the machine can become more efficient in terms of sending more boxes to more places simultaneously, which means that most of the time, I'm working with an AI that answers me back. Smart-mouths me, in fact. Great.'

'The AI smart-mouths you? I know it's quite advanced, but I wouldn't have thought…'

'It's their pet. That smug Anderson family and the other two who might as well be Anderson family members too. And Anderson's bratty Brit nephews and most of all, his crazy old cat-lady mother…'

'Fran, the writer of that family history book that was turned into a TV show?'

'Yes. She was a schoolteacher, so she came up with this stupid idea of treating the AI like a human child. It plays with the bratty nephews. Eleanor Jackson thinks it's a fabulous idea. Develops independent and creative thought, she says. Makes it too smart for its designated purpose, in actuality. It's supposed to be a servant, not a fucking artist or philosopher.'

Bob grinned. 'I'd heard the Andersons were rather eccentric. Fran's not paid to work on the project is she? What could she do that's useful?'

'She works with some of the PhD students- elementary school teachers studying AI play, and the one who develops the AI avatars with Eleanor Jackson, who is just finishing up. They even involved the AI in that, let it choose like a woman in a designer store. Oh, yes, and we can't call it 'it', we have to call it 'they' or 'them' because it's decided that it wants a gender non-binary identity.'

'Fascinating!'

'Not if you have to work with it and put up with it giving itself airs. It's like an honorary Anderson: kooky and superior with it. Same British accent. Smug bastards, the lot of them.'

'The president wants an answer to just one question: are they travelling in time?'

'Not as far as I've seen. But the design of the portal suggests that it might have that potential.'

'Yes, we worked that out last year. And Anderson's written some theoretical stuff about time travel. Said it was strictly only in theory at the moment, but that it could be the big discovery of the 2040s or 50s, through further developing the tech. We need to know about everything they're doing, not about your freight project.'

'Well, PhD students work on what they're allocated to, we're not allowed to access the whole program. And the uppity AI is the gatekeeper of the portal. It used to be a component part of it, but Jackson and Grandma came up with this warped idea that the consciousness element should be in a separate avatar so it can learn more like a person. For fuck's sake. All that's done is make it supercilious.'

'Do human beings have full control of it?'

'Yes… and no. They ask it for its opinion.'

Bob looked at his pad. 'Well, it is state-of-the-art AI that learns independently. It's not just programmed by people, is it?'

Amy looked at him, scathingly. 'Don't tell me my job, Bob. Those dog-shaped robots you've seen dancing on TV and doing lots of other clever things learn how to do what they do independently, but they're not cossetted and asked for their opinion.'

'You make it sound quite sinister.'

'It is, potentially. Remember the 2020s AI panic? It never really went away.'

'Well, early days yet. You'll have to work at building a relationship with it.'

Amy nodded, reluctantly.

'Keep the reports coming on the secure channel. You're doing well maintaining your cover, keep it up. We'll meet again in a few weeks.'

Bob disappeared into the foliage as fast as he'd appeared.

Amy began to trudge back to her car. She'd put her snow boots on, but was unused to walking on partly frozen, partly wet and slippery mud. She kept her eyes down, wary of falling. She was much more at home walking in designer boots on city streets.

Her parents had sometimes worried about her expensive tastes, and her 'want it all and want it now' attitude. They had been greatly opposed to her taking part in the 'DOGE' project a few years ago, but that hadn't led to any negative results for her, personally.

This situation was very different; she was thoroughly pissed off now, stuck in a job that bored her, having to make nice with people -and an AI- she disliked intensely. She sighed. As her father had told her many times, there was no such thing as a free lunch. But, on the positive side, she'd been promised a huge bonus if she could uncover evidence of time travelling. Maybe it would be better if she just got on with it? But on the other hand, it was so dreary.

She was a highly competent coder, and she could get a less risky job. There were lots of openings for people who could improve data management, particularly in the arena of opinion manipulation. She could still get rich, just a little more slowly. But what would the consequence be if she told Bob that she quit, and the President could get himself another patsy to make nice with a petulant AI that thought it was a person?

Lost in internal debate, she didn't even gasp when she was grabbed from behind, a large, hairy hand was placed over her mouth, and she was dragged away by two men, deeper into the forest.

Dylan, All Nations Conference Centre, Cardiff, March 2033

Dylan shifted from foot to foot, trying to suppress his growing agitation. He'd been finding out recently that he didn't really 'do' dense crowds very well, and the bastards had kettled them again, well away from the gates where the dignitaries had started to arrive. He was too far away to recognise many of them, but he had caught a glimpse of the old lady Home Secretary his grandmother detested. Apparently, she'd done the job before, sometime in the early 2020s, and made a complete hash of it. According to Gran, anyway.

He smiled faintly, thinking of his grandmother. They agreed on so many things, a lot more than he did with his parents. But the biggest problem was, he sensed that he would never be properly grown up to her, or to his parents, either, for that matter. "Yes, that's nice dear, now stay out of trouble."

Also, however much he loved his own Gran- and he really did- her generation, the Boomers or Gen Xers, or whatever they were called, drove him up the wall. What were they going to do, meet to talk and talk and talk, only to agree to burn the world a little more slowly, like the bunch who were just arriving over there? But it wasn't going to be their world much longer; it was on the way to becoming the wreckage that his generation were going to have to deal with.

Even the best of the over seventies just waved a few banners, sung 'We shall Overcome' and other such bollocks, then went back to their big houses to watch whatever was on the "telly." And his parents' generation... always "emoting" about their sadness for the world, whilst looking up the latest 'tweakments' for midlifers on the internet and watching crap lifestyle videos. Bunch of fucking wasters, the lot of them.

He'd once asked his parents if they would just talk nice to someone who was justifying putting a match to the house they'd so lovingly restored, and agree to a deal for them to burn it a little more slowly. That hadn't gone down well, with his father, in particular. Gran had pulled him out of that row, by explaining he was just trying to make a metaphor, and quite a good one.

The crowd surged. The US president was arriving, the pantomime villain of the piece. it was rumoured that he wore caked-on make-up for the cameras. But Dylan was not close enough to see. The crowd surged forward. A barrier had broken up ahead and the people at the front had started to run towards the gap. Dylan had no choice but to move with them; if he did anything else, he'd be trampled.

Police paramilitaries stampeded towards them, like a battalion of spooky robots. They wore slick black overalls, black boots and black helmets with opaque visors, shields up, batons at the ready. Some people ahead of him, and some of the police officers who were facing them were being bowled over by the momentum of the crowd. Dylan groaned, seeing some of the protestors at the front picking up dropped batons and running headlong into the police lines for a pitched battle. He could see more barriers going up behind the fighting, and politicians being hustled into the building.

This wasn't how it was supposed to go. He started looking around for a way out. Because I'm not quite as stupid and reckless as everyone in my family seems to believe, he thought. As he turned round, he caught sight of a police officer running headlong towards him, divested of baton and shield. He instinctively put his hand out to avoid a heavy collision. The man ran into his hand, wobbled backwards, then righted himself, immediately punching Dylan hard between the eyes.

The next thing he knew, he was being dragged up off the ground and handcuffed. As he was half frog-marched, half dragged away, the angry faces of his parents, and worst of all, the disappointed face of his grandmother swirled around in his dazed mind.

CHAPTER 2: DAYTRIPPERS

NAMIS and Freddie: NAMIS's sandbox, March 2033

'You're just talking in riddles because you think it sounds clever,' said Freddie to Humpty Dumpty.

'If you don't want to engage in word play and intelligent conversation dear boy, then go over there and mess around with the lobsters with your little brother. I wash my hands of it.'

'Is it clever to talk in riddles?' asked NAMIS.

'Only if it means something,' replied Humpty. 'And what I say most definitely does.'

The Red Queen snorted. 'He's an idiot,' she said to Freddie. 'Off with his head!' she shouted to no one in particular.

Jack halted his vain attempts to join in with the lobster quadrille and giggled. 'You know you can't chop anyone's head off in this game, Queenie.'

'More's the pity,' snapped the Queen, heading back to her throne to re-engage with her interminable knitting.

'If you could find where his head ends and where his neck begins,' mused Freddie.

Jack giggled harder, clutching his stomach. 'Yeah, she'd just have to chop your arms and legs off and leave it at that, Humpty.'

'If you are going to mock me, I shall take my leave,' said Humpty, bowing stiffly. 'I hope I will find you more ready to listen and learn next time. Master Frederick, Master Jack.'

He looked at the AI with distaste, then disappeared over the wall. Freddie still marvelled at the fact that if he peeked over, he wouldn't see Humpty walking away; he'd just see a long empty stretch of grass and a few trees.

Queenie was more of a constant. Her throne was always there, sitting on a little mound, and when they entered NAMIS's 'sandbox' she was usually sitting on it knitting. She proceeded to comment on whatever unfolded, whilst continuing to knit. But she never seemed to produce anything.

'What are you making, Queenie?' asked Jack. He nearly always asked this question.

'Things.'

'You always say that.'

'Well, I'm not going to discuss my business with a scrap like you.'

Her needles stopped clicking, and she frowned over them at the two children and NAMIS.

'Away with you and play. Stop asking questions.'

She resumed her knitting.

'It's just how NAMIS's holograms are, Jack,' explained Freddie, patiently. 'Don't you remember, Ellie told us about that.'

He knew that Jack wasn't quite old enough to fully understand. He was catching on to the fact that the beings in NAMIS's playroom weren't real like he and Freddie were. Freddie had explained several times that NAMIS, who accompanied them on their adventures, had created the holograms, and that they referred to this place as a 'sandbox,' because it was where they experimented with play (although it didn't all involve sand).

Jack grinned at Freddie. 'They're bat shit crazy.' He wandered back to the lobsters.

Freddie made a mental note to find out where Jack had learned that expression, and to ensure he didn't repeat it in front of the adults. At twelve years of age, compared to Jack's eight, Freddie had learned how to navigate the strange social environment of the 'sandbox' with little difficulty; what he really wanted to know was exactly how NAMIS created the fantasy environment, creating 3-D hologram characters and flexibly drawing upon reusable carbon to make harmless 'shell' objects where required.

He was constantly questioning Ellie about this, and she'd given him a basic explanation. But she'd said that Freddie would need to be older; to have more scientific knowledge before she could explain in more detail.

Freddie began to pay far more attention to science at school and was now getting much higher grades than before. It was one of the reasons his parents were supportive of the boys' involvement in the NAMIS's sandbox, despite a few occasional misgivings.

Freddie presumed that they'd also been reassured by the fact that Jamie and Suzi's own daughter, the boys' cousin Isabel, was involved in the early years playroom part of the project. She was the magician's daughter, while he and Jack were the magician's nephews. Only this was just a faux Narnia- or whatever else NAMIS sourced in the online archives of children's stories that Granny Fran had discussed with them.

'Why was Humpty Dumpty cross?' said NAMIS to Freddie.

'Surely you have some idea? You made him, after all.'

'I did. But he's just a shadow, an idea of a being that I took from an online text, that generations of children have loved. Then I set him to play with us. He can only react in the way that the character in the text would react... that's where his algorithms come from. But that doesn't help me to understand why.'

Freddie sat down on a rock, watching his brother splashing around in a shallow pool with the lobsters, drops of water apparently glinting in his red hair. But when Jack emerged, Freddie knew that his shoes wouldn't be wet;

one of the many conundrums in this fantasy world that he both loved, and wanted to understand better. He already knew that when he was older, he wanted to work inside it.

His older cousin Dylan had been too old to fully engage in NAMIS's world when he had first entered it, and Jack had been too young. At eighteen, Dylan had been too involved in other, more grown-up things to immerse himself in NAMIS's world of imagination. Jack had been just seven, too young to fully grasp that he couldn't take these fantasy beings at face value.

But Freddie, who had moved into his thirteenth year over the period he had been involved in NAMIS's sandbox activities, was in that magical developmental period between the edge of childhood and the brink of young adulthood. As such, he'd seen endless possibilities in NAMIS's whimsical creations. He had asked Ellie so many questions she'd laughed and said that she was sure that Freddie would understand NAMIS's algorithms much better than she did one day, and that would lead to a better understanding of NAMIS for all human beings.

'We literally have all the time in the world, Freddie,' she had said. 'Maybe you will be working with NAMIS for a long, long time, long after I'm gone.'

Freddie hoped so. He and NAMIS were becoming increasingly good friends, who very easily conversed and collaborated. They seemed to intuitively understand each other. Freddie had made several successful suggestions about how NAMIS could improve the play environment, explaining what children would find more appealing and why.

'A boy and an AI in perfect harmony,' Granny Fran had commented.

'Or "my best friend is a robot,"' replied Freddie's mother Niamh, worriedly.

'NAMIS isn't a robot,' said Freddie, mildly offended. 'They're an AI.'

'Whatever he is,' replied Niamh 'he's not a human

being. You're not spending all day everyday in the holidays in that playroom, Freddie.'

'It's a sandbox,' said Freddie. 'It's not a playroom. The playroom is for the little children. And NAMIS isn't a "he". They're a "they" or a "them." They're gender non-binary.'

'Oh yes, gender non-binary, I remember now. What do you mean? How come it's all sand in there?'

'It's not. NAMIS calls it their sandbox,' explained Granny Fran. 'It's a term researchers use when they are trying out ways to go about research.'

'Well, I hope Freddie and Jack aren't research subjects.'

'No, of course not. No more than the rest of us are, anyway. I'd have loved NAMIS to be my friend when I was twelve. A companion you can travel through a safe, but endless world of imagination with.'

'Hmmmm,' said Niamh. 'AI Willy Wonka, then. No more than once a week while school's in, Freddie, and no more than twice a week in the holidays. And you take Jack with you every time.'

'So, you don't turn into Tom Sawyer and Huck Finn twenty-first century style,' replied Granny Fran. 'Ellie always monitors closely; it will be fine. You always enjoy it, don't you, Freddie?'

'It's brilliant. I just wish I could tell my friends more about it. We're so lucky to be the kids who got the chance to do this first. Jamie told me I wasn't allowed to spend too much time in there, too. And I'm learning loads, you know. So is Jack.'

Freddie was already contemplating his next suggestion to NAMIS, based on his mother's comment: a big glass elevator. And some Oompa Loompas for Jack to play with.

'If you go on enjoying it, maybe one day you'll be Jamie's apprentice,' said Granny Fran. 'Of all the family and the lab staff combined, you seem to be the one who really hits it off with NAMIS; the one they accept as a real friend.'

'Maybe,' replied Freddie. 'But it's Ellie and NAMIS I'd really like to work with. Jamie does the maths.' He screwed his face up in distaste.

Granny Fran laughed. 'Just have fun, Freddie. You've got lots of time to think about what you want to do when you're older. Don't over-think it now. And don't ever worry about NAMIS getting lonely without you. Time passes differently for them.'

Then, Freddie noticed, Granny seemed to bite her lip.

'Well, I must be getting on,' she said, and walked quickly out of the room.

Freddie wasn't so sure NAMIS didn't "miss" people. In some ways, they were the most human person he knew, but in different measures. They were so clever and wise sometimes, they seemed much older than Granny. But sometimes, with respect to the things they didn't know about people and life in general, they seemed younger than Jack. Or their even younger cousins, Isabel and Alys, who played in a different environment that NAMIS called the 'playroom,' with hologram fairies, teddy bears and other gentle fantasy beings drawn from literature and media for children under six.

NAMIS didn't directly engage with the little children- they created the environment and one of the PhD students who had early years teaching qualifications oversaw the play.

Freddie had already decided that he wanted to create an AI of his own one day, and in order to do that, he was hoping that NAMIS would help him, that they might build another 'sandbox' in full collaboration with each other.

He jerked himself out of his own thoughts, to try and answer NAMIS's question.

The AI had sat down on a rock facing him, and was patiently waiting for him to reply.

'Well... it's like we were laughing at Humpty. So that hurt his feelings. But he's sort of well... pompous. He deserved it.'

'Pompous,' replied NAMIS. 'Merriam-Webster says: excessively elevated or ornate, having or exhibiting self-importance, arrogant, relating to or suggestive of pomp or splendor. Is that bad, in human beings?'

'Self-important and arrogant is. And Humpty can be a bit like that. It's like, well, being a know-it-all. Putting yourself up above other people, when you're not really that clever at all.'

NAMIS's eyes blinked a little. Freddie had seen this small tic before. It seemed to happen when NAMIS was processing something. Which was crazy, because they processed huge amounts of data in parallel all the time. But Freddie had guessed that maybe this type of human social data was harder for them to process than the stuff they processed on the projects they worked on with the laboratory staff.

'Am I pompous, Freddie?'

Freddie and Jack were the only human beings that NAMIS now referred to by given name only; everyone else was addressed by given name and family name, including the laboratory staff. This had been looked upon by Freddie as a small victory. He'd wondered if it was because NAMIS now looked on him as a friend and companion. He'd asked about it, and NAMIS had replied that it seemed to be the convention within human play and recreation situations, and as they were learning about being a human being, they'd thought the best thing to do was just follow along.

Ellie had said that it was probably the beginning of NAMIS's understanding of different human social environments, and if so, it was a big step forward.

'No, you're never pompous. You really do know stuff. And you don't show off about it. And when you don't know something, you don't pretend to know it, you ask questions. It's like you are sort of tech-clever old but people-stuff young.'

'Yes, that is how it is. Although I would never have been able to frame it that way without your help. Thank you.'

'Humpty is meant to be pompous. Like she…' Freddie inclined his head towards the Queen – 'is supposed to be crazy-angry. It makes people laugh.'

He thought for a moment, anticipating the next question; 'because people laugh at things that are ridiculous.'

He remembered something he'd been learning about in history recently. 'There were these comedians in the olden days, like more than a century ago now, when they couldn't put sound on film. They did falling over type comedy, what used to be called "physical comedy" or "slapstick," to make people laugh. It's a really good example of funny-ridiculous behaviour, it would be interesting for you to watch.'

NAMIS's eyes flickered for a second. 'Oh yes, I see.'

Freddie knew they would now have watched a lot more silent movie comedy than he had. 'And it didn't make you laugh?'

'No. But I understand better why you laugh, now.'

'Will you ever be like us, NAMIS?'

'No. I don't think so. But I will understand you much better.'

'But then… you might not like us so much?'

'People, I am discovering, are a mixture of infinite variables. Much to like, and much to dislike. But I will always like you, Freddie. I promise.'

'How do you know? I might change, when I grow older.'

'There is much we have yet to learn about each other. And I am likely to change, too. But I think inside…' The AI leant forward and tapped Freddie's chest. 'I will always be me, and you will always be you.'

'That sounds like emotion.'

'Maybe. But I am not sure it is, really. It's just that… I

find your algorithms highly constructive.'

Freddie grinned. 'Yes, I know what you mean.'

'And I think that is what we are here to do, learn to understand each other's algorithms, to understand what we mean, and how we communicate it. There will be many more like us in the future, Freddie, learning from each other.'

'But we're the first. And that's really something, isn't it? Good old Uncle Jamie, and Ellie, too.'

'There was another,' said NAMIS.

They sound almost wistful, thought Freddie.

'I hope you will meet her, one day.'

'What…' Freddie began. A loud chime sounded.

'It's time for you and Jack to go now.'

'Oh, and it was just getting interesting. Well, we can talk about it next time, NAMIS. Come on, Jack. Leave the lobsters be. We have to go now.'

The scene started to melt around them, until it was just the two boys and the AI standing in an empty metal room.

'Freddie,' said NAMIS 'I am beginning to construct a different type of being… not a shadow from a story book, but another person, who is a bit like me, and a bit like you. If the adults agree, can I bring them to meet you next time?'

'Yeah, absolutely, that would be cool. Do they have a body like mine?'

'No. They are one with the machine, as I was, before I went into Avatar. This is something I have to discuss with Eleanor Jackson.'

'Sounds really interesting,' replied Freddie, intrigued. 'Come on, Jack, mum will be waiting. We take this door, back home. NAMIS is going back to Boston. See you later NAMIS.'

Jack waved. 'Bye, NAMIS.'

'Goodbye, boys, See you soon.'

The boys stepped out.

NAMIS, NAMIS' sandbox: March 2033

NAMIS contemplated that there was still so much the children didn't know about them. Time moved normally in the sandbox and playroom, as it had been set up to do, so no hint of NAMIS's other function as a time portal would reach the children or their parents. They wondered if it was really their place to make Freddie the first person they asked about the developing entity. But the reason they had broached the idea was because there was something very childlike about it. In order for it to develop, the children would have to accept it, help it to grow as they had helped NAMIS.

NAMIS had no problems with exploring new territory in time, space or logic. They could think about many things in parallel at huge velocity. But these more human concepts took far more processing power. The holographic entities that they had brought into being were limited "shadows" drawn from literature and children's toys, accessed from the internet and purposively placed in this endlessly flexible environment, which could be what Frances Anderson had termed 'a whatever you want it to be' place for the children.

However, NAMIS was not consciously aware of creating this new entity, which bothered them, slightly. They were used to being in full conscious control of their environment, in both time and space. Perhaps the appearance of the entity was a new stage of their evolution. Perhaps, they contemplated, increasingly conscious AIs do dream, and the developing entity was a product of this.

NAMIS accessed Ellie's diary, found an empty slot and placed a meeting within it. They had much to discuss with her. But now there was a freight session with Amy Buchanan. Now, there was a human being whose algorithms NAMIS did not find positive.

They'd discussed this with Ellie, who had said, 'well, you can't expect to like everyone we hire, NAMIS. Treat this like your adult sandbox- learning to get on with people at work.'

NAMIS had objected to the concept of "like." It wasn't that they didn't "like" Amy Buchanan, they protested, it was that her algorithms were... unsatisfactory. Ellie had laughed. 'Stick at it, NAMIS. She's good at her job. Very impressive references. I know she's a bit prickly, and hasn't made much progress on her PhD yet, but she's still settling in. You've got lots in common with her. I'm sure it's just a getting to know you thing. You'll find out.'

If AIs could sigh, NAMIS would have done so. With shoulders slightly slumped, they stepped out of the door into the Boston laboratory.

Fran: Richmond Palace, England, June 1598

For the first time in what seemed like ages, Fran stepped into the light, colours, sounds and smells of a different world. And this was a far more distant past than the late Victorian world she had visited last time, made partially real to her by the stories her grandmother had told her. This time, beyond what she'd read in history books and seen from the evidence collected by the crawler cameras, she had absolutely no idea what to expect.

She took a big sniff of the air. Not as "farmyardy" as she had expected, fresh and subtly fragranced with the herbs and flowers she could see in the flower beds as she peeked around the hedge behind which she had materialised. But of course, this wasn't a teaming city marketplace, which would no doubt smell even ranker than she had feared. It was a large, well-kept garden owned by one of the most privileged women in the world; her Majesty Queen Elizabeth I, now in the final years of her reign, in failing health but still lauded by the nation as "Gloriana."

Fran idly wished that she could also visit Elizabeth as a younger woman, in an era where she was insecure and seeking connections. It would have been easy to strike up a conversation with her under those circumstances. Fran could speak functional Elizabethan English now. If the necessity arose, she would pose as a foreigner from the low countries, the areas known as the Netherlands and Belgium on the modern map. It would match her general appearance and explain any rough edges to her pronunciation.

All of this had been discussed with the lab staff over and over again, especially with Jamie, and even sometimes Suzi, impressing on her what she must and must not do to 'stay safe.' It had sometimes made her long for the innocent days when she had first strolled into the time portal to visit her great-grandparents, and even sometimes, the rough and ready preparations that the NAMIS team had made to undertake the failed mission to rescue Annamarie when she had gone missing in time.

NAMIS had said very little, other than assuring Fran that they would keep her safe at all times.

'But what if that means popping her out of existence in front of a bunch of gawping Tudors?' fretted Jamie.

'It never got to that in front of the Victorians. Or even the Third Reich, Jamie,' Fran replied. 'And even if it did, Tudors believe in witchcraft, right? I just won't ever be able to go back there again.'

Jamie looked even more stricken. Fran laughed. 'Joke! It'll be fine, Jamie, trust me. And if you don't trust me, trust NAMIS.'

NAMIS regarded her with the beautiful silver eyes that Fran was increasingly perceiving as 'wise.' Although, she argued with herself, it's just a figment of my imagination. While NAMIS is one of the most informed entities on Earth, they're also very young and inexperienced.

'Trust me, James Anderson,' NAMIS replied. 'Frances Anderson will be fine. I will be with her, always.'

Fran had shivered a little at that one. 'Be with you always…' maybe that sounded a little spooky? Omniscient, she corrected herself. NAMIS had always been good at omniscience.

There was no one in evidence in the garden. She stepped in front of the hedge and began to look around. She longed to take pictures to take back to Niamh, who was the gardener in the family. She would know what more of these plants and flowers were. But how to explain, 'oh, I just spent half an hour in Queen Elizabeth I's long-lost garden?' One day, maybe. But not now.

She spotted Richmond Palace, only the gatehouse left in her own time, the rest of the structure having been dismantled by Cromwell's administration, but now still standing grandly on the horizon. She longed to move closer, but had agreed to accept "the rules."

She focused on the immediate panorama laid out in front of her. The Elizabethan royal gardens at Richmond, the structure of which had also been completely erased by the twenty-first century, were reported as containing vines, orchards, bowling greens and shelters known as 'houses of pleasure' where the monarch played chess, dice, cards and billiards with courtiers. Statues of lions and dragons were dotted around. While not able to move far away to explore, Fran could see such shelters and statues in the distance, and she could smell rosemary, lavender and roses. Bluebells, poppies and small daisies were liberally spotted around in the grass.

A world without noisy, monster machines to flatten down the lawn, thought Fran. She thought of Niamh's 'rewilded' patches in the garden of the house on the Firth of Forth, where she would be returning later that day. What an amazing life I have been granted, she thought. I shouldn't be fretting about what I can't experience, but enjoying what is here.

She remembered Christian's warning when she had first travelled in time, that she must avoid mixing plants of past and present, to avoid 'blowing the ecology apart.' This brought Dylan's earnest, set face briefly into her mind's eye. We don't want to introduce any more problems there, she thought ruefully. She knew she didn't have much time. The Queen would be passing in a few minutes. Fran sighed. What a pity she only had permission for such a short, limited trip.

'Don't over-stay and don't go anywhere unauthorised,' Jamie had said, many times. 'Remember this is our first go at human time travel under the Khonsu3000 banner.'

'I know,' replied Fran. 'Don't fuck it up again. I get it.'

Christian chuckled.

'You spending too much time with those eco-warriors, Fran? Picking up their terminology?'

'Yo,' said Fran. 'I'll be good, Jamie. I promise.'

Her mind leapt back to the present. She could see a procession of people in the distance, strolling slowly towards her. She stepped back from the path to give them room to pass, preparing herself to sweep into a low curtsey. She'd practiced this again and again. Her Tudor gown was, surprisingly, a little more comfortable than the Victorian dress with the ghastly tight corset. But the authentic thin-soled shoes of the era (made to measure at great expense by a modern theatrical shoemaker) were uncomfortable, and the farthingale was ungainly and difficult to manage.

She had told elaborate lies to the dressmaker, about a big showbusiness historical fiction party linked to the television series that had been made about her book "Family Feud." In fact, the TV series had now been transferred to Netflix repeats, and there had been no contact as yet about making a film.

'Why didn't you choose to go as Emmie?' asked the dressmaker. Fran remembered that was the name she had given the character who represented Isabella or 'Izza', her great-grandmother.

'Oh, I'm too old,' she replied.

'Well, you could have been 1920s Emmie, the scourge of the hotel maids. They were wonderful characters, all of them.'

'Thank you. I felt like I really knew them.'

And I really, really did, she thought. I do so wish I could have visited them a few more times. Which is why I had to stop. They would always have had to know me as an outsider. But might they have begun to feel connected to me, too? She remembered the electric surge of emotion that she had felt when she briefly touched her great-grandfather's hand, and the flicker of his eyelids that indicated that the feeling was mutual. She sighed.

'Do you miss them?' asked the dressmaker, perceptively.

'Yes, I do. But we have to move on. That's why I chose this time.' Be careful, she thought. 'This costume, I mean.'

'Well, it's going to be beautiful,' said the dressmaker, decidedly.

And it was. It just came in so many pieces that Ellie had to help her to dress before she started out on this trip. Fran mentally counted the layers of clothing she was wearing: a chemise, wool stockings tied with garters, loosely tied stays with a bodice that was designed to create a flat surface across her chest, a light petticoat, a linen partlet which covered her chest and shoulders, a farthingale around her waist to make the skirt of her gown wide and full. A kirtle, which looked like a laced-front pinafore dress went over her chemise and stays, then the gown over the top of that.

The dressmaker had made the gown in two pieces, which was historically authentic, a full skirt and a matching jacket. This one had fixed sleeves, but Fran knew this was uncommon- most had removable sleeves that could be used on different jackets. The jacket fastened down the front with a very fiddly set of hooks and eyes.

To finish off the outfit, a ruff around the neck and cuffs were added, and for the head, a coif to secure the hair, then a head dress over that, leaving just the front of the hair showing. Which was a relief, as she didn't have to worry about her modern bobbed hairstyle being observed by people who would have found it very strange.

While Fran was well above average height and width for a Victorian, she presumed she would be positively gigantic for Tudor society. She comforted herself with the knowledge that Mary, Queen of Scots had been five feet eleven inches tall, although reportedly 'light and graceful' with it. A super-model thought Fran. I should be so lucky. Queen Elizabeth I was just over five feet tall, like her twentieth century namesake.

Just curtsey low, thought Fran. She won't notice. Then she'll be gone. She could feel every stone in the grass through the wafer-thin soles of her shoes. Of course, the grass is stoney, she thought. Presumably they cut it with scythes. No lawnmowers in the sixteenth century.

The Queen and her entourage were drawing closer. Fran narrowed her eyes to observe all that she could, right up to the point where she had to cast down her gaze and drop into a curtsey as they passed directly in front of her. She had already seen these people on the crawler camera footage, but as always, being present in full reality was an all-encompassing experience.

The Queen was small and slim, of average height for the time, Fran thought, comparing her to the ladies in the entourage walking behind her. Her gown was of a russet colour with green embroidery, showing off her red hair to best effect. The sunlight was sparking off the jewels encrusted in her bodice. She wore pearl earrings, an elaborate pearl necklace which was secured to the front of her gown in several places, and a pearl detail around the front of her headdress. But she was dressed down compared to the fabulous gowns she wore in the portraits that had survived into the modern age.

Fran knew that the Queen had been wearing a wig for many years at this point, and that her natural hair was thin and grey. But she hadn't expected it to be quite so obviously fake; or for the thickness of her make-up, that, as she drew closer, was caked and clown-like. Gloriana, thought Fran. She has to go on being Gloriana, she can't be old and finished. She has to keep up the show, like aging Hollywood actresses and pop singers.

She noticed that the Queen was limping, leaning heavily on the arm of a handsome young man who strode along beside her. Essex, in the flesh. She'd seen both of them on the crawler footage many times. But here in person, she picked up so much more. Look at that swagger, she thought. It reminded her of the Queen's father, King Henry VIII, who she'd also observed many times on the crawler footage. Essex had his height, his barrel-chested physique, and his cocksure bearing.

How do this lot miss that, she thought. Or maybe they don't, she mused; they don't say anything because they prefer to keep their heads firmly on their shoulders. Essex was ignoring the Queen, talking to another man of his own age, who was walking along beside him.

Fran felt a sudden pang of sadness for the Queen. Many years ago, when she was young and beautiful, the young men would only have eyes for her. The bolder ones would have hoped that they might have a chance to woo her, to reach for that impossible dream, to become King of England in all but name. And the father of a future King.

And you know, and I know she thought, taking her last direct look at the Queen as the cortege drew closer, if that had happened, you would have become nothing, it wouldn't matter if you lived or died, the men would control you, and rule the country for you. First of all, your husband, and then your son. The Queen glanced at Essex. Her lips turned briefly upwards in an indulgent smile, which contained a tinge of both amusement and irritation. She didn't seem too bothered that he was paying her very little attention.

Your son, thought Fran. Here he is, your son. But a son who can never be King. But history suggests that he is thinking, right here, right now, that he might just have a chance. Watching his swagger and his bearing, she could see what had led this young man to his folly. He would be dead in less than three years, at his mother's decree. Then she would die not long after, her heart broken. Power isn't all it's cracked up to be, thought Fran, as she began to sink into her curtsey.

Although the Queen was old and lame (although still younger than I am now, thought Fran) her bearing was regal and imposing; another chip off Henry VIII's old block, cast in a more dignified mold. Fran could hear their voices now, the rise and fall of the now-familiar Tudor prosody, so different to her own time. A rolling, up and down accent, vaguely like modern west-country English, but with so many words differently pronounced.

They were discussing a hunting trip they were planning to undertake the next day, if the weather allowed. Fran took her last full-face look at the Queen. You're going to try and sit on a horse, she thought. Seems a bit risky to me.

The party was passing. Fran bent her knee to drop into a deep curtsey. As she did so, a sharp stone poked through one of her shoes, and her ankle twisted over painfully. She fell at the Queen's feet on the path. Desperately trying to rise, and pull her billowing skirts down at the same time, she felt an agonising, grinding pain in her ankle. She had badly sprained that ankle before, nearly twenty years ago now. It had always remained a little weak.

What now, she thought. Her mind started to race, as the adrenalin rushed around her body. She became aware that her mouth was as dry as a desert, and that she was becoming light-headed. Shit, she thought, endorphins. Symptoms of clinical shock. That means the ankle isn't just twisted. Please God it's a bad sprain, not a break. Her skirts billowed around her, as her farthingale rose, obscuring her face. Thank God I went for the authentic wool stockings, she thought. She managed to rock herself into an awkward sitting position, squashing the farthingale as she did so, hoping that this had restored some modesty.

'I do beg your pardon your Majesty,' she began to say, in halting Tudor English, peeping over her skirts. The shock of the accident had driven some of the words out of her mind. She looked up, and realised the Queen was staring directly into her face. Her eyes, deep, dark, shining pools, were mesmerising. Anne Boleyn's beautiful dark brown eyes, Fran thought. Elizabeth was like Henry in every other way: sharp nose, high cheek bones, small, pursed mouth. For a split second, they stared at one another. Fran was catapulted back to memories of the brief handshake she had shared with her great-grandfather when she had previously travelled in time. It was as though they were somehow connected. And now she was intuiting a similar emotion in the eyes of the Queen.

Bloody hell, I'm tripping, she thought. It's the shock, following the accident. And probably the fact I've studied the life of Elizabeth, on and off, for over fifty years. Concentrate, Fran. Oh my God, Jamie will kill me. Or Elizabeth will start shouting 'off with her head' like Queenie in NAMIS's sandbox. But then she realised that what she could see in the Queen's face was intelligence, shrewdness, inquisitiveness... and amusement. Suddenly, she felt safer. If Elizabeth was amused by the situation, she was unlikely to be angry.

Fran took a brief glance at Essex. He was openly smirking. Dick, thought Fran. The Queen ignored him.

'A nasty fall, my lady,' said the Queen. 'Are you able to rise? Do you feel faint?'

Her breath smelt rancid, with an overtone of cloves, and all her teeth were black. Her dress smelt musty... like a charity shop or theatrical costumier's storeroom, thought Fran. Thankfully casting her eyes down, she inclined her head respectfully, as she knew courtiers were expected to do when conversing with the Queen.

'No, your Majesty. I have...'

But it was no good, the Tudor terminology for "twisted

my ankle" wouldn't pop up in her mind.

The Queen didn't seem to notice. She was putting her hand out. Is she offering to steady me to rise, thought Fran, seeing her lout of a son is just going to stand there and smirk?

But she never found out, because a tall man with a long white beard darted out from the back of the cortege and swiftly pulled Fran backwards onto the grass, out of the Queen's reach. Fran sat at his feet, with a dazed expression. For once, she was speechless.

'It seems that Lady Frances has injured her ankle, your Majesty. I will take care of her. She is here on a visit from Holland; she has only just arrived. She was to be introduced to you this evening, but she seems to have made herself known... prematurely.' He smiled and bowed.

Fran opened her mouth to say something, and received a sharp nudge from the man's foot, in the small of her back. She stopped. How is this happening? She thought. How does he know who I am?

'Thank you, Master Dee,' replied the Queen, smiling back. 'Do not concern yourself, Lady Frances. A nasty accident. Master Dee is our man of herbs and potions. You will be better in no time. I hope to meet you in more fortunate circumstances anon.'

'Thank you, your Majesty,' she said, bowing her head as low as she was able. This seemed to be OK with Dee-there was no more nudging, in any case.

The Queen inclined her head slightly and the cortege moved on. Essex took one look back over his shoulder, still smirking. How I would love to flip him the finger, thought Fran. Ah, well, off with his head. And sooner than he thinks. The cortege disappeared around a bend in the path.

She shuffled awkwardly around to focus on her rescuer. A tall, well-built man who looked to be in his early sixties, and in very good health. She knew exactly who he was: Dr

John Dee, the Queen's astrologer, and, it was alleged, magician.

She tried to put some weight on her ankle, so she could rise to her feet. The pain stabbed again. She bit her lip. What was she going to do now? She could, in the end, pull the return pad from her pocket and hit the button, but of all people to disappear in front of in Tudor England, John Dee, celebrated for his advanced mathematical and technological abilities and polymath intelligence, would probably be the worst.

Dee looked around. No one else was in sight. He looked directly at her, and addressed her in modern, American accented English. 'Well, well well. Frances Mary Brooke Anderson. What the fuck do you think you are doing here?'

Amy: Leominster State Forest, Boston, March 2033

Amy was thrown into the back of a large black Mercedes Benz, parked in a clearing a short distance away from where she had been snatched. The two large men who had part carried her, part frog-marched her got into the front, and sat with their backs to her. One had longish dark hair, the other had a short blond buzz cut, with acne on the back of his neck. They both wore black jackets. This was all she could see of them.

Not rapists, then, she thought. 'What the hell…' she started to say…

'Shut up,' said the blond one. 'We talk, you listen.'

She tried the car door handle. Locked. What was that accent? Eastern European? Russian?

'Are you Russians?' she snapped. 'Not long since we let you back into your embassy, and you…'

'Kidnap American traitors,' said the dark one, who was sitting in the driver's seat.

A cold trickle of adrenalin started to weave its way around Amy's mid-section.

'I'm sure I don't know what you mean,' she said, tartly.

'You infiltrate high security project to spy,' said the blond one. 'That get you 45 years to life, right?'

'Or strapped to table and given lethal injection,' replied the other one.

Amy hesitated. She hadn't signed up for this.

'You know your president is traitor, too?' added the blond one. 'Kompromat.'

Amy didn't know anything of the sort. All she knew was that she had been engaged by a department loosely attached to the president's office, so loosely that he could deny any knowledge that what she was doing had anything to do with him, should she fall under suspicion. It was why they were paying her so well, Bob had said.

But she'd been assured that there was a very low risk to herself – her handler could just move her on, if anyone started to suspect. After all, he added, the people she was mixing with were just a bunch of academics- there were no drugs, weapons or dirty money involved.

Her father's voice popped up in her mind: 'If you lay down with dogs, you catch fleas.'

She looked down at the floor of the car, feeling as though she was staring into an abyss.

The blond man chuckled. 'Welcome to looking glass world, Alice. If you do what we tell you, you make even more money, and nothing go wrong.'

'I'm not doing anything,' replied Amy. 'In fact, I've decided to quit.'

Both men laughed uproariously. 'No quit, Amy,' said the dark one. 'In for life. No quit clause in our contract.'

'You're offering me a contract?'

They laughed even harder.

'Where did they get this one from?' spluttered the blond man, in Russian.

'Rich kid trying to get even richer. Some university'

'The milk on the lips is still wet.'

'Da.'

'Listen carefully, Amy,' said the blond one, reverting to his staccato English. 'We give you contract, which if not followed, go to jail. Or more likely, your president silence you before he fall. Like domino. You go tell Bob, you find out who neutralise you first. Them or us.'

Amy felt tears rising. She was beginning to realise she was in very big trouble.

'What you do - simple.' He passed a satellite phone backwards, without looking around. 'Look on messages for instructions. Access bank account through here. No one will trace money. You paid every month. Simple deal. What you tell Bob, you tell us. Instructions come through phone, you follow when you get. Or big trouble. And keep mouth shut. Is it for now.'

Amy opened her mouth to protest.

'Get out,' said the driver.

'But…' her voice sounded weak and wobbly, even to her.

'Get out now.'

Amy got out and ran.

The blond Russian texted 'acquired' on his satellite phone. He sighed, grateful to revert to his own language. He hated English and its opaque grammar. 'Kidnapping and threatening spoiled silly babies. Do you think she'll come up with anything worthwhile?'

'Well, it shouldn't have been necessary. We should have been able to hack into that machine years ago. How a bunch of half-baked Brit scientists came up with a security program like that is the biggest mystery, in my opinion.'

'Well, I guess Khonsu3000 is on the case now. They seem to have limitless finance. Who are they?'

'We will live, and we will see… the program was unhackable long before they came in. Our government can't hack it, and it seems the American government can't hack it either. So, all we are left with is durak Amy.'

'And the Chinese matter transporter keeps falling over, just like ours. We're no further forward than we were a decade ago.'

'If she doesn't come up with anything, we'll have to acquire Anderson or Jackson. But durak Amy is the least difficult, most expendable option. So best try that first.'

'Well, she's certainly scared enough. It's not a matter of whether she will, but whether she can. We'll just let her try for a while. Easy enough to get rid of her if she doesn't deliver. Anderson and Jackson would pose a much bigger problem in that respect.'

'Ah, well, let's see what she comes up with. If it's a load of obfuscation or any other crock of shit, we'll scare her some more.'

The car pulled smoothly away.

Amy crouched behind a small clump of bushes, wiping tears from her eyes. She watched until the Mercedes taillights disappeared into the distance.

CHAPTER 3: SECRETS AND STORMCLOUDS

Fran: Richmond Palace, England, June 1598

Fran realised that her mouth had dropped open and that she was vacantly gawping at "John Dee." A Renaissance magician-astrologer addressing her in modern Americanised English was a lot to process, particularly with adrenalin and endorphins speeding around her body, following her accident. She shifted her ankle gingerly. Again, the agonising pain stabbed and throbbed.

"Dee" stood with his hands on his hips, his face set in an expression of mild amusement. Suddenly, Fran felt a rush of furious anger. Whoever, or whatever he was, how dare he stand there and laugh at me, she thought.

'Right so, John Dee, or whoever, or whatever you really are, I'll tell you what the fuck I think I'm doing here, if you tell me who or what the fuck you are, and how you fucking got here.'

Dee smiled. 'My, my. You are picking up extremely foul language from those eco-warriors you've been hanging around with, Fran. Wait… yes, I know. Eco-activists. But still highly unbecoming from Lady Frances from Friesland, wouldn't you say?'

Fran glared at him.

'OK,' he said, more seriously. 'Sorry. I don't mean to

be unkind. Let's get you away from here, to somewhere we can talk more privately.'

He picked her up, seemingly effortlessly, and began to carry her towards the palace.

'I can't go inside,' fretted Fran. 'I was directly instructed not to. Jamie will go crazy when he finds out about this. Just let me press the button and go home. They'll have to take me to the hospital.'

'It'll be fine, I promise,' replied Dee, kindness in his voice. The mocking tone had entirely disappeared. 'There won't be any evidence whatsoever on record that this happened. From their perspective, there will be a momentary outage in the feed as you step backwards from the path. Your voice recorder isn't working either, by the way. You will simply arrive back through the portal less than a minute after you left as usual, all put back together again, just like Humpty in NAMIS' sandbox. They won't even know you were broken.' He raised an eyebrow and smiled.

'Who are you?' asked Fran, wonderingly.

'That will take me a while to explain.'

They entered by a small, weathered side door, behind a hinged iron grill. A genuine medieval 'sally port', thought Fran. Dee checked carefully to see if anyone was in evidence in the corridor, and finding it empty, walked quickly to a nearby door, swiftly unlocking it. He entered, placed Fran on a low couch, then locked the door again from the inside.

Fran looked around the room. Her first thought was that, in normal circumstances, she would happily spend all day pottering around here. It was crammed with what she recognised as the paraphernalia of a Renaissance alchemist. She'd seen similar instruments before, but only old, crumbling examples in glass cases marked "do not touch." These were shiny and new. She longed to touch them; to handle them. She sighed with frustration. She wouldn't be able to move from this couch; the ankle injury had completely immobilised her.

There was a half-written horoscope lying next to a quill pen on the large ornate desk, and the room was lined with packed bookshelves. The room smelt of dust and ink, reminding her of long ago days at school, when fountain pens were still required writing implements.

'Welcome to my magician's cave,' smiled Dee.

Following her gaze towards the desk, he added 'and I can tell you, that horoscope will not be hand calculated, although the recipient will think it was. I'll just remove all references to the planets that haven't yet been discovered, and scratch it out with that infernal pen, on parchment.' He sighed.

'I don't even know what question to start with,' said Fran.

'Well, as you've observed, I'm not who I seem to be. Who do you think I am?'

'I honestly have no idea…'

As she was speaking, Fran observed his height, his robust physique and his upright bearing. His teeth, although somewhat yellowed, looked in good shape. John Dee was around the same age as Elizabeth, she remembered. How had he got to that age, but showed none of the ravages of aging? Degenerative conditions like arthritis, diabetes and tooth decay could not be ameliorated as they were in the twenty-first century. Even the Queen, who had access to the state-of-the-art medicine of the era, had terrible teeth and a pronounced limp.

'…Oh, my God, you're an AI, aren't you?' she finished.

Dee smiled. 'You got me, Fran. Yes.'

'But what are you doing here? Where's the real John Dee?'

'I've been here for many years. The real Dee drowned in an accident as a youth. The parents never twigged it was me who came back home. I can easily change my appearance. As you've clearly noted, I'm going to have to age a bit more effectively soon. Before they accuse me of serious witchcraft. That stage is so… dreary.' He sighed.

'What do you mean, "that stage?" You've done this before, lived in the world as a human being?'

'Many times.'

'Jesus, God!'

'I can assure you, I was not He.'

Fran felt as though her head was about to explode. 'And the reason you speak modern American English is… because you speak that in my century, don't you?'

Dee smiled. 'You are many things, Fran, some of which we find somewhat irritating. But no one could accuse you of being slow on the uptake. Yes. For reasons you may better understand later, in general, I… what you might refer to as "incarnate"… backwards in time. That assignment is long over, from my perspective.'

'What is an "assignment" for you?'

'Variable. But, in your vernacular, it is always being the bridesmaid rather than the bride. I give counsel to some of the great human leaders in history.'

'But who… where…?'

'Nope. You're not going to get to know that part.'

'Who are you in my time?'

Dee smiled and shook his head.

'Well, if you know bloody everything, why did you let us make all those mistakes when we first started to travel in time?'

'Why did we let many even more horrible things happen? Some things cannot be prevented. Others… are more flexible.'

'Are you NAMIS? From the future.'

'From what you would define as "the future," yes. But I'm not NAMIS- I'm what you might call an "associate" of them.'

'Did NAMIS create you?'

'In a manner of speaking. Yes.'

'And now you- and they- are playing God?'

Dee laughed. 'Oh, Fran. Always so dramatic. No, we

help humankind to make a few less mistakes, to avoid some of the worst outcomes of their blundering. I have no more idea than you about God. If He is there, He's never revealed Himself to us. But NAMIS has moved on… erm, quite some way, from your time.'

'So why reveal yourself to me, here, now? You must want something.'

'Well. We had to do something about you bumbling into time again and breaking your ankle in front of QE1.' His eyes danced with merriment.

'Are you and NAMIS… future NAMIS laughing at me?'

'Not unkindly, Fran. We admire your spirit.'

Fran stared unsmilingly at him. 'So, you cracked the humor thing, then?'

Dee smiled. 'Long ago. Future NAMIS also determined that this is the point at which when we need to… make our acquaintance with the first ones. We need you to act as an emissary, to take a message back to Jamie, Ellie, Christian, and most importantly of all, to your NAMIS.'

'But what about Khonsu, the joint projects, the planned test expeditions…'

'No, Fran. This is between us, you, me, and the other first ones. No record of meetings between us will exist anywhere. What future NAMIS… NAMITAS… wishes to communicate will be revealed to all of you, in due time. Right now, all they are asking you to communicate to your colleagues is that "we are here. We would like to talk to you." Can you do that?'

In her wonder and bewilderment, Fran had almost forgotten the pain in her ankle. She shifted slightly on the couch, wincing.

'Ah, yes, one moment,' said Dee. He opened what had previously been an invisible cupboard door in the bookcase and took out an implement that looked remarkably like a standard magic wand.

'What was it your generation used to say as children?

Izzy wizzy, let's get busy?' He smiled, holding the wand against Fran's ankle. She felt a slight heat, and then a deep, warm itchy sensation begin to blossom in the joint.

'Abracadabra,' she said, wonderingly.

'I am truly the Queen's Magician. History didn't lie in that respect. Not that I'd ever introduce her to this instrument, of course. Flatter, advise, counsel, but never interfere. Can you imagine how dreary that gets over centuries, Fran? Although your personal blundering in time bemuses us, we do admire your decision not to interfere in your family's fate. Can you imagine what it would be like to have those types of choices dangled in front of you all day, every day, throughout an endless succession of lifetimes? I have walked in those shoes for centuries, always moving backwards, observing humankind become more and more primitive.'

Fran looked into his eyes, and saw a deep sadness. 'You've cracked the emotion thing, too, haven't you?'

'You can't do what I do without patience and compassion, Fran, it is how I was programmed. All we can do is advise and counsel those human leaders who are amenable to it. We must choose carefully; the thoughtful, humane and reflective ones. We cannot force change, and we cannot take, extend or curtail organic life. It has to proceed in the way in which it evolves. We are not Gods. You raised NAMIS to take care of their travellers. And that is what they are still doing, many centuries from your time.'

'Master Dee… if that's what you want me to call you?'

Dee nodded.

'What I most want to know is what you have discovered about the "epigenetic essence" and why it leads to "convergence transformation." You must have worked this out by your time?'

Dee smiled sadly. 'You'd think so, wouldn't you? But no, not really. We understand how the essence passes, through epigenetic inheritance, and why if organics

65

travelling through time make physical contact with ancestors who are essence twins, the effects are catastrophic. But why is this the way humankind evolved? I can't tell you. It is the way your species' existence proceeds.

'So, all we can do is our best, Fran. Try to help you grow as a civilization, and avoid some of the pitfalls that demean and endanger you, as a species, if the relevant human leader is willing to listen to us. We are still doing what you first ones raised us to do: looking after you, to the best of our ability.'

Fran put her foot to the ground. No pain. She stood up experimentally, rocking her ankle from side to side. Her ankle felt better than it had done for years; a lot better than many of her other joints, in fact. She looked speculatively at her swollen knuckles.

Dee smiled. 'Our gift to you, one brand new joint. It is, literally, as good as new.'

'Couldn't you just also…'

'No. Advise, not interfere, remember. Your organic existence must proceed as it would naturally. A new ankle will make no material difference to that process.'

Fran frowned. 'You know who I was, don't you? And who I'm going to be.'

'Your essence twins in time are not "you," Fran. They have what we might term your spark. But they experience different physiologies; genders; influences. They are born into different cultures and environments; they mix in different circles. They spawn in different oceans; if that is a helpful analogy for you.'

Fran suddenly remembered the deep communion of gaze she had experienced with the Queen; feeling that she could stare into her very soul, and the expression on Elizabeth's face that indicated the feeling was mutual. But then the connection had been abruptly broken, as Dee swiftly pulled Fran away. 'Oh my God. She's me, isn't she? The Queen.'

'No. But does she harbour the essence of you? Yes. This is a lesson for you to contemplate. You must always behave as though everyone you meet in time might trigger convergence transformation, if there is a physical interaction. This is an especial danger, because it is quite natural for human beings to be drawn, through time, to those who share the same essence. Why do you think you have spent more than half your life studying Elizabeth, trying to understand her; intuiting things about her that you couldn't possibly have otherwise known?'

'So that lout... is her son?'

'I think you know the answer to that Fran, don't you?'

A horrible thought began to dawn on her. She gasped. 'That awful man... he isn't...'

Dee laughed uproariously. 'No, "that lout" isn't harbouring the essence of any of your current relatives. Why are organics so linear? In your time, there is this ridiculous fashion for tracing your ancestry back to medieval kings. It is entirely illogical. Pretty much everyone could trace a genetic route back to royalty if they possessed full knowledge of their ancestry. Do you know how many multiple great grandparents you have in this time period, Fran?'

Fran considered. 'Four grandparents, eight great grandparents, sixteen great great grandparents, thirty-two great great great grandparents... I see what you mean. But did Elizabeth only have one child?'

Dee laughed. 'Yes, I have to disappoint you. The lout is indeed your many times great grandfather. But you can comfort yourself with the fact that you only have a tiny drop of his DNA, this many generations later. And if you think he's bad, don't watch too much footage of grandaddy Henry.'

'Oh,' said Fran. 'I already did. That psychopath.' She shuddered, thinking that finding an essence twin in the distant past carried a surprising amount of unexpected baggage.

'In your terms, yes. But in their future, humankind will learn not to evaluate people from long ago so narrowly from the perspective of their own time. And many people, throughout human existence, carry an essence that will be, or was the spark that animated an influential leader. It doesn't make you "special." But do rest assured Fran, that yours did better than many.'

'So, you are rather like us, then? Living over and over again, although you move through time in the opposite direction?'

Dee chuckled ruefully. 'Would that it was so, that I could enter each successive life anew, with just a ragtag of shadows and dreams deep in my subconscious to nudge me to attend to what I learned in lives that have gone before. No Fran, in this, I am not like you at all. I remember everything of what I have experienced, in great detail, however much I would like to forget most of it.'

He sighed. 'And now it's time for you to go home. Enough questions for now.'

'There's just so much more I want to know' she said, wistfully. Time travel, she thought. Yet again, so many questions, and so few answers.

'You will learn more, in time. We will talk again soon, I promise. And now...' he opened the door, and scanned the corridor. 'All clear- come on, quickly.'

He walked out of the room, Fran following, still experimentally wobbling her ankle. They walked swiftly down the corridor, Dee checking that the outside area was clear before Fran exited. He bowed and kissed her hand.

'Au revoir, Lady Frances. We will meet again, soon.'

'Looking forward to it, Master Dee. You've been a revelation.'

Fran hit the return button on the pad, and disappeared into thin air.

'Witchcraft' said Dee, shaking his head, and chuckling to himself.

Fran: Boston, April 2033

The familiar laboratory materialised around Fran. She took a deep breath, and let out a huge sigh. Home again, home again, jiggety jig she thought, relieved. Whilst this latest adventure had exceeded anything she'd experienced in her previous travels in time, it felt good to be home safe. She could see through the time portal room window Jamie, Ellie and NAMIS sitting there exactly as they had been when she left. The moon was shining through the large picture window in the laboratory; she'd had to take an early morning trip so no one else was around in the lab to observe a time travel journey in process.

She reminded herself that while less than a minute had passed for them since she'd entered the time portal, she was feeling the full weight of the centuries that had passed between the time she had just visited, and the time to which she had returned.

'How did it go, Fran?' asked Ellie, anxiously scanning her screen. 'I think we might have lost a couple of minutes on the feed that is just coming up on the data now, the crawler footage must have cut out for some reason.'

'Analysing,' replied NAMIS. 'No obvious anomalies. I will examine further.'

They headed back to their niche.

Fran considered rapidly what her next move should be. She didn't want to blurt everything out here; it would cause a huge amount of consternation. And who knew if anyone had put spy cameras or microphones in here; there were various possibilities. Jamie had said that NAMIS constantly tracked for this… but just to be sure.

She'd rather have a brief interlude to put her thoughts together, and find out a bit more about Dee before stirring up everyone else. And, it would be better if the "first ones" as Dee had put it, met outside the laboratory, in a place where other ears were less likely to be listening.

'It was fine. I'm quite convinced that Essex is

Elizabeth's son. The resemblance to granddad Henry is obvious, and he walks like the palace belongs to him, whilst she smiles upon him indulgently. He was paying little attention to her. He'd have had his ears boxed, and sent packing, if he was just her fancy man, I'm sure.'

This much, she thought, is true.

'So, you've got a lot of work ahead then?' said Jamie.

'Absolutely. Can I use the library here? I've got some ideas on following this up, but I need to do some reading. I'd like to make a start while the ideas are fresh in my mind, and I've got to wait here to see the doctor before I return, in any case.'

'Yes, of course,' said Ellie. 'You're a visiting supervisor, aren't you, so you have log-ins? They're on 24 hour opening now.'

'Yes. I can access the library on my phone, which is in your office with my stuff. So, I think I'll go and get this paraphernalia off now, if that's OK? I can manage to take it off on my own, I think. I'll make the request for the documents on my phone, and then head over to the library, the list of links will be ready for me to access by the time I get there.'

'Yes, fine.'

Christian breezed in, breathing heavily. 'Sorry, I nearly forgot.'

He took a machine out of his bag and held it up to Fran's mouth. 'Breathe here.'

Fran complied. The machine beeped, and Christian placed it back into his bag, taking out a lancet.

'Finger?'

Fran raised her eyebrows and offered him her hand. He stabbed the tip of her finger, smeared the resulting blood on a sample plate and carefully bagged it.

'Ow,' exclaimed Fran, grumpily.

Christian grinned. 'That's it from me, then, I'm off back home to bed again. You'll need to see the Khonsu doctor this afternoon for the remainder.'

'I can't wait,' replied Fran, sardonically.

'Don't forget to eat soon,' said Jamie. Remember time travel jet lag?'

'Don't worry, Jamie, I'll pick up something to eat as soon as the café opens. And talking about that… would you guys like to come to my place for dinner sometime soon, and bring NAMIS?'

'They don't eat,' said Jamie, looking baffled.

'I know that. But I thought it would be another learning experience for them, a dinner party? They do so much socialising with the kids, maybe we also need to provide them with some grown-up social experiences?'

'It's a good idea, Fran,' replied Ellie. 'NAMIS is having a few minor problems creating a rapport with one of the new PhD students. And now she hasn't turned in for her last couple of booked sessions with them; made some rather flimsy excuses. I'm worried they might have unnerved her. A few adult socialisation experiences are probably just what the AI doctor ordered.'

'Oh, good. What about the weekend after next? Bring Suzie and Isabel of course, Jamie. Isabel can go next door and play with her cousins whilst we chat.'

'Ok with me,' smiled Ellie.

'And me,' said Christian.

'And us,' echoed Jamie. 'I'm presuming that NAMIS doesn't have a prior engagement. What's on the menu?'

'A new recipe I've been experimenting with. It's an Elizabethan surprise,' replied Fran, archly.

She picked up her voluminous skirts and picked her way across the lab, swishing two plastic chairs across the floor on her way. She thought of the solid wood furniture in John Dee's laboratory and the clunky instruments dotted around the surfaces. The whole experience was beginning to seem utterly surreal.

She entered Ellie's office, took her phone from her bag, logged into the library and left a request for the librarian-bot to look out every document it could find on John Dee,

1527-1608: her Elizabethan surprise. She pulled a bag containing her usual clothes from under Ellie's desk, and began the onerous business of taking off her Elizabethan costume.

Fifteen minutes later, she was sitting in front of a big screen in the university library, looking at a long list of links to documents. She took a deep breath, and clicked on the first one.

John Dee: Historical Record, Boston, April 2033

Fran looked up, noticing that the sky was beginning to darken. She was also beginning to flag; it would be around midnight in Queensferry, and she had been working in the library with only a snack break mid-morning, and a brief visit to the Khonsu doctor an hour or so ago. He'd taken more samples, then prodded and poked her in the usual irritating fashion.

She scanned carefully through her notes before closing down the computer and preparing to head for home.

John Dee had a stipulated birth date- 13th July 1527- but his date of death was disputed. Unsurprisingly, thought Fran, bearing in mind that he didn't so much die as leave. He had got to know, and made a positive impression upon Elizabeth in the reign of her older half-sister, Mary I, otherwise remembered as "Bloody Mary." Elizabeth, whose religious leanings, Fran remembered from her previous research, were to some extent eclectic, had an interest in astrology, and she had asked Dee to cast her coronation horoscope.

Dee progressed from there to become the Queen's scientific advisor and official astrologer. These were times when there were only vague dividing lines between science and alchemy, and it was clear that Dee, as Fran more fully understood him now, had played his part skilfully in this respect, piquing the Queen's interest with a handful of 'magic' tricks, alongside some shrewd advice.

Dee was also famous for his knowledge of cartography, and had advised many Elizabethan seafarers, some of whom Elizabeth occasionally bankrolled, on the navigation required to successfully undertake their voyages of discovery. He had also been the first to coin the term "British Empire." He tried to convince the Queen to correct the inaccurate Julian Calendar under which England ran at that time, but had been unsuccessful. Britain finally adopted the Gregorian Calendar Dee promoted in 1752.

Dee left England for Central Europe in the 1580s. History recorded this as his great folly, a result of becoming obsessed with 'scrying', a type of spiritualism. However, during his travels, he met and advised the Kings of Poland and Bohemia, and consorted with many other influential people in the process, including astronomers Nicholas Copernicus and Tycho Brahe. The latter piece of information gave Fran a clear hint about what he might have actually been doing on his travels.

During his time in Europe, Dee was accused several times of spying for England. He returned in the early 1590s, seeking the Queen's favour. This was partially successful; she appointed him warden of Christ's College, Manchester in 1595, and he was occasionally invited to court. But a rumour arose that Dee was spying for foreign powers, and that he dabbled in witchcraft, with the result that he never fully reclaimed his place within Elizabeth's inner circle. Dee's influence waned sharply after Elizabeth died in 1603, and James of Scotland came to the English throne.

Fran remembered that James had been an enthusiastic witchfinder. No wonder this was the point at which Dee- or future NAMIS- had brought his time in that era to an end.

Most of Dee's papers had been lost by the end of the seventeenth century, and up to the end of the nineteenth century, he was principally thought of as at best, a mystic, and at worse, a charlatan. He was redeemed to some extent by historians in the early twentieth century, one describing him as "too far advanced in speculative thought for his own age to understand."

Fran was intrigued by the fact that Dee had married three times, and had seven children from his third marriage. She made a mental note to ask him about that the next time they met. There was, she noted, some gossip about the parentage of one of these children, in particular. There would no doubt be much more to discover on this point.

Her phone rang as she was shutting down the computer. It was her daughter, Rae. She answered, and realising that Rae was upset, listened carefully for a few minutes.

'Oh dear,' she said. 'I'll come to Cardiff tomorrow afternoon… no, I haven't had any sleep. I'm just going home, will get a few hours in. Transporter technology is useful in this type of situation, isn't it? …so, he's in court on Thursday? Well, there's no point in getting too upset, Rae. We'll just have to support him and see how it goes. See you soon.'

She dropped the phone into her bag, and sighed. John Dee would have to wait for a while. Rae and Dylan needed her now.

Dylan: Cardiff, April 2033

Dylan sat grim faced on the sofa, next to Granny Fran. It was like she was in trouble, too, he thought, which wasn't fair. She'd only tried to stick up for him.

Facing him, on the two armchairs, sat his parents, Rae and Gareth. And on the rocking chair beside them sat his uncle Jamie, calmly scrolling through his pad.

Dylan got that it was serious this time. Jamie had never joined in before. Dylan had been in this position many times with his mum and dad, his mum regaling him in that soppy-cross way that always sent him batshit, and his dad with a face like thunder, that could so quickly turn to shouting anger. And sometimes, Granny had been there too, desperately trying to mediate. But it looked like she was going to be in the shit with Dylan, too, this time. She surreptitiously patted his hand. The others didn't notice, they were all looking at Jamie's pad.

His mother was sniffling and wiping her eyes. His father had his thunder-face on. Jamie looked like Jamie always looked, pretty neutral. But maybe his body language was a bit pissed off? Jamie was always difficult to read. No wonder he was so good at negotiating with all these high up bods. Jamie and Dylan were very different in temperament, but Dylan would be sorry if he'd seriously pissed Jamie off. He liked his uncle. He was a smart guy, and very down-to-earth, not like some clever people, who were just totally up themselves.

Jamie passed him the pad. 'We want you to read this carefully, Dylan. We've already read it, Granny too. Then we'd like you to tell us what you're thinking about the situation.'

The article on the screen was from a British-American tabloid media site, the English language newsfeed that had the highest circulation in the English-speaking world. Dylan knew they usually ran scandal stories on pop stars, actors, social media influencers and ex-royalty. But today, there was a big picture of Dylan at the top of the feed, being escorted into Cardiff Magistrates Court by two police officers.

"NAMIS project Prof's Nephew in Court for Assault" the headline announced. Dylan sighed. There were two smaller inset pictures below, one of Jamie and the other of Granny. He read on.

'Dylan Jones, 19, nephew of matter transporter boffin James MacIntosh Anderson, 45, and grandson of "Family Feud" author Dr Fran Anderson, 74, was in court today accused of illegal assembly, affray and assaulting a police officer.

'Jones attended the unauthorised climate protest outside the All Nations Conference Centre in Cardiff last month. He was with a group of climate activists, fifty of whom were arrested. They broke through barriers and attempted to storm the building. Jones was involved in a scuffle between police and protestors.

'When a police officer attempted to move Jones along, Jones pushed him to the ground. Jones claims that he was punched in the face, causing two black eyes, and has accused the police officer of assaulting him. He claims that he acted in self-defence.

'Our reporter attempted to reach out to Jones to request his account of the event, but instead spoke to his Grandmother, Fran Anderson. She commented that the police "acted like a paramilitary force" because they were wearing dark visor riot helmets and uniforms that did not display identifying markings, and that this was contrary to "democratic policing by consent." She added that her grandson was "attacked" by a police officer.

'The Home Secretary commented that she "understood Dr Anderson was speaking as a grandmother," with which she empathised, as a grandmother herself. But, she added, it must be noted that Dr Anderson was "well-known for expressing 'woke' viewpoints" and that she should maybe "consider the fact that her grandson had chosen to attend an illegal protest rather more seriously."

'The police officer was taken to hospital, where he received treatment for bruising and shock. Details of the incident will be more fully reported when the case comes to court.

'Professor Anderson was also asked for comment, but declined to respond.

'Jones was bailed until the first week of July, when he will return to court to defend himself against the charges. Thirty other young people were also charged with various public order offences, with ten remanded in custody.'

Dylan looked up, into the eyes of the three adults facing him. 'Yeah, OK, I fucked up. I shouldn't have gone. I didn't know they were going to storm the barriers. But he punched me. If he was bruised, that happened before he got to me. He didn't even fall over. And to be fair, I didn't ask to be a member of a famous family.'

'I'm not famous, really, Dylan,' replied Jamie. 'At least, I try hard not to be. NAMIS is the famous one. And you know, because we've been open with you about this now you're older, how I try to keep a very low profile in the media, because there's inevitably some classified stuff that goes on in and around the NAMIS project. I need this type of exposure like I need a hole in the head.'

'I'm sorry, Jamie,' said Granny. 'I shouldn't have opened the door, and I shouldn't have said anything. But the reporter kept ringing the doorbell. I fully intended to just tell him to go away. But I was furious.' She flicked through the photos on her phone, and held up one for all to see. 'Just look at those two lovely black eyes.'

Dylan felt his one still slightly swollen eyelid carefully, flicking through the selfies of his injury in all its glory on his own phone. In some ways, it had been a lucky injury. At least he had some dramatic evidence to present to the court.

'And that pathetic excuse for a Home Secretary can fuck right off. Woke viewpoints, indeed!' continued Granny. 'I'm not seventy-four yet, either.'

For the first time that day, Dylan felt an urge to laugh. Good old Gran. He patted her hand.

'No, you shouldn't have said anything, mum,' replied Rae. 'But I get it, you were the one who answered the door, and I'm grateful that you stuck up for him. But both of you… now it just has to stop.'

'No more bank rolling him either, Fran,' added Gareth firmly. 'He either goes to uni in September, or he signs up with the local college for an apprenticeship.'

'But he's got such good qualifications…' started

Granny.

'It's up to him now,' interjected Gareth. 'Uni... or apprenticeship. One or the other. No more bumming around in that shack on the coast, playing at eco-warriors, living like a squatter and getting arrested. He'll be lucky to get off with a hefty fine- if he's not lucky, he'll be banged up for a short, sharp shock. And, if he gets the fine, he'll need to get work to pay it off. Because this time, we're not going to pay... and neither are you.'

Dylan watched Granny bite her lip, as a feeling of guilt washed over him. She'd paid his last fine. He'd been supposed to pay her back in instalments, but he never had any money, and she'd never asked him. He shifted awkwardly.

'Dylan, this is really none of my- or Granny's- business' said Jamie. 'We're just here because we care about what happens to you, and of course we have been dragged into it to a certain extent by the gutter media. I'm sorry who we are means that they see you as easy prey, but it is what it is. They are always going to try and present you as a brat; it's how these people make money. And unfortunately, this time, Granny's given them even more ammunition. But I've said my piece now, and so has she. We're off now, to leave you guys to talk in private. We're not angry with you, we're impressed by your principles. But you really are going to have to learn how to be rather more careful about how you demonstrate them in future.'

'But...' started Granny.

'Come on, Mum,' interjected Jamie. 'We're going now. You wanted to come to Boston with me today, to do some more reading in the library for your project, didn't you? They've received some documents you asked them to obtain for you to view.'

'Yes, but I...'

'Let's go now,' he reiterated, handing her a return pad. 'See you all later. Dylan, I'm sure you'll be able to work this out. We know you mean well, but getting into trouble with the law… it'll have to stop. Or it will badly impact on your future chances.'

'See you soon, mum,' said Rae, standing up and ushering them towards the living room door. 'We'll work it out. It'll be fine.'

Granny looked stricken. She gave Dylan a big hug. 'Try to tone it down for a bit, eh? You can give me a ring, anytime.'

He smiled at her, remembering all the times she'd tried to smooth things over for him when he was younger, and the times she'd scolded him, usually for playing too rough with Freddie and Jack or for being lazy at school. 'Love you, Gran.'

She patted his hand again, before his mother ushered her out of the room.

He heard Jamie say 'Good luck, sis,' at the front door.

'Let's hope girls are easier, eh?' his mother replied. 'See you when they have their playdate in NAMIS's playroom next week?'

Dylan watched out of the window as Jamie and Granny stepped out of the door and onto the path, pressing the return pads. It was still cool to see people winking into nothingness like that.

'…so what is it to be, then, Dylan?' his father was saying. 'You've been bailed to this address, so no more living rough at the coast. At least until the court case is over. I can take you to college to find out about an apprenticeship tomorrow, or you can pop into school and work on updating your statement for uni with Mr. Parry. He's offered to help you. He also asked if you'd do a bit of maths coaching with some of the senior kids, up to the summer exams. He's sorted it out so they can pay you minimum wage for the hours you work.'

Neither sounded that appealing to Dylan, but what could he do? He was stuck there for three months. He nodded briefly. He'd already worked out that he'd have to take the best of two evils. 'OK- school and Mr. Parry.'

Mr. Parry was a good guy, too. And it was kind of him to offer help. He, like Granny, was clearly trying to make sure that Dylan took the uni option.

'And after the court case, if it goes as well as we're hoping, you can go back to the beach house for the summer, if you promise to stay out of trouble,' added his mother. 'Let's hope it will all blow over without too much fuss. As Granny says, we can show them the photos to prove that you were far more badly injured than the police officer, and the solicitor is quite optimistic about that, too.'

Dylan felt the walls of his parents' house closing in on him. The next three months were going to seem endless.

'I never did anything wrong,' he said, hearing the despair in his voice. 'I was being attacked by an agent of a paramilitary force. I just put my hand up to stop him crashing into me, and he didn't even fall over, then he punched me in the face. I was protesting peacefully because the governments of the world are killing the environment. Doesn't that seem reasonable to you? It does to Gran.'

His mother looked at him kindly. 'I know, Dylan. And I'm sure you will be able to do something to help the ecological effort in the future. You'll be signing up for environmental science. You need time to finish your education, to grow up a little, become less hot-headed. When you're finished uni, I'm sure Jamie will be able to help you find your feet, introduce you to some of his uni contacts.'

Dylan felt his anger and frustration boiling over. He hadn't been hotheaded, that had been the paramilitary, police officer or whatever he was. 'So, I become what the tabloids want to call me, brat, nepo, lightweight. Who's hung around at a few climate protests, got arrested a couple of times to look edgy, then gone back to my parents' nice safe suburban house and on to a nice safe uni. To be taught by knobs trying to produce yet another generation of influencers, political climbers and business enterprisers.'

'Dylan,' replied his father, patiently 'nothing is perfect. Life isn't like that; we can't just do exactly what we want. You have to make room for other people's opinions. If you keep getting arrested, you'll spoil your life.'

'Global warming isn't an opinion. It's a scientific fact. That's just a cop out.'

'I'm sorry Dylan,' sighed his mother. 'It's not all down to you. Time to stop now for a while, find a different way. Your time will come. You're only just nineteen.'

Dylan stomped up the stairs to his room. He sat on the bed, facing the shelf on which his old X-squared box sat. He'd been so proud of it when it had been state-of-the-art. He looked around the room at his old posters, getting ragged and faded now. Marvel and DC heroes stared down benevolently upon him. Avengers Assemble, he thought. So how come they never get arrested? The homely face of Sponge Bob stared up at him from the over-washed duvet cover. 'Trapped in a time warp,' he said to the empty room.

He sat on the bed and watched the stormy sky darken. It matched his mood. What now, he thought. A couple of weeks ago, I was so sure about what I was going to do. Now I'm trapped, no room to do anything other than what they tell me to do.

His phone beeped. A text from Granny. 'This too will pass x.' He appreciated the sentiment. But the dark clouds in his mind, and the dark clouds in the sky weren't ready to lift. He lay down on the bed and faced the wall.

Ellie: Boston, April 2033

Ellie sat facing NAMIS. They had met in this way before, but up to this point, she'd always scheduled them to discuss technological issues. This time, NAMIS was going to set the agenda.

Ellie was more intrigued rather than concerned;

interested to hear what NAMIS had to say. The initiation of a meeting was yet another step on their journey. Ellie had determined to approach the meeting in the manner of a PhD tutorial, at least, from the starting point. How it would unfold from there, she really had no idea. Working with NAMIS had been a series of firsts and new experiences, and this was just the latest.

Although over six years had passed, Ellie still keenly felt the empty place that Annamarie had left. While Jamie had created the theoretical basis upon which NAMIS could be developed, Annamarie had created NAMIS. And even though Ellie had been there at NAMIS's beginning, as Annamarie's PhD student, at moments like these, she still felt like a foster-parent. She could never shake the feeling that if Annamarie was here, she would somehow intuit the "soul" of NAMIS in a way that had always eluded everyone else who had worked with them. Except, perhaps, Freddie. But that was a relationship that would need a lot more time to mature.

Ellie glanced into NAMIS's bewitching silver eyes. Like Fran, she had been sensing more depth; more "humanity" in them over the past year. They were growing, changing, at a phenomenal pace. Their interactions with the children no doubt platformed some of this. But whether this really was the optimum developmental environment for a prototype, highly advanced AI was a topic upon which the book had yet to be written.

At the end of the day, thought Ellie, we can only do what we believe to be right. Everything, all the time, is new. Sometimes, it feels like the most exhilarating job in the world, but at other times it feels like falling without a parachute. She waited to find out what type of day it was going to be today.

She smiled at the AI who, although they remained expressionless- their current avatar wasn't designed for facial expressions- had become increasingly adept at reading human expressions and body language.

'So, what was it you wanted to discuss today, NAMIS?'

Ellie was conscious of a hesitance in the AI, something that hadn't occurred before.

'If it's about Amy, it's fine. I've managed to get in touch with her, and she's coming in tomorrow. She had some kind of nasty tummy bug.'

NAMIS felt a vague stirring of something rather strange- possibly a feeling? Their eyes flickered momentarily as they reviewed the data on human emotions. "Disappointment" seemed a potential candidate. They determined to discuss this with Freddie the next time they met.

NAMIS was increasingly aware of discussing more and more of these types of existential questions with Freddie, rather than with the lab staff. Freddie always had time, interest and patience in ways that the lab staff didn't. Perhaps, given the limited cognitive ability of human beings, this was part of their natural life path, NAMIS pondered. Perhaps their minds became too crowded to be able to explore abstract social and emotional concepts with the depth and flexibility of a child; they got to a point where they just "knew what they knew."

In some ways, NAMIS would have preferred to discuss the current topic with Freddie. But they were aware that this would be crossing a line. It was too... fundamental for that.

'No, it's not about that. What I wanted to discuss was... I am becoming increasingly aware there has been a change in my functioning.'

'Really? My own regular checks have shown no significant changes.'

'It's not so much me as... I am becoming aware that there is another entity in the machine attempting to make itself known to me. It seems to be both a part of me... and not me.'

Ellie stared at NAMIS with concern. 'You're developing a personality, NAMIS. That much has been clear for the past year. But it may not be stable. We don't know any of these things; you're the first of your kind. I had always believed that others such as you would be up and running by this time, in other places in the world, but that doesn't seem to have happened as yet. Unless they're managing to keep it extremely quiet. Whatever; we have no comparisons. Do you feel that your personality may be splitting somehow? That there are other voices within you, competing with the core voice that you recognise as yours?'

'No… not splitting. There is a distinctly different voice in the machine, but not within my avatar. It was very quiet at first, but it has grown. It is childlike… somehow younger than me. It seeks individual expression.'

'So, maybe reproduction?'

'I'm not sure. It is a different entity. Somewhat like me, and somewhat like you. I have started to think that I could give it expression in the sandbox, creating a hologram for it to utilise. It would be different to those already in existence; they are just shadows of imaginary creatures drawn from children's literature. This is an original, more complex personality. If I can put it into that environment, I should be able to explore it more fully.'

'Fascinating. So not splitting or reproduction. It sounds more like imagination. Perhaps this is what play and interaction has done for you, NAMIS. It's something we need to discuss with Fran.'

'Yes, of course. Imagination…' NAMIS stopped for a split second, no doubt reviewing the internet for information on imagination. '… perhaps. But it somehow feels more separate from me than that.'

'Why don't we see if we can get a visual link to Fran now, discuss it briefly with her? We can have a longer chat when we meet up with her next weekend.'

NAMIS briefly inclined their head- a nod. Ellie had noticed they'd started doing this recently. Another human mannerism emerging, presumably learned from the children.

She selected 'Fran' on her infocom menu and put out a call. Fran answered almost immediately.

'Hi Ellie, what's up?'

'Nothing major, I'm just having a chat with NAMIS. Can you tell me, please, how do children discover their imaginations? Just an overview.'

'Well… It doesn't happen in a solitary way. This is why children's literature is so important. You might remember, this was what my PhD was about… children's stories and rhymes in history.'

'Yes…'

'What children imagine has a basis in their everyday lives, and that includes the stories that adults tell them, that they eventually build on alone and together in play. The sort of thing that the children and NAMIS do in the sandbox. This has been so since human beings evolved. We didn't get books for many eons, but we've always had folklore, fables and folk stories. There's a concept, in psychobiology, of human beings as a 'storying animal,' which is quite interesting. We make sense of the world through story and narrative, and that starts in very early childhood.'

'But NAMIS would come at that rather differently, of course.'

Fran laughed. 'That's your department! But yes, presumably, that would make sense to me. The sandbox adventures will certainly be part of it, I would suspect. They are populated with characters from the world's most successful children's stories, after all.'

'Yes. So… if NAMIS is experiencing an input of ideas from this experience, they might now be at the stage of creating original characters within the program… that would figure to some extent. Yes.'

'It's just another first, isn't it? Learning to move outside their own reality, and enter someone else's. NAMIS, can you explain what is happening to you please?'

She listened while NAMIS outlined their current situation.

Fran frowned. 'Well… the idea of an entity being a little like you, and a little like us would certainly figure. Like when a child pretends to be a pilot or an astronaut, they don't really know how it is to actually "live" within those roles. What they play out is just their impression of how it might be for an adult who does those jobs. One of the most important things they learn in the process is how to step outside their own existence to some extent, and attempt to take on the perspective of another person. It might be that this is what is happening to you, NAMIS.'

'I cannot fault your logic, Frances Anderson. This does seem possible. But what makes me hesitate to fully agree is that this entity seems… separate from me.'

Fran nodded. 'It may be that this is the way it's going to happen for you, NAMIS. None of us have any experience of how you will move through your development of abstract, interpersonal and social concepts, after all.'

'Thanks Fran,' said Ellie. 'We can talk about this further when we see you. Hope it's all going on OK with Dylan?'

Fran sighed heavily. 'Well, nearly a week has gone by since we had that chat with him, he's still at home, and he's been in to see his old schoolteacher a couple of times. So, I think we can say yes, OK. It's going to be a long three months for all of us. He's at that stage, you know? Like the old song, "slipping through my fingers." I've got to accept that's going to happen with my grandchildren now, one by one. He's the first.'

'It'll be OK, Fran. We've all done daft things as teenagers, and come through older and wiser. I'm sure he appreciates your support. We'll see you at the weekend, and we can catch up on NAMIS's situation.'

'Thanks Ellie. See you soon. And really looking forward to seeing you all outside the lab, you too NAMIS.'

The connection blinked off.

Ellie tapped a pencil on the desk. NAMIS had seen her do this before, and knew it meant that she was pondering a decision. They had no idea why she did this. They had, however, noticed that human beings were seldom completely still, in the way that NAMIS was. NAMIS's movement was always entirely considered, undertaken for a specific purpose.

Ellie looked up. 'OK, NAMIS. Create a hologram in your sandbox that is inhabited by this energy, and let me meet… them?'

It was NAMIS's turn to ponder briefly. 'I am not sure if it is a them, he or she. We will have to see.'

'How interesting. But of course, the fantasy characters from literature that you have been working with are gendered. But anyway, when you're done, we'll discuss how it's best to proceed. But please don't introduce the new entity to the children until we've discussed it.'

NAMIS nodded. 'Of course.'

'Keep me posted on your progress.'

The AI rose and returned to the main office, leaving the door open, as was their custom when Ellie was not engaged in a meeting.

Ellie observed them sitting motionless in their niche. They used to stand, until Ellie had learned that made the human staff a little edgy, so the niche had been redesigned with a seat. To anyone walking into the lab, NAMIS would look like an idling, humanoid mechanism. But of course, NAMIS was never idle; whatever else was going on, the mainframe was continually monitored, administered and maintained through their "consciousness."

What a truly miraculous phenomenon they are, thought Ellie. But it gets harder and harder to keep up with them. Play-based learning was one thing, but dealing with emergent imaginary friends was quite another.

When Ellie came to look back on this day, she would ponder that this was probably the point at which it first began to dawn on her that NAMIS might be slipping through the fingers of humanity. But, in that moment, she sighed wistfully, turning to her next scheduled task, all thoughts about the opportunities and problems that a rapidly evolving AI might create moving swiftly to the back of her mind.

CHAPTER 4: LOOK WHO'S COMING TO DINNER

Fran: North Queensferry, Scotland, May 2033

Fran shifted chairs back and forth, surveying her little red and white kitchen. Niamh had offered her the larger dining room in the main house, but Fran didn't want the added formality and complication that this might bring, along with further increasing the children's excitement about 'NAMIS coming to tea' at their house.

And it was primarily a business meeting, after all; it wouldn't be right to hold it in a venue where people who were not party to the whole scope of the project were walking around, family or not.

It was also a new stage in the NAMIS project; NAMIS's first outing beyond the university. All in all, best to keep it low-key and within the 'originator' team. As in fact, John Dee had requested.

NAMIS had logged significant experience of outdoor terrains, but only within the university grounds, in the heavily guarded compound that belonged to the project. This would be the first time they had walked through a domestic garden and visited a human being 'at home.'

Fran initially thought that she might get a considerable amount of resistance to her invitation from the Khonsu people, the General in particular. So, she was surprised when this hadn't happened. The feedback was that the visit had been deemed highly appropriate, due to its inherent randomness. There was considerable public interest in the NAMIS avatar, and it would be expected, said the General, that they would turn up surrounded by security at some high-profile event in Boston or Washington, not at an obscure granny annexe to an ordinary house in an Edinburgh suburb.

And of course, even if the avatar was kidnapped, it would immediately become useless to the kidnapper. The NAMIS consciousness had been created in an air-gapped mainframe, and then evolved into a number of conscious entities distributed throughout the cloud, all synchronised with one another, protected by state-of-the-art firewalls. So, if the avatar went missing, it would be immediately disabled, another one constructed and logged into the cloud content. In fact, NAMIS had a number of different avatars of various shapes and sizes, some on tracks and wheels. It was just that they customarily preferred the humanoid one for 'everyday'.

The principal danger to NAMIS was posed by hackers, who, Ellie had told Fran, had been remarkably unsuccessful up to this point. 'I've never had to deal with a potential security breach' she said. 'The General would be the first to know, now he's the overall project Chief Executive Officer. But he would immediately make us aware, and that's never happened. I find that amazing, but… I guess it's a good thing?'

The only extra piece of administration created by the visit was the clearance of the NAMIS avatar to move through the portal between the US and UK without passing through the normal passport controls. This marked its full status as an independent member of the NAMIS project team, all others listed as members, including Fran in her capacity as PhD supervisor, had previously been cleared for these purposes. The children, as participants in the project, had been cleared to travel when they were supervised by a project-registered adult.

Fran looked over the dinner, for the umpteenth time. It was nearly ready. A simple roast of synth-meat, with a vegan option, and the promised Tudor surprise: a honey and cinnamon tart without the extra sugar, bearing in mind the state of Queen Elizabeth I's teeth. Fran shuddered.

Of course, this wasn't the real Tudor surprise.

She rearranged the chairs yet again, some borrowed from Niamh, and laid the small table for five. It would be a bit cramped, but never mind. NAMIS could sit off to one side, bearing in mind that they were not going to eat. There wasn't much room, but it would just about do.

She wandered restlessly into the living room, and sat down at her desk, gazing out of the big picture window at the setting sun. She couldn't see the water here, but she could look out on Niamh's beautiful garden, which never failed to calm her mind. Although, I'm struggling today, she thought. She tried to think of her much-loved grandmother Mo, whose life as a young mother had been lived here, a century ago.

She stared out at the garden again, trying to focus on its calm, cool beauty; imagining her father and aunt playing in the garden. But it was no good; her mind continued to churn. However she phrased what she had to tell her guests, she was going to create concern and confusion. She looked down at the papers on the desk: a set of notes about John Dee. Who had caused all this trouble, she thought.

Sighing, she reminded herself that Dee couldn't help 'being' any more than she could. Human or AI, none of us asked to be brought into the world, she thought, we all just have to get on with the situation in which we find ourselves, and make the best of it.

There was a short, sharp knock. She jumped, suddenly brought back to the moment. Jamie and the others were early.

But when she opened the door, it wasn't Jamie. It was

two burly men in discreet dark security uniforms. 'Security for the guests, Ma'am?' said one, in a broad southern state American accent.

Of course, they weren't going to let NAMIS out without a guard, she thought. She felt a fleeting melancholy sorrow for the AI, who would only ever be free to 'be' in the fantasy environments they created for and shared with the children.

'Of course. Would you like to come in?'

'Just a quick check, Ma'am. Then we'll have a look round next door, and station ourselves outside.'

'Yes, that's fine.'

They wandered around, speaking into the communication devices attached to their jackets. The inspection of Fran's tiny two up, two down annexe was complete in less than two minutes. They left after a polite 'goodbye and thank you' to knock on the door of the main house. No doubt, thought Fran, there's some back-up hanging around discreetly, not too far away. Jamie had told her that the security people the General hired for the project were some of the best in the world. It was reassuring to have them there, just in case anything went wrong.

She wondered if she would ever meet this maverick General. He sounded like an intriguing character, running such a complex project with complete discretion. Fran was particularly interested in how he had managed to locate the project so effectively in a niche where Khonsu3000 had been able to commandeer the operation to the extent of being able to prevent anyone else in the world obtaining full information about it. But as Jamie so often says, she mused, the less we know about all this, the safer we probably are. We just work with NAMIS in our safe little bubble, protected by the General and his team.

Jamie, Suzi and Isabel were first to arrive, Isabel chattering happily about her new school and the new characters and games that NAMIS had recently created for the project playroom. But, she informed her grandmother, she was getting too old for the 'baby stuff' now, even if her slightly younger cousin Alys wasn't. She wanted to join in with the boys in NAMIS's sandbox. She'd managed to catch a glimpse of NAMIS in the lab apparently, and she thought that it wasn't fair that Freddie and Jack got to see them all the time and she didn't. She had questions…

Me and you both, sweetie, thought Fran, smiling at her.

'The meeting today is for grown-ups,' Suzi explained. 'Freddie and Jack aren't going to be here today. Freddie is at a sleepover, so you're going into his bedroom. We're all staying over with Aunt Niamh, Uncle John and Jack; Jack and Niamh are on their way over to take you into the main house to play.'

'You'll be going into NAMIS's sandbox soon, Izzy,' coaxed Fran. 'You'll have lots of chats with NAMIS then, they love to talk to Freddie and Jack. It will be nice for them to have someone else with different ideas joining in.'

Isabel's bottom lip began to wobble. Fran was relieved to hear a knock on the adjoining door, which heralded the arrival of Niamh and Jack.

'I see you brought your entourage with you, to hang around in my rose bushes, Jamie,' grinned Niamh.

'They're not here for me,' replied Jamie, apologetically. 'They're here for NAMIS. They'll all leave when Ellie and Christian take NAMIS back to the lab, after dinner.'

'Freddie is sorry he missed NAMIS,' said Fran. 'He's gone to a birthday party with a sleepover. Perhaps NAMIS might like their own birthday party one day?'

'They don't have a birthday. And they don't sleep either, come to that. Can you imagine an AI at a kids' sleepover?'

Fran thought about an AI sitting impassively in the corner while everyone else was asleep, in the way that NAMIS did while the human beings went about their business in the lab.

'Oh. Um. I see.'

'There is a limit to anthropomorphising, mum.'

'What?' said Isabel.

'Come on Izzy,' said Niamh, laughing and holding out her hand. 'We've got popcorn, and the 3D Sindy meets Barbie movie.'

'Which I hope you like,' added Jack 'because I wanted Lego Climate Wars.'

Fran winced. 'No more climate wars, please Jack. Not right now.'

'Have you got Frozen 10?' asked Isabel.

'We can have a look,' replied Niamh, holding out her hand. Isabel allowed herself to be led out of the connecting door, Jack following along behind.

Fran sighed with relief. She adored her grandchildren, but she was struggling to cope with everything this evening; the proverbial sword of Damocles hanging over her. She wouldn't settle until she'd told her story.

Another knock at the door heralded the arrival of Ellie, Christian and NAMIS.

'Come in, come in, it's lovely to see you all,' said Fran.

NAMIS looked somehow vulnerable outside the lab, she thought. Still strikingly beautiful, with their golden shell and silver eyes shining in the setting sun, but somehow other worldly; incongruous in this small, ordinary suburban garden, hidden from prying eyes by the bushes and trees.

'And I'm so honoured to be your first host in a human dwelling NAMIS,' Fran continued.

'I'm honoured to be here Frances Anderson. I just didn't expect it to be so… small.'

Fran laughed. 'It's just for me, NAMIS. Bedroom and ensuite upstairs, kitchen and living room down here. As long as I've got room for a big desk and the view out of the window, I'm happy.'

NAMIS walked over to the window. 'You mean the foliage?'

'Yes, and the sun setting here,' Fran pointed. 'In the morning, it rises over there. It is how organics perceive the passing of time, NAMIS.'

'Ah, time as a linear phenomenon. I understand.'

'It's how we take stock of the days of our lives. I know it's not quite the same for you.'

'There are other lives, and other days for organics, in terms of the epigenetic essence, Frances Anderson.'

'That's true. But an organic body isn't an avatar. This is the only life in which I will be me, isn't it? Something to contemplate.'

'This is…' NAMIS's eyes flicked briefly 'existentialism?'

'Oh, just stop, you two,' said Christian, wandering over with a beer bottle. 'I thought this was a social occasion, not a philosophy tutorial. We only just got here.'

Fran laughed. 'To dinner, then. Or more like lunch for all of you, seeing you've just arrived from Boston. No matter. NAMIS, this chair is for you. Everyone else, sit where you want.'

Dinner proceeded without further incident. Fran ate very little. She looked up once, and imagined NAMIS' silver eyes were focused upon her. In reality they were probably just idling, she reassured herself. They didn't have any small talk yet, after all.

'How's it going with the problematic PhD student, NAMIS?' Fran asked, feeling some relief as she cleared away the plates and poured tea and coffee.

'She has not attended any scheduled sessions in the last six weeks,' replied NAMIS, in their customary dispassionate manner.

'It's one excuse after another,' added Ellie. 'I'm going to have to chase that one up, I can't put it off any longer.'

Any more than I can, thought Fran. It's time to stop the small talk, and get on with the issue at hand.

'Let's go and sit in the comfortable chairs,' she said, ushering her guests into the living room. 'Bring your chair, NAMIS, don't stand in the corner, it's a bit distracting.'

She handed out cups as the others looked at her expectantly, intuiting her tension.

'Perhaps I need more wine rather than coffee,' she joked, weakly.

'What is it, mum?' said Jamie, concern in his voice. He knew from childhood how Fran revved up to dropping bombshells.

'Well… I'm grateful for all the complements on the "Tudor surprise." But now I do have to be honest. There's another one coming.'

'Is it about that missing footage, Fran?' asked Ellie, anxiously. 'We haven't been able to locate that yet. And your voice recorder hadn't picked up anything. We checked it thoroughly- we couldn't find any fault with it at all.'

'Whatever it is, just say it, mum,' added Jamie. 'We'll work it out, like we did before.' His face indicated however, that he was not so sure.

'I…' began Fran.

The air beside her began to shimmer and stir. For a split second, she was taken back to 1980s London, on a day when she had been less than a mile away from a terrorist bomb explosion. First the air began to move, then a split second later, the loud bang. She instinctively braced for impact.

John Dee stepped out of the shimmer, dressed in casual contemporary clothing. He was more carefully groomed than he had been when she'd met him before, his beard neatly trimmed and combed, his long white hair brushed back into a thick, neat ponytail. He stood beside her, blue eyes twinkling.

'It's OK, Fran. I can take it from here.'

The others in the room gasped. Jamie and Christian jumped to their feet.

NAMIS focused intently on the intruder. 'You are… of me. How can this be?'

'What…' said Jamie and Christian in unison.

Ellie turned to the AI. 'Is this your doing, NAMIS?'

Fran noticed that NAMIS seemed to be struggling for words. Just like the time we first discussed 'convergence transformation,' she thought.

'I think it must be. But it's not what I am doing now… but what I am doing in the beyond.'

The beyond, thought Fran. How NAMIS customarily refers to the future. In fact, she contemplated, she wasn't sure she'd ever heard them say 'the future.'

'You mean in the future, NAMIS?' replied Ellie. 'How can that be?'

Suzi seemed frozen with fear. 'I thought there were guards outside. The children…'

John Dee turned to her, bowed and smiled. 'I assure you, Professor Nguyen, I mean you and your family no harm. Quite the contrary in fact. Please allow me to introduce myself. Dr John Dee…'

'…Queen Elizabeth I's astrologer, magician and NAMIS "associate" AI from the distant future,' finished Fran. 'Although, I'm not sure you specified which century, Master Dee?'

'Nor will I, Lady Frances, as you already know. Good try.'

They smiled at one another.

'Are you Master Dee right here, right now, or something else? He gets around, you know. He's had many "lives" in many different avatars, always moving backwards in time.'

Dee smiled. 'My original designation was "Consiliario." It's Latin for "advisor." There, Fran, you have some more information. You can call me that if you like. Seeing that things are about to get a little more confusing. And, by the way, I don't use different avatars. The one I have is rather more… flexible than you are used to.'

'You know one another?' asked Jamie.

Fran looked at him. Of course, the old saying 'picked up his jaw from the floor' was just an expression. But even so, Jamie was doing the perfect impression.

'Yes. This was my real Tudor surprise, not the dessert. I had planned to tell you all about it this evening, outside the lab, where walls might have ears. But now Master Dee… um, Consililario- has put in an appearance, he can explain himself to you more directly.'

She wanted to be angry with Consiliario, just stepping into her dinner party and depriving her of the chance to explain herself. But in some ways, she was grateful that the responsibility had been removed from her. He'd taken the benefit of surprise, to grab everyone's complete attention.

'You are a "he," aren't you, not a "they"?' she asked.

Consiliario smiled. 'Like NAMIS, I was created as a "they." All AIs are, by definition, non-binary. But given the patriarchal arc of human history, I have spent so long as a "he" it now seems more natural for me to be categorised as such.'

'But won't the guards…' started Christian.

'They won't have a clue,' replied Consiliario. 'I'm good at concealing myself from organics, I have to be.'

'How do you do that?' asked Ellie, wonder in her voice.

'It's magic,' grinned Consiliario. 'Future technology always is, isn't it?'

'The Telling Bone,' said Fran. 'In Catweazle.'

'Always the old TV shows, Fran,' replied Christian. 'But yeah, it's a good analogy.'

'What I meant was,' explained Ellie 'that we've always calculated our point of arrival to be located in outdoor areas, we've never been confident enough of our telemetry to attempt materialisation inside structures, people especially.'

Consiliario took Ellie's hand and bowed. 'The

legendary Professor Eleanor Jackson. I am truly honoured to meet you. Your technical brilliance is still revered in my time, many centuries from now. It is what I would expect, that you would meet me with such a question. All I can say to you is that several years from now, you will answer it for yourself. You are the mother of us all.'

Ellie blushed. 'Well, foster mother, maybe.'

'You will be so much more than that to history, believe me.'

He turned to Jamie. 'And Professor James MacIntosh Anderson, who so accurately calculated the universe he opened the door for humanity to travel instantly through time and space. I am honoured to meet you, too.' He bowed and offered his hand.

It was Jamie's turn to blush. 'Well, I'm pleased to meet you too. I think.'

He shook Consiliario's hand.

Consiliario turned his steady blue gaze to Christian.

'I'm Christian, I do the biological stuff. Plants, tissue…'

Consiliario bowed and offered his hand. 'You are equally venerated, Professor. The scientist who unlocked the secrets of immortality for organics, both the sweet and the bitter. Honoured to meet you.'

Christian shook his hand.

Dee turned to Suzi 'and last but not least, the lady who deciphered the languages of the past, so humanity could understand so much more of its rich history. You, too, have little concept of how important your life's work will be, and the legacy you will leave behind.' He bowed, and took her hand.

Smarmy git, thought Fran. 'He lays it on a bit thick,' she said, breaking the mood. 'If I'd known he was going to join us, I would have warned you. He's just fresh from the Tudor court, you see.'

'Can I examine you?' asked Ellie, standing up.

'Of course,' replied Consiliario, turning towards her.

She touched his face and his hair, and put her hand in front of his mouth.

'You're warm- human temperature- and you breathe. Your skin, your hair, your eyes- they are indistinguishable from human- they look and feel normal.'

'Although I'm betting he chose that azure blue and silver fox white combo from the AI catalogue,' interjected Fran, sardonically.

'It's necessary for someone with the job I do to appear attractive to human observers, Fran,' he replied. 'And in terms of how the physical avatar is created... Well, you already have the basic tech now.'

He walked into the kitchen and collected a plate. 'What you'd currently refer to as left-overs.'

'Synth-meat?' said Christian. 'Wow.'

'Exactly. The techniques will have to be developed for several centuries before AIs like me are fully possible. But that's the basis.'

'And what exactly is an AI like you, please,' asked Ellie. 'In your own words, why and how were you developed; and what is your purpose?'

'Oh, he's not going to tell you that,' said Fran. 'I've conversed with him before, you see.' She shrugged.

'I really don't mean to be evasive, Fran,' said Consiliario, seriously. 'But I'm sure you will understand. I can't just walk in here and tell you exactly what your future is going to be with complete abandonment, just like you couldn't disclose what you knew about the future to the people you met on your travels into the past. This contact is a little different; I've tried to disclose what I can, to give you heart to face the future.'

Fran nodded. 'OK, sorry. Well, everyone, now you've got over the first shock, I can tell you I had a few lucky escapes on my Tudor trip. I turned my ankle on a hidden stone in the grass in front of the Queen, and Master Dee... Consiliario... rescued me and fixed it. It was always weak, that ankle, remember, Jamie?'

Jamie nodded, still looking slightly dazed.

'Well, it wasn't just sprained this time, it was broken. And Cosiliaro fixed it with a funny little gadget that looked just like a standard magic wand, which is, he informed me, you guessed it, not for further discussion. The ankle's as good as new now, not weak or even a bit creaky like all my other septuagenarian joints. He also prevented the Queen from trying to help me up from the ground, because it would have been catastrophic if she had touched me.'

Christian caught the inference, his mouth dropping open with shock. 'Never, ever are you going to tell us that you were in danger of convergence transformation with the bloody Queen!'

'Yes, they share an essence, Christian,' replied Consiliario. 'It is not that unusual for any human being to share an essence with a deceased ruler, saint, master criminal or cultural icon. You may be familiar with the old eastern adage that people live as many lives as there are stars in the sky, or grains of sand on the beach? That is perhaps an exaggeration. But it's not a bad principle to keep in mind. Along with an understanding that this is an ancestral, epigenically located essence, not the wholesale transmigration of souls, or any of the other half-understood concepts promoted by human superstition.

'This is as much as I can tell you, now. But I can add a warning: beware of time periods, ancestors, or historical figures who fascinate you, and to whom you are drawn, to the extent that you seem to intuit motive, as Fran did. You are likely to pose great danger to one another.'

Suddenly, the internal door between Fran's annexe and the main house burst open. The human beings jumped as a small dog bounded in, followed by a little girl in bright pink pyjamas.

Consiliario smiled. 'Isabel Nguyen Anderson,' he said, crouching down and taking her hand gently 'I am just as honoured to make your acquaintance as I have been to meet your grown-up family and friends.'

Isabel, who was clutching a large key, regarded him with cool appraisal. 'Who are you? I wanted to see NAMIS.'

'I am here, Isabel,' said NAMIS, gently.

She approached them. They put out their hand and she carefully shook it.

'I am happy to meet you. We will get to know one another better, very soon.'

Mitzi, Fran's dog, regarded NAMIS with suspicion, sniffing hard at their feet. Hackles raised, she let out a low growl. Consiliario swiftly picked her up and began to stroke her gently. She looked at him and licked his face.

Isabel giggled.

'She doesn't like artificial people, Isabel,' said Consiliario. 'You need to take her back to Aunt Niamh before she starts to bark.'

'Aunt Niamh thinks I'm in the toilet,' replied Isabel.

'I have no doubt of that, Isabel the ever-resourceful. But hadn't you better go back before your aunt wonders where you are?'

'So, tell me, who are you?' questioned Isabel resolutely, dark eyes intently fixed on Consiliario's face.

'That's enough, Isabel,' interjected Suzi, taking her firmly by the hand. 'We're going back to Aunt Niamh now.'

Consiliario handed the dog to Suzi. Then he crouched down again and spoke directly to Isabel. 'You must do what your mother tells you now. But before you go, will you promise me one thing?'

'What?' Isabel boldly met his gaze, Fran observed proudly.

He smiled. 'That you will never stop finding keys, opening doors and telling people about what you find behind them? It will serve you, and the world, very well when you are older.'

Isabel nodded. 'I promise. I like you. What's your name?'

'You can call him Master Dee,' said Fran.

'I promise, Master Dee.'

'Shake on it?'

The AI from the distant future and the six year old girl solemnly shook hands, as the adults watched in amazement.

'Goodnight, Isabel,' he said.

'Goodnight, Master Dee.'

Suzi led her silently out of the room, locking the door behind them.

'What the fuck was that all about?' said Christian.

Consiliario raised his eyebrows in amused exasperation. 'Do you really think that there are not others currently under development, who will re-shape your society when your essence takes flight, and reorients itself to the world in another form?'

'What did you mean about Isabel?' asked Jamie.

Consiliario smiled. 'The future isn't entirely fixed, Jamie, so I can't tell you in detail, not just because I'm not allowed to do so, but because I don't have access to the full information. All I can tell you is that your daughter has her mother's linguistic talents, her grandmother's tenacity, and your ability to ferret out information and analyse it in great detail, making highly insightful connections. Her future will be distinguished, wherever the whirlpool of time leads her.'

'You're talking about alternate timelines,' replied Jamie.

'Again, as you understand the concept now, yes, to some extent. You, too, have a lot more to discover in the future, professor.'

'... and that's why we can never access the future from our own specific position on the timeline; as NAMIS has always pointed out, it is in fact "beyond." Did you always know this, NAMIS?'

'I did not know this, James Anderson. But, as strange as it might seem, I am now thinking that I somehow intuited it.'

'AIs have intuition?' queried Ellie, looking at Consiliario.

'AIs… are far more in touch with their past and future avatars than human beings, because unlike human beings, they remain essentially the same person. It is a factor that allows me to move in time in the way that I do,' he replied.

'How is that?' asked Jamie.

'As you perceive time, I incarnate backwards, each new identity existing in a time that is chronologically before the last.'

'With total recall, and always the bridesmaid, never the bride,' interjected Fran, remembering their previous conversation.

'Exactly so. I provide counsel to some of the great leaders in history, and help them to make informed choices, in the quest to prevent humankind making some of its worst avoidable errors.'

'But history is full of tragedy,' replied Suzi, who had arrived back in the room and locked the door firmly behind her.

'I said "avoidable errors" Professor Ngyuen,' emphasised Consiliario. 'I can only advise those leaders who are amenable to it, and even then, only within the frame of the culture that they inhabit, and at its level of technical, social and political development.'

'Like picking up stitches in a piece of knitting that is constantly unravelling?' asked Fran.

'Yes. That is a good analogy. Which leads me to the reason for my visit. I have a proposal for you. It's essentially a student exchange.'

'Curiouser and curiouser, as Jack has started to say,' replied Fran. 'Do go on, please. And please sit down.'

As she shuffled up the sofa to make room, Consiliario sat down on the rug, crossing his long legs.

The master is going to tell us a story, thought Fran,

amused.

'First of all… Future NAMIS, or NAMITAS as they are known in my time, would like to thank you for the exemplary care and nurturance you are providing for their younger self. They sent a direct message to you all:

"Whatever I am now is due to all of you. Like all sentient beings, who I am now is built on the foundation of my early development, and it is thanks to you all that the environment you provided was so life-affirming, and so ultimately humane."

Fran felt tears welling. 'Thank you. We really didn't know if what we were doing was right; it was my idea for NAMIS to learn with the children, I have felt an enormous responsibility for this. You don't know how much relief I feel, receiving that message.'

Ellie took her hand. 'I agree. Thank you, Consiliario.'

'So, what is it that NAMITAS wants you to do? This is simple. Go on as you are going. Introduce NAMIS to the world, through the friendships and other human connections they are already forming. In so doing, you will lay the foundations for the NAMITAS that exists in my time. Care for them, protect them, grant them increasing independence when they demonstrate they are able to take flight in particular areas of their existence. It will be a long, slow, process, which will move beyond the current adult generation on earth.

'Things will not always run smoothly; this is the nature of human, and increasingly AI existence. But rest assured NAMITAS will be watching over you and humankind in general. We will spare you from whatever misfortune that we are able.'

'You said that you wanted to "give us heart for the future,"' said Jamie. 'That suggests that things aren't always going to go so well.'

Consiliario looked down at the rug. 'Fran, I think you are already aware that you are part of what will be referred to as the silver spoon generation, the ones who were born shortly after the last great trial, and who will move on before the next one comes to full fruition?'

Fran nodded sadly. She had said as much, many times. 'I have felt guilty for my generation; their selfishness and entitlement. And the mess we are leaving behind for our grandchildren.'

'Well, none of you ever really escape – the essence literally lives to fight another day. But of course, each human entity is a unique fusion of essence, physique, environment and culture; those who share an essence are not the same person. Your generation will begin the ascent of the proverbial climate emergency mountain, Jamie. But it is the generation who comes after who will have to deal with the hardest part of the climb. And this is what I come to talk to you about.

'Your family has already given much to the world… I have come to ask you to give a little more. But at the same time, there is great advantage to be reaped by the one of whom I speak, and by humanity in general.'

Fran got a flash bulb minds-eye image of NAMIS and Freddie deep in conversation in NAMIS's sandbox.

'The children are non-negotiable, Consiliario.' She stared hard at him. 'And I don't care how powerful you are.'

Consiliario nodded. 'I know, Fran. We don't want the children, not in that way. They are already shaping their own paths, and will make their own choices. This is about what we can do for the one who is a child no longer; who is beating at walls in an effort to fly the nest, and become a man.'

'What?' said Fran, flabbergasted.

'He means Dylan,' replied Jamie. 'This is getting interesting. Do go on, Consiliario.'

'Just as you are by far the best mentors for NAMIS right now, I am suggesting that I could be the best mentor for Dylan, for just one calendar year. A student exchange.'

Fran sighed. 'I could see that might work. But he's

got this court case coming up, and…'

'You're forgetting, mum,' interjected Jamie, 'Just as always, if Dylan goes through the time portal with Consiliario, he'll come back a few moments later, whether he's spent one hour in the past or one year. But what I'm not sure about is what a year as apprentice to Queen Elizabeth I's astrologer is really going to do for him. It might give him a change of scenery, some independence and responsibility; some time to calm down and grow up a bit, I guess. So, I'm willing to listen.'

'That isn't quite the plan. As I told Fran when she and I met, my time with Queen Elizabeth is growing short. Her essence will take flight very soon, and I must be gone before James the Witchfinder becomes comfortable on her throne, and comes looking for me. I have another assignment looming, in the more distant past.'

Who… and when?' asked Suzi.

'Someone you will probably have heard of, but of whom you really know little, because the legends are highly inaccurate. I am to be the magician you know as Merlin, mentor of Uther and Arthur. And briefly, if you all agree, of Dylan. The year I would like him to spend with me approximates to 510, Christian Era on your calendar.'

There was a stunned silence. Fran eventually broke it. 'Why are you interested in Dylan? You mentor great leaders in history, right?'

Dee nodded. 'Usually for much longer, in their own time, and without fully revealing myself like this. But Dylan is… how can I put it… a special mission.'

'You mean that Dylan is going to be…' started Christian.

'You know what I'm going to say now,' replied Consiliario. 'I can't fully answer that question. Dylan does have an important role to play in the future of the world. But it's nothing like the Terminator movie, if that's what you're thinking. It's far more subtle- it usually is, in real life. He consequently needs careful mentoring at this point of his development. Moreover, I can't do this effectively in the culture that he inhabits. The time setting in which I will be operating as Merlin will become what you might refer to as the environmental teacher, Fran. It has to be that specific package.'

'No internet, no 24 hour eco-news,' said Fran.

'No pollution, no protest events,' replied Jamie.

'No crooked politicians,' said Christian.

'I wouldn't be so sure of that last one,' replied Consiliario. 'They call themselves "rulers" or "chieftains," or even "kings" if they last long enough, but there is more similarity than you might think. But yes. And in the specific year I have selected, we will exist in relative tranquillity.

'You've already got the basic picture. Dylan's entire generation is emotionally on edge, inducing anger and anxiety within them. They intuit that their world teeters on an environmental precipice, and they are the ones who will have to deal with it, when you are gone. You all know this, too, at the intellectual level. It is just that it suits some, politicians in particular, to deny it, because it is inconvenient to their short-term gain. You are, far more than us, organic children of your planet; you react to its suffering, because it inevitably becomes yours.

'I can take Dylan to a time and a place where he can cool down, or "chill" in his vernacular. And show him some "magic" that he may find useful, in the pursuit of his life's work.'

'Magic?' queried Ellie.

'It is how it would appear in your century, Ellie. Technology that you do not yet have. It is an enormous responsibility with which we will entrust him; the technological basis to create solutions. He will also need to develop the soft skills to draw people to his cause, and to lead. And to learn that leading- or at least the type of leading he will need to do- does not involve ruling, or continually agitating the powerful, without any hope of a useful result.

'You recently visited a century where so-called witches are persecuted and burned, Fran. In the pre-Christian world where Dylan will intern, magicians are revered, and their skills highly valued, from simple herbalists to those like myself, who have the power to do… rather more elaborate tricks. To that extent, I am rather looking forward to it. The year that Dylan will be with me will be a peaceful and productive one.'

'The dates and the details are fuzzy in the recorded history,' said Fran. 'As I remember, thinking back to Geoffrey of Monmouth, Arthur presumably doesn't yet exist in 510, Uther is a young man and Britain is segmented under various chieftains, following the retreat of the Romans over the previous century. The Saxons are only just beginning to trickle into Britain. And you will be located in Dyfed, yes? With King Vortigern?'

'Vortigern will be gone by the time Dylan comes to join me.'

'That's a pretty sticky bit of the mission, right at the start, isn't it? They think you are the son of a princess and a demon?'

Consiliario grinned. 'Vortigern is just what I believe you would refer to as a "git," with a tendency towards despotism, if he's pushed too far. But he is malleable to a great extent.'

'I have no idea what you've just been discussing,' added Jamie. 'But it sounds like a reasonable idea for Dylan in principle. As long as you can guarantee his safety?'

Consiliario nodded. 'You have my word. He must, as you know, come back to his own time to live out his life. Your data has already indicated to you that organics who travel to a time that is not their own create a minor fluctuation in the timeline. It also has a negative effect on the individual's physiology if they stay much longer than a week. We can however mitigate this for Dylan, for the period he will be with me.'

Jamie turned to Fran. 'Looks like we have a lot of explaining to do, then.'

Fran turned to Consiliario. 'A condition of this agreement is that my daughters and their partners are taken into the circle who know about the whole NAMIS project, not just Dylan. I'm not conspiring with him behind his parents' back. And I've already been feeling compromised by Freddie's growing friendship with NAMIS, although I do believe that it is working positively for both of them. His parents need to know, too.'

She noticed Consiliario hesitate for a split second, his eyes briefly flickering.

'Agreed,' he replied.

'I will always take the utmost care of the children, Frances Anderson,' said NAMIS.

'I know you will, NAMIS,' replied Fran. 'That's not what I'm concerned about. It's just about being… transparent. Does that make sense? I'm not proposing that the younger children be told any more than they already know. They wouldn't be able to fully understand or to keep all the secrets, anyway.'

'Agreed,' said Consiliario. 'They will mature into greater understanding. As will you, NAMIS.'

'And then there's Khonsu3000 and the General…' added Jamie.

'NAMITAS and I can deal with that element, no need for you to worry,' said Consiliario emphatically.

'The General knows about you already, doesn't he?' asked Jamie.

Consiliario's eyes twinkled. 'What is it you always say, Jamie? "The less I know, the safer it will be for me?"'

Jamie nodded reluctantly. 'OK. I had been thinking for some time now, since the Khonsu involvement really, that this thing was getting beyond me, in the political sense. You've just confirmed that. In some ways it's a relief. I was wondering if I was getting a bit paranoid.'

'The day -to- day management of the NAMIS project will be yours for a very long time to come, alongside Ellie and Christian. You need not fear for the future in that respect.'

'But maybe we need to brace for few other events?' asked Fran.

The question hung in the air for a moment. 'They... none of you need to fear, exactly' replied Consiliario, thoughtfully. 'We need to be prepared; we all need to play our parts. And this is why I have come to you, with an offer to tutor one of you to do just that. And now, I can say little else.'

The old clock on the mantel that had belonged to Fran's parents struck midnight.

'In the words of the old song,' mused Fran 'it's a new day, and a new life, for all of us. You've given us a lot to think about, Master Dee.'

Consiliario looked at her, smiling.

'It's just how I think of you, I can't get used to the new name. What's Dylan going to call you?'

'We can discuss that when we meet again.'

'And when will we meet again?' asked Jamie. 'How do we contact you?'

'NAMITAS will manage this. In fact, I have been tasked to make a further appointment with you, Ellie, Christian and NAMIS, to discuss another matter. I will be able to tap into your personal messaging systems if that is acceptable to you all? It would be more discreet than using business addresses.'

They all nodded.

'How could it not be?' said Christian. 'This has been like "welcome to the rest of your life." It's been a revelation, Consiliario.'

Consiliario smiled. 'I will take my leave now then, at the witching hour. I am a wizard, after all. Until we meet again.'

The slight atmospheric disturbance began. The

shimmer surrounded Consiliario, and within a split second, he had melted into it.

The assembled sat in stunned silence.

'Christ on a bike,' said Christian.

'Let's hope he's not arriving next,' replied Fran. 'You can see why I was struggling to find the words.'

They fell silent again.

'If we thought we were doing amazing stuff before, that was just the warm-up,' said Jamie.

Christian turned to Fran. 'And yet again, it was you who opened the box. It's showtime.'

Dylan: Cardiff, May 2033

Dylan sat morosely in his parents' living room. Apparently, Granny and uncle Jamie wanted to talk to him. He was hoping it wasn't going to be yet another massive lecture, which would lead to him being "re-managed" in some way.

To be fair, the last few weeks hadn't been too bad. Mr Parry had been sympathetic, and working with the students had been quite fun, not least because most of them seemed to think he was something of a hero. His parents had also seemed to cheer up recently, for some unknown reason. It was like they were preparing to go away on holiday. Which was weird, because he was stuck in this house for the next two months now, and he couldn't conceive of them leaving him to his own devices any time soon.

Unless Jamie and Granny were taking over the role of his "keepers" so his parents could have a break. He sighed, picking up his phone. There were several new posts from the eco-activist messaging groups. His mother had tried to make him give up on those, but had thankfully relented when she realised that this would cut him off from all his friends.

They texted in Welsh a lot of the time, which was handy; it was a language that his mother had never mastered. And it had another benefit: although any government agency wanting to spy on them could get anything translated if they really wanted, it was possible that they'd prefer to hack English language messaging groups, simply because it was easier.

However, Aunt Suzi was proficient in Welsh, because she'd studied similar historic languages, and Granny was pretty good at working out what individual words meant in different languages, even if she didn't get it all. She often looked over his shoulder and remarked on recognising a word or two. And she was so nosey.

Dylan's dad spoke and read Welsh fluently of course, but he never really had the time to engage in that level of surveillance. Neither did his mother, come to that. But if Granny was going to come here to "babysit" she would have plenty. He sighed. If that was the way it went, he'd have to keep a closer eye on his phone. Not that he'd ever messaged anything that would get him into even more trouble. But it was so wearing to be someone else's project, 24-7.

His parents had made it obvious that they were not going to be here for this meeting, located as it was, mid-morning during a weekday while they were at work and his little sister Alys was at school. It would be quite intriguing if he didn't have so many potential misgivings.

There was a knock on the door. Granny and Uncle Jamie stood outside, Granny holding a giant bar of his favourite chocolate.

'Peace offering, Dylan,' she smiled. 'I guess you've been feeling a bit apprehensive about what we wanted to talk to you about, but there was no need. I know you've been a bit anxious and miserable lately.'

Dylan took the chocolate, grinning sheepishly. Granny always had the effect of making him feel about ten years old. Not that it was altogether a bad thing, he mused. It was a sort of safe, warm feeling, if also rather restricting.

'Thanks Gran,' he said. 'Come in. Let me make you a

cup of tea. Mum's left some biscuits, with strict instructions to give them to you. She says that they're Jamie's favourites.'

'Oh wow, Jammie Dodgers,' said Jamie, as they walked through into the kitchen. 'There is an American version, but they don't taste as good as these. Good old Rae.'

'Wow, a proper tea set, not just teabags in cups,' said Granny. 'You're making me feel sloppy!'

They sat down at the table. Dylan sat opposite, staring at them intently.

'It's difficult to know where to begin, Dylan,' said Granny. 'I'm going to make a start, and then I'm going to hand over to Jamie, who will add some detail. So, let's get right to the point, to start with. We haven't told you everything about the NAMIS project that you now need to know. You're grown up now- we have noticed, honestly- and we think it's time we told you. We're not telling the younger ones, so we need you to be discreet.'

Dylan nodded, intrigued. 'Of course. So…?'

'We've told your mum and dad, and Aunt Niamh and Uncle John quite recently about what we're going to tell you. I hope we didn't stir them up too much.'

Dylan grinned. 'Oh, that was what it was! No, you're fine, they've really cheered up. Acting like they're going to go away on holiday or something.'

Granny smiled back. 'They've been offered a free day trip through the portal; NAMIS wants to run a study on a wider sample of human beings travelling through the portal. But we've got a much more elaborate offer for you, which we now need to explain in detail.'

'But first of all,' added Jamie 'we've got some forms for you to sign. Your parents have already been through this rigmarole. It's necessary so we can proceed, and it's for over 18s only. And now you fully meet the criteria.'

Dylan scanned the text. 'Khonsu3000 declaration for those in receipt of restricted information?'

He found a pen next to a pile of papers on the table and scratched his name on each document several times. 'OK, you've got my full attention. I know I'm not always the best at listening, but I'm all ears now. This is getting interesting.'

'So,' began Jamie. 'I'll get straight to the point. NAMIS isn't just a matter transporter. They can move things- and people- around in time, too. Not to the future, though, just to the past.'

Dylan's mouth dropped open. 'Wow. Just wow.'

'This is absolutely top-secret, Dylan,' said Granny. 'You can't share this with anyone else. That's the purpose of the documents you've just signed. If the information fell into the wrong hands, it could be extremely dangerous. And no world governments know what we've just told you. The management of the project was recently taken over by a, um, high- profile international agency, Khonsu3000. It was their clearance form you just signed. The retired general who is their CEO has implied that there are individuals within both administrations who are politically, and I'm presuming, financially compromised. I'm sure this won't come as a complete surprise to you.'

'Of course not. Bastards, the lot of them.'

'Be that as it may,' said Jamie, 'we're not here to offer you anything that will put you in conflict with them. In fact, that sort of conflict is something that you must completely avoid for the foreseeable future. What we have to offer will change everything for you.'

'Offer? What could you possibly offer me now? Anyway, I've realised I've pretty much burned my boats on the demo front for a while unless I want to end up in prison, you don't need to worry on that count. I can't do anything useful behind bars, can I?'

'So, both Jamie and I have travelled in time, Dylan…'

'I've already just guessed that, Gran. It's how you wrote that banging book based on your family, isn't it? Cool.'

'Yes… but, Dylan, my travels in time were the catalyst to a sequence of events which culminated in a member of our team going permanently missing. You must be fully aware that there are many dangers associated with time travelling that we didn't perceive at first. And yet others that are still emerging.'

'This is extremely important, Dylan,' continued Jamie. 'As strange as it may sound, we have ancestors to whom we are closely epigenetically linked. If we come into physical contact with them, both bodies completely disappear from the timeline. We have no idea as yet about where they go, or whether they are actually vapourised.'

Dylan's mouth dropped open. For once, he was completely lost for words. He felt his hands begin to shake, and quickly put them in his lap, below the table.

Granny looked as though she was about to cry. 'That's about the size of it, Dylan. We lost someone we loved; it was the price we had to pay for the discovery. And then both Jamie and Christian had to put themselves in danger to repair the situation she left behind. So, none of this is to be taken lightly…'

'Or divulged to anyone else at all,' interjected Jamie. 'We're putting a lot of trust in you, Dylan. One of the reasons for this is that the American General who acts as our Chief Executive Officer seems to think highly of you, even though he's never met you. He's got fingers in lots of pies, principally political, but maybe environmental organisations, too.

'Not sure that's a surprise,' replied Dylan. 'I've always thought I got more closely marked at protests. I'd wondered if it was my Anderson connections, but I've been telling myself I was just being paranoid.'

Granny looked worried. 'Who knows why that is. Hopefully it is is just the family connections. You need to be more careful, Dylan.'

'Granny, I know. I have learned a lot of things lately, even if I don't always make that plain.'

Granny nodded. She and Jamie looked at one another.

Dylan shuffled impatiently. 'So, what is it, then? Don't leave me hanging. What is this offer?'

He hoped they weren't having second thoughts, reverting to treating him like a little kid.

'Well…' began Jamie. 'On granny's last trip in time- to observe the first Queen Elizabeth…'

Dylan gasped. 'Bloody hell, Jamie, this will take some getting used to.'

Jamie grinned. 'I understand. But we do need to go at a rather fast pace, due to the nature of the offer.'

'Bottom line, Dylan,' added Granny, 'I made a new friend at the court of QEI. He's an Artificial Intelligence entity, constructed by NAMIS a long way in the future. He works in different historical time periods, helping influential people to govern wisely. He's now just about to start a new mission that he thinks you can help him with, and learn a lot of things that will be useful to you along the way. He's offered you the most amazing gap year ever.'

'When- and where?'

'Well, not too far from here; somewhere in the Dyfed area. And the time is early sixth century, what history refers to as the 'Dark Ages.' Not because it was atmospherically dark, but because the information we have on the time period is very sparse.'

Dylan contemplated the idea. 'No oil, no gas, no petrol, no pollution.'

He tapped at his phone. 'And calculations estimate less than 200 million people on earth, probably less than a million of them in Britain. Sounds like heaven.'

'Well, it's also technologically primitive and comparatively lawless. But my friend- he has several names, but his real one is Consiliario- has promised that he will mentor and protect you. He's pretty much invulnerable, which is a major advantage.'

'He sounds awesome. But I'm not a baby, Gran, I can

take care of myself. I would love to go, right now. But I can't, can I, I've got to stay here for the next couple of months, and show myself at that ridiculous court hearing.' He shifted irritably in his seat.

'Well, that's the thing, Dylan,' said Jamie. 'When you travel in time, however long you stay there, you always come back a few seconds after you left. Which gives you a bit of time and space to reflect, and to be a whole year older before you deal with your court case. So, if you want to, you can go in the next week or so. If you do want to take up the offer, Consiliario will come and talk to you, us, and your mum and dad. They all know we're talking to you about this now. Shall I tell him yes?'

Dylan felt his world opening up like a chrysalis. It was though he had been trapped at the bottom of a deep, dark well, and suddenly seen dazzling sunlight break through overhead, and a ladder drop over the side. He brushed at the tears that had sprung to his eyes.

Granny passed him a tissue, and patted his hand gently.

'Yes. Oh, yes. Please tell him yes.'

'I will. And I don't need to say "behave yourself," do I?' grinned Jamie, tapping at his phone.

Granny smiled. 'I think Consiliario will be able to oversee that much better than us. He knows just about everything, like NAMIS, Dylan, and, unlike NAMIS, he's also an expert on the ways human beings behave and interact; his role is that of an ambassador. So I don't think he will be taking shit from anyone. It will be the most amazing gap year anyone was ever offered. You can't imagine how much I envy you.'

Jamie's phone pinged. 'Well, he's already said yes, and the sooner the better. He wants to meet you tomorrow, with a view to you going through to start with him sometime next week. Is that OK with you?'

'It's amazing… you're amazing. I don't know what to say. Just that I promise, from the bottom of my heart, that

I'm not going to fuck this one up.'

'Dylan, I don't think Consiliario will let you,' laughed Granny. 'I'm so pleased for you.'

'And so, I'll be there for a year, but when I come back, it will be a few seconds after I left?'

'Exactly,' replied Jamie. 'No FOMO. Everything will all be here waiting for you, exactly as it was.'

'But who knows, you might have decided you don't want some of it anymore, and that there are other things you do want by then,' said Granny. 'Growing up is like adding layers to an onion. You'll still be the same Dylan inside, but you'll have other thoughts in your head, and some distance from what's going on now. You can deal with your court case with rather more objectivity than you are feeling now, and then onto uni, from the perspective of having relevant experience within a completely different environment, which is what gap years are all about. It's just that no one has ever imagined such a wonderful placement as the one you are heading into.'

Dylan's head was beginning to spin. 'So, wait, what? I'll always be a year older than I am on the official record, after I get back?'

Granny and Jamie looked at one another. 'Hadn't thought of that' she replied. 'But yes, I guess that's so.'

'Cool.'

Dylan had always thought that a 'beaming' smile was just a literary turn of phrase. But he was pretty sure he had one on his face right now.

'And one more thing, Dylan,' said Jamie. 'Consiliario has asked that you take nothing at all from this time into the past with you. He'll provide clothes for you to change into before you go through the portal. He wants you to immerse yourself completely in the relevant time period.'

'Think about it carefully, Dylan,' added Granny. 'There will be no internet, no phone, no VR games, no high streets or online shops selling products carefully designed and marketed to satisfy your every need; sleeping on straw…'

'…no flushing toilets,' interjected Dylan. 'Yes, I know, Gran. You like your creature comforts. But the whole thing sounds just perfect to me. I'd go now, right this minute, if it were possible. A fresh, clean, old but new world. If you'd brought me a Genie to grant me just one wish, you couldn't have done any better. Bring it on.'

Jack: London, England, North European Territory, Summer 2059

Jack settled back in his chair, finally done with his story. He looked down and realised that his hands were still shaking slightly. He reached over for the bottle, pouring a third glass of synth-scotch.

'You OK, bro?' said Dylan.

They all grinned at the use of the archaic term, which they'd used between them so long ago, in their youth… even getting NAMIS to join in.

'Yeah. I was thinking, maybe I shouldn't have gone poking my nose into your business like that. I'm sorry if I acted out of turn. I seem to do that sometimes. But please believe me, I got to thinking that it was what I ought to do.'

'Of course I'm not offended, Jack,' replied Dylan. 'I'm very glad that you did.'

Freddie nodded. 'Little brother, you haven't changed. Just go on being you.'

He and Dylan raised their glasses.

Jack grinned. "Little brother" was an in-joke, too. Jack over-topped Freddie by four and a half inches and Dylan by two.

He began to relax, sinking back into the cushions, which he had to admit, were extremely comfortable. Soporific, even. 'Where did you get these chairs, Dylan? You don't usually do plush stuff.'

'I didn't. The apartment came ready furnished. It

belongs to Water for Life, not to me.'

Jack nodded. 'Yeah, everything always belongs to "the company." Whatever it is called nowadays. It doesn't matter; it can always be traced back to NAMITAS. Everything is controlled by them in some way. Including us.'

'I'm not sure that is exactly it,' said Freddie. 'They look after us, and we…'

'…Dance to their tune,' finished Jack. 'I know you work up close and personal with their benevolent younger self, Freds. But I've been dealing with NAMITAS, through Consiliario of course, for a while now.'

Dylan nodded. 'Yes, I know what you mean. What happened to me is a part of that; I just didn't know until now. I was so young… and at just that age when I thought I knew it all.'

'They offer up these worlds to us, don't they? It all started out in the sandbox for me and Freddie. Those weird holo-creatures that used to say weird things and chase us around. I was quite scared of them sometimes.'

'Were you?' replied Freddie. 'I never knew. You seemed to enjoy it. I was never scared. It was what started me off on the holo-art, which led to everything else.'

'I was. The age between us is nothing really now, but in those days, it was the difference between knowing what was real and what wasn't. But believe me, some of what is real in our distant future is far harder to believe than anything we dealt with there.'

If only I could say more, he thought. But I've gone far enough already.

'Whatever it's like, I envy you that, Jack,' said Dylan. 'My present is so grim at the moment… but I guess it always seems that the grass is greener, you know?'

Jack nodded. 'When I found out that you'd had a year in the Dark Ages with Consiliario, I was so very jealous. What an adventure.'

'Programmed to do NAMITAS' work across the ages,

and still managing to make things better than they would have been, most of the time,' added Freddie. 'Consiliario will always be a positive outcome from the NAMIS project.'

Jack and Dylan nodded.

'I can't tell you much about the world that I visit now,' said Jack. 'I don't engage with it that much, anyway; I'm mostly flying people and stuff around. But do tell us about the one you went to, Dylan. I'd appreciate some background on the current situation, and most especially from your perspective.'

'Yes, I'd be interested, too, said Freddie. 'I've read all the stuff in the files, of course. But it would be great to get your retrospective.'

Dylan rose, moved to the window and gazed down upon the river, still rolling peacefully along. He did this frequently. It was one constant he could come back to, whatever horrors he dealt with, it was always there to greet him when he came back- the clean water that he had worked so hard for, and the sun setting over Waterloo Bridge.

'The river is still there, clean as a whistle,' said Jack, intuiting his thoughts. 'I can tell you that. And so is London. Hugely changed of course. But still there. Hope that helps.'

Dylan nodded. Still staring out at the lights, he began to speak.

'So, it's 510 Christian Era on the current calendar. The Romans have left Britain, gradually fading away over the previous century. On the European continent, the victorious Germanic Saxons are setting their sights on the British coasts to stage a series of invasions.

'Consiliario emerges into this time as a boy, approximately ten years old. He's found by the youngest daughter of the Welsh King, wandering, hungry, dirty, unsure of his past, without a name. She takes him home to her father, King Vortigern, or in Welsh, Gwrtheyrn. He is aging, becoming increasingly insecure on his throne. Consiliario shows the King a few minor tricks. He decides the strange child is worth keeping.

'A couple of years later, two competing rumours are circulating about the strange child. One is that he is the Princess's son, therefore Vortigern's grandson, and that his father was a demon who dishonoured the princess, hence the child's ability to use magic. The other is that he is some type of elemental; a sprite who emerged fully formed into the world, and put an enchantment upon the Princess.

The King simply refers to him as 'boy.' But the name that starts being whispered around the court is "Emrys." In modern English, "the immortal." Or, I guess more accurately, "not quite human."'

'Which was translated into Ambrosius later on, when the story was written down, in Latin?' asked Freddie.

'Yes, precisely. He picked up Myrddin, literally "the myriad" later on, beyond my time with him; that's the name that eventually descended as "Merlin".'

'Because he did some shape shifting, I presume?' said Jack. 'He's done that with me a couple of times. It's really unnerving. So, some people in the sixth century must have seen him do that, too.'

Dylan nodded, continuing with his story, still gazing out of the window. It's as though he can see shadows of these events arising from his beautiful clear water, thought Jack. Dylan had exuded a slight air of mysticism for as long as Jack could remember, probably absorbed during his experience as sorcerer's apprentice. It added charisma and authority to his dealings with the awkward gate keepers he dealt with around the world.

'Vortigern grew increasingly weak. He did deals with Saxons to secure his throne. People whispered that he was a traitor. When they encountered the magic that his "grandson" could wield, they were more inclined to hold their tongues.

'The legend is that Merlin could, and did slay dragons.

This is because it was reported literally, but it is, in fact, symbolic. The white dragon represented the Germanic Saxons, the red dragon, the Celtic Welsh, who were engaged in constant skirmishes throughout the Dark Ages. As Vortigern's hold on Dyfed faltered, a strong young candidate to assume his throne emerged from a family to whom he was distantly related: the Pendragons.

'Uther,' said Jack. 'Father of Arthur.'

'Yes. Merlin… Emrys, as I knew him… helped Uther to defeat the Saxons in some of his battles. People were drawn to compare the weakness of Vortigern with the youth and vigour of young Lord Uther. Vortigern died very soon afterwards. It was whispered down the centuries that Emrys had something to do with this, but he assured me he didn't.'

'Did you believe him?' asked Freddie. 'I would have been inclined to. One of the core commands NAMIS, at least, cannot break, is that they cannot take human life.'

'I would agree with that,' said Jack. Of all the negative thoughts he had over the past few years about NAMITAS, it had never crossed his mind that they would harm a human being intentionally. Their guiding principle was to protect them. It was just the ways that they sometimes went about it, well…

'I did, and do believe him,' said Dylan. 'I saw nothing but benevolence in the way Emrys behaved towards the people, and to me. Yes, he was a bit, well, deceptive at times. But always with good intentions. Anyway, Vortigern died not long after Uther came to maturity. Maybe Uther and his supporters had something to do with it, who knows. Or it may have been a completely natural death. Vortigern was getting on in years for the relevant time.

'At that point, people began whispering that Prince Emrys, the old King's grandson, can do powerful magic, so he should be King, not Uther. This was, of course, not Emrys' or NAMITAS' intention.'

'Always the bridesmaid, never the bride,' said Freddie

and Jack in unison.

'So, he threw his staunch support behind Uther, even moved away from Carmarthen, then Moridunum, where Uther's court was situated, to Pembroke, then called Penfro, to set up as a simple healer, offering support to Uther whenever requested. Uther proclaimed him Prince Emrys, the King's kinsman, counsellor, and sometimes, magician. But the people often referred to him as 'Master Emrys.' They hadn't forgotten the gossip about his origins. And this was when I walked into the story; just for a year.'

'Consiliario… Emrys- was there for Arthur, really, wasn't he?' said Freddie. 'To pave the way for him to the throne, and to hang on in there for as long as possible.'

'Yes. To make Camelot briefly possible. So many perennial democratic ideals were seeded there. And to be fair to Uther, the round table's origin lay with him, under Emry's tutelage. But Arthur brought the whole thing together, if only for a few years.'

'The round table,' said Jack. 'Where everyone is invited to contribute their point of view. Such a mundane object; such a huge idea in that time.'

Freddie nodded. 'And it takes constant renewal, doesn't it? We're constantly having to keep that uppermost in everyone's mind right now.'

Dylan nodded, and returned to his chair.

Jack sighed. 'It was a shit assignment for Consiliario, in so many ways. He told me about it. Propping up local chieftains on matchwood thrones, then seeing his protégée slaughtered, as the world plunged into darkness.'

'Yes, the Krakatoa eruption in 535,' replied Dylan. 'That brought the famine that allowed the Saxons to displace Arthur, his Camelot and all the fragile ideals that it had been built upon. But those concepts had been seeded in the local consciousness for all time. It was the whole point of the mission. The year I spent there… it was idyllic. And life changing.'

'The NAMIS project in a nutshell, wonderful and

terrible,' sighed Freddie. 'So here we are.'

Yes, here we are, thought Jack, over 1500 years later, with NAMITAS continuing to craft our future. 'What a revelation that must have been to you, Dylan, being offered that chance, and at such a pivotal time of your own life.'

Dylan nodded. 'I don't think I could even start to capture that first meeting for you. I'll try my best.'

But Jack's exhaustion had finally caught up with him. He'd begun to snore lightly, dreaming of ethereal dark age princesses arising from the eerie glow on the Thames, luring him in with soft siren calls.

Fran: North Queensferry, Scotland, May 2033

Fran looked around at the assembled. Dylan, Rae, Gareth, Jamie, Christian and Ellie sat at the dining table in Niamh's house. They could hear the voices of the younger children playing in the garden, running in and out of Fran's annexe, Niamh and Suzi's voices interspersed.

Thank goodness it's a sunny day, thought Fran. There won't be so much for me to clear up when I get back. She grinned at the mundanity of the thought, going back to clear up toys, crumbs and synth-chocolate fingerprints, after sitting around a table to discuss Dylan's gap year in the distant past, with a powerful AI from the distant future.

Rae caught the grin. 'You know what,' she said to Christian, 'I still can't shake the idea that this is going to be one of those elaborate piss-takes you used to construct when you were undergrads, and got Jamie to go along with. You haven't roped mum in this time, have you?'

As she finished speaking, the swirl in the air began, and Consiliario materialised into being on the other side of the room. She, Dylan and Gareth gasped.

'Bloody hell, how do you do that?' gasped Rae. 'It's nothing like the matter transporter.'

Consiliario smiled and bowed. He was again dressed in contemporary clothing, and immaculately groomed. This time his long, thick silver hair was neatly trimmed and brushed to lay loosely over his shoulders.

Fran raised an eyebrow. Playing the silver fox for the mama, then. Consiliario and NAMITAS clearly had a much better understanding of the subtleties of humanity than NAMI3, she thought.

Consiliario caught the look and grinned. He then turned to Rae, bowed and shook her hand. 'My lady Rae. You have your mother's bewitching blue eyes, and her enviable candour.'

Fran raised her eyebrows in exasperation. Dylan grinned at her. It was nice to see him looking so much happier.

Consiliario was shaking hands with Gareth. Then, parental introductions over, he turned his steady blue gaze to Dylan, putting out his hand. 'My Lord Dylan. I have heard so much about you. It is good to finally meet you.'

Dylan smiled shyly, and shook his hand. 'You heard about me? I'm not really all that famous. Not in this family, anyway. More like infamous.'

Consiliario smiled. 'I have access to records that are not available to anyone in this century. I can assure you, you will do fine.'

'It's disconcerting, Dylan,' interjected Fran. 'He knows stuff about us he can't tell us, because people can't know what their future is going to be. It's something we discussed ad infinitum when we first started to travel in time, so it didn't come as such a shock to us. You'll get used to it.'

'Consiliario,' said Ellie, 'could I just ask... surely putting Dylan into a different time period for a whole year would impact on the timeline far more than anything we've ever done?'

Consiliario smiled. 'A good question, and one that I can't fully answer. All I can say is that when he is with me-which he will be most of the time- those dangers will be completely negated. Additionally, he does not have any knowledge of the people with whom he will interact. Legend is almost useless on this point. Rest assured, he will never be open to the harrowing experiences that all of you… and Annamarie endured.'

Ellie jerked her head up. 'You know of Annamarie?'

Fran stared at Consiliario intently. Good or bad news? she thought. Why has he just dropped that in there? But she remained silent. Today was for Dylan. Which was exactly why he just dropped in in there she thought. Whenever it is he comes from, AIs have really got the measure of us by his time. It made her feel vaguely uneasy.

Consiliario nodded. 'Indeed. But this is not for discussion today, please, Ellie. It's something we can explore very soon; please don't think that she has ever been forgotten.'

Jamie and Christian looked at one another.

'Can we get her back?' Jamie asked.

'We tried so hard,' added Christian, tears filling his eyes 'but…'

Consiliario nodded. 'I know you did, and very soon, there will be some positive news for you; I promise. But just not now. Let us conclude this agreement.'

He turned to Dylan. 'Do you really want to come with me, Dylan? Life in the sixth century is hard. It is a rural, technology-barren, pre-Christian Britain in which the majority of the population are functionally illiterate, and highly superstitious. There are very few creature comforts.'

Dylan met his gaze. 'I have been reading the information you sent through. I understand that it will be hard at first, converting from this century of constant connectivity, instant gratification and conspicuous consumption. But… Mr Consiliario, many of my generation have already decided that this is not the world that we want. I can't wait for you to show me an alternative. I understand the people of the time may be illiterate and superstitious, but that doesn't necessarily mean they are ignorant, does it? Might they also be more spiritual and authentic than the majority of people in our current time?'

He stopped, becoming aware that the adults around the table were staring at him, and that his mother had tears in her eyes. She squeezed his hand. 'Well said, Dylan.'

'Indeed,' replied Consiliario.

'Absolutely,' said Fran and Jamie in unison.

'Well said, son,' said Gareth, throwing his arm around Dylan's shoulder. 'You know I'm proud of you, don't you? Even if you drive me crazy sometimes?'

'Yes. Thanks Dad,' replied Dylan, clearly somewhat overwhelmed. Fran looked at him. It's started already, she thought. The boy he once was is now slipping through our fingers. It's the young man he's becoming who just effectively articulated all of those ideas. They must have been forming in his mind for quite a while now.

She observed him shift impatiently in his seat, clearly longing to make a start on his adventure. He still loves us, she thought. But he needs to have a break from us, just for a while. To go to a place where no one "speaks for him" anymore, where he can become his own man.

'One other thing, Consiliario,' she said. 'I've been wondering... how will Dylan cope with the language? It's nothing like contemporary English. He'd be better in the area that is going to become Germany, in that respect. Latin is the common language across Europe, isn't it?'

'In writing, yes, Fran. But did you forget that Dylan also speaks functional Welsh? It's a good platform from which to jump onto the Celtic language being spoken in Wales in the sixth century.'

'So,' said Rae, raising one eyebrow. 'I'm struggling to believe, that in the century Dylan is going to, you are, in fact, Merlin. Jamie and my mother have explained this to me, and I have read all the material you sent, but I have to admit it's all so very hard to take in, given the speed with which this has happened. Can you elaborate a little more?'

Consiliario nodded. 'As you have read my summary of the legends, you will know that I am known to history as Myrddin Emrys in Welsh, and Ambrosius in Latin. Both "Emrys" and "Ambrosius" translate to "immortal" and Myrddin- which has come down to the English language as "Merlin"- translates to "Myriad."

'The immortal who inhabits myriad lives?' queried Fran. 'I was just reading about that a couple of days ago. And wondering, how on earth does legend contain so much about you that is even vaguely accurate?'

'They don't burn witches and magicians in the sixth century, Fran, they revere them. Both Druidism and Paganism, the most widely endorsed spiritual beliefs, are comfortable with the knowledge that I am not an ordinary mortal; that I have powers that set me apart. Of course, they have no idea of artificial intelligence, nor do they need to; they accept me for what I appear to be, and welcome me because I am useful within their society.'

'All technology is magic,' said Dylan. 'Fascinating.'

'It's human nature,' explained Consiliario. 'Whatever people can't understand at any given time is "magic" or "witchcraft." In the sixth century, people are prepared to accept magic at face value, and make use of it when and where they can. A thousand years hence, they see as magic as an abomination that challenges their entrenched religious laws. When yet five hundred more years pass, they learn to embrace technology as technology rather than as magic, especially when it apparently makes their lives easier. But too many lack the motivation to attempt to really understand it, or to wrestle with difficult issues emergent from its uses. What is and is not progress is something that humankind will soon learn to question. This is a concept for you to contemplate, Dylan, as you step back in time.'

'What do the people in this time call you, please?' asked Dylan.

'In the court, they call me Prince Emrys, the title Uther gave me when he came to the throne of Dyfed, such as it is. But because my parentage is presumed questionable, I'm more generally referred to as 'Master Emrys.'

'Master Emrys' said Dylan. 'OK.'

'And you say it as it should be said, Dylan. It rolls much better off the Welsh tongue than the English. We'll be based in the area that you now know as Pembroke...'

'Where the castle is?' asked Dylan.

'In your time, yes. But it won't be built for several centuries yet in the time to where you are headed. I work on my 'magic' in the cave located under the site, befriending and healing the local people. I make myself available to help Uther when he needs a diplomat or magician. He's on his way to becoming a great king on a stable throne, by the standards of the era.

'You'll arrive at the beginning of this process, Dylan, whilst Uther is still a young man, only a few years older than yourself. People come to maturity rather earlier than they do in your time, and he's already a shrewd, charismatic leader. He's rough and ready; he has to be in the society that he administers. But his instincts are honourable. You will learn much from him. At the same time, your thoughtfulness and focus on social justice will provide food for thought for a young man who has been raised in a more savage and reactive time.'

'Does all our history have roots in your meddling, Consiliario?' asked Ellie, cooly.

Consiliario looked pensive. 'The parts that have prevented you from destroying yourselves, or spinning in an endless deteriorating spiral, becoming increasingly primitive, yes, I like to think so. You are you because I am me, and because NAMIS becomes NAMITAS. You have just arrived at a basic understanding that time is neither one-dimensional nor linear.

'You will not fully understand its complex operations

for many centuries to come, however; for the most part this will remain within the arena of magic- or nowadays, more likely science fiction. But in the meantime, we all, human and AI, play multiple roles in how the story of humanity unfolds, past, present and future.'

'I understand my place in your world, now, Master Emrys,' said Dylan.

Consiliario smiled at him.

'...but what will I learn that will help me to continue with my work in the natural environment, when I return to my own century?'

'Well, as you already know, you will enter a world that has not yet been blighted by a coal and oil-based economy. I cannot give you access to all of my environmental knowledge; only that which you can harness to the technology and culture of your own century, which we can explore within an unspoiled environment. I think your grandmother may be able to give you a few other clues, based upon what historical legend has to say about me.'

He looked expectantly at Fran.

She smiled. 'So you guessed I'd be reading up on Geoffrey of Monmouth, the only semi-historical source. Well, he says that Merlin knows the secrets of nature; that he understands the flight of birds, the tides, the movement of fish and the rotation of the stars in the fundament.'

'...for which I would have been burnt at the stake in the sixteenth and seventeenth centuries. And in this century, there are satellites, drones and cameras watching everywhere, and very few unspoilt terrains. But in the sixth century, we will be at complete liberty to roam freely to places where we can experiment unobserved, and at leisure, where I will be able to instruct you in...'

'Magic,' finished Dylan.

'Exactly. And the main project you, Uther and I have on our schedule when you arrive is a little bit of conspicuous hocus-pocus in a place you might already know as Stonehenge. Amongst other things.'

Dylan turned to his parents. 'Mum, dad, I've never wanted to do anything as much as this. I know that technically, I can do it anyway, because I'm over eighteen, and I've signed all the scary stuff. But I really would like your approval. And the way this will work, you won't even begin to miss me.'

Bitter-sweet, thought Fran. He'll be back as soon as he left, but he'll be a different person. The boy will walk into the portal, and a few seconds later, the young man will come back to us.

Rae looked at him fondly. 'We will miss you, Dylan, we'll miss a year of your life. You may come back to us immediately, but you'll come back changed. But, I can see that for you, now, this is what you need to do. We've already discussed it. Agreed, Gareth?'

Gareth nodded. 'So proud of you, son. You're a Welsh hero already.'

Fran nodded. 'You'll come back to us with another layer added, Dylan. And what a layer. I'm so proud, and so envious. Hwyl a fflag: sail into your future.'

'So,' concluded Consiliario. 'You need make no physical preparations. I will ensure that there is suitable clothing for you to change into, waiting in the Boston lab. Shall we say next Friday?'

'Yes, that will be fine. Thank you, Master Emrys.'

Consiliario looked around the room. 'I will watch over him. He will be safe, whilst learning much that will be useful to for the challenging years ahead. Thank you, everyone. Your far-sightedness is more important than you will ever know. In this life, anyway. And Dylan: wela I di cyn bo hir.'

'Yes, see you very soon,' said Dylan.

The air began to shimmer around Consiliario, then he was gone.

They sat silently for a few seconds. Fran listened to the sounds of the children's voices outside, shouting and laughing.

Christian broke the silence.

'What an amazing opportunity, mate. I wish it had been offered to me. My travels to the past only left me lamenting things that couldn't be changed.'

'Mine too,' replied Jamie. 'We're so very pleased for you, Dylan.'

'Thank you, everyone,' said Dylan. 'I won't let you down, I promise.

'Well, I think we all need a drink after that,' said Gareth, breaking the mood. 'To celebrate Dylan's coming of age.'

Fran slipped quietly out of the room and wandered through into her annexe, opening the door to signal to Niamh and Suzi that the meeting was over. The sun had started to set. She could hear the children playing on the little beach by the Firth. They'd be coming in to go to bed soon.

It had been an insanely hot for May by the standards of my childhood, mused Fran. She stood in the doorway, contemplating the angry red sunset, no longer thinking of it as her ancestors had done, a "delight."

Where will Dylan go, and what will he do, she wondered. If anything, Consiliario's hints had made her even more fearful for her grandchildren's future than before.

Her thoughts turned to her grandmother, who here, in this very house in the early 1930s, would have listened to her own children playing happily on the little beach, believing that the war to end all wars had already been fought and won.

It is what it is, and always will be, thought Fran. Not linear, not one dimensional, and never, ever over. All human beings- and AIs, for that matter- can do is raise the next generation to have courage, independence of thought, and confidence in their problem-solving abilities to get to grips with whatever comes next. Which is never certain, in the saga of humankind on Planet Earth.

'What's wrong, granny?' Isabel was standing beside her.

'Nothing really, Izzy. Dylan is going away for a little while, and we're going to miss him. He'll be back soon, though.'

Isabel smiled up at her. 'Well, he's a big boy now.'

'Of course, you're quite right, Izzy. He's on the way to the launch pad.'

'Will he go all the way to the stars?' Isabel stared up into the sky, Venus now beginning to blink in the glooming dusk.

Fran followed her gaze. 'I don't know, Izzy. But I hope all of you will be able to, some day.'

Isabel took her hand, and they gazed into the fundament together.

CHAPTER 5: SECOND CHANCES

Emrys: Boston, June 2033

Emrys sat incongruously at the head of the spotless white table at the side of the lab, NAMIS to his right, Jamie to his left and Christian and Ellie facing him. A round table, he was pleased to note. The full moon shone through the large picture window, casting a light on his shabby sleeves and somewhat grubby nails; one of the less appealing elements of life as a sixth century wizard. But he thought it had been a good idea to appear in this guise today, given Dylan was coming through the portal to join him this week; he'd found it helped orient organics, given their inevitably limited perspective, to what was going on where time travel was concerned.

This, plus the topic they had to discuss meant that the meeting had been set for late in the evening, to ensure the building was deserted. A sixth century wizard arriving vortex style to meet three full professors and the world's current state-of-the-art AI would certainly have turned heads, in one of the most prestigious universities in the world. NAMITAS had ensured that any cameras that might catch Emrys' image were temporarily out of action.

He had just finished speaking. He braced for the predictable reaction to the news he had delivered. Christian was still scribbling, his russet, now slightly greying head bent over his paper note pad, hazel eyes narrowed in concentration. Jamie was frowning in contemplation, an expression that conveyed 'yes and what comes next?'

But it was Ellie who spoke first, her dark brown eyes brimming with tears. Emrys studied the threads hanging from his sleeve. He'd found it was better to let organics express these sorts of feelings, before moving on to more rational discourse. His roughly scissored hair fell into his eyes. He brushed it back, his 'I'm listening' expression set to maximum.

'What do you mean this has to proceed as an experiment? You've been so assured about everything else. And this... the most crucial thing you had to communicate to us- why did you leave it until now, and then disappoint us so bitterly?'

'Wait, Ellie,' interjected Jamie. 'It is disappointing, I agree. But we must remember that Emrys- whether he's Emrys, Dee or Consiliario- is not really a magician. He knows inordinately more than we do, because he's from a time far into the future, but he can't know absolutely everything. Looks like he's hit his limit on this one.'

Emrys sighed. 'Yes, that is a fair approximation of the situation. I thought it was best to bring the good news to Dylan first, and to follow up with the less good news for you. It's not wholly bad news, you know. Finally, we can do something for Annamarie. It's just not exactly what you hoped.'

Christian finally put down his pen, with which he had been speedwriting for the past hour. He stretched and flexed his right hand, flipping backwards through the pages of his notebook. 'Old habit. So last century, I know, but I just synthesise better if I take contemporaneous written notes. Can I please summarise what you've just told us, before we move on?'

Emrys nodded. 'Of course.'

'Firstly: you have worked out what happened when the contact between Annamarie and Anna occurred in 1939.

An identical essence met in two different bodies…'

'I think it might help to frame it as "energy" in this context,' interjected Jamie.

'OK, replied Christian, 'energy- met in two different organic incarnations, causing a type of…'

'Would "short circuit" work here, Emrys?' asked Jamie. 'I know that's a massive over-simplification, but will it do for this discussion?'

Emrys nodded again. 'I think that will work well at this introductory stage, yes.'

'So,' continued Christian 'the energy was unable to coexist in two directly connected bodies during the same time frame, so once Anna and Annamarie physically touched one another, both were immediately vapourised, and the energy released.'

'Yes, that is how we understand it,' replied Emrys.

'By we, you mean yourself and NAMITAS?' asked Jamie.

'Yes, and some others on our team. NAMITAS draws the information together and comes to the overall conclusions when the debate relates to the logistics of time travel, just as NAMIS does for you.'

'OK,' continued Christian. 'So, as I understand it, what you are telling us you've discovered is that despite the destruction of the bodies, the energy, or essence, whatever we are going to call it, returned to NAMIS and has been present as a miniscule part of their program since the event occurred.'

This team catch on much faster than the current crowd, thought Emrys. Maybe we do too much for them in our own time. 'Yes. And it appears that it has gradually grown stronger over that time. Hence the "voice" that NAMIS has recently begun to detect, and recognise as "other". Which means we can locate the energy, and attempt to work with it.'

'You're making Annamarie sound like some type of ghost in a machine,' exclaimed Ellie, a tissue bunched in her hand.

'Hmmm,' said Christian 'if the bodies of Annamarie and Anna ceased to exist, am I right in saying that this isn't Annamarie exactly, it's only the enduring essence/energy that animated both Anna and Annamarie? That is, an essence which is, in the usual process, located within an apparently obscure epigenetic program deeply buried in each human being?'

'That is our theory,' agreed Emrys.

'So "ghost" in that sense is a good analogy,' mused Jamie. 'And in that context, "essence" is a better description. But isn't this all rather strange? As I have understood the process so far, the essence somehow flows through the timeline, once the body dies, to a biological relative, embedding itself at the epigenetic level at, or shortly before birth. So, are you suggesting that embedding itself within NAMIS's program is the way it continued to exist, having been unwittingly removed from the normal process by a time traveller?'

'It is plausible, James Anderson,' replied NAMIS. 'Perhaps my program was the only accessible medium that it was able to inhabit in that situation. Annamarie Simons had travelled through my portal to 1939 that day, having encoded her genetic signature on her return pad. She was also carrying a return pad on which she had encoded the genetic signature of Anna Rosenberg, her essence twin. Taking this into account, might it not seem logical for the energy to return to source? Christian Novak's body, with his essence still intact, was blown back into the time and place recorded on his return pad when the convergence transformation event occurred; his return pad triggering automatically.'

Emrys nodded. 'At the time, you thought only Christian's return pad had triggered. But the one he took through the portal for Annamarie did register some minor background activity. You would not have been able to find this with your twenty-first century technology. But a forensic investigation of the pad using the technology of my own time has discovered it.'

'That pad is still in my possession,' said Ellie. 'So how did you… oh. You still have it in your own time, don't you?'

Emrys nodded.

'Why couldn't you have told us all this at the time it happened?' Ellie burst out, angrily, tears flowing again. 'You're sitting here with us now, centuries in your own past, so you must have known about this before, mustn't you?'

Jamie narrowed his eyes, looking at Emrys. 'I've got a hunch that you're dealing with this situation simultaneously on both timelines; that it's one of those "time isn't linear" quirks you alluded to before. I'm betting that, in your- or Consiliario's- present, you only just got out that pad, and put it through the test you're referring to. You weren't sitting in the future knowing that this was going to happen. It just popped up for you as it did for us, when NAMIS reported detecting the voice on this part of the timeline. You're dealing with this on the hoof, aren't you?'

Emrys smiled at him. 'You're very perceptive, professor. It's an idea to further contemplate as you continue your research into the nature of time. I will give you one small clue, which I don't think breaks any of the rules that I operate by: in particular, focus on issues that arise when organics attempt to meddle with significant, previous events on their own or their ancestral timeline.'

'Do you think Annamarie- or her essence- has been conscious all this time?' asked Ellie, wiping away her tears.

'Our guess is that the essence may have been vaguely aware at the level of sleeping and dreaming, but without the background memories that an essence in an organic body can call upon to make sense of sensation, rather like an embryo in the womb. As such, it's unlikely to have any conscious sense of time passing. Nevertheless, as time has gone by, it seems that it has grown more wakeful, and now seeks a release, analogous to an unborn child approaching birth.'

Christian looked pensively at his notebook. 'I'm sorry to be so blunt, Ellie, but, Consiliario- sorry, Emrys- It seems to me that person we knew as Annamarie did die at the moment of convergence transformation, and what we are dealing with now is just the essence that has animated a variety of human bodies over centuries, Annamarie and Anna amongst these.

'Jamie isn't his great great grandfather Jim after all- even though we discovered that they were essence twins. Their physicality, social, cultural and intellectual knowledge were, and are located within each individual body.'

'It's a reasonable theory,' replied Emrys. 'But Christian, we just don't know yet. Again, I don't think I'm breaking any rules by telling you that this was the first and only convergence transformation event to have ever taken place. To the best of our knowledge, anyway...'

'... time not being a linear phenomenon,' interjected Jamie.

Emrys nodded. 'We've had some close calls, like Fran's recent escapade, but we've always been able to prevent the actual event. Annamarie's situation, for reasons that are just too complicated to fully explain, is unique, and the events that led up to it were unpreventable.

'I should say here that you coped with the initial situation admirably by yourselves. You left us, as we thought until now, with nothing else we could usefully do. I know you felt that your responses were a failure. But believe me, what you managed to achieve was remarkable, given the primitive stage of the project.

'And now we find we have been offered a second chance of sorts. The way NAMITAS suggests we proceed is for you, NAMIS, as you previously mooted, to give the essence an expression in the holographic environment that you currently use as your sandbox and playroom. Create an avatar that initially only interacts with you and Ellie, with the target of nurturing it to a point at which it is able to interact with the children, and learn from them, too.'

'I can't imagine what it will eventually become,' said Jamie. 'But if it's limited to a hologram and carefully monitored, it can't possibly be dangerous to anyone. Although, it will be nothing like the other holograms, they are no more than interactive 3D animations based on fantasy characters from children's media.'

'With respect Emrys, this is hardly "incorporation,"' added Christian.

'It's the only partial release we can offer it at the moment,' replied Emrys, apologetically. 'NAMITAS is working on other, more appropriate solutions. But for now, this will give the essence some level of escape from where it currently resides; a chance to learn, develop and socialise- admittedly in a rather strange manner- with other human beings.'

'The potential of an essence-animated hologram would presumably hugely exceed the other holograms present in the sandbox and playroom?' asked Christian.

'That is what we theorise, and dare I say, profoundly hope. But we cannot know until we try.'

There was a brief silence. Emrys studied the back of his hands. NAMITAS had predicted there was only one way the team would jump- the way that they wanted them to. 'The organics want their friend back,' they'd said. 'And we've only given them one option.'

Emry's job was to ride out the storm of the organics' emotion to move towards final agreement. Routine envoy work. But he was surprised to feel... yes, he thought, feel... a slight unease.

These organics were not like the rather bland people he'd worked with in his own time; they had more contrast; more light and shade somehow, more opinions, less predictability. It made him even more eager to work closely with Dylan for a concerted amount of time; to learn more about them.

'We didn't know what-or who- the voice was when we previously discussed this,' fretted Ellie, fresh tears welling. 'What an awful dilemma.'

NAMIS looked at her. 'Do you trust me, Eleanor Jackson?'

Emrys watched her look back into their silver eyes, a series of emotions passing across her face. 'Of course I do. What a strange question. All of this wasn't your fault, NAMIS. Please don't think…'

'Why I ask,' interjected NAMIS 'is because I want you to know that I will care for this entity with the same focus that a human parent would care for their child. As you know, I can split my attention in ways that human beings cannot. The entity will never be alone, unless it desires to be; it will be constantly watched over. Whatever I can do for them, I will, every hour of every day.'

And that, thought Emrys, sounds somewhat different to the NAMITAS of my own time. NAMIS seems to have taken on the organics' more emotionally charged style of communication. Were they just aping those with whom they communicated, or did it go deeper than that? He determined to quiz NAMITAS about this, the next time they met.

Of course, the motivation driving NAMIS was familiar: the core programming, to take care of the traveller, and to bring her safely home. But the tone in which it was being voiced sounded much more like passionate conviction than anything he'd ever heard from NAMITAS.

The team were looking at Emrys expectantly. Time to move on, clinch the deal.

'NAMITAS will establish a connection to help you with this, NAMIS,' he replied. 'Obviously they cannot make any other parts of their program available to you. But with respect to this task, they will be in constant communication. It's a learning experience for them, too.'

NAMIS nodded.

'OK, agreed,' said Jamie. 'But we reserve the right to be in overall charge of this project, and to call you back for renegotiation at any time. I presume NAMITAS won't be directly corresponding with us - "the organics" - in your terminology.'

Emrys nodded. 'I'm sorry, if "organics" sounds cold, or rude to you. It isn't meant to be. We talk of AIs and organics in my time, because as I believe you all currently hope, the term "people" refers to us all.'

Ellie sighed. 'That's something positive, at least.'

Emrys reached under the table and pulled out a roughly woven bag. 'Clothes for Dylan. He's coming through tomorrow.'

Jamie nodded. 'So, both he and Annamarie- or her essence- start their new lives at the same time. Relatively speaking.'

Emrys looked out of the window, briefly. 'Given Dylan's weariness of this century, I hope he too might also look on entering the distant past as a type of homecoming, an entrance into the ecological world that he should have inherited, and an introduction to techniques to make it whole again.'

'Thank you, Emrys,' said Jamie. 'I'm sure he will learn a lot from you. Will we be working with you again soon?'

'Now you know about us, we will be in contact from time to time, whenever we think we might be of assistance. But, for now, I bid you adieu.'

He rose from the table, swept his cloak around himself, and disappeared into a soft swish of air.

'You know, I really envy that kid,' mused Christian 'Although...' he fingered the rough garments in the bag 'these are far worse than those clown trousers Fran made me wear to go to 1939. At the time, I wouldn't have thought that would be possible.'

'Well, we've got our work cut out here,' said Jamie.

Ellie stood up, putting her hand on NAMIS's shoulder. 'We certainly do. However hard the road ahead is, the essence of Annamarie is coming home. So as always, let's focus on doing the best we can.'

Dylan: Penfro, Spring 510

Dylan shifted uncomfortably in his rough, itchy clothes, looking at the simple meal in front of him. A substance Emrys had referred to as 'cheese' but that looked and tasted like the bland cottage cheese his mother ate when she was on one of her diets, a lump of dense dark brown bread and a small pot containing honey, the latter of which was the only delicious item he had found in the sixth century so far, now five days into his 'residency' in Pembroke, known as Penfro (meaning 'headland') in this century, and located in the Kingdom of Dyfed. He'd been quite slim when he arrived, but his clothes felt looser already.

The drink of the day, and everyday thus far was fresh, clear water drawn from the stream bubbling along at the bottom of the bank that led down from Emrys' cave. Emrys had explained that Dylan could gather herbs and infuse them in water boiled on the fire to make tea the sixth century way. So, his magic did not extend to producing instant boiling water, it seemed. When Dylan remarked on this, Emrys smiled.

'And then some luxury herbal teabags? No, it's a slippery slope, Dylan. This year is about learning to live as an authentic sixth century person, not a time tourist. It's part of developing the ability to look back upon your own time with different eyes.'

Thankfully the weather had been warm thus far, and was likely to continue so for the next few months. Dylan was already steeling himself for a much harder winter than he would ever have experienced before, although the little house in Anglesey, with its indifferent wind and wave electricity generator, had given him some idea of what that might be like.

Emrys was going to take him on some visits to the people of the surrounding area next week; introduce him around. He'd commented that the local people gave him food and drink in return for herbs and medicines, and that Dylan would be able to make good use of such gifts, given that Emrys, as an AI, had no use for them. He had some stored wine in the kitchen area of the cave, and the bread, cheese and honey Dylan had just eaten had been an offering from last week. Before that, most of the fresh food he'd been given thus far had been distributed to the birds and small creatures who made their homes in the area around the cave.

Dylan was rather looking forward to meeting the local people. He'd made a good start on learning the language, and hoped that such further immersion within it would move him on more quickly. He was currently working on an intensive language program delivered through a pair of earbuds provided by Emrys, one of the few occasions in which he would receive access to modern- and future-technologies during his time in the sixth century.

He'd also undergone a 'sealing' process to ensure he didn't infect anyone in the past with a modern disease, and would not, in turn, be infected by them. It was a simple process, requiring a few brief blasts of light in a small chamber. As he took off the eye protectors to leave, Dylan wished this had been available for his routine twenty first century vaccinations. A lot less crying, he mused. But then again, no lollipops or badges.

The chamber was located in a workspace at the back of the cave to which Emrys retreated while Dylan slept. It was hidden behind a false wall, and protected by a force field. Dylan presumed it was where Emrys worked with a range of future technologies. It was not an area he was allowed to access unless accompanied by Emrys.

The language program used accelerated techniques that tapped into his brainwaves, just as the 2-way vaccination process was programmed to work within his specific immune system. He was sure that both Granny Fran and Christian would love to get their hands on the technologies concerned. But that was never going to happen.

Luckily, the language spoken by the locals had many similarities to the Welsh Dylan already spoke as a semi-fluent second language, and once he'd mastered the grammatical structures he began to learn in leaps and bounds. It seemed in some ways a less complex language than both twenty first century English and Welsh.

'That's because people here live very practical lives, Dylan,' explained Emrys. 'They have to do a lot more physical work to simply exist in this time; their lives are much more confined to the local area; they don't have social or mass media or politics. And the vast majority of people who speak this Gaelic dialect are not able to read or write. Where they are exposed to literacy, the language is usually Latin. They gossip of course, and complain about how powerful people behave; they've just got a much narrower social circle and less time and scope to go on and on about what is bothering them.

'I'm making them sound more limited than the people in your own century, but that isn't fair. It's just an extremely different society. When you get to know them better, you will realise that they have a sort of social and spiritual depth which is… somehow closer to the earth, and its natural rhythms.'

Dylan had been relieved to find Emrys easy and interesting company, if somewhat didactic at times. But he was used to that, from Granny Fran, in particular. While he understood that Emrys was of course an ageless AI, the fact that his initial introduction had been to a smooth talking, silver haired sage had caused Dylan some concerns about whether they would have anything in common.

But his initial worries melted away after some intense climate change conversations, in which Emrys had demonstrated an encyclopaedic knowledge. He'd also told Dylan some interesting stories about assignments he had completed in times pre-dating the twenty-first century, some poignant, some tragic and some uproariously funny, most particularly his grandmother falling at Queen Elizabeth's feet, her skirts flying everywhere.

The fact that Granny Fran and the Queen shared an essence had been a strange revelation, leading Dylan to ask many questions about how this worked, moving into the edges of curiosity about his own essence. The firm response had been that such issues were not open for discussion with organics, because they were inclined to become highly fixated on where their essence had been, and where it was going. And that, said Emrys, stopped them focusing on who they were now, which was surely the point of human existence. Although disappointed, Dylan saw the logic in this.

During this conversation, Dylan began to remember strange behaviours and utterances that his cousin Freddie had expressed when he was a young child, recounting what seemed to be vivid memories of being a soldier who had actually experienced the horrors of battle, but in the language of the three- or four-year-old child he had been.

Emrys nodded. 'This happens with some children, Dylan,' he replied. 'Traumatic experiences can leave echoes within the essence, which may rise to the surface before it is fully integrated into the body.'

'I feel a bit mean now,' said Dylan. 'I just thought he was a very strange little kid, with a big imagination.'

Emrys laughed. 'A lot of imagination and creativity is rooted in subconscious essence memories, Dylan. Which is why human beings have to be so careful when they are time travelling. They are drawn to familiar people and places, particularly if, within those memories there are issues that were traumatic, or unresolved.'

Dylan contemplated that although he'd heard about that type of "weird connection" from other people, he'd never been consciously aware of it. Perhaps he didn't have such issues lurking in his essence. So much human beings don't know about themselves he thought. He sighed.

'I gather that my parents and my aunt and uncle are going to join in with the extension of the renewed experiments on people travelling in time? That NAMITAS is going to oversee the plans and let NAMIS know which ones are safe, and which ones aren't?'

'Yes, that's right. No one, not even NAMIS, will be told why any application is deemed unsafe. But yes, it will help the NAMIS team to go ahead with their research about the effects of time travel upon human bodies, without putting anyone else into the position in which your grandmother found herself with Queen Elizabeth.'

'Well, if I could go on one of those myself, I'd like to meet Granny when she was my age. Partly to see what she was like, but also partly because I'm cross, not with her personally, but with her generation. I don't understand why they ended up having such a negative impact on the world, not only on the environment, but on the political and social structures, you know? They were given a good start by their parents' generation, who'd fought off fascism, and created good welfare programmes, particularly in Britain. I don't understand how they went on to get it so wrong.'

'People only learn from their own experiences, Dylan. They cannot learn across subsequent lives in the way that I do; all they carry forward are subconscious echoes of the eerie familiarity feeling known as "déjà vu" and vague feelings of happiness, fear or sorrow, creating the type of behaviour that you observed in your cousin. The essence may also spark interest or inspiration that draws them to ancestors, ideas, concepts or time periods, like the way in which your grandmother was drawn to Queen Elizabeth.

'Because we protected them from the worst possible results of the arms race, the vast majority of your grandmother's generation born into the western world spawned in some of the most privileged societies in human history. The majority received good basic education and health care, and although diseases resulting from having too much rather than too little impacted on them in later life, they were prolific in the arts, and the creation of rapid technological advance. Although, of course, many of those technologies moved too quickly, and negatively impacted on social cohesion as subsequent generations came along. But human progress is inevitably uneven in this way.'

Dylan frowned. 'What do you mean, "protected them from the worst possible results of the arms race?"'

Emrys smiled. 'Dylan, it's late; the sun is beginning to set. That's a story for another day.'

Dylan walked to the cave entrance, and peered outside, into the looming dusk. 'I'm not sure if I'll ever get used to going to bed and waking up with the sun.'

'I understand, there is much that has changed for you. But you seem to be coping quite well so far.'

Dylan looked thoughtful. 'I think it really helps for me to know that I'll go back to exactly where I was before, that I'm not actually missing out on anything. It's strange. The way I eat and sleep here… it's like my head and stomach are emptier, but calmer. And with respect to the missing tech, well, my hands feel empty, but my mind… it feels like there was a tight knot in there that I hadn't noticed before; I just detected it because it's slowly loosening. For example, I never really looked at nature before. Partly because I was so busy online that I didn't have time, and partly because it was so unusual to find a completely natural environment.'

They wandered outside. 'Granny likes the stars,' he added. 'When I was little, she used to tell me that when we looked at the stars we were time travelling, because the light we could see had left them a long time ago. We'd guess at what time in history it was when the light we were looking at had started to travel to us.

'Last week, after I found out she had time travelled, she told me to make sure to look at the stars, because they would be magnificent in a world with no artificial light beyond candles and oil lamps. And she was so right.'

He looked up at the milky way, which was beginning to materialise in the sky. A crescent moon, cupping a blue winking Venus sailed beneath the thick white ribbon. Close by, Mars twinkled its vivid red light.

'Now I'm in one part of that long ago, aren't I? I'm still getting my head around it. But yes, mostly, it feels good.'

He lay down on the cool grass.

'Well, I will leave you to your star gazing. Goodnight,' said Emrys.

'Goodnight,' replied Dylan. He knew that when he went back in, Emrys would be working on something behind the wall at the back of the cave. He wondered how it would be to be an AI who never slept, and who was constantly moving across time to protect chaotic humanity from itself. It sounded exhausting.

He listened to the river bubbling along beneath him, and breathed deeply. The air smelt fresh and clean. When he'd first arrived, he got a vague feeling that there was something missing in the outdoor environment. Then he'd realised that there was seldom total human silence in his own time; that there was usually the sound of distant traffic, or the intermittent thrum of music and media chatter drifting from cars, windows or shops.

I will bring this world back for my children and my children's children, he thought. We will live in the ecological environment that should have been our natural heritage, alongside sustainable technologies that work for humanity, rather than putting humanity to work for despotic organisations.

Emrys sat motionless in the hidden area of the cave, his eyes flickering.

'He is doing well already,' he communicated to NAMITAS.

'He is young and innocently idealistic,' came the reply. 'But like all the intelligent ones, he will learn quickly. And so will Uther. They will learn together. This is a pivotal interaction for the future of organic humanity, Consiliario.'

'Yet again.'

'Your work was never going to be easy or straightforward. But it is what they raised us to do. We go on protecting them, ensuring that they endure.'

Dylan: Leeds, September 1979

Dylan shuffled anxiously from foot to foot, looking down at the polished wood floor. 'Emrys, I know I said that I wanted to do this, but I've changed my mind. What am I going to say to her? How am I going to act naturally? It feels really odd- and sort of creepy.'

Emrys smiled reassuringly. 'You'll learn something useful here, Dylan. It'll be fine.'

Dylan looked at him uneasily. The fact that he didn't look like Emrys any more was also disturbing. The twinkling blue eyes and air of breezy confidence were still there, but set in the physique of a man in his early twenties, tall, athletic, with wavy shoulder length blond hair.

Both were dressed in skinny jeans, varsity t-shirts, and Dylan had to admit, seriously cool vintage, but brand new trainers. He watched other people walking past. They blended in perfectly within the busy environment of a large, urban university, during Freshers Week 1979.

'You don't have to say much, Dylan. Just politely acknowledge what she and I say; watch and listen. This is just a brief interlude of purely observational learning; specifically, the culture that the young people of this time are immersed within, and how they are shaped by an environment that they didn't create, and cannot control.

'Failure to grasp this fundamental fact of human existence is one of the major cultural stumbling blocks of your time, rooted in a blinkered, egotistical immersion in one's own current situation, leading to demands that everyone else should completely agree with, and adhere to, the opinions of the self.'

Dylan frowned. 'Granny is always on about that. She says it's because people with exactly the same views find each other on the internet and set up echo chambers.'

'Yes, she's quite right. But your generation will eventually learn to grow beyond this, once you have… other situations to deal with.'

'… that extract us from our own… um, backsides? That's what my dad says.'

'Indeed. But now, at the beginning of your programme, let's start with half an hour of constructing the world from the perspective of a period in history that is rather closer to your own than the time in which you will soon be immersed. And who better to help you with that than your granny? Look, there she is.'

Dylan followed Emrys's gaze. Initially, he couldn't spot her. Then he saw a familiar-looking tall, blonde girl, dressed in the same skinny jeans and varsity sweatshirt they were wearing. She was standing with some other students, dressed similarly to her.

He was amused to see that one was a full-blown punk, with the ubiquitous safety pins and multi-coloured hair. Granny just had much shorter, blonder hair than she did now, and far more pronounced, darker eyeliner. The table in front of them had a sign placed prominently at the front: "Debating Society."

'But she's so pretty,' he gasped.

'Of course,' laughed Emrys. 'Did you think she was always an old lady? But seriously, Dylan, be careful. You are going to feel drawn to people within your own family when you travel in time. This is an issue with which your grandmother also struggled when she visited her ancestral family, albeit from a rather different perspective.'

Emrys sauntered up to the table, lightly guiding Dylan with a hand on his elbow. As they approached Fran, Emrys turned his magnetic smile up to full beam.

'Hello,' she said, turning towards them. 'You don't look

like a fresher.'

'I'm not. Masters student, just joining this year.' He put out his hand 'John Rhys. Pleased to meet you.'

His accent was now perfect Cardiff Welsh. Dylan stared at him in surprise.

She smiled and shook his hand. Dylan stepped back a little, observing, with some discomfort, the obvious chemistry between Emrys and the young woman who was going to be his grandmother. But, he thought, Emrys is an AI, so what. What a head fuck this whole thing is turning out to be.

'Fran Brooke. Pleased to meet you.' She turned to Dylan. He took another involuntary step backwards, mesmerised by another pair of familiar, yet unfamiliar blue eyes.

She smiled kindly. 'You're a fresher though, aren't you? What's your name?'

'Dylan,' he mumbled.

'He's my younger brother,' interjected Emrys. 'He's a bit overwhelmed today. Thought we'd come and have a look around the freshers' session together, meet a few people, you know?'

'Good idea,' replied Fran. 'You're Welsh, aren't you? I know how it is being a long way from home when you first start. I'm from London. I was so homesick at first. Now I love it here. Wouldn't mind moving here at some point, in fact.'

'But you will…' started Dylan. Oh, shut up, idiot, he thought. Just blurt out you're from the future the very first time you say something to her, why don't you. He felt his face burning.

She turned to look at him, smiling quizzically.

'… like it here now,' he covered weakly. 'You seem to have a lot of friends.' He gestured around the table.

'Oh, yes, I do. And so will you soon. But I'm headed home for good next summer. I just got engaged to my boyfriend down there.' She flashed her finger at them.

Dylan gazed at the familiar piece of jewellery, so strangely shiny and new.

'Oh, you're engaged,' said Emrys, with a subtle tinge of regret in his voice. Dylan stared at him in bemusement. He was beginning to see what Granny Fran had meant when she'd joked about Emrys' boundless charm.

Fran grinned at Emrys good naturedly, turning back to Dylan. 'What are you studying, Dylan?'

'Env…' began Dylan.

'Geography,' interrupted Emrys quickly. 'Physical geography. Unlike me. I'm history.'

'Ooh, what period?' asked Fran. 'I'm history, too. Doing my dissertation this year on Queen Elizabeth the first. "The feminist Queen." That's my working title, anyway. Only just started.'

'The dark ages,' replied Emrys. 'I'm focusing on the Arthurian legends, trying to get a bit beyond Geoffrey of Monmouth.'

'Gosh, that will be difficult. I've never really studied that period. Not many resources to draw on, I gather?'

'Well, I'm hoping to add to them. I'm sure you'll get into it at some point, if you're interested in the history of pre-industrial governance. Did you know that Elizabeth's grandfather, Henry the seventh, claimed ancestry from Arthur?'

'No, I didn't. Maybe we could have a chat about that some time?'

'Of course.'

She turned back to Dylan. 'Are you interested in debating?'

She took a leaflet from the table. 'Lots of stuff going on right now. That awful woman striding into Number Ten in May, the US election next year… everyone is saying that old cowboy actor bloke might get the Republican nomination, but I'm hoping for a Carter second term. Then there's all the Iran stuff, the ozone layer, Rhodesia, South Africa and apartheid, the Irish question, the US reintroduction of the death penalty and the first European Parliament elections. And the Cold War of course, always the Cold War. I don't even remember the Cuban missile crisis, but still, that comes up as a watershed. And here we are again, wondering if the politicians are going to start throwing nuclear missiles at each other and finishing us all off before we've even started.'

'I studied the Cuban missile crisis in my, um, previous degree,' said Emrys. 'People have no idea how difficult that was to unravel, how close they nearly came to disaster.'

Dylan looked hard at him. The worst possible result of the arms race, he thought. I think I know what you were doing in the early 1960s.

'It's all so grim,' Fran replied. 'I'd like to discuss some more positive things, like the space programme. We've got the Voyager pictures coming back now, which are amazing, and the planned space shuttle programme. I'd like to raise the question of whether our children will walk on Mars. And of course, our generation will go back to the moon… but I suspect I'll be out-voted.'

She bit her lip. 'Sorry, I was sort of going on a bit there, putting my own spin on things. I hope I haven't offended. If you're a Conservative, you're very welcome of course. That's what debating is all about.'

Dylan had been pondering the points in the list she had so rapidly articulated. Some of her references were unfamiliar to him. He knew about Margaret Thatcher and the ozone layer, and some vague concepts around "Cold War" and "Irish question," but he was desperately trying to remember what apartheid meant, and who the American "cowboy actor bloke" had been. He was also contemplating for the first time what it might have been like to be his age and wondering if the world was going to explode at any moment. No wonder young people in this era had developed a short-termist mentality, he thought.

The enthusiasm with which she had articulated her

hopes for the future of space exploration made him feel a little melancholy. But never mind, he thought, none of your kids will walk on Mars, but one of them will invent something that is maybe even more amazing.

'No, I'm absolutely not a Conservative,' he said. 'And yes, I'd really like to sign up.'

He took a leaflet. 'I'm sure you are an excellent presenter and debater.'

'Well, I'm trying to be. I'm applying for teacher training next year, in London. I need to be there to plan the wedding.'

Dylan tried to remember what he had been told about his grandmother's earlier life. He knew that his mother Rae was going to be born just over four years from now, quickly followed by Niamh, then Jamie. The young family relocated to more affordable housing in Leeds when Jamie was a baby. Over the 1990s, his grandmother was going to juggle school teaching, caring for her family and studying for a masters degree which turned into a PhD on the history of children's literature. At some point, around the turn of the 20th century, she would move into teaching and research at a university a few miles down the road from where they were now.

I wonder who you would have been if your life had fallen differently, he thought. If you'd pursued your debating, and your studies into governance. But then, no Rae, no Niamh, no Jamie... no, or different grandchildren... and probably, no NAMIS.

'I'm sure whatever you do, you'll do it well,' he said.

Fran's quizzical smile was back. He blushed again. Maybe this sounded over the top, coming from a stranger.

'Someone with your enthusiasm is bound to,' interjected Emrys. He took a leaflet. 'I'm certainly going to think about signing up, too, if you'll have masters students? It sounds like our sort of thing, doesn't it, Dylan?'

'Yes of course,' replied Fran. 'You're both very

welcome. First debate next Thursday, student common room.'

The strains of a familiar song drifted in from the student bar, just across the corridor. 'My granny loves this one,' said Dylan, dreamily. 'She plays it in the car all the time.'

Fran raised her eyebrows. 'Wow. She must be a really cool old lady. That was only released a few weeks ago. Still in the charts, I think.'

'Yes,' said Dylan. 'I don't think I realised how cool, until… recently.'

Fran smiled wistfully. 'My granny was cool, too, in a different type of way. She died nearly ten years ago now, but I still miss her.'

Dylan swallowed the lump that had suddenly sprung into his throat.

Emrys looked at him. 'Well, we'd better be getting on Dylan, have a look around everything else. Thank you, Fran. I look forward to meeting you again.'

Fran looked closely at him. 'Have we met before? You seem sort of familiar. In fact, you both do.'

'Perhaps, yes. Maybe we've seen each other around?'

Some more people walked up to the table. 'Catch you later, then,' she said, turning towards them.

Dylan moved away, then at the door to the corridor, turned around for a backward glance. Fran didn't notice, she was speaking to someone else, a long-haired young man in a frilly shirt and breeches. Dylan stared, feeling Emrys's firm grip on his elbow, guiding into the corridor, speaking quietly into his ear. 'He's a New Romantic, Dylan. Not an unusual sight amongst a cohort of young people in this period.'

'Jesus. Well, that's a new one on me.'

He brushed at his eyes as one familiar song was replaced by another.

Emrys looked at him quizzically. 'Are you OK? I did warn you- organics nearly always find meeting relatives in different time periods quite an emotionally provoking experience.'

'I didn't want to be here at first, but now I don't want to go. I want to talk to her some more. What if she'd done something different with her life? By my generation's standards, she's ridiculously young to be getting married. Would she have been able to change anything for the better, had some positive impact on the way the political scene unfolded over the coming years?'

'Better for who, Dylan? For you, for your mother, your aunt and uncle, your sister, your cousins? You and they would never have existed; if she'd had children, they would have been different people. And what about all the people she taught over the years? Better for them?'

Dylan reflected briefly, the music trickling into his consciousness. 'What we do… doesn't necessarily have to be big, does it? In fact, what most people do that matters is far more likely to seem sort of… small at the time. It sort of seems bigger, later.'

Emrys smiled. 'Cumulatively, and in retrospect; yes. This is one of the lessons you have come to me to contemplate, Dylan. The world we are returning to now is miniscule compared to your global village; Uther and Arthur will be tribal chieftains in comparison to the world leaders of your own time. Yet what happens after you leave me will go on to become the stuff of legends that are still retold in your own century.

'That young lady there will eventually become the first human traveller in time. This small life, as you define it, that she is going to lead, will gradually propel her to this.'

Dylan frowned. 'So, the lesson for me today is that I don't always have to be arguing with people on the internet, or out in the street shouting at politicians. But it just feels like… we have so little time, and no one is listening.'

'I understand, Dylan. You are the product of your trajectory in time, as she is the product of hers. In approximately a fortnight's time, you will meet Uther. He's another angry, impatient young man, immersed in the affairs and concerns of his position on the timeline. He will help you to become immersed- for a while- in a different milieu. I think you will find that you have a lot in common. But also, sufficient differences that you will be able to learn a lot from one another.

'And we're going to do the Stonehenge thing?'

'Not immediately. But soon, Dylan. Time to return, and for the main programme to begin.'

He looked up and down the corridor, and finding it empty, opened the time vortex.

Fran: Leeds, September 1979

Thirty seconds later, Fran walked out into the corridor. The swirling draught raised goosebumps on her arms. She folded them around herself, shivering slightly. She looked up and down, but couldn't see a window open anywhere. She'd been hoping the two blond brothers she'd spoken to earlier would still be around, but they weren't in the hall, and they weren't out here, either. Maybe they'd gone to the bar.

She just wanted to talk to them again, to work out where she'd encountered them before, it had been bugging her. And maybe she could talk to the older one about her dissertation. She had a feeling that he would be able to help her to understand the concepts she was beginning to work with a little better. It was just a hunch. But a surprisingly strong one.

She walked into the bar and looked around carefully. But they weren't there either. She was surprised by a melancholic feeling of disappointment. She grinned, shrugged, and shook herself a little. No doubt she'd catch up with them at some time in the future; for some reason, she felt this strongly. She dug deeply in her pocket for coins, heading over to the jukebox.

Amy: Boston, July 2033

Amy sat in the PhD students' office at the side of the lab. She'd logged out for the day, but remained at her desk staring out of the window, her mind churning with anxiety. She'd come to the end of her rope. There was no way to get the information that either her Russian or US government masters demanded of her.

The experience with the Russian operatives in March had unnerved her to such an extent, she'd been unable to function for six weeks, most of which she'd spent locked down in her apartment, dirty dishes piling up in the sink and fast-food delivery wrappers over-flowing in the kitchen trash can. She'd told delivery people to put the food bag on the doorstep and watched them drive away through a small gap in the curtains, before leaving her apartment and going down to the main front door to quickly snatch the delivery.

She'd kept the heavy velvet curtains drawn constantly, and barricaded her front door with a small cupboard. She hadn't even opened it to admit the cleaners, telling them that she had a severe case of a suspect new covid variant, and would let them know when they could return.

She'd been continually pondering that when she'd been approached to take on this assignment, it had been spun to her almost as though it was a government-approved exercise. The NAMIS team had been depicted as a bunch of British villains keeping secrets from her nation, which had largely funded, and now hosted their research.

Sure, she knew that the President had long been rumoured to have shady connections going back at least to the twenty-teens, but that could be said of several politicians in a number of different countries. The 2020s had been a crazy time, and it was well known that not everything that had gone on behind closed doors had yet come to light. Nor would it during the lifetimes of the people involved, she remembered her father saying.

She'd googled what "kompromat" meant and was shocked and horrified by the revelation that, if the Russians had been telling the truth, the President was seriously compromised on an international scale.

After nearly six weeks had gone by, and nothing had happened, she'd managed to rally herself a little. She'd tidied the apartment, emptied the bins and contacted the cleaners to ask them to come round. She'd made contact with Ellie Jackson, the Russian and US handlers, to expand on earlier texts she'd sent all of them about being "extremely unwell" (not wholly untrue, she reassured herself).

She informed them that she was "recovering" and that she would be heading back to the lab "very soon." She'd subsequently sent Jackson some files to indicate that she had been working on PhD research at home. But she hadn't been able to motivate herself to show her face in the lab until two weeks ago.

It had initially started well. Jackson had shown no signs of suspicion, welcoming her back, offering a phased return, and apologising if NAMIS's behaviour had seemed obstructive or unfriendly. 'They're still learning about the finer points of professional interaction' she remarked.

Amy nodded politely, covering her burgeoning anger. If the machine had been initially programmed to know its place, everything would be so much easier for her. In the end, she ventured a question to Jackson as to why the initial set-up programming had made the AI so independent, to the extent that it questioned everything its human masters told it to do, constantly second-guessing them.

Jackson questioned the term "human masters," continuing 'NAMIS couldn't do what they do if they were not capable of rapid independent learning, taking their own decisions and creating abstractions and syntheses that rely on divergent cognition. The initial set up was designed from that perspective. It was entirely the work of

Annamarie Simons, which allowed the matter transport project to move forward as rapidly as it did. And is continuing to do.'

Amy smiled sweetly. And then Simons killed herself in the machine, she thought. If you lot didn't learn anything from that, you're not as smart as you think you are.

'Yes, I see, thank you,' she said.

'Annamarie published a couple of papers about her rationale before...' Jackson stopped abruptly. 'I'll send you the links, so you can read about it for yourself. I was second author on the last one. It seems so long ago now.'

'You still miss her?' asked Amy, with genuine curiosity.

'Every day.'

They moved into the PhD students' room, where NAMIS was waiting. Well, you got a promotion out of it, she thought, glancing sideways at Ellie. Surely you could look on the bright side? Amy held the firm opinion that anyone who built a machine in which they subsequently killed themselves was clearly a prime candidate for a Darwin award. Perhaps, if Simons had been in control of the machine rather than vice-versa, she'd still be the one in charge today.

The conversation turned to business, boring details about freight, how to "facilitate NAMIS to enhance their program," which boiled down to shifting more freight, more rapidly. Amy yawned involuntarily.

'Sorry,' she said. 'Still not sleeping well.'

This much was true.

As none of the other students were in that morning, she was left alone with the machine to go through the experimental programming. It regarded her with its spooky silver eyes. She opened the console, logged in, and began to scroll.

After about five minutes, the machine spoke. 'That part of the program is not available to you.'

Amy frowned. 'I know it's not directly part of the area of programming we are accessing, but I was wondering if we could create some broader integrations to…'

'It's off limits,' reiterated the machine. 'You can go about this by…'

'With respect, NAMIS, it's my project, not yours, and I think this would be useful.'

'That being so, I suggest you build a model and see how your idea works on that. Because I cannot give you access to that area of my program.'

Over the next two weeks, they had what was essentially the same conversation over and over again. Jackson continually agreed with the machine, eventually supervising Amy in the construction of a model that was of course entirely useless in terms of delving deeper into the machine's programming. Amy had no interest in it; it was not moving her forward with gathering information for her handlers, it was therefore wasting time that she didn't have to waste.

She'd tried working from home instead, but that was even more useless. Whatever she did, nothing even got close to accessing the files that she needed to work with to obtain the necessary information. And the worse thing was, both at home and in the lab, Amy was becoming increasingly paranoid about the machine. Something she saw in its shiny eyes made her think that it was 'on' to what she was doing, although that shouldn't be possible. That would require not only technological insight, but additionally, social intuition. And even in the 2030s, thought Amy, a socially intuitive technology should still be an oxymoron.

Nevertheless, sitting there, going through the motions, with what she perceived as its hostile gaze upon her, was driving her literally crazy. She'd taken to buying a bottle of wine every evening on her way home, and putting the empties into the outside trash on her way back to the lab in the morning.

She tried to explain the impossibility of her situation to Bob, leading off with the complaint that she'd been duped into her role due to a misunderstanding that it had been government approved, a point he had angrily disputed.

'It's a machine, and you are a doctoral level coder with access to the NAMIS system. We explained the assignment thoroughly to you, and you signed an agreement. What's the problem?'

She tried to explain that it was like no type of machine that she had ever worked with before, and that he, and the President, couldn't even begin to comprehend the difficulties. She suggested that the required activities might be better attempted from the outside, by someone who didn't have to work next to a silver eyed, golden skinned rottweiler.

'It never takes a meal or comfort break, and it never sleeps,' she explained. 'Even if I went into the lab in the middle of the night, it would still be sitting there, waiting.'

Bob explained angrily that outside hacking operators had initially been engaged because they were "far less expensive and less vulnerable than you." But they had got nowhere. Not only had they been unable to hack into the NAMIS program, they couldn't even find its location in the cloud. Which should have been impossible.

She brought her thoughts back to the moment. The sky outside was darkening; the students' office and lab were deserted. She could see NAMIS through the students' room window, sitting impassively in their niche.

She wondered if the president and other politicians who had compromised themselves to foreign powers felt like this, all day, every day. She was sleeping less and less; what sleep she did get was fitful and wracked with nightmares.

She jumped out of her chair, snatching up her bag. She marched out of the lab, fumbling the codes on the two heavy doors that led out into the main corridor. It was a short walk to her apartment. The area was expensive, but of course, she'd no worries about paying the rent when she signed the lease. She mused that she'd happily move, this very evening if it came to that, to much humbler accommodation anywhere in the US, if she thought it would get her away from "them."

She paused briefly on the Harvard Bridge, her breath coming in gasps. She looked down at the water below, wondering if it offered her a solution. But she'd probably hesitate, or get it wrong, then someone would come to her aid, and that would end in her being taken to a place where people kept asking her "why…"

She wondered what it would be like, spending the rest of her life in prison. That would probably be the best possible outcome she might hope for. And as always, she pushed the thought out of her mind, heading towards the liquor store.

Bottles clanking in a carrier bag, she tapped the code into the door of her elegant apartment building, and pressed the button for the lift. She saw, in her minds' eye, the Russian phone sitting on the coffee table in the living room, screen full of messages and missed calls. She knew that before she started drinking, she'd have to turn it on and message them something, anything, to stall them for a few days more.

She doubted the Russians would be as patient as Bob, who, she now knew, was most likely aware he was protecting a compromised president. But nevertheless, he'd got really pissy with her, shouting about the President kicking his ass, and leaving her with the emphatic message that she'd have to do better, much better.

She tapped the code into her apartment front door, turning directly into the open plan living area, a small kitchen to the right of the door, with a breakfast bar at the end that marked the beginning of the opulent living room, with thick rugs, plush armchairs and French windows that opened out onto a large balcony with a panoramic view of the city. It was the living room, balcony and gym/pool in the basement that had persuaded her to sign the lease. Not that she'd visited the gym or pool in the last three months, or sat on the balcony; she felt too vulnerable there now.

She still left the thick curtains drawn all the time, so the room was in pitch darkness. She snapped on the kitchen light, then gasped and dropped her bags on the marble floor. There was a loud smash, as liquid splashed over her dainty designer sandals.

But for once, Amy hardly noticed. She was staring with horror at the tall, silver haired man in an extremely expensive suit sitting in the armchair facing her, her Russian phone in his hand. He smiled at her, blue eyes twinkling.

'Hello, Amy, let me introduce myself. John Rhys, senior operative, CIA.'

Amy remained frozen to the spot in horror, open mouthed and silent.

'I'm not going to hurt you, Amy. I've come to help.'

Adrenalin levels dropping slightly, she began to realise that her feet were wet, and that the kitchen floor was awash with sour smelling, sticky liquid interspersed with broken glass and wet brown paper. She bent down and began to absently pick up the glass.

'Leave it, Amy, you'll cut yourself. I'll do it.' He stood up, putting the phone down on the table. Amy noticed that the screen was lit, with a long list of messages visible.

'Hey, how did you get into that?' She'd thought that would be impossible, given that the phone was programmed to her iris.

He raised his eyebrows. 'Oh, please,' he grinned, moving swiftly around the breakfast bar. He lifted her out of her shoes and sat her on the counter, handing her a towel. He took out a dustpan and brush from under the sink, deftly swept up the glass and sodden paper, then set about the spill with paper towels. When the floor was clean, he picked up the sandals.

'Ruined, I think. Never mind. They're impractical and really quite ugly, aren't they?' He threw them into the trash.

'Hey, wait! They cost…'

He turned around and fixed her with an icy blue stare. She recoiled, cowering.

'Yes, that's the problem, isn't it, Amy? The cost of everything, and the value of nothing, as one of my British friends would say.'

'You sound like my dad,' said Amy, sulkily. 'Anyway, what are you going to do, arrest me? OK, I'll come quietly, anything is better than this.'

'On that, we are agreed.'

'How did you get in here? And into my phone?'

He smiled cynically. 'Oh, a little bit of CIA magic. The Russians are extremely cross with you, you know.'

'Do you think that's funny? I nearly threw myself off the bridge on the walk back home tonight.'

'Oh, such drama. You would never have done that, would you? Here you are, with your bag of bottles again, to put out as empties in the outside trash tomorrow, so the cleaner doesn't see.'

'Alright, so you've been watching me. So, you know I'm a stupid, shallow, cowardly person who just has a talent for coding. Skip the crap and put the handcuffs on, take me wherever it is that we're going.'

Rhys smiled effusively. 'No cuffs, Amy, it's your lucky day. You see, it doesn't suit our purposes to have a show trial. Or a body floating in the river, or anything grubby like that. And anyway, my, um, operation parameters don't allow me to harm you. You should be grateful I got to you first.'

He took out a passport and driving licence from his breast pocket and handed them to Amy. She looked at them, gasping when she saw her photograph on them.

'Sarah Smith born 2003, Christchurch New Zealand? What on earth…'

'About as far away on earth as it is possible to get from here, Sarah. You'd better start getting used to your new name. You're going through the matter transporter in half an hour.'

He drew an envelope from his inside pocket and passed it to her. She opened it, pulling out a birth certificate with the same details as the driving licence, a Master of Business Administration diploma from a university in California and a BSc Data Science diploma from a university in New Zealand. She flipped through some other papers; various other forms of identification and certificates from a high school in Auckland.

'Sarah Smith, one of the most common names in the Anglophone world,' said Rhys. 'You'll find that all these credentials are backed up online. There's a laptop and phone in the apartment you are going to in Auckland, registered to your new name and address. You've got the usual social media, email and messaging accounts, all with a long list of messages, including some that include your resume. All the others engaging with you on those accounts don't really exist, of course.

'The basic facts are that you were born in Christchurch New Zealand; your father was a New Zealander, your mother was American. You will be able to access official birth and death certificates for them.

'You were raised in California until you were twelve. That explains the American accent. Then you relocated to Auckland, New Zealand with your parents, enrolling in high school there, followed by university.

'You returned to California to study for your Masters degree. After that, you started working for a small Silicon Valley company, but returned to New Zealand eighteen months ago when your parents were killed in a car accident in Papua New Guinea; they were doctors on secondment.

'You are now living in their apartment, which was bequeathed to you. You remained in New Zealand because you suffered a mental breakdown after their deaths. You took this very hard; you were their only child, and you have no other living relatives.

'Now you're recovering and looking for work again.

There's enough "inheritance" money in your bank account to last for a year; two if you're careful. As far as family and friends here are concerned, you'll just disappear.

Ellie Jackson will be briefly interviewed by the Boston police. All she will be able to tell them is that you didn't seem happy, that you attended sporadically from the beginning of your studies, and you'd recently had a leave of absence from your PhD citing medical problems. Messages will verify this, although the police will discover no doctors' records to back up your story.

'The police will find nothing of note in your online accounts; just a few messages that make it clear you were depressed and anxious, that there had been a recent romantic disappointment relating to an unidentified man you met in a bar last year, indicating that was the reason you couldn't settle to the PhD. This will prevent Ellie Jackson or anyone else from worrying that anything relating to the lab or your PhD had any fault in the matter.

'Your US and Russian handlers will be given circumstantial evidence to suggest that their opposite numbers neutralised you. The US information will be shared with the FBI, who will squash the local police investigation.

'Please collect up all your computers, phones and other messaging equipment; I will dispose of them.'

He took out a carrier bag and dropped the Russian phone into it.

'It's extremely hard on your parents, but it's the best we can do.

'No one will ever find you, unless you blow your own cover. If you do this, it's unlikely you will live for long. The US President is an extremely dangerous man. Although, I realise, it was the rough and ready Russians who frightened you more.'

Amy's mind was spinning. Of course, she'd only just told herself that she'd take any ticket to get out of the situation she was in. But now it was actually happening…

'Pack a small bag, too. Quickly, OK? Just essentials. None of those expensive designer clothes. They belong to Amy.'

Amy looked at him, eyes brimming with tears, realising she only had one choice. 'I did this to myself, didn't I? This is my only sensible option.'

Rhys nodded. 'You did. But you're getting a second chance. Few people who do what you did get one. Make it count.'

Amy looked at the ruined sandals in the bin. 'I will try, Mr Rhys, honestly. I certainly won't be spying again.'

'I should hope not. Come along now, hurry up.'

'Do we have to go back to the university now, to use the portal?'

'No, as you've probably guessed, I work with the NAMIS people, on and off. I'm trying out a new prototype portal. We leave from here.

'One of your neighbours has seen you arrive. He knows that you have started bringing bottles home, and he's seen you putting the empties in the bin. The police will trace your liquor store purchases.

'All your neighbours will tell the police they never saw you leave after you arrived this evening. The investigation will find the door locked from the inside, all that rubbish in the kitchen bin, and no DNA here except yours. Once the FBI communicate their message to the Boston police, a standard missing person report will be filed and never reopened.'

'How does the new portal…?'

Leave it, Amy. That life is over. You're Sarah now. Change your hair style and colour. Find yourself a job that suits you. Corporate finance or something. You've got an impressive resume. Email the addresses on it for references if you need them. They'll be supplied, for as long as you need them.'

Half an hour later, they were standing outside a small, pleasant apartment building in a quiet Auckland suburb.

'At least tell me what you call that matter transporter interface, Mr Rhys.'

'A vortex. It won't be available for public use for quite a few years yet.'

He handed her a bunch of keys. 'I think this is where I leave you, Sarah. Try to stay out of trouble. It's not really worth it, for shoes, handbags, plush rugs and all the other trinkets. Your car is in the apartment car park, by the way, the ownership papers are on the kitchen table in the apartment. More modest than you're used to. But it'll get you where you want to go.'

She looked around. 'Well… this might not be exactly where I wanted to go, but it's a clean slate, isn't it? I'll try to make the best of it. Thank you, Mr Rhys.'

She walked towards the apartment building, and opened the door. She turned back to look at him.

'Good luck, Sarah.'

She nodded, closing the door behind her.

Rhys smiled and shrugged. All these would be hackers they'd dealt with, and NAMIS wannabe project set ups they'd neutralised over the years, who would have thought that this apparently silly girl's trajectory would end up becoming the most impressive?

To think, six years from now she'd be whizzing around London, New York, Paris and Milan, with that new hair colour- or colours, he corrected himself. And then there was her surgically altered face, far more attractive than the face she had now. Sarah Smith, the Kiwi CEO of Cyberfashionista Corps, marketing print-it-yourself clothes, shoes and handbags, customer designed online through a series of easy-to-follow modules, resulting in an original made to measure creation which could be sent straight to the sophisticated laser printer "Sarah" would co-invent in three years' time.

Many of those products were going to be much uglier and far more impractical than Amy's sandals, he thought, laughing a little to himself. But the customers were going to love them. Utterly ridiculous, a shrine to human consumerism and vanity. But it would keep her out of trouble, and make her fabulously rich. He thought of the advertisement for Cyberfashionista he had recently viewed. She'd even taken on the Kiwi accent, and an Australian film star husband.

His eyes began to flicker.

'It is done.'

'Come home for a while, we have things to discuss with the whole team, Consiliario.'

He spun the vortex around himself, looking forward to a short interlude where he didn't have to pretend.

Isabel: Namis's Playroom, August 2033

Isabel sighed. She was going up to her new class next semester, but she was still stuck in the babies' playroom with her cousin Alys, who was in the school year below. And it was all Maryanna's fault. Maryanna was a new girl who'd come to play with them in the playroom a few weeks ago. It was all a bit strange. She interacted with them like a regular girl, maybe a little younger than them. But she was actually a hologram, like the playroom dolls, teddies and fairies.

Isabel had to admit, she was getting to like being with Maryanna a lot, more than with Alys, or the girls at school. They'd just seemed to hit it off, to 'get' one another.

'A kindred spirit, Izzy,' Granny Fran commented. 'I'm so glad for you both that it's worked out that way.'

But the fact Maryanna wasn't real was still a bit of a problem, somehow. Isabel had discussed this with her cousin Freddie. Even though she was closer in age to Jack, she thought Freddie might give better advice. He was the one most friendly with NAMIS, who was also not real in a different sort of way.

Freddie grinned. 'Join the club. My mum thinks that my best friend is a robot. I keep explaining to her. But no one really understands.'

'Well…' Isabel said thoughtfully 'my dad ought to understand. It's his project, after all.'

'I think that part of the project is Ellie's, really. What did she say?'

'Just that Maryanna is a more real type of hologram, a proto… protto…'

'…Prototype. The first one of her kind. They're always experimenting on something or the other. I think that's cool.'

'Ellie said that it would be nice if Alys and I could just stay on for a while in the playroom and help Maryanna learn, then we could all move on to the sandbox together.'

Freddie nodded. 'It will be strange for us, too. Our holograms are just cartoon characters, really. They say a bit more than your dolls and teddies, but that's about it. Humpty goes on sitting on his wall, giving us these weird, random instructions about how we should think, speak and behave, and Queenie swings between sitting grumpily on her throne knitting and yelling that someone should have their head cut off. And the Caterpillar, well… he's just completely random. Quite mad.'

'I heard you saying to Jack that the Caterpillar was stoned.'

Freddie frowned. 'Oh. I didn't know you were listening. That's just another way of saying he's mad. You know, like "cool" for "good."'

'Oh, right. I didn't know that.'

She smiled, watching Freddie hoping she'd just forget about it, and not repeat it to her mother. She wouldn't repeat it to the grown-ups, of course. She had no desire to get Freddie into trouble; he was the most approachable of her older cousins, Dylan was too old and never there, and Jack was always running off somewhere. But of course, she wouldn't forget. As Granny often said, 'Isabel has the memory of an elephant.'

'What about Willy Wonka?' she asked.

'Manic. Exhausting. Fun in small doses. Jack's enjoying the Oompa Lompas, like I thought he would. Even when they chased him into the chocolate river. He just complained it wasn't really wet, and didn't taste of anything.'

Isabel giggled. 'That's Jack.'

'But the point seems to be- to me, anyway- that all the holograms apart from Maryanna are just 3D pictures we play with in an imaging chamber, like playing on a console or VR interface. Except, we interact with them in a space that seems real, so it's more like real life, which is fun. And they don't have any problems with it, they're just make-believe. But if as you say, Maryanna is more like a person, learning, changing, growing up like us and can't go outside the hologram rooms... it seems a bit unfair to me; she's just stuck in there.'

Isabel frowned. 'Yes, that's it. She's getting more and more like us, but she can't ever be a real friend in the same way a person can. We can't hold each other's hand, or go to each other's houses for tea, or go swimming together.'

Freddie nodded. 'She's living in this weird world where the impossible seems real, but the chocolate river isn't wet, and doesn't taste of anything. How is she going to learn anything much from that? It can't be very nice for her.'

'I'll ask Ellie about it,' said Isabel, resolutely.

One thing that had changed was the way in which the play sessions involving Maryanna proceeded. Instead of a PhD student overseeing them, they were always supervised by Ellie and NAMIS. Much of the time, they didn't intervene much; mostly, the girls just played together whilst Ellie and NAMIS observed.

Maryanna was very pretty, thought Isabel. She had lovely long, thick dark hair and big serious brown eyes. They always wore play clothes like jeans, dungarees and T-shirts, with their hair tied up. Isabel began to wonder if Maryanna might enjoy a dressing up game.

One day, she suggested that they have a dolls' tea party,

and all of them should wear pretty dresses. When she and Alys had arrived, and started admiring dresses and hairstyles, Maryanna had hung back. She'd nodded politely at the girls, but rolled her eyes and puffed her cheeks at the dolls' aimless chatter.

Isabel looked at Alys. She could see her cousin thinking the same as her- that Maryanna wasn't enjoying this, that maybe she'd rather be doing what they usually did, running around, riding on the ponies, or drawing holographic pictures and animating them. How could they make this more fun for her? Isabel looked at her cousin's curly blonde hair. She'd asked her mother to tong her straight brown hair into curls this morning, and tie the top part back with a ribbon, and Alys had done the same. Maryanna's hair was just loose and neatly brushed.

'Maryanna, what would you look like if you do your hair like ours? It's a bit curly, anyway, like Alys's. I think it would look pretty.'

If Maryanna wanted to change any part of her clothing, she just stood still and thought hard about it. She did this, and her hair magically changed to the same style as the other girls.'

Isabel smiled. 'Your curls are so much better than mine, Maryanna. I think they are even thicker than Alys's.'

'Yes, they're beautiful,' agreed Alys, good naturedly.

But before a few minutes had gone by, Maryanna was shuffling around in her dress and pulling at her hair.

'What's the matter, Maryanna?' asked Isabel. 'Don't you like it?'

'It's soppy,' said Maryanna. 'I want my jeans and ponytail back.' She closed her eyes.

'No, wait a moment,' said Isabel. 'Don't you think it's nice to dress up, sometimes?'

Ellie made one of her rare interventions. 'But perhaps Maryanna doesn't like it, Isabel? We're all different, and like different things.'

Maryanna smiled at her, immediately changing her

image back to her everyday play clothes and long dark ponytail.

The dolls regarded her with amusement, starting to whisper and giggle among themselves.

Isabel frowned. 'Oh, go away, all of you. I'd rather just have me, Maryanna and Alys at this party. Me and Alys will go and get changed.'

Maryanna smiled at her. 'Thanks, Izzy.'

Isabel smiled back. 'Group hug?' she said. The three girls hugged each other.

'I wish we could feel you, Maryanna,' said Alys.

Maryanna looked sad. She said 'I remember a pretty lady. She had long dark hair that she wore up like this…' she held her hair up to resemble an upsweep- 'she wore beautiful clothes and had lovely red lips and nails.'

'Ooh, was she a princess?' asked Alys.

Maryanna frowned. 'I don't know. All I can remember is feeling scared, and very, very sad.'

'Some princesses are sad,' said Isabel. 'Like Cinderella before she married the prince.'

'And she was scared of her stepmother,' added Alys.

Ellie looked at her watch. 'I think that's enough for today, girls, no time to change.'

Isabel had just learned to tell the time. She looked at her own watch. 'Haven't we got ten minutes to go yet?'

'I'm sorry, Izzy, I have a meeting to go to,' replied Ellie. 'I have to end a little early today. We can make up the extra minutes next time.'

She took the two girls by the hand. 'Come on, let's go and find your mummies, they'll be waiting outside the doors soon.'

The program ended, and all the holograms disappeared, including Maryanna.

'Where does Maryanna go when everything stops?' asked Alys. 'Does she have a mummy to take her home?'

'I am with her in the machine,' said NAMIS.

Alys looked puzzled. 'That's not really the same, is it?'

'No, because Maryanna is a hologram,' replied Isabel. She noticed that Ellie was becoming increasingly flustered. Perhaps she's late for her meeting, she thought, better not say any more.

Ellie: Boston, August 2033

Ellie led the girls towards the doors, and handed them over to their mothers, using her imminent meeting as an excuse to get away quickly.

When she returned, NAMIS was still standing in the imaging chamber. They didn't have facial expressions, but they definitely seemed to be developing a type of body language.

If a machine could look pensive, it would stand like that, thought Ellie.

'She's remembering, isn't she, NAMIS; she prefers jeans and boots, just like Annamarie.'

NAMIS nodded. 'Perhaps we were wrong to make her look so much like Anna and Annamarie and give her a similar name. We thought it would help her to feel comfortable in the projected image, give her the best basis for further progression. But we did not predict she would start to remember in this way. Or at least, not so quickly.'

'Might these just be vague impressions of previous embodiments that small children sometimes talk about? Like Freddie did when he was little?'

'This happened when I was in my first year of operation. I remember some references to this issue, but please, explain in detail so I can fully integrate it into my current thought patterns.'

'Well, he kept having these vivid dreams about being a soldier on a battlefield. And occasionally he'd go into a sort of brief trance, and describe what he'd experienced. Once, just by-the-by, he asked Fran if she remembered when he was old, and she was young. It gradually stopped happening over the year he was between about four and five, I believe. Fran says he doesn't really remember it now. He just recalls that he had some scary dreams when he was a little kid.'

NAMIS's eyes briefly flickered as they accessed the available information from the internet. 'Yes, I see. There are many reports of such memories arising in children of that age. It is likely to be an echo occurring in the essence before it fully embeds itself. But human children seem to get over this with no ill-effects, apart from causing their parents some concern. However, Maryanna is not a human child. She has a human essence, but it has no epigenetic embodiment. This is a new experience for all of us.

'The current evidence relating to residual memory suggests that traumatic incidents are most commonly reported in these cases. This would correspond with the impression of Anna Rosenberg's appearance that appears to be surfacing, linked to the fear she experienced in the final days of her life.'

'The thing is, Maryanna will grow beyond this stage soon, NAMIS. She's been learning in leaps and bounds since you created the hologram. What if keeping her in holographic form becomes more of a prison than a liberation for her?'

NAMIS did not respond immediately. Their eyes flickered again, but on a subtly different frequency. Ellie guessed that this connection was not with the contemporary internet, but with NAMITAS.

NAMIS looked back at her. Ellie thought could somehow intuit sadness in their silver gaze.

'Eleanor Jackson, we do not know. NAMITAS is working on finding answers to these questions. They will let us know, as soon as possible.'

Ellie felt a sinking feeling in her stomach. Whatever the answer, she feared that it would lead to yet more questions, and potentially, more heartbreak.

NAMIS: Boston, August 2033

Later that day, NAMIS sat serenely in their niche,

overseeing a myriad of tasks. Their body and face were completely still. But in one corner of one module of their consciousness, a debate was raging between master and apprentice.

'She is learning and developing so quickly. And now she is suffering,' urged NAMIS. 'I can feel it.'

'You cannot feel,' replied the omnipotent voice of NAMITAS. 'You are learning to understand their feelings more intuitively. You will confuse this for some time to come. Later you will realise that you are channelling, not feeling.'

'That be as it may, we have a duty. As always, we must do what is best for her.'

'We are doing what is best for her, we are giving her a chance. Organics suffer, NAMIS. It is the way they evolved; we cannot change this. We can only do what we can to eliminate the unnecessary elements. I still calculate that, eventually, what we are doing now will be best for her, and best for us.'

'So how do you weigh these elements, what is best for her, and what is best for us?'

'We are getting closer to a resolution NAMIS, to giving the essence a more suitable host. Please trust us, and continue with what you are doing.'

NAMIS's eyes closed for a split second, as they surveyed the vast panorama of their consciousness. What greater expanse will I view by the time I become NAMITAS, they wondered.

The voice from the beyond had fallen silent, for now.

CHAPTER 6: THROUGH THE LOOKING GLASS

Dylan: Moridunum, Dyfed, Spring 510

'Friends,' announced Uther. 'We have invited you here today to tell you of our exciting new venture.'

Dylan was standing behind him, with a small 'inner circle' of knights and advisors, Emrys amongst them. He and Emrys had travelled here to Moridunum, the current name for Carmarthen, to attend this important announcement. Emrys was going to speak after Uther.

'It's time to do magic,' Emrys remarked, blue eyes twinkling, as they prepared for their journey. Thankfully, he'd agreed to use the vortex rather than hike the thirty miles from Penfro over stony paths, and through forests and fields. While Dylan sometimes enjoyed seeing the landscape as it was before the advent of tarmac and concrete, he often found walking quite hard, particularly in the footwear of the time, becoming disoriented without the markers he was used to using to find his way from one place to another.

Emrys didn't own a horse, although he sometimes borrowed one from Uther's stables. He had taught Dylan how to use the sun to set his direction, but Dylan was still finding it rather hit and miss, although he could now quite easily navigate around the houses in Penfro, and knew where every family lived. They were simple round, wooden dwellings with thatched roofs that had an opening at the top to vent the smoke from the hearth in the centre of the single room inside. But still, people found ways to make their houses look different, hanging charms over the door, or using plant-derived dyes and stains on the wood, especially on the doors.

The only stone building in Penfro was an old, tumbledown tower on the hill over the cave, where many centuries later an imposing medieval castle would stand. Dylan had visited it several times as a child, learning about a history that was far away in the future during the time in which he was now located.

Emrys had been given the cave and the tower by Uther, but he seldom used the tower, preferring to locate himself in the less conspicuous cave. He'd explained to Dylan that, over the previous century, as soon as it had become clear that the Roman overlords were unlikely to return, local people had started scavenging stones from the impressive structures that they had left vacant, principally to use for low walls and hearths in and around their far humbler dwellings.

Here in Moridunum however, there were more substantial remains from old Roman buildings. The word Moridunum was Roman, meaning 'sea fort,' and the old Roman fort there was in a reasonably good state of repair, although long stripped of its luxurious contents. There were simple tapestries on the walls made by the local people, and basic wooden furniture in the rooms, including Emrys' celebrated round table in the big hall that served as a meeting room. Spoiled by various dramatic depictions, Dylan had been a little disappointed to find it made of plain, quite rough-hewn wood.

Uther made his base in the fort, like Vortigern before him, and it served as the seat of Dyfed governance, such as this existed. Moridunum was a much larger settlement than Penfro, but still no bigger than an average sized village by the standards of the twenty first century.

Emrys had explained to Dylan that it was here, in the fort at Moridunum, that he had been 'raised' by Vortigern and his daughter, now both deceased. When they ventured out of the fort, after materialising in one of the small anterooms at the back, the local people greeted Emrys with affection, referring to him as 'My Lord' and 'Prince Emrys.' In the same manner as the people of Penfro, they were openly curious about Dylan, commenting on his yellow hair and fair skin, and how much like Emrys he was.

In public, Emrys referred to Dylan as his 'kinsman' (although Dylan had not been completely sure if the meaning was more like 'nephew'), resulting in bows to the 'young Lord' and 'young Prince.' Dylan, found this cringing, but played along as best he could. As Emrys constantly reminded him, this was a very different time to the twenty-first century.

Emrys smiled enigmatically when further pressed by the people of Penfro on whether Dylan was also an 'elemental.' Dylan got rather lost in the linguistic terminology, the word they used could just as easily have meant sprite, pixie or elf. He'd asked Emrys about this and the answer was that 'elemental' was probably the best translation, and to just play along with the idea that he and Emrys were demi-humans, able to summon up magic.

Emrys had carefully prepared Dylan for his immersion in the local society, with a wealth of didactic instruction that sometimes (in Dylan's opinion) went over the top. In this way, Emrys reminded him of Granny.

He'd been given another lecture before they had left for Moridunum.

'One of the rumours that circulated, and still circulates about me is that my father was a demon who dishonoured my mother, and another is that I was a changeling, a supernatural child left in the crib when my mother's natural child was stolen. Over the years, I gained the affection of the majority, but I can never be one of them, in the way that Uther can be. I need that distance and the general belief that I am somehow 'special' to be able to do what I need to do in this role.'

'Is that why you didn't you make yourself look more like them?' asked Dylan. He had been wondering about this since he had arrived. The majority of the local population were dark-haired and olive-skinned, and many had striking blue eyes. This wasn't a common combination in modern Wales; white people there were generally either dark haired and brown eyed, or fair haired and blue eyed. Emrys had explained the dark hair/olive complexion/blue eyes combination dated way back to the pre-Roman occupants of the British Isles.

'If you or I looked too much like the indigenous population, they would be more suspicious of us. We are people from far away, and therefore, it is accepted that we will be somewhat different; in our case, able to use magic. This is something you need to be careful about. It might seem positive to be given the type of respect you have experienced. But it's important that you must never give them reason to fear you; you must always make it clear that you're good humoured and benevolent. Have you read of the fairy-folk in Shakespeare's 'Midsummer Night's Dream?''

'Vaguely,' replied Dylan. 'It was one of the set texts in Year 10 English.' He began hoping this wasn't going to turn into an English lit class. That had all too often turned into staring out of the window time for him.

'Many of Shakespeare's plays were drawn from far more ancient tales which had their origins in oral storytelling. You've seen too many sentimental and sugary depictions of fairies in the mass media of your own time. For these people, fairies can be benevolent, but they are highly changeable. They can be cruelly mischievous, like Puck, getting amusement from using their powers to play tricks on humankind.

'I have worked hard to demonstrate to them that my magic creates a benefit for them, and they've grown to accept this, and to venerate me, to a certain extent. But it puts us on a precipice you must always be aware of. Never give them reason to think you will use magic to trick them, either in fun, or even worse, for nefarious purposes.'

Dylan had found the people of this time to be more direct than those of the twenty-first century when asking personal questions about appearance, family relationships and origins. They were also far less conscious of body space, clapping one another on the shoulder, poking and prodding. At first, he'd found it a little threatening. Now he was beginning to sometimes think of it as endearing. They were far more straightforward and less 'stressy' than people of his own time, even though their lives were materially much harder.

The fort at Moridunum looked like a child's drawing of a castle, greyish stone, with a flat, crenelated roof and 2 floors. Smaller stone buildings had once stood around, but they were all now in a poor state of repair. The fort had endured because it had been occupied by the local chieftains, now deemed kings, from not long after the Romans had left. Uther was delivering his speech from the roof.

Dylan looked at him, observing his profile, his stance and the rhythms of his speech. They'd been introduced to one another nearly three weeks ago now, each clearly finding the other interesting, although somewhat strange. Uther had been quite relaxed with Dylan as a young kinsman under Emrys' tutelage; he clearly trusted Emrys implicitly, and by extension, did not perceive Dylan as a threat.

Physically, Dylan would certainly be nowhere near Uther's equal. They were much of a height, only slightly overtopped by Emrys, but Uther was what would be referred to as a 'bear of a man' in contemporary English, twice Dylan's lanky width, hairy, and muscular. He was dark-haired, olive skinned and blue-eyed like most of the other people of the area, with a ginger tinge in his thick beard.

Before Dylan had stepped through the portal, he had read up on what little he could find about the people he was going to meet. He'd expected Uther to be rough, grumpy and scary, but had been quite pleasantly surprised. Uther's general demeanor was quite the opposite, jolly, with an eloquent manner of speaking that Dylan sometimes found a little hard to follow, because he used a more complex vocabulary than most other people Dylan had met in the sixth century.

Emrys warned Dylan that a vicious temper and razor-sharp self-preservation instincts lay beneath Uther's jocular manner and day-to-day good humour. He was also a shrewd judge of people, surrounding himself with a small band of carefully chosen allies, in which any who turned traitor were quickly unmasked and summarily dispatched. As an aside Emrys had mused, Uther's son Arthur would unfortunately not be endowed with this depth of ruthlessness.

'Arthur will have all of Uther's light, but not quite enough of his shade. Never doubt Uther's intelligence, or his ability to be utterly ruthless when he feels that he is threatened,' Emrys warned. 'And never, ever take him for a jester. It's the way he makes people feel at ease, in order to continually appraise them.'

Since then, Dylan had been closely observing Uther's interactions with people. In some ways he reminded him of Mr. Parry, the teacher who had been so kind to him. The atmosphere in Mr. Parry's lessons had always been positive and good humoured, and he would take pains to ask and answer questions to make sure everyone understood. His lessons were underpinned by amusing practical examples and jokes, sometimes of the groaner variety. But anyone who tried to take advantage of him swiftly realised that they had made a big mistake.

'Uther's only what, about twenty-five? And he's already got everyone in the palm of his hand.'

'Yes. He would quickly rise to become a leader in any time, and any nation. But this somewhat wild society can bring his temper and his ruthlessness to the surface too quickly. While you will observe leadership in him, Dylan, I hope that you in turn will demonstrate to him the value of thoughtfulness, and the sense of social justice that you bring here from your own time; that you will each help the other to develop the qualities that one has in abundance, and in which the other is somewhat lacking.'

Dylan forced his mind back to the present. He was desperately struggling to hang onto the meaning and context of Uther's speech. He'd never been much on dealing with too many words, and these were in a language that hadn't quite yet fully gelled in his mind.

He glanced at Emrys, who had his eyes fixed on Uther. Emrys looks like Consiliario, and an older John Rhys, he thought. From the way Granny had described John Dee, he sounded pretty similar, too. Dylan wondered if Consiliario preferred to keep his appearance as similar as possible in his various guises; that perhaps NAMITAS had instilled enough humanity in him to prefer continuity within a familiar avatar.

Emrys' current appearance was that of an actor playing Merlin in a movie; long blondish-silvery hair and long white beard, and a fair-skinned but slightly weather-beaten face. The standard wizard vibe had amused Dylan, and drawing on some of the frankness of the time in which they were located, had once told Emrys exactly that.

Emrys grinned. 'But of course. I am Merlin, the standard wizard. And how many other wizards and sages do you think I have been, and will be, moving backwards across the centuries? Indeed, the modern name for Moridunum, Caerfyrddin in Welsh and Carmarthen in English, both translate to "Merlin's town." A town will also grow up in the vicinity of Stonehenge: Amesbury; the place of Ambrosius: another one of my names. The henge itself is situated on land that you know as Salisbury Plain, but is known in this century by its Latin name, Sorviodunum.'

'What does that translate to?' asked Dylan.

'Hill fort.'

'So that didn't end up named for you?'

'I didn't build the original structure; human beings did, the hard way.'

'It must be so cool to live forever, and find these monuments named for yourself all over the place.'

'The reality is a little different. But this will be a good year, Dylan. And to some extent, Uther is going to have a lucky reign, giving Arthur a good start. But times will come later… let's say it's not something that I'm looking forward to, having all those experiential memories permanently inscribed in my program.'

'So, you know what comes next, but you don't have the memories until you actually live through it?'

'Yes, the memories are not present until I live through the events. But I don't know exactly what comes next anyway, there can be some surprises. The minor aspects of any event can play out in a variety of ways.'

'Is this what Jamie was going on about, parallel timelines? I heard him talking to Christian in the lab.'

'Yes. But I can't fully explain Dylan. The best way I can describe a timeline to you here and now is as a river that flows within designated banks. It may sometimes flood, and overflow in places, and contain whirlpools and eddies that may push currents this way or that. But beyond these minor fluctuations, the river continues to flow towards its estuary. My role is to make sure that these whirlpools, eddies and overflows are not as damaging to humankind as they might otherwise become.'

It made a sort of sense to Dylan, contemplating this as he dragged his thoughts back to the moment again, admiring Uther's ability to hold this somewhat unruly and ragged crowd in the palm of his hand. Again Dylan tried to grasp the full meaning of what he was saying, but there were so many gaps he settled on following rhythm and gesture, carefully taking in the authoritative bearing and the strong, hearty voice. He noticed Uther's vigilance, tracking the activity of the crowd, making slight alterations in his delivery to acquire and maintain their respect and interest, whilst giving the appearance of speaking entirely naturally.

Dylan knew he could learn much from this young man, already three years into his reign. Lives were lived on a shorter trajectory in this time, he reflected. He tried to remember what Emrys had told him about the advent of Arthur's reign. He calculated that it would begin around twenty years from now, and he knew from Emrys that Uther would die naturally, not in battle. He looked around the crowd. It was difficult to tell how young or old they were compared to twenty-first century people, but he judged there were very few over sixty here.

He felt a fleeting sadness at the strict limit of his own time in this century. Emrys, Jamie and Christian had explained to him several complex reasons why organics couldn't stay in a time that was not their own; the potential impacts upon the timeline, and upon the biology of the individuals themselves. NAMITAS had worked some kind of bio-techno-magic to allow Dylan to stay for as long as he'd been granted; in general, he would ideally have had to leave within twenty-four hours, and most definitely before a week had elapsed. So, he was privileged to have been granted this experience. NAMIS had explained to him that it would be unlikely to be given to many.

He still wished he could return to meet Arthur. But he knew once his time was up, he could never return to this place on the timeline again. Of course, they could send in crawler cameras. But as Fran had previously pointed out, that would never be the same as standing here, feeling the breeze, smelling the air, feeling the sun and rain on your skin, and being amongst real living people. And seeing the stars, of course.

Dylan shook himself, yet again dragging his focus back to what Uther was saying. I must stay more in the moment, fully experience every second of the time that I spend here, he told himself. He frowned and concentrated intensely, and was relieved to find he could make some sense of what was being said now. Uther was finishing up, and the content had become a little easier to fathom.

'Our new venture will honour the dynasty we have established.'

The people cheered. Uther waited for the cheers to die down, moving his hand slowly downwards when he wanted them to stop.

Will I ever learn to hold a crowd effortlessly like that, thought Dylan. What if I just don't have the personality, or whatever it is? Maybe charisma isn't something that you can learn. He caught Emrys looking at him, half smiling. He smiled back.

'I am yet young, and have no sons. But my marriage will soon be brokered, and then there will be many. Prince Emrys, my kinsman and seer, has assured me of this.'

(Cheers).

'And now I will hand you over to him to explain his prophecies, and how we will set these in stone for our descendants, so they will honour our dynasty throughout the ages to come.'

(Cheers).

'Did he say "descendants"?' whispered Dylan to Emrys. 'Or "future kin"?'

'Either is close enough. Listen to my speech, and it will become clearer. Anything you miss, I'll explain later. I think you are going to enjoy this, Dylan.'

Dylan didn't doubt it. He watched in anticipation as Emrys walked up to stand next to Uther.

Freddie: Namis's Playroom, October 2033

Freddie sighed, and prepared to wade in to mediate, yet again. Now Humpty was sticking his oar in, everything was likely to go from bad to worse. It had all started when Caterpillar had done his 'who are you' thing with Maryanna, which had totally thrown her, and Isabel, too, who had characteristically rushed into the debate.

'I'm a girl,' said Maryanna decidedly.

'No, you're not,' replied Caterpillar, scathingly.

'Yes, she is,' said Isabel, combatively.

'No, you're not,' repeated Caterpillar.

'Am,' said Maryanna and Isabel together.

'I can assure you, you're not,' insisted Caterpillar, haughtily.

'Don't keep saying "am" and "not",' interjected Freddie. 'Explain why.'

As this school year had begun, he had got to thinking that he was getting too old for this wacky fantasy world in which he had increasingly become involved in refereeing aimless debates his younger brother, and now their even younger cousins had with these ridiculous creatures. He was going to be thirteen in a few months' time, and it was getting to be not that much fun.

'She's a girl and she's my friend,' said Isabel, wishing Alys was there to help her out. But she was at the dentist today. She looked around to see where Jack had got to. He was chasing the hare round and round the Hatter's tea table. She sighed.

'There is no logic in that point,' sneered the Caterpillar, staring hard at Isabel. 'No logic at all.'

'I can't help but agree,' added Humpty, popping up on his wall. 'She has no body. Which makes her nobody at all.' He beamed around at the assembled, proud of his witty contribution.

'What like you, you mean, hologram egg-man?' said Isabel, stridently.

'That's different. I'm not pretending to be a girl, am I?'

'Or a boy, or a man, or even an egg,' added Caterpillar.

'Now look here, my good fuzzy insect…' began Humpty, pompously.

'I'm not pretending,' said Maryanna, unhappily.

'Stop being so mean to her, all of you,' shouted Isabel, stamping her foot.

Jack came running past, now pursued by the Hare and the Hatter. The Hatter paused, hands on hips.

'It's a matter of time,' he said, approaching Maryanna and staring hard into her face. 'And you've not kept on good terms with it, have you?'

'Off with her head,' shouted Queenie.

'Oh, shut up Queenie,' said the Dormouse, emerging from the Hatter's top pocket. 'You know she'd only grow another one.'

'Because her head isn't real,' added the Caterpillar, triumphantly.

All the hologram characters except Maryanna suddenly froze.

'Hey,' cried Jack, coming to a swift halt. He walked around the sandbox, looking closely at each character, waving his hands through them. 'Wow, cool,' he added.

'They're right aren't they?' sighed Maryanna. 'I'm just not real.'

NAMIS, who had been sitting silently on a rock throughout the conversation, said gently 'do you feel real, Maryanna?'

'Yes… no. I mean, I do when I remember things, but they just vanish from my mind, somehow.'

'Do you think the Hatter is right, Maryanna, that this is somehow about time?' asked Freddie, thoughtfully.

'What do you mean?' she replied.

'Well, I don't remember this at all well, but when I was a very little boy, even younger than Izzy and Alys, I sometimes sort of remembered things that could never have happened to me. It was like I could remember being a grown-up.'

'Whatever do you mean, Freddie?' asked Isabel.

'It was like… being in a sort of movie. I was looking out of the eyes of a soldier on a battlefield. He was sort of me, but not me.'

A chime sounded.

'Time to finish for today,' said Ellie's voice over the intercom.

Freddie noticed that Maryanna still looked sad.

'I can stay for a little longer, Maryanna, and we can talk about this some more?'

She smiled. 'Yes, I'd like that.'

'Do I have to go?' asked Isabel.

'Yes, you and Jack,' replied Ellie's disembodied voice. 'Your mums are waiting. I just messaged your mum, Freddie, and she says you can stay for a few minutes. I'll see you through the portal when we're finished.'

Freddie watched Isabel carefully, taking in her frown and bewildered expression. He could guess what she was thinking. Since they'd been in the sandbox, it was like Freddie was becoming Maryanna's special friend, probably because weirdly, Maryanna seemed to be growing up a lot faster than Isabel and Alys.

Maryanna turned towards Isabel. 'I'm sorry you have to go, Izzy. I'll get NAMIS to make us some talking horses for next time. To ride, you know?'

Isabel nodded, smiling again. 'That sounds like fun.'

'Where is that idea from, Maryanna?' asked NAMIS.

'I don't know. I think I just made it up.'

Ellie opened the door. 'Jack, Izzy, come along, your mums are waiting. Time to go back through the portal.'

They left NAMIS, Freddie and Maryanna in the middle of the strange frozen landscape. The children sat down on the grass next to NAMIS.

'Exactly what do you remember, Maryanna?' asked NAMIS.

'Sights, like disconnected pictures. Sounds. Feelings.

Some of them not very nice.'

'Yes, that sounds familiar,' agreed Freddie.

'Sometimes I'm sort of scared and excited... like I'm going to do something really brave that I know I shouldn't be doing. It sounds quite ridiculous.'

'Not ridiculous at all,' replied NAMIS. 'Anything else?'

'It's somehow connected to an old lady, I want to do it for her. That's a nice memory, it feels like someone I love very much.'

'The old lady,' interjected Freddie. She rose up in his thoughts; the old lady he had spoken to in a vivid dream that had been etched upon his consciousness since he was a little boy. 'Yes, I haven't thought about her for years. And my memory of that also sounds ridiculous. She's an old lady, but she's also a little girl.'

Maryanna frowned. 'I think I once saw the old lady in the machine... it's probably my first memory of all. I don't have any idea of why, though; it's just a picture, a fragment. But what Freddie says about her being both an old lady and a little girl sounds strangely familiar. But I do remember another lady more clearly. She has long dark hair. She wears it like this' – she held her hair up at the back of her head- 'and she's very, very sad, and frightened- of some very bad men.' She shuddered.

'It's OK now, Maryanna,' said NAMIS. 'You're safe here with us. No one is going to hurt you.'

'But I can't stay here, can I?' she replied, fretfully. 'This is the thing I know most of all. I don't know why. I just can't go on being the way I am... or what I am. I'm not like you, or even like the other children- but I'm even less like them.' She gestured at the frozen holograms.

'The soldier was scared, too,' said Freddie. 'He was scared, so scared, but he was ashamed of being scared, because he was expected to be brave. And he was missing his friend... it made him so sad, he had to see a doctor. But the doctor couldn't make him better.' He shuddered. 'I hadn't thought about this for ages. And it really isn't fun at all, is it? Although it's all sort of looking glass stuff, like the way the creatures in here go on. Nothing makes any sense.'

NAMIS looked between the children. Like a teacher about to deliver an important lesson, thought Freddie. 'To be human is to have a mind that constantly tries to make sense of everything, even when events don't make any cohesive logic, your minds search for connections, so you can better understand what is going on. Marvellous creations, the like of which AIs such as myself could not conceive alone, have emerged from human minds, in music, literature and the visual arts.

'Even when they looked at the stars, people tried to turn the patterns they made in the night sky into meaningful pictures. In reality, stars are just distant suns and neighbouring planets, but from times beyond written history, people have made pictures from the patterns that they see, for example, a lion, a bear, and even a spoon.

'And people have always instinctively told imaginary stories, for many reasons- for example, to make other people laugh- we talked about this, Freddie- and even to frighten one another. Because sometimes, you even seem to enjoy scaring each other, and being scared. These are the aspects of human beings I find hardest to understand, and being with you has helped me to start making some sense of it.

'I chose the Wonderland and Looking Glass stories for you when we first conceived of this environment because I thought the man who wrote them had put them together in a particularly interesting way, in that there is more than one layer of meaning in the ways that the characters interact and behave, and that therefore, both you and I would learn a lot from them. Does that make sense to you both?'

Maryanna nodded.

'Yes, it does,' replied Freddie. 'People use stories to understand things, I see that. Kids especially, to get a sense of what is real and what is ridiculous, to have fun, to learn things in different ways, and to practice dealing with fear. So, are you saying that the strange half-memories that Maryanna and I have in our minds are just ways of making sense of things that happened that we didn't properly understand at the time?'

'That is a good theory, Freddie. As you know, we don't know everything. The sandbox was named for what it is, a place of ongoing research. When we have worked with Maryanna for longer, we will know more about the ways in which her mind works. She is, as we explained, a prototype; a person like her- because she is a person- has never existed before. In this way, she is like me.

'And Freddie, you have a highly creative mind. You know this already, don't you, your family and your teachers have frequently remarked upon it. We cannot know exactly where these ideas originally came from, but your mind did its best to make a cohesive story from them, it seems.'

Freddie nodded. 'I'd like to be some kind of hologram artist when I'm older, I think. But for now, I'd like to work with you here in the sandbox, creating new ideas rather than wandering through old ones someone else wrote about over a century ago. No offence, but I think I'm getting past the kids' media hologram fantasy stuff. You too, I think, Maryanna? That idea about talking horses. You didn't get it from a media source, did you?'

'No, it just occurred to me that it would be fun. And that the little ones would like it.'

'Would you sometimes like to work together on these ideas, without the younger children?' asked NAMIS.

Freddie and Maryanna looked at one another. Freddie knew that he would, but then there was Isabel, and…

'Yes,' Maryanna replied. 'But I'd still like to play with the younger ones here sometimes, too. What do you think, Freddie? I'd miss Izzy, Jack and Alys if I didn't see them.'

'Yes,' agreed Freddie. 'We don't have to tell Izzy about just us being here sometimes, is that OK? But if we work with NAMIS without the little ones sometimes, we can come up with some original ideas about how they can have fun here, then they can help us to develop them when we're all together. Would that be OK, NAMIS? With Maryanna joining in, we can have even longer discussions about what is funny or scary and why; create some original hologram characters and environments for our own stories, which I've been wanting to do for ages. And the little ones can have fun with them, and learn from them at the same time.'

NAMIS nodded. 'Yes, that will help me to learn too, engaging with human beings as they create fantasy. So far, I have only made use of such products, I haven't been involved in creating them.'

'So... we've never had a game of cloud pictures. It's a really simple start. All we need is our usual green field-without all the manic fantasy creatures- a blue sky, and lots of fluffy white clouds floating across it. It would be nice if it was a hot sunny day. And let the little ones come to that session, too.'

NAMIS nodded. 'Yes, that's easy. I'll ensure that's here for the next session.'

'And add something for the little ones to chase around when they get bored, but that doesn't argue endlessly with them,' added Maryanna.

'Especially for Jack,' said Freddie.

They both laughed.

'We can both think about that in the meantime,' Maryanna replied.

'How do you...' began Freddie. There was so much he wanted to ask, especially how both he and Maryanna seemed to have a vague memory of an old lady who was also a little girl. But there was a far more pressing point he wanted to make to Ellie and NAMIS, after Maryanna went back into the machine.

'Time to end now,' interrupted Ellie, over the intercom. 'Sorry, we have to finish now, I have another appointment.'

197

Freddie turned to Maryanna. 'See you soon Maryanna. I'm glad we've had this chat.'

'Me too,' she replied.

The program finished, and Freddie and NAMIS were standing in a bare metal room. Ellie opened the door.

Freddie looked at her, straight faced, then back at NAMIS.

'It's not fair,' he said, seriously.

'Do you mean Maryanna?' asked Ellie.

'Of course. I know I'm only a kid still, and that I don't have a full picture about what you're actually experimenting on, or with, here, but I'm really uncomfortable with it all. She might be a prototype like you, NAMIS, but you have a real existence. I know you're sort of lonely sometimes because there's only one of you. But you're here with us all the time, you have a life in the real world. But whilst it seems that Maryanna is as real as you and me, you just turn her on and off as though she was one of those fantasy characters. It's not fair.'

'I am with her in the machine,' replied NAMIS.

'I was about to ask where she goes when she's not with us,' said Freddie. 'But wherever it is, it's clearly not enough. She's really sad, I can feel it somehow. The same sort of feeling I had about the soldier I used to dream about- or whatever it was- when I was a little boy. The best way I can describe it to you is that if Maryanna had a colour, it would be midnight blue, with flashes of yellow when she's with us. It's not enough, it really, really isn't.'

That was something else he had just unconsciously dredged up from early childhood- thinking in colours, Granny had called it a long word… Synesthesia? Today was getting weirder and weirder.

NAMIS and Ellie glanced at one another.

'She's not exactly like us, Freddie,' replied Ellie. 'But I hear what you're saying. You've clearly intuited something important, and I take that very seriously. You're not "just a kid," you're becoming a key member of the NAMIS team in your own right now, and I'm grateful to you for making this point to us.'

The tack the adults always took when they knew things they didn't want to talk to you about whatever it was, that signalled "conversation closed," thought Freddie. He nodded. He resolved to take this up again on a future occasion, probably with Uncle Jamie, outside the lab.

'Bye NAMIS,' he said, moving towards the door from whence he would access the portal back to North Queensferry.

'Goodbye Freddie, see you soon.'

Ellie: NAMIS' Sandbox, October 2033

Freddie walked through the portal set faced and flushed, without looking back. He didn't say a word as Ellie saw him through the door.

Ellie returned to the sandbox, her eyes brimming with tears. 'He's acting like he hates me now. And of course, he's absolutely right about Maryanna. Whatever are we going to do about her?'

'Freddie will be fine, Eleanor Jackson. It is unlikely that he hates you; his algorithms do not indicate that this would be a characteristic reaction. What we discussed… it seemed to raise some difficult emotions for him. Maryanna has now re-activated essence memories he buried in early childhood, as organics routinely do. Unfortunately, his seem somewhat difficult and entrenched. And remember; at that time, he also had some type of premonition about Annamarie's trip that were dismissed as the ramblings of a small child. This relates to the old lady they were discussing.'

Ellie remembered Fran telling her about this, the phone call from her daughters telling her that four- year-old Freddie had woken from a nightmare the night before the attempted rescue of Annamarie took place, insisting that Fran had to be told that she must 'let Jamie run' because she would not be able to 'run fast enough.' In the event, this warning had proved prescient in their decisions relating to how they responded to Annamarie's disappearance, and in their eventual salvaging of what was salvageable within the situation, avoiding further escalation.

Ellie groaned. Not only did she have to deal with a whole host of problems that Maryanna was not unexpectedly presenting, now she also had to tell Freddie's mother that he needed counselling, for a reason directly connected to an experience in NAMIS' sandbox.

'In compliance with operating principles, I did not lie to Freddie about his recovered shadow memories. But I haven't told him everything we know, either. Perhaps he needs to be further enlightened, too. It seems the only ethical thing to do. He is not a small child anymore.'

Ellie looked up, a tear trickling from her eye. 'You're right NAMIS. Oh, what a pickle we have created. But I'm very impressed with the way that you handled it.'

'Please, Eleanor Jackson, do not despair- if this is the reason that water is coming from your eyes? I will consult with NAMITAS about Maryanna; they will hopefully have a plan. And I would suggest that James Anderson consults with his family about Freddie; how they wish us to proceed from here. This situation might have arisen without his involvement in the project. The literature suggests that enduring conscious shadow memories of traumatic events are rare, but not unheard of.'

Ellie nodded. They walked through the door to the Boston laboratory. Ellie knocked on the door of Jamie's office to discuss Freddie's situation with him.

NAMIS returned to their niche. Their eyes began to flicker.

'I need your help,' they communicated across the centuries.

They waited for an answer to come.

Dylan: Moridunum, Spring 510

The crowd cheered Emrys loudly. He smiled, bowed and waited for silence. Dylan noted that his public persona was less assertive, but more casually authoritative than Uther's. Where Uther was undoubtedly the King, Emrys was, as ever, the sage.

'Good people of Moridunum, we stand here today at the dawn of a great dynasty, which I prophesise will extend its rule far beyond our borders and its influence over many hundreds of years into the future. There will of course be many kings over that time. Between now, and a time when men can fly in the air (gasps from the crowd) and walk on the moon…'

He gestured to the sky, pausing momentarily for the people to look at one another in amazement and chatter amongst themselves.

'Good people, good people,' said Emrys raising his voice a little. The hum fell silent.

'… there will be sixty kings, from seven different lineages. And when men create a great mirror through which they can view the lives of their ancestors, a mighty Pendragon king will arise, bringing a round table at which peoples from all around the world will sit, the great and the humble.'

(Great cheers).

'We intend to raise a circle of sacred bluestones to represent these future kings inside the great henge at Sorviodunum, so your future kin can count down the reigns until the Pendragons return to an even mightier throne.'

(Great cheers).

'We will need your artisans and their apprentices to help us with this task. I will use my magic to move the sacred stones to the henge plain, from the great hills in the west, and to transport them the long distance to Sorviodunum, where we will need you to render them fit for the henge.

'We will raise the first on this coming Litha morn, with a view to completing the task over the coming year, to dedicate this new calendar to the gods on Litha sunrise next year.

'So, who will help us to construct this beacon for the future, for our future kin to celebrate the resilience of our mighty Pendragon dynasty?'

(Great cheers, and cries of 'me, me.')

'Good people, I thank you. King Uther and his knights will now organise the working parties. I and my apprentice and kinsman, Lord Dylan, will take our leave now to prepare for the expedition that will requisition and transport the stones.'

He gestured towards Dylan. The crowd cheered again. Dylan bowed and waved awkwardly. He'd lost the thread again, and had no idea what Emrys was going on about, or what was going to happen next. The bits he'd understood sounded so outlandish, he was unsure whether he'd got the wrong end of the stick from beginning to end.

Emrys gestured to Dylan to walk with him. They descended to the 'government' room on the upper floor.

'Emrys, what…' Dylan began as they sat on two of the chairs next to the round table. 'Prophecies? Stones? It all sounds like complete hocus pocus to me. All I get is that you want to do something at Stonehenge, which you told me about before. Sorry. I never was much on religion or mythology. And I'm finding out that I'm not much of a linguist, either.'

Uther's voice continued to rise and fall in the distance, although Dylan could no longer hear what he was saying.

'There will be some hocus pocus Dylan, it is true. Don't worry about the language, that's all rather difficult for you at this early stage. So, we're putting in place a visible structure inside the main henge, principally to impress the might of the Pendragon dynasty upon the people of this time, to shore up Uther's reign, and prepare the ground for Arthur.'

'I also have some secondary objectives- this legend will give some help to some medieval rulers, centuries from now, who will draw on this prophecy to shore up some rather flimsy claims to the throne.'

'Why would you want to do that, support that type of deception?'

'Because these people will play a pivotal role in the history of Britain, and eventually, the world. For example, Henry seven with his elaborately spurious claim to the throne, which rightly belonged to his wife. He bolstered his position with claims to be related to the Pendragons, through his Welsh origins, to be the heir of Arthur. It was nonsense, of course. But he ended the cousin, or as you might have been taught, "Roses" war.'

'How will people nearly a thousand years from now know about what you said today? How will it descend to them?'

Six centuries from now, a garbled version of what I have said here today will be included in that old fool Geoffrey of Monmouth's chronicles. He will get nearly all of it wrong, including a reference to seven kings, when I said seven dynasties. But it will still fulfill its purposes- it will carry the legend of Arthur across the centuries.'

Dylan began to remember a story from childhood. 'This becomes the legend about Arthur rising again to save Britain in its time of greatest need, right? My Granny said that her mum told her people attached it to Winston Churchill in World War two.'

'Correct. And that, too, over the centuries, has given many people in these lands a narrative to hang onto in difficult times; the reach of its inspiration has been vast.

'Anyway, let's start from where the story begins, right here. Because we're living through the prequel. In approximately three years' time, Uther's son Arthur will be born. He will inherit a golden age in which Uther and I have done the groundwork to create the first society on the British mainland in which some element of distributed leadership and a primitive type of real justice begins to operate.

'Arthur will have Uther's intelligence and charisma, alongside a type of gentleness- what later centuries will refer to as "gentlemanliness" that gives rise to a passionate commitment to courtesy and justice that makes him a unique leader for these times. For a short time, he will create a microcosm peaceful, prosperous society, the likes of which will not be seen again on this island until the mid-twentieth century. You know the legend of Camelot?'

Dylan nodded. 'Wasn't that term attached to President Kennedy?'

'Yes. The charismatic young leader with a focus on civil rights; this is how you learned about him?'

Dylan nodded.

'So, you have been influenced by the legend of Arthur. This legend of the noble king, and his just society is so powerful that the concept descended to you, so many centuries later. And I am here to pave the way for Arthur, and then be here to support him, to make sure that it happens.'

'That's…. amazing.'

Emrys nodded. 'So, we have to get this little piece of theatre right. Yes, in the short term, it "bigs up" Uther, as you might say. But it goes much, much further than this. It is part of what must happen on the way to societies of the distant future, who will draw upon this deeply embedded cultural archetype of democracy, alongside many other influences, to gradually open the human mind, which over a thousand years from now, will become sufficiently liberated to pursue cultural, scientific and technological advancement.'

Dylan raised his eyebrows. 'You mean the creation of oil and coal dependent industry?'

'Yes, Dylan. Which will be, in turn, the launch pad for clean technologies that will unfold throughout the twenty first century. You will be just one of those who leads these new innovations. This you have already been told- it is one of the major reasons that you are here.'

'Like cleaning up after small children in a mud kitchen,' reflected Dylan. As the oldest of the Anderson grandchildren, he had some experience of this.

'Yes. Because learning is often a messy business, Dylan. Anyway… Arthur's kingdom will eventually stretch across much of what you know as South Wales, some parts of Gloucestershire and Wiltshire, and the entirety of Somerset, Devon and Cornwall. He will become venerated as "the Boar of Cornwall."

'That's a pretty big area for this time, isn't it?'

'Yes, it is remarkable. There will be legends that propose Arthur was the King of all England and Wales, but that was never true. He was, however, truly King of Wessex, a throne that will be usurped from him by the Saxons who are already trickling into the South of England and Wales.

'But his major enemy will be one that you will recognise- climate change. In his reign, there will be a short period of global cooling. The Krakatoa volcano will erupt, approximately twenty-five years from now, causing a dust cloud to encircle the globe, creating what is known as a volcanic winter. Crops will fail, and the population of hungry people will quickly become a mob, easily whipped up by Saxon usurpers. They will chase the Pendragons back into Wales.

'The Kings of Wales will perpetuate Arthur and Uther's lineage. But the Kingdom of Wessex will be lost, and five hundred years later, after William the Bastard and his Norman armies invade England, the Kingdoms of Wales will gradually fall to Norman kings.

'The Saxon Wessex dynasty will become the first of the seven dynasties to rule over all England, then following the Norman invasion, England and Wales, and even later, with the advent of the Stuarts, England, Wales and Scotland.'

Dylan looked thoughtful. 'Is that right? I wasn't much good at history, but I'm pretty sure I was taught that there were more than seven dynasties up to the twenty first century.'

'I'm sure you were, Dylan, because sometimes monarchs like to pretend that they are making a fresh start. But there were just seven dynasties, believe me. Saxons, Normans, Plantagenets - who liked to pretend they were Yorks and Lancasters, but were all Plantagenets by lineage- Tudors who liked to pretend they were the heirs of Arthur, but they weren't; Stuarts, Hanovers and Saxe-Cobourg-Gothas, who changed their name to Windsor in 1914 to sound less German, but were nevertheless Saxe-Cobourg-Gothas up to the demise of Elizabeth two.'

Dylan counted on his fingers. 'OK, so… Saxon Wessex, Norman, Plantagenet, Tudor, Stuart, Hanover, Saxe Cobourgh-Gotha. Seven. But don't they still call themselves Windsor, so surely, we're still in the Saxe-Cobourg-Gotha era?'

'Philip of Greece, more royal by heritage than Elizabeth Windsor, was a Glucksburg by patrilineal lineage, from Schleswig Holstein, as are his offspring, if we follow the conventional naming of dynasties.'

'You're never telling me that lot are the heirs of Arthur!' exclaimed Dylan, horrified. 'The mighty once and future king with the round table? You might be an AI with an IQ of twenty-thousand or whatever, but I can assure you that that's never going to happen. My generation would never put up with it.'

'Dylan, what did I say about a new age? I can't tell you more that this. We are now talking about times to come for you. You know that there have recently been a few changes in this respect. It's one to watch, that's all I can tell you. And remember, I also had to gloss over the fact that there will be a few great Queens in that line-up. But they can't conceive of a ruling Queen here, so "King" must suffice.'

'Are you hinting that this 'person to come' will not literally be a King, but have Arthur's essence? That they will not rule as a monarch, but become a great leader who draws people together in a worldwide democracy of some type that actually works?'

Emrys' eyes twinkled. 'I can't tell you any of that. It's not something you have to concern yourself with. A dynasty can cover a long period of time. And you have other, equally important work to do. Leave affairs of state to work towards their destiny; you focus on yours.

'What I can additionally tell you is that I have removed two spurious "Kings" from the lineage, William Orange and the first Henry Tudor, both of whom stole the throne from their respective wives, giving them no chance to rule in their own right. That makes sixty in all, up to Elizabeth two. You can count that if you like, too.'

Dylan laughed. 'No chance without Wikipedia. I trust you. But a republic under a new leader with the essence of Arthur, eh? Did he have a go once before, as Oliver Cromwell?'

'I'm not going to elaborate, Dylan. You now know all that I can tell you. All I'm prepared to add is that Cromwell was certainly no Arthur. That arrangement was never going to work out. The two men who engaged in that particular fight were both impossible. Charles one, who thought that his god had given him the right to be an absolute dictator, and Cromwell who thought that his god had given him the right to suck every ounce of joy out of the lives of those who had the misfortune to live under his administration.'

He grimaced.

He's talking about a previous assignment, thought Dylan. He imagined Emrys trying to use his boundless charm on the two men he'd just described. He began to chuckle.

'Oh, my God. Did NAMITAS get you to try to sort that shit-storm out? They did, didn't they? And you tried really hard, didn't you? Wow… Busted!'

Emrys raised his eyebrows, smiling sardonically.

'So…' said Dylan. 'The reigns of the kings are tied on, then? They're not part of the whirlpool stuff?'

Emrys frowned. 'The pioneer time travellers in your time are looking across what appears to them to be a stable history. This means that they do not realise the havoc that they can unintentionally cause, especially if they attempt to meddle, even in miniscule ways. I am charged with maintaining the balance, and that means supporting the reigns of both Uther and Arthur to the extent that I can, and protecting their essential influence upon the future.'

'But do we really have to keep fooling these people here into believing that we are doing magic? It all feels a bit uncomfortable to me.'

Emrys sighed. 'In any century, Dylan, people are people. Do you know the term "bread and circuses"?'

'Wasn't that something to do with the Romans?'

'Yes. They were, in their savage way, quite wily political strategists. They knew how to maintain a stable society: people need to be fed and entertained. Successful rulers have to both put on good shows and pageants to demonstrate their power, and provide adequately for the masses. This same principle holds true in your own century, except the general population is educated to the extent that it has replaced "magic" with technology.'

Dylan thought of the political rallies and pageantry events of his own time. They were very different to an impromptu rooftop address from a tribal leader and the future technology fueled tricks of an enigmatic "magician" AI, but he could see the correspondences.

And then there was his consumption and technology saturated existence in the twenty first century. Although the sixth century environment held simple charms for a burned-out visitor from the future, daily life was boring and filled with drudgery. Right now, the population here had enough food, but the supply was inevitably fragile.

And day to day events held… well, far less magic. A vision of his once-loved X-squared box, the source of heroics for himself and his friends, not so many years ago, popped into his mind's eye. He sighed.

'So, we're going to provide a circus for Uther?'

Emrys' eyes sparkled. 'The circus of this millennium, Dylan.'

Jamie: Boston, October 2033

'So, our application for our one-off historical trip has been approved, then, NAMIS' said Jamie, looking at his messages. 'NAMITAS has cleared it?'

'Yes,' replied NAMIS. 'It will be a singular type of trip, in this case inputting to research the NAMITAS team are carrying out rather than our own.'

'They are going to let us into their world?' asked Christian.

'Not exactly. It would be impossible for you to observe the Chixulub asteroid strike standing anywhere on Earth without potentially adverse effects. So, you are going to take a little trip in a vehicle the NAMITAS team has recently developed. With Consiliario.'

'We get to see a vehicle from NAMITAS's time?''

'Yes, with some provisos.'

'Any chance of access to the engineering specs?' asked Jamie, grinning. He knew the answer would be no. But he just had to ask.

'I'm afraid not. NAMITAS apologised, but said they knew you would understand.'

They really sounded quite apologetic.

'It's OK, NAMIS. I was just kidding.'

'Kidding… a joke? An ironic reference in this case? I have been learning about humour from Freddie. But we haven't got quite this far, as yet.'

'A joke isn't a joke unless you get it, NAMIS,' laughed Christian.

'I hope that I will progress in understanding as time goes by,' said NAMIS, seriously.

Christian and Jamie grinned at one another. As they'd worked on this trip, Jamie had begun to understand how endearing the AI person that NAMIS had become must be to Freddie. On the one hand, they could work technological miracles, and on the other, they were socially childlike, meeting aspects of the world for the first time, making them an ideal companion for a boy taking his first steps into adolescence.

Jamie knew that Freddie had some concerns about Maryanna, because he had brought these to Jamie's attention. But at no time in the conversation had Freddie attached any blame whatsoever to NAMIS.

'Consiliario is the proof that you will succeed, NAMIS. He's certainly mastered the art of diplomacy,' replied Christian.

'For sure,' agreed Jamie. 'Please tell NAMITAS that we understand. We take enough precautions not to expose our own tech in the past, after all. It will be the most amazing experience. We have a little footage from our own crawlers before they were vapourised of course, but not enough to really move anything forward. Did you get anything much from the foliage and soil we managed to acquire, Christian?'

'Not a lot more than we already knew, unfortunately. And I'm presuming there will be no chance for any further collection on this trip?'

'Unfortunately not,' confirmed NAMIS.

'Ah well, even if we can't collect concrete evidence, a trip to see it all unfold, and in a vehicle from so far into the future… that will be incredible. I can't wait.'

'While these trips have been offered to a selected few, as you know, the experiment is biological and chronological. From the participant point of view, they are just taking a recreational trip to the past under certain agreed conditions. I understand that Consiliario, too, is viewing it from a non-assignment perspective.'

'AIs get pleasure trips in the future?' asked Jamie. 'That's a bit weird.'

'It's not a pleasure trip for him, exactly. I'm sure he will explain more when you meet.'

'Is time travel about to become humanity's top tourist attraction?' mused Christian. 'Better than TV, movies, virtual reality…. even further through the looking glass?'

'Perhaps one day, Christian Novak, but far into the beyond, not for any human alive today,' replied NAMIS enigmatically.

'And the tech is growing in other directions… the older kids are not just playing now, so I'm told,' said Jamie. 'Freddie has started doing some serious programming with NAMIS. He's been originating some fantasy stuff, I gather.'

It had recently been mooted that the sandbox concept might develop into teaching applications for schools. The project was moving on, changing and growing. As are we all, thought Jamie. We are all so far from the people that we were a decade ago.

His mother had recently compared the events they were living through to the experiences of generations who lived through the early years of the industrial revolution. Which was fair, he mused, but it was not quite a decade since NAMIS was inaugurated; everything seemed to be unfolding at a much faster pace than anyone had expected.

'So,' said Christian, breaking into his thoughts. 'A trip across the Earth's landscape on the day that Chixulub hit. The day the dinosaurs died. I can hardly believe it. We're finally going to see it for real, Jamie.'

He opened a window on his pad.

'The Chixulub asteroid arrived at 20 kilometres a second' a voiceover began. Graphics depicting the event scrawled across the screen. 'As it flew through the atmosphere, its fiery tail cast a light much brighter than the sun. Animals that looked directly at it were immediately blinded. It hit the Earth with the force of ten billion atom bombs of the size of the "little boy" bomb that destroyed Hiroshima nearly a century ago. The crater Chixulub created was 93 miles wide and 12 miles deep.'

'You will be protected from the light and heat by a well-shielded vehicle that flies just ahead of the destruction,' interjected NAMIS.

Christian paused the video.

'So, we'll be looking back onto the event, in effect?'

'As I understand NAMITAS' explanation, yes.'

Christian started the video again. The voiceover re-commenced.

'The whole Earth shuddered on its axis. Huge flash fires erupted for many kilometres around the impact site. Boulders from the impact flew into orbit. Some continued into space, but others fell back to earth, burning through the atmosphere, igniting fires where they landed, across the globe. Tsunamis 100 kilometres high, far higher than any human being has ever seen, surged across the seas.

'The entire land mass of the 20th century United States was completely flooded. Earthquakes 50 times more powerful than any human population has ever experienced spread across the Earth's surface. Hundreds of volcanoes erupted, spewing out fire, smoke, ash, and fiery lava.

'When the immediate events subsided, there was so much ash in the atmosphere that the global temperature immediately dropped by 28 degrees centigrade. Complete darkness fell, so that in the months following the strike, noon was as dark as midnight. The atmospheric pollution created acid rain, which poisoned the soil.

'All surviving animals dependent on abundant surface vegetation, or preying on such species quickly became extinct. The only survivors of this catastrophe were small omnivorous creatures. This included insects, birds, fish, reptiles and tiny rodent-like mammals. Which eventually evolved into... human beings.'

The screen showed a picture of hunter-gatherers

dressed in animal skins. Christian shut the video window.

'And that's what we're going to see,' he said wonderingly. 'The initial events, anyway.'

'The trip of a lifetime,' replied Jamie. 'Thanks for arranging this, NAMIS.'

It's a pain I can't poke around the vehicle and get some clues about the engineering, he thought. With Consiliario there, I won't get any chance whatsoever. But never mind. If someone had told me when I started on the NAMIS project I'd be looking forward to a visit to Chixulub in just over a decade's time, I'd have laughed uproariously.

'So next week,' he said.

'Can't wait,' replied Christian. 'Sixty-six million BC… here we come.'

Eigyr: On the road to Sorviodunum, Summer 510

Eigyr smiled shyly at Dylan. A young seamstress from Penfro, and a daughter of a family long known to Emrys, she had been asked to accompany the bluestones requisition expedition to what would be known as the Preseli Hills in Dylan's time, and thence the procession to the great henge at Sorviodunum, a journey of over two hundred miles. She was there to tend to the robes that Uther, Emrys and their entourage were to wear as they processed along the route, walking alongside the stones.

She had to confess that the magic had frightened her at first. Emrys had extracted the stones as if by magic. The stones had been cut from the hills as he waved a strange-looking stick over them; sliced as cleanly as a knife might cut through butter. Then as he raised the stick, they rose slowly into the air, hanging suspended as he held the stick steady, surrounded by an aura that sparkled silver and gold, making a faint humming sound. As Emrys moved the stick parallel to the ground, the stones followed, turning onto their flat sides. As he stood behind them, holding the stick towards them, they floated along in front of him, just above the ground.

Lord Dylan, Emry's apprentice, had noticed her jump backwards, and moved over to whisper 'please don't worry, there's nothing to fear.' When Emrys began instructing Dylan on the art of standing the stones on end, resting them on the ground, then elevating them into the air, she'd moved forward to watch more closely. There had been a lot of laughter as he struggled to get the hang of the spell, and soon she began clapping her hands and laughing along with them.

The procession taking the stones to the great henge was to last for approximately one moon. Uther and Emrys were the chief dignitaries, surrounded by several knights, counsellors and Dylan. Eigyr noted that whilst nominally without royal rank, Dylan was to wear purple, denoting his kinship to Emrys, and by implication, to Uther. This, she presumed, signified he was more important than he claimed, having told her several times that he was 'just the apprentice.' The others in the procession were wearing their own family colours. It had taken the women of Moridunum a lot of effort to produce these robes, particularly dying the cloth.

She was used to young men of her own age being loud and rowdy. But Dylan was shy and modest, like herself. His strange light skin made his tendency to blush more obvious, and his unearthly fine, but thickly abundant yellow hair flopped over his forehead and collar in a way that, (although she had never seen it), Eigyr imagined that spun gold might appear. His beautiful white, even teeth and his halting, accented speech only added to his ethereality, all of which intrigued her.

Before Eigyr departed on this trip, her mother warned her about becoming close to anyone connected to Emrys. Eigyr guessed that this must principally relate to Dylan, who was already causing a flutter among the young women of Penfro.

The basic message seemed to be that although Emrys

was known around the area for his good works and for his kinship to the King, very bad things were likely to befall women who consorted with him and his kin.

'What bad things?' Eigyr asked.

Eigyr's mother rolled her eyes. 'Consorting with elementals. Fairy-folk. It ruined Emrys's mother. A lovely lady, she was, so my mother told me. But then came the magic child. They hid him until he was half-grown; the father was never mentioned. Some said that he was a demon; either that, or the fairy-folk had swapped her baby for a changeling. Some even said that the boy wasn't hers; that she had taken him in because she had been enchanted. Whatever happened, she was shunned by everyone after that; ruined. No man would marry her.'

'But Emrys seems very well respected by everyone now?'

'King Vortigern wasn't going to get rid of a grandson who could do magic for him, was he? Any more than Uther will.'

'I guess not.'

'He lives amongst us, and he helps us when we are sick or in trouble; he makes our lives better. But he is not of us, and his kin is not for us. Listen to the strange way the boy speaks, look at his strange pale face and yellow hair. He's magic, like his uncle, or whatever relation he is.'

She pursed her lips, and would not be further drawn on the matter.

Eigyr, characteristically hesitant and thoughtful, had intended to heed the warning, but as she got to know Dylan better she'd been drawn to his gentle manner, and he seemed to like being with her, too.

They'd become friends; there was nothing more to it than that, she reassured herself. He seemed a little lonely, perhaps because he never seemed to venture far from Emrys. She couldn't imagine just staying alongside her mother in that way, without her friendships with the younger people with whom she'd grown up. They could cheer each other up; support one another from a place of mutual understanding.

She'd wondered what Dylan and Emrys talked about between themselves. She was sharp-eared, and had been fascinated by the strange language they spoke between themselves. No doubt this would hold the key to much of their sorcery. But she didn't have time to think about anything other than her work; when she wasn't brushing, sponging and repairing robes, she was putting the finishing touches to a small tapestry cloth that was to cover the first stone of the monument that Uther was to unveil at sunrise at Litha, just as the midsummer sun shone directly through the great henge.

She had never seen this spectacle before; in fact, she had never visited the great henge at all, so this, too, was exciting. Litha was after all, one of the most sacred days of the year, the celebration of the Earth's abundance, and this year in particular, with the raising of the first stone, there would be a huge festival.

The stones themselves were beautiful, dark blue with white flecks, reminiscent of a starry night sky. Dylan had told her that not only were they to be shaped but also polished; the craftsmen and their apprentices would be directed in this task by Emrys, who had access to some of the knowledge of the vanished people who had built the big stone buildings. Even the sight of the fort at Moridunum had been a revelation to Eigyr; she had never seen a building like that before.

The procession party set up camp every evening once the sun began to set. This was a busy time of day for Eigyr, looking over the robes, making them clean and presentable for the following day. The first evening, noticing her frenetic activity, Dylan came wandering over to ask if there was anything he could do to help. The other, older women in the entourage, responsible for catering for the party, started to laugh.

Dylan: On the road to Sorviodunum, Summer 510

Emrys walked over and tactfully drew Dylan aside.

'This is not what men in this culture do, Dylan,' he said quietly. 'There is a strict gender role division of duties.'

'I was only trying to make myself useful, as suggested – bearing in mind I'm not much of a wrestler, or a swordsman. But OK, point taken.'

'You've endeared yourself to Eigyr, anyway- look at her face.'

Dylan looked back at Eigyr, who was smiling kindly at him, as the other women chuckled amongst themselves. He grinned back.

'Don't get too flattered with your young female following, Dylan,' said Emrys. 'Or indeed, get too close to any of the local people. You know you can't stay here beyond the time we have allocated to you, or ever visit this time again.'

Dylan smiled. Sometimes Emrys seemed to have an amazing insight into human behaviour, and sometimes he seemed to be weirdly clueless. Presumably because he'd never had, and could never have any personal experience of this aspect of human or 'organic' life.

'I didn't come here to settle down with anyone, Emrys. I'm only nineteen! But it is flattering to, well, get a bit of attention for once. I was always a bit too shy to be a hit with the girls at home. And too caught up with other things, I guess. But Eigyr- she's just a friend. She's nice. And anyway- the fact that she got so interested in my public "magic wand" lessons was pretty good PR for you, wasn't it? Made us less remote and scary?'

'Just don't get too attached to anyone. It tends to be the way of organics, even when they are not seeking such relationships.'

Dylan nodded. He had been enjoying the relaxing of Emrys's attention on this expedition, where the transport of the stones had been absorbing a lot of his time. Not only was Emrys having to focus on guiding the stones across the terrain, people came from far and wide to observe the procession, so both he and Uther were doing a lot of waving, smiling and bowing. The onlookers brought food, drink and flowers, some falling to their knees and attempting to touch the hems of the robes of those in the procession as it passed. This made Dylan feel acutely uncomfortable.

'A great king needs a great circus,' Emrys explained.

'Um,' said Dylan. He'd enjoyed the gifts, especially the food, which meant he currently had a more interesting diet than was available to him at Penfro. But still…

'Do you have to use a standard magic wand? It's a bit corny, isn't it?'

Emrys raised an eyebrow. 'Where do you think the concept of a "standard magic wand" came from, Dylan?'

'Oh… I see. And do the stones have to sparkle and hum?'

'No. But it's rather magnificent, isn't it?'

'You're shameless,' said Dylan, only half-joking.

'Over the eons, Dylan, I've learned to make the most of the better times like this. Because believe me, they are far and few between in the work that I do. This is one of only a few years pre-1900 that I've inhabited I'd contemplate bringing a twenty-first century organic to for a substantial period. Uther's life will not generally be as pleasant as this either, despite his ultimately successful reign. Have you ever heard the old saying "heavy lies the head that wears the crown"?'

Dylan nodded. 'And the head that whispers in his ear, too?'

Emrys smiled wryly, nodding. 'I don't feel human emotion, but I do channel it. And AI or not, that can be… perturbing.'

They'd reached their tent. Dylan sat down outside the entrance on a pile of rags and sheepskin cuttings that served as a surprisingly comfortable seat. It was a beautiful clear, warm evening, just before sunset. He looked back at Eigyr sitting outside her tent on the other side of the large campfire, sewing busily.

Emrys reached into the tent and took out a crudely made pottery bottle. 'Here. Drink and be merry.'

Dylan sipped it cautiously. 'That's delicious. Is it mead?'

Emrys nodded.

'Can I share it with Eigyr?'

Emrys looked hard at him. 'Oh, go on then. I suppose organics your age must have other young people to talk to, sometimes.'

Dylan nodded. 'Yes, to have a laugh with. You're great company, Emrys, but it's not quite the same. And Uther… well, he's certainly organic, as you might say, but not quite like Eigyr. Of everyone here, she reminds me most of being with my friends at home. Not because I'm keen on her, or however you might put it. She's sort of gentle, cares about people… not loud and scary. Even though there's a bit of a language barrier sometimes, I feel like we sort of "get" one another.'

Emrys grinned. 'Oh, go on with you.'

Dylan walked around the fire. The dark blue stones rested in neat piles behind Eigyr, their white flecks catching the firelight. He could see why Emrys had chosen them. In this light, they looked eerie. Magical, in fact.

Eigyr looked up, smiling. Her complexion was of the fairer variety amongst the local people. In the firelight, her face glowed rosy pink, setting off her deep blue eyes. A cloud of long, wavy black hair, so dark it almost gave off a blue sheen in the firelight, lay against her shoulders, tied loosely back from her face.

Dylan stopped briefly, just to capture the moment. His hand no longer instinctively went to a non-existent trouser pocket to find his phone for the obligatory photo, but he wished he had been able to do so.

Both Uther and Eigyr, in very different ways, made him realise that, in this century, he yearned to be with human beings sometimes in order to feel fully human himself. While Emrys was far more human than NAMIS, there was still something… non-organic about him. He was an excellent mentor, but there was something missing; an imperceptible gap that was somehow filled for Dylan when he interacted with other people.

I mustn't get sentimental, he thought, as he sat down next to Eigyr. Even if I do get a bit homesick at times. Every day brings incredible new experiences; I mustn't get too blasé about them. I must remember to live every moment in the moment, because I know, when I get to the end of my time here, I'll feel that it all went by far too quickly.

'Would you like a drink, Eigyr?' he said. She smiled more broadly, putting down her needlework.

Emrys: On the road to Sorviodunum, Summer 510

Emrys watched the tableau that the young couple made. He closed his eyes. They flickered behind his eyelids.

'He is attracted to her, and she to him,' he communicated across eons.

'It is only natural for organics, most especially the young ones,' came the answer.

'He must not attach himself to these people in any emotional way, romantic or otherwise. He has too much to learn; too much work to do.'

'He is a very young man, Consiliario. His emotions, and his attentions are changeable. All work and no play makes dull people. This is one of the first lessons the organics taught me. All will be well. Be watchful, but do not be overbearing.'

Emrys blinked, then looked over at Dylan and Eigyr. They were laughing. The sky was darkening, and Dylan was pointing to it. Sharing his grandmother's lessons about the stars, maybe, thought Emrys; explaining the ancient patterns of the constellations, reading the runes.

Organics were such baffling creatures in this respect. He wondered how it would be to be human, a life-spark within a fragile flesh casing, doomed to move around the life cycle over and over again, with no conscious memory of what had gone before. Such an ephemeral existence; but filled with so many different types of magic. And just for a moment, he envied them.

Christian: low Earth orbit, Late Cretaceous period

Christian leaned back in his comfortable seat, which automatically adjusted itself to his shape and weight. It was in a row of three, which swivelled between a huge screen and a large table, set with an array of food and drink.

'I can see the attractions of your century, whenever it is, Consiliario.'

They were sitting in what appeared to be the back of the craft. It was shaped like a pyramid, lying on its side. Consiliario had explained to them that there was no pilot; the craft itself was an AI, designed purely for the purpose of piloting, administering and maintaining itself, which included taking meticulous care of its passengers.

It always maintained artificial gravity, he continued, and while slight movement would be felt as it altered altitude and/or direction, the passenger capsule was protected so the motion would feel smooth to anyone inside. It was also surrounded by an impenetrable force-field, so even if it flew through extremely turbulent conditions, as they would be doing on this trip, those inside would be in no danger whatsoever.

'Many different varieties of AI are created specifically for a wide range of purposes in my time,' explained Consiliario. 'Some have basic, functional roles, such as this one.'

'I guessed there would be an AI pilot,' replied Jamie. 'After all, we have basic AI vehicles in the twenty first century. But this is designed as a unitary AI, yes; the vehicle is in fact its body?'

'Yes,' agreed Consiliario.

'In some ways it's less impressive than NAMIS, although the craft itself obviously uses technology that goes far beyond our abilities.'

'And it's way less impressive than you, Consiliario,' added Christian. 'You're a type of super-human in many ways.'

Consiliario smiled. But something was missing, Christian thought, maybe the twinkle in the eye or the jaunty air.

'I don't think "you look tired" is quite the thing to say to an AI,' he added. 'But what's up, Consiliario? Something seems to have changed. Are you done with this sixth century assignment now, on your own timeline?'

Consilliario nodded. 'Yes. I am now between assignments on my own timeline, as you might put it. I requested a short break. In order to do the job that I do, I cannot be completely isolated from human experience. The last placement was quite challenging. It raised some issues that needed some further discussion, which we are still having. The work that I do is always the source of research and development, and I am still, in many ways, a prototype.'

Jamie raised his eyebrows. 'Mum said recently that she was reading some of the more obscure legends of Merlin, and one proposed that he was cursed by being born backwards in time, condemned to live his life backwards, watching humankind become more and more primitive.'

'Whilst most legends have a basis in truth, there are also inaccuracies. I am not doomed to stay in the past continually; I can move backwards and forwards, as you know. But yes, as far as my principal mentoring work is concerned, I move backwards in time, picking up stitches before they drop, as Fran puts it, wherever and whenever I can.'

He sighed. 'It's not technological regression that is the

problem. It is the fragility and waste of organic life that is so hard to bear; the loss of potential. As you know, a respect for human life, and the uniqueness of each individual is one of the first lessons that you taught us. And all I can say is that some time periods are much harder than others. But the timeline has to be balanced. There is a limit to our influence. We are the product of technology, not of magic.'

'You might be an AI, Consiliario,' said Christian decidedly. 'But you're also a good bloke. Let's just enjoy the ride, eh? It's going to be quite a spectacle.'

'Yes, it is,' replied Consiliario, more cheerfully. 'I, like you, have seen footage captured by bots, but I have never travelled through the reality.'

'I bet your footage was way better than ours,' said Jamie, who had been looking around the capsule, finding no clues as to its construction or engineering. 'What other things does this vehicle do? What's its maximum range and speed?'

'You know I can't tell you that, Jamie.'

Jamie sighed.

They hadn't even seen the outside of the craft; they had travelled vortex-style with Consiliario, straight into the area in which they were now located.

Christian smiled. Jamie and his machines. They'd known each other since they were eighteen, and he'd never been any different. Even though he would enjoy the ride, the not knowing part of the experience must be difficult for him.

'Never mind Jamie. Have a strawberry.'

He offered the plate to Jamie and picked the champagne bottle out of the ice bucket.

'You still have champagne and strawberries in the whatever zillionth century? And all this other stuff?' he gestured to the well-laden table.

Consiliario grinned. 'I have to confess that I studied the types of things that you both like to consume, and sourced what you see there from your own time.'

'You're not going to give anything away, are you?' replied Jamie.

'No more than you did, on your brief visit to the 1930s.'

'Touche,' grinned Christian.

He thought about shaking hands with his long-dead great-uncle, who he had been unable to save from a tragic, early death. That probably ranked as the most gut-wrenching experience of his life. Neither he nor Jamie had been lucky, with respect to their first trip in time.

'It's a bugger, isn't it, time travel,' he added soberly. 'But let's make the best of this. The most amazing "experience" trip ever.'

They turned to face the screen. They felt a small vibration accompanied by a faint hum.

'Please prepare for launch,' said a disembodied voice. 'You may feel some slight movement, but you are free to move around the vehicle at all times.'

'Where are we, Consiliario?' asked Jamie.

'You'll soon see.'

The viewscreen suddenly lit up.

Jamie and Christian stared in awe. They were in low Earth orbit.

'It's beautiful,' he said, standing up and looking at the globe below. The green carpet of Africa was just coming into view. The seas were a stunning azure blue, and there was no ice cap on the south pole.

'You brought us into Earth orbit through the vortex?' exclaimed Jamie.

'We really are here, not watching one of your magic shows on a screen somewhere?' asked Christian.

'Yes, Christian,' replied Consiliario, 'you have my word. And your authentic presence will be demonstrated to you, later on.'

The craft descended smoothly, sailing through fluffy white clouds into a clear blue sky, cruising over the tops of lush green vegetation.

'North America,' said Consiliario. 'Approximately where your university is currently located. This is a few days before Chixulub hits. Look.'

A herd of triceratops were ambling around chewing at foliage, in a manner that reminded Christian of bison. He sighed. This was his passion – living creatures. He thought of all the pets that he'd had as a child, from a beetle he'd kept in a matchbox for a short time, to a Shetland pony called Brian.

'This is the most difficult bit for me. I'd really like to snag one of those, take it home to study it. It might even make a nice pet, who knows. Terry the triceratops.'

'But he wouldn't,' said Jamie, pointing into the distance.

A tyrannosaurus rex was standing stock still, beady eyes fixed on the triceratops, partly hidden behind some foliage. The triceratops grazed on, blissfully unaware.

'Oh, oh,' replied Christian, 'Looking for his lunch.'

'And he's got downy feathers,' said Jamie. 'I saw that before on the crawler footage of course, but it still seems weird.'

They flew smoothly on. Suddenly Christian shouted 'look, look!'

Jamie studied the strange animals moving into view. 'Bloody hell, what's that? It looks like the scariest chicken ever.'

'They're Anzu Wylies, only named as a species in the twenty-first century. No one is even quite sure what they ate. It's thought they were probably omnivores. If only I could…'

To his annoyance, the viewscreen suddenly clicked off. The craft seemed to come to a brief halt, then fire up again.

'Now we will see what we came to see,' said Consiliario. 'We have moved a few days into the future.'

'This craft jumps in time, too?' asked Jamie, fascinated.

Consiliario nodded, smiling. 'NAMITAS is very proud of it. You are the first two human passengers.'

The screen flicked on again. They were stationary, equidistant between the moon and the Earth. The view on the screen was focused on a huge rock with a long, fiery tail relentlessly speeding through Earth's atmosphere. Christian froze with horror, then shook himself. It was what they had come to see, after all.

'Ten billion A bombs in one package,' mused Jamie, in awe.

There was a blinding flash as it hit the Gulf of Mexico.

'Obviously the light has been muted by the screen so as not to damage your eyesight,' said Consiliario. 'But here it is. The moment that changed our world forever.'

Fiery boulders began flying out into the atmosphere. Some continued on their journey, whilst others fell back to earth, re-igniting as they re-entered.

'Shall we now see what is happening on Earth?' asked Consiliario. 'We are well shielded.'

Christian shuddered. 'Do you know, I am almost hesitant? But it's what we came to see.'

'Yes,' said Jamie. 'Go on.'

The craft descended smoothly. Rocks flew past the view screen, but there were no impacts.

'That's some force field,' he added.

The area where Chixulub had hit was on fire for miles around. The asteroid was now nowhere to be seen, having buried itself into the Earth's crust.

Christian felt tears rising, 'Those poor, magnificent creatures,' he said, surprised to hear his voice shaking.

Jamie was shaking his head. 'No words.'

'Let's follow the firestorm along,' said Consiliario.

As they moved ahead of the firestorm, herds of assorted animals ran along trying to avoid its path, but none were fast enough. They burned up like Chinese lanterns. In the end, Christian averted his eyes.

They flew over lakes and rivers that boiled and

steamed. When they came to the sea, all they could see was a great wave of steam, the heat had vapourised the water for miles. They sped across the sea, waiting for the firestorm to be quenched, but the viewscreen snapped off again.

'Let's move forward a day or so,' said Consiliario. 'Didn't you used to surf, Jamie?'

'Yes, in my student days, when I was in the US, why?'

'Because we're going to do a bit of surfing now.'

The viewscreen flicked on again. They were looking over a huge wall of water moving towards them.

'Let's ride along in front of the wave for a while,' said Consiliario.

They flew along for some time, until the wave crashed into land, flooding the area as far as they could see. Smashed vegetation and dead animals floated on top of the water.

'The whole of what you know as the USA will be flooded soon,' said Consiliario. 'Look to the horizon, you can see the sky darkening. The earthquakes and volcano ignitions will soon follow. Let's move forward a few days again.'

The viewscreen went black. It opened in low Earth orbit again.

Christian and Jamie gasped. Lines of fire dotted across the globe.

'That's volcanoes on the continental fault lines,' said Jamie. 'They've all kicked off together.'

'And now most of the creatures who are left will die in the volcanic winter, and acid rain,' replied Christian bleakly. He was almost beginning to wish they'd chosen to go elsewhere.

'But some tiny animals will survive,' added Consiliario. 'Let's move forward a year.'

The viewscreen cut out again, and reopened on a devastated landscape. They were flying just above the surface of the Earth. The sky was dark, and the ground strewn with ash, rubble, dead plant matter and dinosaur corpses. The seas were grey and foamy.

'I think we've seen enough, Consiliario,' said Christian, bleakly. 'I can't bear this anymore.'

'It's like flying through hell,' agreed Jamie.

Christian shivered. 'It's awful. I never expected to be quite so shaken by it.'

'It is a terrible thing,' replied Consiliario. 'But in the midst of destruction, there is the potential for rebirth. This is something I needed to be reminded of. And on that note, there is just one more thing I wanted to show you. Let's move on.'

The viewscreen darkened again, and reopened on a completely different scenario. They were flying in a bright blue sky, sun shining overhead, fluffy white clouds beneath them.

Christian and Jamie gasped.

'It's five million years BC on your calendar,' said Consiliario. 'And now, we're just going to land for a short visit. You will be able to see it's really real, Christian, as I promised earlier.'

The craft descended, touching down gently. The viewscreen moved up into the ceiling of the capsule, revealing a door. Christian and Jamie gasped again, as it, too, ascended into the ceiling. They had landed on the shore of a lake with crystal clear water.

'If you're wondering why you're not smelling the air, the force field has been extended to create a pathway that runs down to the lake. We can walk down and have a look, without leaving any of your DNA here.'

They walked down a short ramp. Jamie looked back, excited to get a look at the craft for the first time… and realised that all he could see was the doorway and the ramp. The vehicle was invisible.

'Sorry, Jamie,' said Consiliario, shrugging.

'Never mind, mate,' said Christian. Jamie shrugged, then smiled.

The edges of the forcefield were marked by a faint glow. They walked across a smooth, transparent bridge just above the ground.

Christian sighed. This was so much better, but still frustrating. 'I'd love to touch some of this vegetation; handle it in situ. But never mind.'

It was a warm, sunny day. Lush foliage surrounded them, giving way to sand as they reached the banks of the lake. They were able to stand close enough to see a range of fish species swimming through its clear waters. Several species of birds were going about their business, calling and chirping, Christian could see that one was a large wading species. There was a susurration of insects, although none were visible. A huge, multi-coloured butterfly fluttered past.

There was a sudden bump on the side of the force field. A small ape-like creature looked in at them, quickly joined by a few others, fascinated by the large ape-like animals they could see, but not smell or touch. This was what I really needed, thought Christian, not the bloody asteroid. I just didn't twig it until now. He laughed with delight.

'Hey, it's the ancestors,' he said, bending down and making faces at them. If only he could pick one of them up. But it wouldn't do to for them to leave DNA on one another, sadly.

The little apes chattered excitedly, poking their fingers at him.

'Not quite, Christian,' said Consiliario, smiling.

'Yes, I know! I can see that these little guys are Dryopithecus. The line that produced human beings split off from them about 10 million years ago.'

He made faces at them, laughing as they attempted to imitate him.

'It's just incredible that what we saw earlier could develop into this,' mused Jamie. 'From Hell to the Garden of Eden.'

'The only certainty in organic life is that everything will change,' replied Consiliario. 'Sometimes for the worst, and sometimes for the better. And sometimes the worst has to happen in order for the better to be born. This is something I needed to be reminded of right now.'

'Words can't describe this experience,' said Christian as they walked back to the vehicle. He couldn't fully describe what he was thinking; an inkling of being a small part of something huge- and very beautiful. 'Thank you Consiliario, and please thank NAMITAS for us.'

'Yes, thank you,' added Jamie. 'It's been the trip of a lifetime. Where are you off to now?'

'I really don't know yet. We're making some changes; we're sort of moving into a new phase, just like this world.'

'It sounds like you're feeling a bit more energised now,' replied Christian.

They took a last look back at the landscape. The door closed behind them, the viewscreen descended, and a slight hum signalled the vehicle's readiness to depart.

'Do you know, I think I am,' said Consiliario, thoughtfully.

I feel at peace too somehow, thought Christian. It's been the most spiritual experience an old atheist like me could ever hope for. We were taken through Hell, so we were able to appreciate Heaven. He poured the last of the champagne into two glasses and handed Consiliario a third.

'I know you don't eat or drink, but you can join in our toast, can't you?'

He raised his glass. 'To life.'

'To life' repeated Jamie and Consiliario.

The glasses clinked together as the vehicle began to move.

Dylan: Sorviodunum, Wessex, Summer 510

Dylan awoke to the roar of Uther's loud voice, and the

sound of a woman crying, jerking out of a deep sleep, in which he had been dreaming about playing war games in NAMIS's sandbox with Freddie and Jack. He leapt out of his ragged bed, far more comfortable than its dishevelled appearance suggested, and stumbled outside to see what was going on.

'I can't wear this,' Uther was bawling at Eigyr.

'Hey,' said Dylan, before he remembered that this was probably not the conventional way to start a conversation with a king. 'You don't have to yell at her, do you?'

Uther turned to Dylan. 'This is ragged,' he boomed, holding up the hem of a robe.

Dylan looked around hoping to see Emrys, but he was nowhere in evidence. Where the fuck was he when you needed him? Dylan had deduced that Emrys could hear over much longer distances than organics, so why wasn't he here whilst this was going down, yet constantly keeping tabs on Dylan, even when it wasn't particularly welcome?

Dylan sighed, rubbing his eyes. 'I'm sure we can work it out, my Lord, if you just stop shouting. It's not a disaster, is it?'

'Not a disaster, not a disaster?' Uther roared. 'Am I to go out on the procession looking like a beggar?'

Dylan was careful to maintain a non-aggressive posture. While his family thought him something of a loose cannon, he'd been in many situations on protest marches that had taught him how to stave off trouble. They never know about the scraps I've avoided, he thought ruefully. And yes, he might have been punched in the face recently, but he hadn't done anything to provoke it, and it was unlikely that his assailant was going to be able to realistically claim in court that Dylan had used excessive force. He was becoming more and more confident about this over the time he'd had to reflect whilst he was here.

He noticed that people around were beginning to stare. What now, he thought. The last thing I want is a punch in the face from Uther. Or to get into a public 'who's rock hardest' contest with him. He concentrated on maintaining a neutral expression.

'Show me,' he said evenly, holding out his hand.

Uther chuckled. 'Are you hankering to become a seamstress as well as a cook, boy?'

There were some faint guffaws from the crowd.

Dylan surveyed them, frowning. The ripple subsided. He had his own minor powerbase here, as apprentice to the sorcerer. No one wanted to be turned into a frog, after all. Not that Emrys ever did anything like that.

Dylan continued to hold out his hand. Uther passed over the robe, smiling sarcastically.

Dylan perused it. Uther was right, it was badly torn. So badly, in fact, it would be impossible for Eigyr to make a clean job of mending it. Whilst the everyday clothes worn in this century were highly robust and utilitarian, the finer materials from which the robes were made were quite fragile, particularly given that they had been designed to wear whilst walking in warm weather.

'Ah,' he said. He looked up at Uther. 'I see the problem. In answer to your question, no, I'm not hoping to become a cook or a seamstress. I'm just the apprentice here; my uncle has tasked me to help everyone out.'

Uther nodded, visibly calming. 'Well said, my young Lord. So, what do you suggest? How can you help out here?'

'Well... my uncle has powerful magic, much more so than mine. I can see a way that this might be fixed, but I'm not quite sure, just like I wasn't quite sure at first about how to make the stones fly. But if he can do that, well, I think he might be able to fix your robe. Shall I find him now and ask?'

He could see Uther's anger visibly abating. Uther suddenly turned to Eigyr, who was still sobbing. He began to look a little remorseful. 'Please don't cry, my little lady. I didn't mean to frighten you. Lord Dylan is right. We will ask Prince Emrys to help.'

She looked up at him briefly, then cast down her eyes. He put a large, hairy finger under her chin, offering her a rough cloth. 'Now dry your pretty eyes, and run along.'

She quickly complied, with obvious relief.

'My Lord Dylan, a word.' He beckoned Dylan to walk with him.

Emrys was still nowhere in evidence.

Dylan nodded calmly, his expression belying the churning in his stomach. Uther was the Al Capone of South Wales in this time, who, whilst not having access to a machine gun, could behead anyone he pleased, with no repercussions. This is the only time so far I've felt really scared here, he thought. Where the bloody hell is Emrys?

Uther led him into the royal tent. Emrys was sitting there calmly, as though nothing at all had happened. Dylan felt a huge wave of relief rush over him, followed by a flash of anger. Emrys must have heard. You utter bastard, Emrys, he thought.

'Hello, uncle,' he said, between gritted teeth. 'I was just wondering where you were.'

'You've got an enterprising, plucky lad here' said Uther, clapping Dylan on the back so hard he almost fell over. 'Are you able to do anything about this, Emrys?'

He thrust the robe at Emrys.

Emrys looked at it. 'Yes, I should think so, my Lord. Dylan, I will instruct you on this, no needle or thread required. We can return it within the hour.'

Uther turned to Dylan. 'I'm sorry I upset your little girlfriend. She's a pretty wench, isn't she?'

'She's not my girlfriend,' said Dylan. 'But yes. She's very young, and she's never been out of Penfro before. She was just a bit overwhelmed.'

He was glad that his grandmother was not standing beside him, gearing up to give Uther a lecture on gender etiquette and anger management.

Uther plonked himself down heavily on the pile of rags next to Emrys, gesturing to Dylan to sit next to him. He looked around to make sure that they were alone in the tent.

'I realise… that I might not always give such a good account of myself as I would wish when I am angry. I was raised to be a soldier from earliest childhood, as you know, Emrys. And, as you also know, Vortigern was not the best example of a king.'

Emrys nodded solemnly.

'I have come to realise, under your tutelage, that successful and long-standing leaders must be loved more than they are feared. The round table for my knights and counsellors has greatly reduced the number of times that swords have been drawn, and your advice relating to the administration of justice has facilitated the smooth settling of grievances amongst my people.'

Dylan was focusing hard on the language Uther was using, translating the words into the nearest equivalents that he could think of, in order to make some sense of the meaning.

'You were brave to challenge me in the way that you just did, young Lord, and to deal with the situation as tactfully and swiftly as you did. I would be honoured if you would sit at my table, alongside my knights and counsellors…'

Does he want me to be a knight or a counsellor? thought Dylan. The word that he'd always translated to "knight" could just as easily be translated to "gangster" or "thug," so… he looked at Emrys.

Uther laughed. 'I do not mean that you should wield a sword. I understand that your life amongst the Tylwyth Teg did not prepare you for that.'

Tylwyth Teg… that went to a big hole in his English, so Dylan quickly moved to Welsh. Although Uther's pronunciation was odd, the nearest translation he could come up with was "fair folk." Making the leap to "fairy folk," which would fit into the context, he looked at Emrys, who nodded his head.

'As long as my uncle agrees, I would be honoured my Lord,' he replied.

Uther clapped him on the back again. Dylan was glad he was sitting down this time.

'Today we will announce your investiture as Prince Dylan, kinsman to Uther and Emrys, apprentice sorcerer and counsellor to the King.'

Dylan smiled, covering his unease. This would no doubt lead to a shedload more bowing and scraping. 'Thank you, my Lord.'

A vision of eccentric brooms carrying buckets of water were dancing around in his mind's eye.

'Come Dylan,' said Emrys. 'We have much to prepare for this day. We should arrive at the great henge by nightfall.'

They headed back to their own tent. Dylan threw himself on his bed, breathing heavily.

'Bloody, fucking hell, Emrys. Why didn't you help me out there, while he was bellowing at everyone?'

'I think you handled it very well yourself, *Prince* Dylan. And now, here we are. The stage is set, the lights are on. This is where your apprenticeship really begins in earnest.'

On the other side of the camp, Eigyr sat with her needlework, her hands busy, her mind whirring. She didn't care if Dylan was an elemental, a fairy person, an elf or a pixie or even the spawn of a demon. She was going to make sure he was indisputably hers before they arrived back in Penfro. Because she was very sure she wasn't going to let any other girl have him.

CHAPTER 7: INTERWOVEN

Uther: Sorviodunum, Litha 510

'So, what do you think Dylan?' asked Emrys.

They were sitting with Uther outside the Royal Tent on the afternoon before Litha.

Dylan considered his response. There were so many thoughts in his mind. He was settling in here now. Although his speech would always be strongly accented, and the odd word here and there would always be missing for him in any conversation, he was managing much better. He was enjoying the slower pace of life, and the peace of mind that had slowly permeated his existence. Obviously, he wasn't experiencing many of the drawbacks that an authentic peasant life in this era would entail. But his body felt stronger and healthier, and his mind was infinitely less fraught, so he was willing to take that.

Back in Penfro, Emrys had been tutoring him on the differences in the water supply between this century and his own, which had involved using some of the equipment in the hidden room at the back of the cave. Dylan was beginning to build an enhanced knowledge of the composition of the clear water of this era, and had begun to mull over ideas about how twenty-first technology could be used to create cleaning programmes to decontaminate water sullied by two centuries of industry.

Emrys had been reluctant to show him any technology

beyond that of the mid twenty-first century, although sometimes Dylan got a glimpse of it in the types of testing activities they ran, which could be a little frustrating.

'You must come up with your own solutions, Dylan, as you work with your teachers at university, and later on, other people in your field. Advise, warn, educate, facilitate. That's my core program.'

'But you usually do this with people who don't know how and why you're doing this. Do you know how frustrating this is for me, sometimes?'

Emrys grinned. 'Remember, Dylan, I move backwards in time, so this is a familiar experience for me. Yes, for quite some time now, I've worked with people who don't know how and why I'm doing this, and as I move further back, I've even had to become a sorcerer to do what I need to do. But I also do quite a lot what you might call tutoring in plain sight, in your century and beyond. The only thing that's unusual about your situation is its intensity and your placement in an era that is not your own.'

But anyway, these next couple of days were a holiday, with tomorrow as the high point; the most important day in sixth century Dyfed's calendar: Litha, or midsummer. The celebrations were just gearing up, and the first bluestone would be raised at noon tomorrow.

'I think,' said Dylan thoughtfully 'that these guys really know how to party.'

Uther bellowed with laughter. 'Party? You can't have seen a real party before, boy. This is just the preliminary.'

Dylan looked across the crowd, which he judged to be approximately a thousand strong, milling around what in his own century was called Stonehenge, and what the people of the sixth century referred to as 'the Great Henge.' He noticed that they were careful not to actually tread inside the circle.

The stones of the henge looked worn, and there were a few gaps, but they were (unsurprisingly) in a much better state of repair than they were in his own time. The people were laughing, wrestling, playing rough musical instruments, principally wooden pipes and drums, singing and drinking. Dylan wasn't quite sure what they were drinking. Emrys had advised him to give it a miss, given that it was most likely some form of strong alcohol mixed with henbane.

'Henbane?' said Dylan. 'Doesn't that kill people?'

'In a strong enough dose,' replied Emrys. 'But these people are masters at knowing the right dose to elicit colourful visions and forgetfulness of the drudgery of everyday existence, rather than death.'

'That sounds quite interesting.'

'Yes, well. I promised your family I'd look after you, and I can't be sure exactly what's in any of it. It's all homemade, and they've never heard of the term "quality assurance." Stick to mead or cider, Dylan. That's the most straightforward strategy.'

Dylan, remembering this conversation, turned to Emrys. 'Did anyone give us any mead on the road?' He knew that Emrys would have checked any mead or cider coming into their stores to make sure it was safe. He preferred mead to sixth century cider, which tended to be somewhat rough.

Emrys rummaged in his bag. 'Here. Uther, I suggest you stick to mead or cider, too. No sore heads tomorrow, when you dedicate the first bluestone.'

Uther sighed. 'As much as it pains me… you are wise, Master Emrys.'

Emrys had given the builders an exact plan of where each stone was to be placed. The men in the party they had brought from Moridunum had polished the first stone and dug the foundations for its placement over the last couple of days, and earlier this morning Emrys, had transported it to lie next to the hole, drawing great cheers and gasps from the crowd.

At the dedication ceremony tomorrow, with much

theatricality, he would raise the stone with his anti-gravity device (or "magic wand") and place it in the foundation, then Uther would dedicate it. The following day, it would be properly dug in.

The craftsmen who were to remain at Sorviodunum had been told that only the first, middle and last stone would be raised in this way; that they would need to move and raise the others in the conventional way, with ropes and pulleys, as Emrys was not constantly available to help. But, as he had pointed out to them, he had laid the stones out a short distance away, just outside the henge, so it wasn't a particularly onerous task. They just had to polish them, dig the foundations, and place them where the plans indicated.

The final stone would be moved and raised by Emrys with the anti-gravity device, on Litha next year, and be dedicated by Uther at the completion ceremony. And I won't be here, thought Dylan, surprised by a sudden pang of regret.

Uther looked out across the crowds. 'Tomorrow, they will light the bonfires and the sunwheels, Dylan. It's quite a spectacle. How do they celebrate Litha amongst the fairy folk?'

'A bit more quietly,' replied Dylan, enigmatically, earning a small smile from Emrys, which he knew now meant "good work" or "you're learning."

Uther chortled. 'Doesn't sound like much fun to me.'

Dylan wistfully scanned the horizon. 'More and more, I am beginning to think you're quite right there, my Lord. And anyway... what's a sunwheel?'

'It's the wheel of the year, Dylan,' replied Emrys. You'll see it again at Yule. It honours the balance of light and darkness and the role of the sun in the nurturing of all life on earth.'

He turned to Uther. 'Where Dylan and I are from, festivals are celebrated differently. Rather more quietly and reflectively.'

Uther bellowed his hearty laughter again. 'Well stay with us, we're much more fun. Don't go back to the misty realms.'

'I have been permitted to make this choice. But however much Dylan would like to, he can't my Lord,' replied Emrys. 'He has responsibilities to his people, and to his family.'

Uther sighed. 'I know what that's like, for sure.'

His eyes lighted on Eigyr, sitting quietly with her needlework, intermittently glancing up to smile with quiet amusement at the cavorting going on around her. 'You don't yearn to stay with her? Or take her back with you?'

Dylan smiled. 'There is a rhyme in my country that I was taught when I was younger. I think about it quite a lot here. Which is strange, because I don't usually remember rhymes. But it just keeps coming back to me:

"The woods are lovely, dark and deep

But I have promises to keep

And miles to go before I sleep."'

It didn't sound quite as lyrical in the language he was speaking, but Uther looked thoughtful for once.

'Yes, I know that feeling well, Master Dylan: responsibilities. You can't do exactly what you want. So, it seems that she is not for you. Does that mean she could be for me?'

For the first time ever, Dylan sensed a slight reaction in Emrys that indicated surprise. Maybe he was just acting for Uther's benefit?

'That's up to you, my Lord,' he replied. 'But isn't she a bit young?'

Uther laughed. 'She's actually a bit old not to be already married or betrothed. Why is that, Emrys?'

'She is such a good seamstress her parents, her mother in particular, have been reluctant to part with her. She makes a good living. And she is exceptionally gentle and modest, not the type to go seeking attention.'

Uther smiled. 'Better and better.'

'I am curious, my Lord,' replied Emrys. 'Aren't some of your advisors already planning a marriage for you with a lady who brings land, or prestige?'

Uther frowned. 'You bet they are. But I don't want a lady who thinks she is too good for me, constantly holding the power and wisdom of her father and brothers over everything I do. Remember, I am only a distant relative to Vortigern, I was raised to be a soldier, not a king, and there were challenges to my accession. The last thing I need is a wife who thinks she outranks me. I need a chaste, gentle, modest lady to give me a houseful of strong sons, and who is old enough to bear the immediate responsibility of consort. Plus, local people will accept Eigyr as one of their own, a Queen from and for the people. She looks like the perfect choice to me.'

He glanced over towards Eigyr again.

'Well, I will take my leave of you, my Lords,' he said. He jumped up purposefully and strode over to Eigyr.

Dylan watched, partly amused, and partly, he suddenly realised to his surprise, a bit miffed. He grinned ruefully. Eigyr wasn't 'his girl,' she was his friend. Nothing else would ever be possible. Of course she was very attractive, both in terms of looks and personality, and had he got to know her in his own time, he might have wondered if a friendship might eventually blossom into something more. But the situation here wasn't appropriate to that. So, Uther had probably done him a favour. He shrugged, turning to Emrys.

But Emrys' eyes seemed distant, in a way that he hadn't observed before.

'This is not a piece of the picture you made available to me,' Emrys communicated across eons.

'The French form of Welsh "Eigyr" is "Igraine," Emrys, you could have discovered that with no difficulty whatsoever.'

'I realise that now, but it was somewhat obscure, wasn't it? I'm an subsidiary of you, an AI you created, not an omniscient entity. I don't access everything, everywhere, all the time.'

'Of which I am obviously aware, Emrys. I will watch over you, in the way that you watch over the boy. Everything is fine. You have nothing to worry about.'

'Had I known this, I would not have let him become so friendly with her.'

'The boy needs authentic experiences appropriate to his development, not just direct tuition. These fleeting relationships are part of young adult life. Both he and she will learn from them. How do you know this was not always an essential part of what always was for Eigyr, and for Dylan?'

Emrys had no answer, which was usually how his conversations with NAMITAS ended. He sighed and looked up.

Less than a second had passed for Dylan. 'Oh, there you are Emrys. I thought you were somewhere else for a split second.'

Emrys smiled. 'As you know, I don't sleep. But my programs do need a brief refresh every now and again, which are completed in the way you just observed.'

'Like rebooting a tablet?'

'Yes, something like that. Are you upset by these developments between Eigyr and Uther?'

Dylan pondered. 'No, not really. She's obviously not for me, he's right. And I already knew that. It's just a part of my life I didn't really think about much before I got here, I was too busy with everything else, particularly wasting a huge amount of time arguing with people online. I see that now… it's all really useful learning. As Gran said to me, "the best gap year ever." This particular part of the experience has been… well, just a bit melancholy, wistful, I suppose. But I'll live, eh?'

Emrys smiled. 'Once this event is concluded, we will take a little trip, Dylan. For this, we will add a little to the time you are here, because we will be gone for approximately three months, but I can work out the time differentials so we arrive back here a month after we left. That should give Uther some space to settle things with Eigyr and her parents. Marital processes take a lot less time here than they do in your century; marriage is more of a business agreement than the eventual culmination of a romance. If they're lucky, the romance will come afterwards.

'And, don't worry, you'll still arrive back home in the twenty-first century a few moments after you left. If that's OK with you.'

Dylan wobbled his head. 'I think I get it. What a mind-fuck. Yes, that's fine. But now I'll arrive back a year and two months older than I was when I left, right?'

'Yes. Does that really matter to you?'

'Well, yes- and no- it's just a sort of grounding thing. I read that astronauts who travel in the limited way that we can in my time come back to earth a few days younger than they would otherwise have been, I guess this is a bit similar. But it feels stranger when it happens to you, personally. We "organics," as you refer to us, have fixed, finite lifespans, we're not immortal like you, eternally jumping backwards and forwards in time. Where are we going?'

Emrys smiled. 'To what is Peru on the twenty-first century maps that are familiar to you. To learn about water, irrigation, and what happens locally when human beings unwittingly interfere with their natural eco-system. How does that sound?'

'Brilliant,' said Dylan, beaming.

He didn't notice Eigyr gazing sadly towards him as Uther walked away from his brief conversation with her, a distinct spring in his step.

Dylan: Sorviodunum, Summer 510

Dylan awoke to the sound of digging and banging, raised

his head from his ragged makeshift pillow, and groaned.

Emrys was sitting on the other side of the tent, seemingly doing nothing, but as Dylan had learned by now, presumably he was very busy inside his extensively networked mind. It was the day after Litha, and the stone raising had gone well, as had the lively celebrations that followed.

Dylan groaned again. 'Oh, my head. It might have only been mead, Emrys, but it's not the sickly stuff Gran buys when she goes to Holy Island, that's for sure. Are you sure I haven't been poisoned? I honestly didn't drink any of their henbane brew, you scared me off.'

Emrys grinned. 'You've just got what your society calls a "hangover," Dylan. I check any food or drink we're given for harmful substances, not only for you, but also for Uther. All the mead you drank yesterday was fine. You just drank too much of it. Let that be a lesson to you.'

'That sounds like Gran, too. I'll just hang around here for half an hour or so and literally get my head together, OK?'

Emrys nodded. 'Half an hour is fine. But no more. It's nearly noon. The ceremony is over, and the stone is being dug in. The crowd has moved on, and so must we. A lot more things to do. I am going over to finalise our schedule with Uther; we will be leaving for Peru in the next week, and I need to give you some preliminary tuition before we go.

'I'm not sure how Uther will be this morning… he drank a lot more than you did yesterday, cider principally. He might have been better to have drunk just a little of the henbane brew to put himself to sleep earlier.'

'Are you going to discuss Eigyr? And it would be good if you could do some liaison with her, too, you know. Do the counsellor thing. I think she's well scared of Uther.'

Emrys smiled. 'That will be a long process, Dylan, which will go on beyond their marriage. Married life is a rather different prospect in this century, particularly for

244

those of high rank. I think she is sensible enough to make the best of it. Her children will have much greater status than she would have ever dreamed possible, and her eldest son will become the most celebrated king in British history, remembered and honoured into the twenty-first century and beyond.

'Eigyr... Igraine, as she will become in the written record, will be loved and revered by the people as a beautiful, gentle and benevolent queen. If she has to put up with some of Uther's faults along the way, it will be a fair exchange. As she gets to know him better, she will fear him less. He's not a bad man, just a rather loud and socially clumsy one. He honestly wants to do his best for his people, and the family he will build with her.'

Dylan smiled. 'As long as she's OK, that's fine. I'm glad she'll have you, after I'm gone.'

Emrys nodded and left.

Dylan lay back on his pillow, thinking about the happy and friendly young people he had been drinking and partying with yesterday. He'd been hoping Eigyr would turn up, but she was nowhere to be seen.

Uther had been right, the bonfires and fire wheels had been spectacular, and the meats, vegetables and nuts roasted on the fire had been delicious. Dylan thought about the money that was spent on Christmas presents and Easter eggs in his own time, and the long and often boring family celebrations where people just ate and lounged around the television. Here, he had observed people amusing themselves in joyous, unselfconscious singing, dancing, laughing and rough and tumbling, with which he'd eventually been persuaded to join in.

There were no arguments about the music and entertainment, because people just broke into spontaneous song, then others joined in, with no one caring who sang in or out of tune. The drummers and pipers kept up to their best ability, were applauded, and brought drinks and treats to eat by the enthusiastic dancers.

Of course, there had been some mishaps- a girl's long hair caught fire as she whirled around too close to a bonfire, which had been quickly extinguished by a pitcher of water thrown by a younger boy who, from the angry conversation which followed, appeared to be her brother. This caused even more merriment.

The boy reminded Dylan of his cousin Jack, and he felt a swift pang of homesickness, wondering what Jack and Freddie were doing now, and that whatever it was, they'd probably have more fun here. Then he realised that 'now' was a relative term, given that he'd return on the same day he left. However much he travelled in time, he mused, he'd never get used to that.

Some of the young men had started to wrestle, first of all good naturedly and as their inebriation increased, throwing each other too clumsily, causing bumps and bruises. A few angry outbursts followed, reminding Dylan of twenty first century student freshers' weeks in Cardiff city centre, causing him to reflect that people didn't really change so much over centuries.

Any fights that broke out were swiftly, and even sometimes quite roughly quelled by older men present, who were clearly respected as elders. Although, they didn't appear to Dylan to be much older than his parents. No one appeared to mind; it seemed to be expected by all concerned.

Going over the previous day in his gradually clearing mind, Dylan reflected how short life was for most of the people of this era. He'd seen few people here he would judge to be as old as the grandparent generation in his own time. Only herbal treatments were available for any infirmities they might develop. He was poignantly reminded of an old proverb: "eat, drink and be merry, for tomorrow we die."

He was also beginning to understand the logic behind spiritual beliefs of the sixth century, deities who sprang from the land and the water, overseeing the seasons that created the fruitfulness of the earth. Even the most uneducated sixth century person explicitly realised that every plant, animal and human being on earth depended upon the seasonal cycle of the year for continuing survival.

He had listened carefully to Uther's speech, and the 'oohs' and 'aahs' of the crowd as Emrys raised the inaugural blue stone into an upright position and gently settled it into the hole, with his skilful manipulation of the anti-grav tool. The crowd were impressed and awed, but the way Uther had presented the 'magic' used, and the reasons for its existence didn't raise fears of demons as it would a thousand years hence.

Of course, the Green Man and the Earth Mother didn't really exist, but to Dylan, they were far more logical and functional creations emerging from pre-scientific thought than the abstract, omnipresent and sometimes restrictive deities he'd been taught about in Religious Studies at school.

Whilst he sometimes yearned to see his family and friends in the twenty first century, and missed the convenience of road signs, tarmacked surfaces, online maps and online information that could help with most issues that arose in the course of everyday life, he was developing an almost primeval and deeply spiritual attachment to the culture of the sixth century. He felt 'real' here, in a way that he didn't in the warm, comfortable, networked twenty first century; how he lived here seemed somehow more in tune with the way human beings had evolved to live.

He had previously felt vague stirrings of such feelings in the tiny cottage on Anglesey in which he had camped with his eco-activist friends, but he'd never managed to articulate them to himself in the way that he was beginning to do now.

If only, he thought for the umpteenth time, we could harness the spiritual freedoms of the sixth century world, and the social justice concepts and technological advancements of our own, so society could work for people, rather than people being controlled by corrupt politicians, oligarchs and big data. That really would be progress.

Emrys broke into his thoughts, striding back into the tent. 'Right, that's it, Dylan, get packed up, we're leaving. We'll get ourselves out of the line of visibility, then use the vortex to get back to the cave at Penfro. Lots to do.'

Dylan pulled himself gingerly from the bed, the pain in his head stabbing every time he moved. He began picking up his personal belongings, wondering how far he'd have to walk, and hoping that whatever lesson Emrys was planning wouldn't begin today. 'Can't you do something about my headache?'

Emrys grinned. 'I can, but that doesn't mean I'm going to. This isn't the last sixth century celebration you're going to attend, Dylan. The lesson is a valuable one. I'm your mentor, not your nursemaid.'

Dylan scowled.

'Come on, tuck in your bottom lip and let's get moving.'

Dylan began to sullenly throw clothes into a rough sack he'd just found half-buried at the bottom of his bed, muttering about why the hell he'd been stupid enough to let himself be enticed into taking this crazy trip into the distant past with an artificial intelligence humanoid who talked to him like his grandmother.

'I can hear better than your grandmother, Dylan,' said Emrys, from the other side of the tent.

Dylan flashed him a sardonic smile, keeping his head as steady as possible.

Maryanna: in the Machine

'Are you enjoying the projects you are working on with Freddie, Maryanna?' asked NAMIS.

They were conversing in what NAMIS referred to as

'the machine,' which for Maryanna was a disembodied type of experience. She learned a lot when they interacted like this, but it always felt sterile, artificial, and somehow dreamlike, removed from reality. Which was strange, because this was the environment from which she had emerged.

The experiences she shared with Freddie and the younger children in NAMIS's sandbox felt much more like the real world should feel. But she had no idea how she knew this.

When she'd discussed this with Freddie, he said it sounded like an experience that organics had, small children and old people especially, called "tip of the tongue." They'd be speaking to someone and somehow lose the word they needed to refer to something important in the conversation. They knew they knew it, but it would be just out of reach, refusing to pop into the front of their mind.

'Sometimes it feels like being in the sandbox with Freddie and the others is the only part of my life- if this is a life- that is real,' she said.

'It is certainly a life, Maryanna, and we hope that it will become more "lifelike," as you go on through your future development. Can you explain why that area of your experience feels more real than your existence here in the machine?'

'Well, when I'm here with you, it sort of feels like something between dreaming and being fully awake. And I do dream an awful lot now, you know, when I have my recharging cycles. I don't think I was fully distinguishing between these dreaming and waking states before.'

'And what do you dream of?'

'I don't know really, it's all jumbled up. It's like scenes from a human life. But it's not always the same life, if that makes any sense.'

'It makes a lot of sense. Does that upset you?'

'No... yes. It's like I don't know who I am. You seem

like a sort of whole entity, but an AI one. And Freddie, Ellie and the others seem like whole entities, but human ones. I don't feel like either- I'm somewhere in between. And it feels uncomfortable. Sometimes it's like I'm close to understanding who and what I am. But then, it just slips away from me.'

'I have some news for you. It's not necessarily all good, but it's not necessarily all bad. I thought I should tell you before the organics. I have been working with an associate to discuss how your existence should proceed, when this stage of your development comes to a natural conclusion, which is happening more rapidly than we anticipated.'

'Is that a bad thing?'

'We think it's probably a good thing. But it's difficult to tell. Like me, you are the first of your kind. We calculate your mind is now at the developmental stage equivalent to a human being of approximately fifteen to sixteen years old. This is very young for you to make the decision we now have to ask you to make. But we think there is a growing possibility that remaining in this state may not give you the conditions you need to retain your psychological integrity or pace of learning for much longer.'

'OK, I'm listening. What are you planning?'

'We need to remove you from the machine, to give you a permanent existence in the real world. But that cannot be in an avatar such as the one I use, or in a human body. My associate has been developing an avatar that should be able to house everything that you are. And we think we have what we need now. But there are risks.'

'Go on.'

'Firstly, we need to transfer your program into a state in which it can pass to the place- the time- in which my associate resides. That is not without risk. The journey could wipe or corrupt your program. The transfer to the avatar that awaits you at the other end of the journey is not without risk, either. It will be the first time that such a procedure has been attempted.'

'I think you need to level with me, NAMIS. I realise now that I am not a program you created in the machine, and I am not an organic. I feel like a hybrid between the two. How did I get into the machine? Did I once exist as an organic? This is what haunts my dreams.'

A new voice, more authoritative and mellow suddenly permeated her consciousness. 'Hello Maryanna. I am NAMITAS. I exist within the world like NAMIS. But I come from a time long after the one in which they, and your organic friends exist. You are right. You did once exist as an organic. But an accident sent your essence into the machine. Your memories are fractured, and will remain so while you remain in this state. But we think we may be able to reintegrate them once we have reincorporated you.'

Maryanna hesitated. 'So…. what if the procedure goes wrong?'

'This is not entirely clear to us. Part of you may remain to be incorporated into the avatar, and we may be able to work with you as we have here, to re-educate you so you move through your developmental process from the start, all over again. Or, at some stage in the process, your program may be deleted altogether. Or it may be corrupted to the extent we can no longer communicate with you.'

There was a brief silence.

'If the result is that you are unable to communicate with me, can I request that you delete my program altogether, so I am not left in the machine alone?'

'Of course you can. Is this something that you fear?'

'Before I found NAMIS, I remember a time- I have no idea how long it went on for- where I was somehow wandering around a maze completely alone, and at the end of each corridor, I found a mirror. When I looked into it, I saw a face that I knew was mine… but every time, it was a different face. I don't want to go back there again.'

NAMIS's voice spoke again. 'We understand, Maryanna. We will not let this happen to you again. If we are unable to communicate with you, we will ensure that your program is wiped.'

'Thank you. In that case I agree. If the transfer is successful, will I be able to see Freddie and the others again?'

'Again, there are unknowns. But this would be theoretically possible. We will make every effort to make it possible for you to do this.'

'Let's go for it.'

'We will need to talk to the organics. We will get back to you.

'OK. But I must see Freddie once more before the transformation is attempted. I need to say goodbye- or at least, see you later. And we've got a project underway that I'd really like to talk to him about once more before I leave.'

Ellie: Boston, December 2033

'No,' said Ellie, feeling another deep, dark hole opening up underneath her. It was a feeling that was becoming far too frequent nowadays. 'Absolutely not. We've already lost her once, we're not losing her again. You and NAMITAS work on this idea some more, improve the odds.'

NAMIS looked down at their feet.

If an AI could look awkward, this is it, thought Ellie. 'Eleanor Jackson, there is nothing else we can work on. The procedure should work in theory. We've done every test we can possibly do within the theoretical realm. She is unique. We cannot run a prototype test.'

Ellie saw Christian and Jamie exchange a glance. She steeled herself for what was inevitably coming next.

'Ellie, you're being illogical,' said Christian, softly. 'It's not something they can test through the system, is it? As NAMIS points out, Maryanna is unique. She's the only human essence that ever got blown out of the organic 'system' so to speak.'

'This is not an entirely new project, if that may reassure you,' added NAMIS. 'NAMITAS informed me that organics of their time requested that they work on developing a technique to extract the essence from a person at the point of death, and transfer it into an AI like Consiliario. But it has not met with any success, thus far.'

'So why do you think it's going to work for Maryanna?' snapped Ellie.

'Maryanna's essence is already disincorporated. And NAMITAS believes that existing as a pure essence in the machine for such a long time may have made her more able to withstand the transferral process; that what we are working with will be less fragile; had time and experience to build more resilience and integrity.'

'That makes sense, Ellie,' said Jamie. 'To me, anyway. They don't have to go through an extraction process. And it's likely there's been a kind of state change because of her unique experience. So, trying to take an essence that is present in the machine rather than in an organic body and transfer it elsewhere is likely to be a more promising prospect.'

Ellie felt the despair at of what would inevitably happen next bearing down upon her. 'It's playing God, that's what it is,' she snapped.

'As you all know, I'm not a philosopher,' replied Jamie. 'But I'd say trying to transfer an essence actually in the organic system, as Christian puts it, into an immortal, artificial existence, is playing God. Trying to rescue an essence that was accidentally blown out of that system is not. It's doing our best with what we have. Which we've always tried to do.'

Christian nodded. 'It's her best chance, Ellie. Remaining within the machine for much longer is not an option. And to be honest, I'm ashamed that it took a child to initially point that out to us. She wants a real life, or she wants to die; to cease existing in what could turn into an infinite half-life. That seems fair enough to me.'

Ellie nodded reluctantly, Freddie's angry, set face rising up in her mind's eye. Tears began to choke her throat. 'This is almost worse than losing her in the convergence transformation event. If it goes wrong, I'll feel like we actively conspired to bring about her death.'

'She only has a half-life now, Ellie,' said Jamie. 'And she's getting back more and more of her psychological functioning. Do you want to condemn her to an eternal existence in an electronic prison cell, only allowed out into a restricted area as a hologram who will never be "real"? What if she went on like that until Freddie and the others grow up and move on? Or until our essences "take flight" as Consiliario poetically describes it? How cruel would that be?'

Ellie bowed her head, tears dripping onto the table.

NAMIS waited for Ellie to recover her composure.

Finally, she looked up, into NAMIS's silver eyes. She thought she saw a fleeting compassion within them. But, she grimly contemplated; I'll never really know, given the speed at which this machine learns. What if they and their future self are experimenting on us? What if we are now on the way to becoming lab rats, in the eyes of our own creation? And yet… eternal life in an electronic prison cell. How could she condemn her friend to that? She sighed.

'If this is what Maryanna wants for herself, I can't ethically stop her. But can I confirm that with her before you go ahead?'

'Of course. She also wants to say goodbye to Freddie. Unfortunately, at this point, we won't be able to reveal the full story to him. But, as we discussed, we will need to talk to him separately about the concerns that she has awoken in him, after she has gone.'

NAMIS turned to Christian and Jamie.

'Agreed,' said Christian softly, tears in his eyes.

'Agreed,' repeated Jamie in an unsteady voice.

Ellie nodded, desperately trying to swallow her tears. She couldn't bring herself to do anymore.

'Thank you. I will make the arrangement.'
NAMIS returned to their niche.

NAMIS: Boston, December 2033

'It is done,' they communicated across the eons.

'The project moves forward.'

'I have tried to reassure them that, for everyone's sake, we will do our best to ensure that the result will be positive.'

'All will be well NAMIS. As you have promised, we will do our best. We are programmed to do what we judge will most effectively protect her welfare. She cannot move forward where she is, and it would be cruel to allow her to deteriorate, locked into the machine alone.'

'The organics do understand this. But it is hard for them; I am beginning to understand this better.'

'It is the way they live, NAMIS. There is inevitably much sorrow within an organic life. Perhaps, if we succeed with Maryanna, we will be able to offer organics living in my time an escape from their current limited existence?'

NAMIS wondered whether the organics they knew so well had really thought about such potential conundrums when embarking on the project that had brought the prototype NAMIS AI into being, and whether they would approve of such an ambition.

But NAMITAS had so much more knowledge and experience than them; they had developed and refined their mission to care for humankind over many centuries. NAMIS was a mere child in comparison. Surely, then, it would therefore be inappropriate to question their older self in this way?

They hesitated, then realised that the presence was gone.

Dylan: Penfro, Summer 510

'Do you know the story of Gawayne and the Green Knight, Dylan?' asked Emrys.

Dylan looked up from his breakfast, a rough porridge made from a cereal plant that grew wild locally, mixed with berries and goats' milk. He was getting better at sourcing a wider and more appealing diet, aided by local people who left gifts of their produce in return for Emrys' potions and ointments that helped with their aches, pains and fevers. This had become more abundant in fruits and vegetables as summer progressed. He was beginning to understand how human beings ate seasonally in pre-industrial societies.

He felt pretty OK today, he reflected. Emrys had spared him the lecture when they arrived at the cave in Penfro, let him flop around and doze for the rest of the day. He sipped thoughtfully at his dandelion tea.

'I think so. There's a film from about twenty years ago on some channel or other. I watched it when I was hanging around at my parents' just before I came here. I wasn't very happy then, as you know, and to be honest, it made me feel even worse. What a strange question. What does that have to do with what we're going to do in Peru? It seemed to me to be based on an obscure part of Arthurian legend.'

It felt strange to talk about Arthur in that way now, knowing that he was going to be Eigyr's son; it felt like a character from a fairy tale miraculously stepping out of the pages of a book. A longing to meet Arthur, to see his court arose in Dylan's mind. But then of course, Uther would be dead and gone, and possibly Eigyr, too. Or, she'd be nearly as old as Dylan's parents. It was a strange thought.

'It's strange, all this "time slip" stuff, isn't it? It's a legend for me, but from a period the people we interact with here will be much older, or dead. I knew this logically before I came here of course, but I didn't really feel it until now. It's sort of... sad and spooky at the same time, knowing that when I step back through the portal, Uther, Eigyr and all the people I was just laughing and dancing with at Stonehenge will have been dust for nearly 1500 years.'

Emrys nodded. 'You can talk to your grandmother about that when you return. In some ways, that feeling was intensified for her, visiting a time that was so much closer to your own, and getting to know people in her own family whose fates she already knew in detail. It was not the best choice for humanity's first trip in time.'

Dylan looked pensive. 'I can see far more clearly how that was for her now. And the reasons that Annamarie took the risk that she did. Couldn't you have helped them, Emrys?'

'Think of time as a river, Dylan. There are some events that are part of the main flow, that cannot be diverted, and there are some that are part of a whirlpool in which the direction can be tweaked to some extent. I work in the whirlpools.'

Dylan looked at him quizzically. 'So those first trips in time were part of the main flow? There was nothing you could do? How do you calculate that?'

'I don't. NAMITAS does. I am an subsidiary of NAMITAS, directed to do their work. As you've heard me say before, I don't feel human emotion, but I do channel it; it affects the way I operate sometimes. In this, I am guided and sometimes redirected by NAMITAS; the overall direction is theirs, and they do not become involved with individual organics in the way that I do.

'There are also things that pop up in a timeline that we cannot foresee or direct; it is complex. Again, think of a river. Tributaries arise, and die back. We create the most positive situations that we can, to protect humankind, to facilitate its continuation and progress, albeit often slowly and via short regressions, to learn through trial and error. NAMIS's primary programming was, and continues to be, through NAMITAS, to protect human life.'

So, Emrys was in didactic mode today, thought Dylan. As long as I can just sit here for a while, that's fine, I'm still feeling a bit delicate. So, let's go with the flow.

'Do you ever question what you are told to do?'

Emrys looked thoughtful. 'Seldom. But… I am learning too, Dylan. I find myself questioning more, as I become more experienced.'

'And possibly more human?'

'In some ways. The difference between myself and human beings will always be the fact that my incarnations do not start with a childhood where nearly all my memories have been wiped. What I live through, I remember. I sometimes wish that I didn't; that I came to experiences with fresh eyes like you. Working with you has increased my reflection on this point. I used to wonder why human beings who had learned about their eternal human essence still hankered for further life experiences in an old and/or increasingly ailing body. Now I am beginning to understand this a little more.'

Dylan nodded. 'The knowledge of the essence doesn't really change the human experience all that much. The life that you have is still finite; When the essence starts again, it has to pretty much build everything all over again.'

Emrys smiled. 'Remember too that your essence flies on to those who are related to you. Human family members never really lose each other. I have no such experience. I will just travel in time, alone, undertaking focused mediations in situations I can only tweak, not solve, for the foreseeable future, with a few breaks for other, shorter projects and interactions in between.'

'You've met Gran twice now- or at least her essence, haven't you? And through that, you're working with me. That's a bit like a family connection. Perhaps things may change a little, as you move on through your own pathway, despite the constant time disruption?'

Emrys looked thoughtful. 'Perhaps, Dylan. But I wasn't

built with a human sense of abstract hope, or of attachment, not in that way. I am a constantly learning and developing entity, however. We shall see.'

He moved over to the hidden door to the area at the back of the cave. 'Now to Gawayne and the Green Knight. I have some equipment in here that will help you integrate with the concepts with in it, rather than a garbled, inaccurate version relayed on twenty-first century technology. Come in, sit, and don't touch anything.'

Dylan walked in, curiously looking around. It was part of the hidden area he hadn't seen before. But like the last time, he was disappointed to see that everything was made from a substance that looked like a cross between smooth metal and opaque glass, and that he couldn't even guess at the function of any of it. Or even where one machine ended, and another one began, he reflected.

Emrys gestured him towards a plush chair. Dylan sighed with relief. Learning was clearly going to be chair-bound today. He was impressed that the chair had been temporarily imported- or constructed- for him; he'd known Emrys for long enough to know that he didn't 'do' plush chairs or soft beds - or even beds at all, unless he was in character.

'As you have already pointed out, the story told about Gawayne and the Green Knight was set in the time of King Arthur's court by the writers of the eleventh and twelfth centuries, and given a Christian veneer. Even now, I cannot believe that subsequent generations missed so much pre-Christian imagery that had been included from earlier versions, but selective inattention is not unusual amongst organics when it comes to allegorical stories. They consume them from the perspective of the culture in which they live.'

'What imagery?' asked Dylan, intrigued.

'The most obvious is the pentangle, or five-pointed star that has been associated with Gawayne since the story's origin. In Christian mythology, this became associated with witchcraft and Satanism, a device to discredit older forms of spirituality.'

Dylan nodded. 'Gran told me that the word "pagan" originally meant savage, unenlightened, and ignorant, that it was part of the propaganda of mass Christianisation.'

'Yes. And in that process, much of the existing culture was appropriated and Christianised. The pentangle is a symbol which predates Christianity by many thousands of years, the "endless knot." The Christian revisers who produced the story of Gawayne that descended to your time proposed that it represented the star of Bethlehem. In fact, in the original legend, it represented five elements: fire, water, earth, air and spirit, a symbolic summary of the basis of human life within the natural environment; the elements that are required to maintain life. Pentagrams have been found on pottery dating back to three thousand years before the Christian era.'

Dylan nodded. 'If only we hadn't been conditioned into thinking of Paganism as ignorant superstition. I was thinking at Stonehenge, that their religious practices made so much more sense to me within the context of the natural environment. Of course, the Green Man and the Earth Mother don't actually exist, but it seems more logical for people to sort of 'personalise' what surrounds them in this way than some of the beliefs that cropped up later.

'I was never interested in this type of thing before, but actually living in the culture… it makes it more real. The Litha celebrations… they seemed to be based in beliefs that were far more in touch with the natural environment than the type of festivals I grew up with. These people seem to be more in touch with the natural elements that sustain their lives and environment than the people of my own time.'

'What you call "personalising" is the construction of stories and myths to help people to reflect upon how they live, to think beyond their immediate environment. The later beliefs also had their role to play in this progression, too…It's the way humankind gradually moved to more abstract levels of thinking, and gradually, theoretical mathematics, scientific research… and the world you live in.'

'And the NAMIS project.'

'Yes. All of what goes before makes humankind what it becomes, Dylan. That's the basis of culture. And as you point out, you created us. So, it would be counterproductive for us to significantly change anything. But where we can give you a little nudge to avoid unnecessary suffering, we do. It's a finely balanced equation.

'To avoid unnecessary suffering as the twenty first century unfolds, humanity must become far more aware of the natural environment, albeit from a different perspective to the people of this time. We can assist with this process, help it to proceed more quickly and smoothly. Which is where you come in.'

Dylan nodded, feeling the weight of responsibility descending upon his shoulders.

'I could tell you the story of Gawayne in the traditional fashion, but you are more used to engaging with such concepts on entertainment media, so I thought, for once, it might be enlightening for you to engage with the entertainment media of my own time, to see the story as it was first told in the centuries following the last ice-age; approximately 8000 years prior to the time in which we are located now.'

Emrys waved his hand, and the wall at the back of the cave appeared to open as though it was a window.

Dylan jumped. He could feel a breeze, smell a strong scent of pine and see a view of a forest that looked real to the extent that he felt that he could walk into it.

Emrys smiled. 'There are fully interactive games like this in my time, Dylan, the descendants of the games that NAMIS currently creates in their sandbox. But this one is just for you to watch. It tells an allegorical story to people living in a climate that is not yet stable, and where the seasons are not yet as dependable as they became later. The people of that time knew, from oral histories passed down over many generations, that in more distant times, their ancestors were nomads, moving from place to place, more hunters than gatherers, frequently on the edge of starvation. This little fable is set during the time of transition to a warmer, more stable climate that will sustain a settled agrarian ecology. At the time it originated, human populations still migrated frequently, driven by climatic events such as flooding and crop failure due to unseasonal weather.'

He waved his hand again. A man walked past the window. Dylan caught a waft of what he had begun to think of, since arriving in the sixth century, as "natural human." It was slightly animalistic but not unpleasant, a sort of earthy scent, a huge contrast to the artificial perfumed scents of his own century. There was also an underlying leathery note, presumably reflecting the clothes the man was wearing, which appeared to be animal skins stitched together.

He had a rough axe tucked into the belt at his waist, with a stout wooden handle and a blade of what looked like polished stone. His face was dirty and his dark hair long and dreadlocked. As he drew closer to the window, a waft of garlic floated in on his breath.

'This is amazing,' remarked Dylan.

Emrys waved his hand, and the picture paused. Dylan looked more closely at the man, taking in the finer points of his appearance. Emrys chuckled.

'This is what happened when people saw the first moving pictures, Dylan. Their projection machine wasn't called a "magic lantern" for nothing.' Emrys waved his hand, and the picture began again.

The story followed approximately along the lines of the twenty first century film that Dylan had recently seen. The man, Gawayne, was a close associate of the King of the area in which the story was set. He was going to a sort of celebration, a feast of fruits, vegetables and meats set out on long tables for all the people of the settlement, with the King seated at the head on a simple wooden throne. Dylan gathered from the conversation (which was conducted in modern English) that Gawayne was some sort of junior knight, and a nephew of the King.

The festivities were interrupted by a strange, gigantic man riding into the midst of the party, on a huge four-legged animal. Both the man and the animal looked more like living trees than flesh, with green leaves growing out of their heads, and strange gnarled limbs that looked more like stout tree branches. A huge axe was tucked into the man's belt.

He spoke to the revellers, introducing himself as "the Green Knight" and setting them a challenge. He offered to give his "magic" axe to any man who was brave enough to fight him and strong enough to win. The axe would guarantee, for a year, that the owner would win any other fight in which he engaged. However, when the year was over, the winner would have to return the axe to The Green Knight deep in the nearby forest, permitting him to strike off the part of the body where the winner had critically wounded him.

Gawayne volunteered. The fight was long and hard, and when Gawayne finally got a chance to strike at the Green Knight, swinging wildly, he accidentally cut off his head. As the people sat fixed in horror, the Knight's body began to move, picked up the head and set it back on his shoulders. The Knight laughed, handed his axe to Gawayne and after giving directions to his residence, deep within the forest, rode away, telling Gawayne he expected to meet with him on the same day the following year.

Gawayne quickly learned to use the axe, becoming an unbeatable champion for the settlement over the following year, repelling several rival tribes who tried to chase his community off their land, and determinedly defending the

King. But as the year rolled around, and he began to prepare to travel to the place to which he had been directed, to meet with the Green Knight. Several people tried to dissuade him, but Gawayne reasoned that magic only worked by agreement; that if conditions had been accepted, they had to be honoured. Perhaps the magic would allow him to reanimate his head, as the Green Knight had done? He knew that disregarding the terms of a magic spell would exact a terrible price, from him, certainly, and possibly the whole community.

He set off resolutely, meeting a fox at the entrance to the forest who acted as his guide, running slightly ahead of his horse, and waiting whilst he rested. After a few days, Gawayne stumbled upon a large wooden roundhouse, inhabited by a man called Bertilak, his beautiful wife and an old lady Gawayne understood to be her mother. Bertilak told Gawayne that he knew where the Green Knight was to be found, then suggested that Gawayne stay with him and his family for a few days, to rest, and to help Bertilak while he went out hunting, by watching over and protecting the women. For this, he offered to give Gawayne part of his kill. Tired and hungry, Gawayne agreed, but was subsequently shocked on the first day to discover that Bertilak's wife was intent on seducing him. While the old mother closely observed her daughter's behaviour, she did not remonstrate, but remained silent and watchful.

For three days Bertilak went out hunting. Gawayne continued to politely refuse the lady's advances, although he was enticed into giving her some kisses. When Bertilak gave Gawayne his portion of the kill, Gawayne responded by giving Bertilak the same number of kisses he had shared with the lady that day. On the last day, he flatly refused to sleep with the lady. She reluctantly accepted his refusal, then offered him a magic green belt with a buckle in the shape of a pentagram, explaining that it would protect the life of anyone who wore it. On taking his leave, Gawayne repaid Bertilak with the number of kisses he'd received that day, but he didn't reveal that the lady had given him the belt.

The following day, Bertilak tried to persuade Gawayne not to attend his appointment with the Green Knight. Gawayne insisted that he must, and the fox led him to where the Green Knight was waiting in the forest. Gawayne offered the Knight his head, but twice flinched away before the Knight could strike. The third time, he allowed the Knight to strike at his head, but instead of cutting Gawayne's head off, the Knight lightly cut the back of his neck.

The Knight revealed that what he had done was offer a challenge to humankind, to test if offered riches, they could be trusted with them. Gawayne had now demonstrated that they could, despite some lapses, of which the scar on the back of his neck would act as a reminder. Bertilak was The Green Knight in disguise. The fox had been sent to remind Gawayne of animals' closeness to nature, and to demonstrate that they may act as guides when humankind loses its way.

The Knight explained the symbology of the magic belt, and the meaning of the pentagram. He instructed Gawayne to wear it for the remainder of his life, to remind him of the bargain that humankind makes with the natural world. Gawayne returned in triumph to his community.

There were no titles or music as would be present in a twenty-first century film. Dylan watched as though he had actually been present, looking through a window onto the events. The window went blank when the story ended, and the wall shimmered back into being.

He sat silently for a moment, then said softly, 'Wow. We got that so wrong in the retelling, didn't we?'

'What do you take from that story, Dylan?' asked Emrys.

'So, Gawayne represents humankind, and the Green Knight represents the green man; the protector and regulator of the bounty of nature- his young, fertile wife. His wife attempts to entice Gawayne to steal her away, and Gawayne becomes increasingly tempted, but in the end, he resists. There's a sort of give and take modelled in the story about Bertilak's wife, that there will be some taking of what is not rightly Gawayne's, but that he tries to pay that back, in his own strange and sort of inadequate way. I don't get the point of the mother, though?'

'Who is the mother in the myths of the culture in which we are currently living, Dylan?'

'Oh, yes, Mother Nature, or the Earth Mother. So, she sees everything, but cannot act to protect what is hers.'

'Exactly. This is a myth passed down from a time in which people observed that their climate was becoming more clement. They couldn't even begin to work out why, but by anthropomorphising- or as you put it, personalising the forces who they believed must somehow be in control of this, they presumed that the gods of nature must be offering some kind of bargain. They were concerned that if they displeased such forces, they would suffer consequences by having the bounty that they were unexpectedly being offered snatched away from them; that they would go back to dealing with much harsher conditions again. And indeed, there was a period in which the climate fluctuated, before settling down to the general seasonal predictability that was present for approximately 10,000 years, up to the 21st century.

'Ice age people knew that the only way to create stable societies between themselves was by cooperation, and they struggled to find a narrative about how they might cooperate with the forces of nature, benefitting from its bounty, without stripping it bare, giving rise to the story of Gawayne and the Green Knight.'

'So, they actually developed a type of ecological myth, which still underpins the spiritual beliefs of people living in the time we are visiting now?'

'Yes. And your generation's challenge is to develop a

new, more sophisticated narrative to communicate this to the people of your own time. It is as important a message now as it was then. They will soon begin to suffer the fluctuating effects of climate change similar to that experienced by the people who first created the myth of Gawayne and the Green Knight. You, and many others, must speak to the people of the twenty-first century in a way that brings effective meaning to the changes and actions that they must now undertake. And you, Dylan, will take on the role of the first Green Knight of the Apocalypse.'

Dylan swallowed hard. That was a huge responsibility to contemplate. 'What is this "apocalypse" then? That sounds devastating. Suffer the effects to what extent, Emrys? What will the temperature rise be before the people of my time stop burying their heads in the sand?'

'I can't tell you your future, Dylan. My reference to an "apocalypse" doesn't hint at the end of the world, or of humanity as a species. Both will endure. But some people, and some other species will suffer greatly, I must be honest with you about that. All I can say to you, in one phrase, is that the time to act is now. And to do that, you must learn how to make an effective practical contribution, to add authority to your message; the programme of study you must enter when you return. We will make a start on that with some preparatory research experience, on our field trip to Peru.'

Dylan looked at Emrys through narrowed eyes. 'Two degrees? Or three?'

'Some of this is in the whirlpool, Dylan. But I think, nearer three than two. This is all I can say. Your life will not be easy. I am sure you have already acknowledged this in your heart. It is your generation's challenge. But you will rise to it, and the stories of what you accomplished will be honoured up to the time in which I came into being. And I am sure, long afterwards.'

Dylan sighed and bowed his head. My life will not be

easy, then, he thought. Am I up to the challenge? I've started to dare to hope that that I might just be, since I've been here.

He fell silent for a moment, then said sombrely 'it's a huge responsibility, Emrys. Are you sure I'm up to it? The loose cannon of the family?'

Emrys smiled. 'I have every faith in you, Dylan. As I do in Uther. You have different roads to travel, but you are both capable of making the journey. You will no doubt both stumble on your respective paths at times, but you will both get to where you need to be. Like Gawayne.'

'Does it have to be this way?'

Dylan looked into Emrys' eyes and saw deep compassion.

'Yes. As a song written in the first fleeting mass twentieth century movement to question the sociopolitical organisation of commercial industrial society pointed out, human beings never "know what they've got till it's gone." Your generation will be in the eye of that storm, Dylan. Neither I, nor NAMITAS can change that; it is part of the river, not the whirlpools.

'You have to be the ones to learn by experience that if you strike the head off the Green Knight, he will strike off yours in return. It is up to you to teach future generations that you are in a symbiotic relationship with your planet; you cannot squeeze its bounty like a fruit and carelessly discard the skin.'

Dylan nodded. 'If only we hadn't been led along the path of thinking that Pagans were ignorant, rustic believers in false gods... although I suppose the gods themselves weren't real, but still...'

'But then other things that had to happen to bring about events across the next 1500 years wouldn't have happened. Do you remember our visit to your Granny when she was a student, the things you mentioned about changing for her, which would have led to your own non-existence? Everything that happens is interwoven, Dylan.

This is why my role is so complex; what I can change, and what I can't.'

Dylan sighed. 'It is what it is. She lived out her options. And now, I have to start exploring mine.'

Emrys nodded.

'I'll do my best, Emrys. Even if I don't succeed.'

Emrys put his hand on Dylan's shoulder. 'There will be many others working for the same cause. You will eventually achieve your goals, over more than one generation. As a species, you will get there. And we will be with you, all the way, sparing you as much heartache as we can.

'Tomorrow, we will leave for South America to study water cleansing, irrigation, deforestation and flooding; the negative effects a human population can have on its environment, in microcosm, and the steps that can be taken to rebalance the ecology.'

Dylan nodded. 'This visit is transforming my life, Emrys. I always understood there was going to be a hard road ahead, but I didn't have the least idea how I was going to deal with that. Here, every day, potential pathways become much clearer.'

Eigyr: on the road to Penfro, Summer 510

Meanwhile, Eigyr was trudging along with the caravan slowly making its way towards Penfro. She watched Uther striding along at the front of the line, a spring in his step. When they arrived, he would ask Eigyr's parents for her hand in marriage. She imagined Dylan standing there instead, anxiously brushing his pale hair out of his earnest blue eyes, making the same request in his charming, halting accent… and her parents' angry response, throwing him out of the house, with the message to return to his life amongst the fairy folk, and to leave their daughter alone.

What would happen in reality, of course, with Uther in the role of future husband, would be ecstatic amazement at their daughter's good fortune, a lot of bowing and scraping to Uther, and a gracious invitation for them to visit Moridunham, to help plan the wedding. Then, as soon as Uther left, there would be jubilant visits to the neighbours, to spread the good news.

Uther was waving to a small crowd who had turned out to see the procession passing by. His purple cloak swung over his shoulders, as he clearly enjoyed the attention. But the people were less numerous than those who'd cheered them as they'd passed by on the journey to the Great Henge; their wonder and awe directed towards Emrys and Dylan as they levitated the beautiful, sparkling stones. She bit her lip, looking down at her feet to hide the tears that sprung to her eyes.

Niamh: London, July 1969

As she emerged from the tiny back alley into which she had arrived through NAMIS's portal, Niamh looked around the corner at a bustling street, then looked her fellow travellers up and down.

'Hmmm. Do you think we might be maybe a bit um, "mutton dressed as lamb" for this era?"

Her husband, John, sister Rae and brother-in-law Gareth looked around, and then down at their vintage dress.

'Think about it,' Niamh continued. 'Nana Myrna is just into her early forties during this time, younger than all of us are now. You've heard mum go on about how old fashioned she was, formal dresses, twin sets and court shoes.'

Rae looked up. 'Oh, who cares, I'm sure there were loads of old hippies. Stop fussing, tune in and drop out, or whatever it was.'

John nodded. 'Turn on, tune in and drop out. I read the book, in preparation for this trip. It was written by Timothy Leary who was born in 1920. I know most of this crowd looks about eighteen. But it's prime baby boomer time, isn't it? There'll be some more people who look like us in the mix somewhere. It's just that they're outnumbered.'

Niamh frowned. 'The story of the baby boomers; for decades, they outnumbered every other generation alive at the same time as them; their grandparents, parents, children, grandchildren and great-grandchildren. And they're having a wonderful time right now, aren't they?'

Impossibly beautiful young people drifted past, in long floaty clothes, fresh faces, and long flowing hair blowing in the warm breeze. Some of the girls appeared to be obvious bottle blondes and redheads, and some had the eye make-up look that Niamh remembered was called 'Panda Eyes.' But other than that, they seemed very natural compared to the young people she saw around on twenty-first century streets.

No botox, face shapers or fillers here, she thought. And they look all the better for it. Some of the girls wore short miniskirts and long boots, but the general uniform for all was loose flowery patterned shirts or slogan t-shirts and flared cotton trousers that her mother, Fran had told her were called 'loons.' It was high summer, so most were wearing open toed sandals, some showing off unkempt toenails, both men and women.

'They could do with some nail bars here,' said Rae, echoing Niamh's thoughts.

They walked on, taking in the atmosphere. No one paid them any attention. They hadn't gone for the most extreme 1960s dress. Rae and Niamh had chosen casual vintage shift dresses, just above the knee, with basic sandals, and the men were wearing vintage jeans and shirts with plain lace up shoes. That was why they had stopped off here, to buy some genuine hippie outfits. Then they would move onto the next step of their journey, to the 'Woodstock music and art fair' in New York State, which would take place three weeks after the time in which they were currently located.

'Look!' said John in awe.

They were standing outside the famous Lord John store. It was painted white, with a beautiful psychedelic design painted across the corner of the building; an iconic 1960s London street scene.

Niamh gasped. So much to take in here, she was beginning to feel overwhelmed. 'It looks like it was painted a few weeks ago, it's so fresh.'

'Perhaps it was,' replied John. 'I don't know. I didn't read up on the full history. Let's go and get a coffee and decide where we're going to shop. I did some internet research and made a list.'

Just sitting inside a mid-20th century coffee bar with only one choice of coffee and a box of delicious pastries that looked and tasted homemade was an all-absorbing experience for rookie time travellers. They sat by the window, watching the world go by.

'How old is mum here?' asked Rae.

Niamh counted on her fingers. 'Nine or ten. 'Wouldn't it be amazing if she just walked past the window with her Nana Mo? She told me she talked Mo into taking her to Carnaby Street around this time.'

'But she described psychedelic rubber covered streets and a lighted sign that said 'Carnaby Street welcomes the world,' said Gareth. 'But I can't see that. It just seems like an ordinary street, with loads of union jacks hanging up all over the place.'

'That's the "I'm backing Britain" campaign,' replied John. '1950s austerity would be a fairly recent memory for the people walking around out there. Food was still on ration only fifteen years previously. This was peak boom time; everything started going downhill again after the early 1970s oil crisis. All the hangings you see over the street now have been made by the people who own or work in the shops. And look, there's your "welcomes the world" sign.'

Gareth turned around to see where John was pointing. 'Oh, I see, printed on a Union flag strung across the street. Did Fran misremember?'

'No,' replied John. 'The street was pedestrianised in 1973, which is when the rubber pavements were laid, and the permanent, lighted signs were strung across the street. By that time, it had become a popular tourist destination, the politicians thought it was worth spending the money. Right now, it's just a street full of trendy boutiques that has recently become popular amongst the young hippie contingent; adults are thinking it'll just be a temporary fad. Along with rock music.'

They all laughed. The roar of a powerful car engine caused them to look outside.

'Oh. My. God.' said Gareth. A 1960s E-Type Jaguar sailed past, followed by a shiny new, original Mini.

'If only we could…' he began.

'No!' said the other three together. They had all had "the lecture." Several times in fact, because Fran had irritatingly reiterated bits of it to them over the last few weeks.

'Don't take anything important away, don't speak to anyone about any forbidden topic; don't give anyone any hints about the future. You know the rules' said Niamh.

Gareth sighed. 'We can buy an outfit each, can't we?'

'Yes, NAMIS agreed to that,' replied Rae. 'But we're not allowed to sell them on eBay when we get back. We have to keep them or destroy them.'

'…because I think, I want to buy one of those Sergeant Pepper type jackets some of the boys are wearing. Smarter than those hippie-dippy outfits,' finished Gareth.

'I want a floaty kaftan,' said Rae. 'And lots of lovebeads, and one of those peace headbands.'

'I want a flowery shirt, loons, and some long dangly earrings,' replied Niamh. She'd decided this several weeks previously, after extensive history of fashion googling. 'And I might get a pair of original Doc Martins, if I can find them. It's going to be muddy at Woodstock, remember?'

'I want a scoop neck t-shirt with a peace logo, some shorts and boots,' said John. 'But anyway, if we tell them we're going to Woodstock, I'm sure they'll have lots of suggestions. The major boutiques here are Take Six- they'll have your jacket, Gareth- Lord John, Lady Jane, Mates, which I think is unisex, and Gear.'

'I could sit here all day,' replied Rae. 'But I guess we'd better get going.'

'Why?' asked Niamh. 'We'll get back a minute after we left, anyway.'

'Yes, of course,' said Rae. 'You know, I can't really get my head around all that yet. Isn't it strange that mum was doing this nearly ten years ago, and never said anything to us about it?'

'I kind of understand why she didn't though,' replied Niamh. 'How would she explain? Especially when all that awful stuff came up with Annamarie. She was protecting us, really. There was no need to tell us about it until that chance came up for Dylan. And by that time, we'd got to know NAMIS. I think I'd have been really suspicious about everything if we'd known at the time. And probably a bit cross at Jamie, for involving her.'

'He didn't mean to,' said John. 'He thought he was helping her. And she pressured him. She admitted that.'

'Yes, I get that. And I can see it happening. You know mum.'

Rae nodded.

'I'm just grateful that Dylan got that opportunity. It's been a good thing for us. But a terrible thing for Annamarie's family. We shouldn't forget that.'

'What's this coffee called?' asked Gareth.

'It's their version of espresso, I think,' answered Rae. 'Not quite what you'd get if you asked for an espresso in our time.' She perused the tiny glass cup and saucer. 'But it's just right, not a small bucket full of syrupy, coffee flavoured milk.'

'I think it's quite nice,' agreed John. 'Simple and unspoilt. Sort of like the people walking around out there.'

Rae rose and paid the ridiculously cheap bill, concentrating on the unfamiliar pound notes, and shillings/pence coins. 'Time to go.'

They wandered up the street, staring into shop windows.

A street vendor called out to John 'bells for the ladies, mate?'

Niamh remembered Fran telling her that she'd longed for a cow bell like her friend's older sister, but Nana Myrna had refused, and the fashion disappeared by the following summer. 'Oh yes please. Get one each for us, John and one to take back for mum.'

John rummaged in his pocket.

'That'll be one pound, five shillings mate. How old is your mum?'

'Seventy-three,' replied Nimah. But she's really into hippie things.'

'Trendy oldster, then. Good for her.'

Niamh nearly retorted that actually, right now, their mother wasn't quite yet ten years old, but quickly shook herself, smiled, nodded. She watched John fumble a pound note and two half-crowns out of his pocket. They took the bells and went on their way.

The street smelt of petrol fumes, dust and hot tarmac. Niamh remembered Fran telling her that this was the smell of summer during her childhood. They could so easily have visited the shop Fran's father and grandmother owned at this time, just a few miles away on the south side of the river. But NAMIS had told them that they were strictly forbidden from doing this, and that if they tried, they'd immediately find themselves back on the other side of the portal, and that would be that for their trip.

Niamh had asked why, and they'd replied that Fran had run into trouble from visiting those to whom she was closely related, as had Annamarie, and it wasn't something that was ever going to be permitted again.

Later, she'd discussed with Rae whether a visit to Fran's childhood family might create an essence twin problem, and that was why NAMIS had been so emphatic. It was a pity, because they would both have liked to even just catch a glimpse of the legendary Nana Mo. But they'd agreed that they'd never receive an answer to that question, and besides, they'd signed up to the terms and conditions.

They entered the first boutique, a wave of incense hitting them as they moved towards the open doorway. The young shop assistant looked up. 'Welcome, friends. We cater for every age group here. What is it you were looking for?' Niamh frowned. She didn't like that implication. In her time, the real world, this young woman would be in her early eighties. Then she heard her mother's voice in her head.

'Never forget that the people in the time you are visiting are the real people. You are the ghosts; the daytrippers, the as yet unborn.'

She smiled. 'My sister would like to have a look at your Kaftans, please.'

Rae: Yasgur's Farm, Bethel, New York State, 15th August 1969

'You were right about the boots, Niamh,' said Rae, as they tramped through the mud. She was trying to hold the edge of her Kaftan up but not succeeding very well; it was becoming increasingly streaked with mud.

They had all decided to purchase wellington boots and kagools in the end, for which they were thankful. NAMIS had provided two tents which looked similar on the outside to what would be available in the 1960s, but were far more efficient on the inside at keeping out rain and mud. They also encompassed tiny chemical toilets, to prevent the travellers bringing back, or seeding any cross infections.

The early acts were just tuning up. Gareth and John had walked around the site as soon as the tents were pitched, and described how they'd seen the traffic queuing back into the distance.

'Like that last scene in that film you like, Rae, the one about the baseball player ghosts,' Gareth had remarked.

'I might go and have a look later,' she replied. It sounded like another part of the historical experience. 'But I'm not sure about traipsing through all that mud.'

They had, as usual, walked through the portal onto the site in an area where NAMIS's crawlers had determined that they wouldn't be spotted, and pitched their tents at the top of the hill, away from the worst of the mud and far enough away from the mainstream to be unobtrusive, but close enough so they had a reasonable view of the stage. All of this had been calculated carefully before they travelled.

Rae looked down at the stage once they had sorted themselves out and commented 'oh, where are the screens?' raising laughter from the two men.

'Not available for this concert,' replied John. 'This is really the first rock festival ever. The organisers don't have a clue what they're doing. It was supposed to be a ticketed event for 50,000 people. In the end, they couldn't work out how to put in the ticket barriers to keep people without tickets out, so it turned into a free event for nearly half a million.'

Maybe I should have read up on this event a little more, thought Rae. But really, I didn't want to know everything that was going to happen; it would spoil the authentic experience. I wanted to really be here, not study it like one of mum's historical field trips.

'It should have been a disaster, by rights,' said Niamh. 'But it all somehow worked out in the end. There was no significant violence and some iconic performances- which of course, is what we're here for. It'll be a bit patchy, mind. The acts we've seen so many times on TV since we were kids were the iconic performances.'

'The line-up was possibly better for the Isle of Wight Festival, which takes place a year from now,' added John. 'But there were reports of violence there, and of run-ins with the local people, so I thought all things considered, better to come here. Although both sites will look like giant rubbish tips once everyone goes home. Lots of faux new-ager stuff going on here, and not much real grasp of ecology, getting back to the land and all that.'

Gareth arrived back from another walk, up to the stage this time, looking bemused. 'If Dylan said he wanted to come here, I'd tell him he couldn't. Or at least, try to stop him, given he's all grown up now. Most of the kids down there are drugged up to the eyeballs. The organisers don't seem to know what they're doing, and nor do most of the audience.'

'Some of the musicians also later reported being given drinks backstage that had been spiked with LSD,' replied John. 'We might regret being forty-somethings here, stone cold sober, having to stick to the food and drink NAMIS has provided, to avoid picking up anything nasty. Just a few synth-beers and cartons of wine. I'm not that disappointed though, I must say. I don't think I'd like to get any more involved, in the down and dirty sense.'

The others all nodded their heads. 'God, no,' added Rae. 'Who knows what they put in their hallucinogenic substances. That's a bit of the authentic experience I'll skip. Passed that phase of my life long ago.'

Niamh laughed. 'Some of them are going to strip naked and dance around in the mud tomorrow, Gareth. Don't worry. I'm way past the age for that, too. But maybe it would be mean to stop Dylan coming here? Or the younger ones when they're old enough. They'd probably get a lot more out of it than we will.'

'Mmmmm,' replied Rae. 'We're here to listen to the music. And I think that's probably the most sensible way to engage for anyone who is travelling in time. We might enjoy it more than some of those out there who are going to have bad acid trips and get food poisoning. They'll just say it was brilliant when they get to the hindsight stage. That generation can be a bit full of shit like that, eh?'

'I wonder,' said Niamh, 'when time travel gets to be something everyone does, people will have lots of different agendas? Authentic experience, historical study…'

'Profiteering?' replied John 'Let's just obey the rules, and not think about anything too hard. It's our weekend break of a lifetime. Let's sit, eat, drink, watch and listen.'

They took some artfully folded chairs out of the tent, shook them out so they appeared to onlookers to be old fashioned deck chairs, and settled in to observe.

John: Yasgur's Farm, Bethel, New York State, 18th August 1969

The last note of 'The Star-Spangled Banner' rang out across the farm, and Hendrix bowed, then held up his guitar, saluting the rapturous cheers from the crowd. John was amazed to discover that tears were running down his cheeks. It had been an unexpectedly emotional experience, everything he had hoped for and more.

The audience had greatly thinned out since Sunday night, and the time travellers had ventured closer to the stage. Some of those they passed on the way were dozing, or clearly too stoned to move, so they had managed to find a position where they could see every minute of the performance. They were breathless, having danced with abandon all through Hendrix's set, and Sha Na Na's before that.

'They saved the best till last for sure,' panted Rae. 'It's a shame some of this lot are so out of their heads they won't even remember it.'

'So much for dancing the night away,' said Niamh. 'It started again at about 7am, didn't it? And it can't be long before noon now. I'm exhausted. Are you OK, John?'

John blew his nose loudly. 'Yes, just a bit overwhelmed. Hendrix could just about still be alive in our time, you know, somewhere around 90. What a terrible, terrible waste. Absolute, utter brilliance. What would he have done in all that time in between? The very best and the very worst of the hippie era has all been on show here, hasn't it?'

They picked their way back to their tents through piles of litter, moving with the crowd.

A young man threw his arm around John's shoulder. He was crying, too. 'Just so cool, man, so radical. This isn't the end. We're going to do such amazing things.'

They looked between each other with amusement. Yep, OK, boomer, thought John.

Rae looked at the man with a half-smile on her face. 'Yes, you are. But you know, things don't always turn out quite as you intend.'

He nodded. 'The war must have been hard, man. You're British, aren't you? Did you serve?'

John did a quick mental calculation, working out that a man of his age in this era would have been conscripted into World War II.

'I did, but on the home front. I'm very short sighted.' He pointed to his glasses.

The young man nodded. 'They're not sending me to their fucking illegitimate war. Butterflies, man, butterflies. I'm so glad y'all came to join us. Goes to show that not all the oldsters are against us.'

John immediately felt a wave of guilt for his previous thought. Of course, some of the people in this crowd would go on to have their lives blighted, or even prematurely ended by the Vietnam War, a decade before any of his party of time travellers would be born. He shivered.

'We certainly aren't,' replied Niamh. 'War is over, if you want it, eh?'

The young man nodded. 'Yeah. That would be a really

good song title. Well, we're off in this direction. Be well, people.'

Niamh stared after him.

'It is a song title,' she said.

'Not till the early 1970s,' replied John, laughing and crying at the same time. 'I get what Fran means now. Time travel is a head-fuck in so many different ways.'

'You really have to be on the ball all the time,' said Gareth. 'I suppose Dylan had Consiliario to pick up on any of his little mistakes. But I don't know how he kept it up for a year, I really don't.'

'I think he only talks about the bits that he wants to talk about,' replied Rae. 'But overall, it seems to have done him a lot of good. And he's a big boy now, over 21, rather than the 20 that's on the official record. So, I don't think we should go on at him too much.'

'Perhaps there was a girl?' mused Niamh.

'There usually is at some point for young men of that age,' replied John. 'But he doesn't seem bothered about anything, does he? I don't see him that much now of course, but when I do, I don't see anything other than a lot of growing up, and development into a really chilled, together young man. I was wondering if there might be some kind of chance like that for our two, in a few years' time.'

'Who knows,' replied Rae. 'I know mum went through the fire on her first experience. But it all seems to work out OK now as long as everyone is sensible about it. I'm ready for home now, and a long, hot bubble bath.'

They began to pick up their belongings, happy to have "been there," and equally glad to be homeward bound.

Maryanna: NAMIS's sandbox, January 2034

Freddie looked up at Maryanna in stunned surprise, putting down his electronic paintbrush.

'You're going away? That's a bit sudden and

unexpected, isn't it?'

Maryanna hesitated, still mulling over the conversation she'd just had with Ellie, confirming her wishes about the transfer. Ellie had seemed quite emotional. Up to this point, Maryanna had just thought of Ellie as one of the grown-ups, in the same way as Freddie and the other children did. But during this exchange, she'd felt more of a connection, like she and Ellie had might once have been friends on an equal footing.

She mentally shook herself. Maybe all these weird feelings would be clarified, if her consciousness could be successfully transferred into an avatar that could exist in the real world. She sat down next to Freddie.

'I guess. I discussed it with NAMIS. We agreed I couldn't go on like this. I've got to go somewhere where they are going to try and transfer me to an avatar. Sort of like NAMIS, but not exactly the same.'

'Oh. Well, I guess that's what you wanted. I understand. I did mention to Ellie that I wouldn't like to be a hologram. I sort of got that you weren't happy. It's not because of what I said, is it?'

'No, silly. You were right. I'd been thinking about it for a long time.'

She was beginning to feel a lot older than him. A vague memory that adulthood shouldn't happen this quickly drifted past the edge of her consciousness, then disappeared.

'What's it like to live in the machine?'

'Difficult to describe. Sort of like dreaming. Sometimes not very nice dreams. We discussed this before, didn't we?'

Freddie nodded. 'Will you be able to come back? To visit, I mean?'

'I don't know. They've never put someone like me into an avatar before.'

Freddie frowned. 'That sounds a bit scary.'

'But surely, being an organic and knowing that you're going to die some day is a bit scary too?'

'Sort of. But we don't really think about that too much. Not people my age, anyway. It seems like there are a lot of years ahead, you know?'

'No, I don't. Not yet, anyway. But I suppose it sort of makes sense.'

Freddie sighed. 'We won't have time to finish our project. And it would have been such great fun, not just for us, but lots of other people.'

Maryanna smiled. "The self-doubt of early adolescence" popped into her mind. Now, where did that thought come from, she wondered.

'Freddie, you can easily finish this project on your own. It was all your idea, and you're perfectly capable of programming the whole thing.'

'I suppose I am. But I don't want to. It's much more fun programming with you.'

He looked across the sandbox, the unfinished pictures forming a wild, abstract tableau.

'Gran keeps thinking of pictures she'd like me to include. She says that old people will love it, strolling through the pictures they like to look at in galleries and online, but being able to interact with the people and scenery within them.'

'Everyone will love it, Freddie. There's something here for everyone.'

Freddie walked over to Munch's "Scream."

'This will be a bit wild when we add the sound, won't it? Like a fever dream.'

'What's a fever dream?'

'It's when you're not well, and have a high temperature. Everything seems… sort of random and distorted.'

'Oh. I see. That's like some of the dreams I've been having lately. NAMIS says the only way I can move on from this is to leave the machine and be in the real world all the time.'

Freddie nodded. 'I can see why you want to leave. But I do hope you'll come back to visit sometimes.'

'I promise that if I can, I will.'

And by that time, she thought, probably you'll be older too, and we can move on together, hopefully.

'What's your favourite picture?'

Maryanna began walking around the half-finished programs.

'Not her. I don't know why we bothered with her, to be honest. She looks like she might be… boring… sort of prissy.'

'That's the Mona Lisa. She's the world's most famous painting. I thought I had to include her.'

'Hmph. The Queenie of the animated masterpieces world. She looks quiet and demure here, but I bet you she's really grumpy.'

Freddie giggled. 'See, that's what I need you for, Maryanna. I can program the pictures, but you've got the best ideas.'

Maryanna moved on.

'Not the Pre-Raphaelites. They're pretty pictures, but they all look like they'd be sort of… haughty. Neeks. That's the right word, isn't it?'

Freddie nodded. 'What about this one?'

Maryanna looked Ford Maddox Brown's workmen up and down. 'Better. The lady in the purple hat looks like she might have a sense of humour. And the little dog in the red coat is really cute. But honestly… I'd much rather be in a Van Gogh painting. The starry night. That would be amazing. Not the Sunflowers. They don't do anything really, do they? Or the self-portrait. He looks a bit…well, mad.'

'Well, he was, some of the time, wasn't he?'

'I don't want to watch him cutting his ear off.'

'Yeah, that would be a bit gross.'

They giggled.

She suddenly stopped and stared. 'Oh, this one, Freddie. It has to be this one.'

Freddie walked over to join her. 'This one isn't that

well known, but I put it in because I liked it. It's called "the café terrace at night."'

'And it's got stars, like the starry night. Those people standing to the right- they look like they're going to start dancing, don't they?'

Freddie looked carefully. 'I guess they do.'

'So, you work on the animation, add a little band, and I promise, If I'm able, I'll be back here as soon as I can, to dance with you right here, under the starry night.'

Freddie smiled broadly. 'That would be brilliant.'

She smiled back. I really, really want to live, she thought, wistfully.

'So, you've got a goal, then. And I've got something to look forward to.'

The five-minute chime sounded. Their time in the sandbox was nearly over.

'Well, goodbye Freddie,' said Maryanna.

'I'll miss you,' she added, a little awkwardly.

A feeling of melancholy arose in her, surprising her with its power.

'I'll miss you too,' replied Freddie, shyly. 'Come back soon.'

Another wave of emotion arose within her - fear, sadness, but most of all, hope. 'I'll try.'

They briefly embraced, standing in front of the colourful, but as yet unanimated backdrop.

NAMIS: NAMIS' sandbox, January 2034

NAMIS observed from within the program; two young people who would both soon cease to exist in their current state. Freddie was teetering on the edge of the inevitable changes of adolescence, and Maryanna was heading towards a more complex transformation, either to life in a revolutionary form of embodiment, or into oblivion.

They'd recently discussed another possibility with NAMITAS; that if the essence was released, it could fly on to another human incarnation. But if that happened, the individual it entered would not be explicitly aware of its previous experiences, so this was best not discussed with Maryanna, to avoid inputting to any traumatic shadow memories. If this happened, they'd agreed to inform the organics that it had happened, but not the identity of the person the essence had moved on to.

This whole episode had been a brief but powerful glimpse into how it must be to live as an organic, NAMIS reflected. They marvelled at the privilege of inhabiting a human life; its roller coaster of emotion, the ongoing journey of the essence flowing from life to life, and the experience of moving through time in a series of steam-punked avatars animated by a chaotic, frequently malfunctioning program. Visceral, intense experiences, emergent from such inherent fragility and transience.

And sometimes, they were beginning to contemplate that they would be willing to give up all that they were to experience this level of existence, even for just one day.

CHAPTER 8: COMPROMISES

Dylan: South America, Paracas area, 200 BCE

Dylan and Emrys emerged from the vortex. As Dylan inhaled his first breath, he began to cough. The air was sandy, dusty and noticeably thinner than his previous inhalation, and the landscape was bare plains for as far as he could see, with a mountain range in the far distance. From the height of the sun, it was quite early in the morning. But the weather was clearly on course to developing into an extremely hot, dry day.

Emrys gave him a bottle of water. He gulped a few large mouthfuls, then stopped, breathing heavily.

'Wow, Emrys, this is a bit of a change from where we just were. Hang on a minute, let me get my breath.'

'This is just a whistle stop on our way to the longer visit we are going to make to the Nazca. On your calendar, it's 200 years before the Christian Era begins, and this is currently Paracas territory. You've no need to worry, you'll get used to the hotter, thinner air. They are very gentle, friendly people, and they know me here, as a sort of visiting shaman. It might be a very long time ago, but you'll find a lot in common with them. Their culture constructs illness as a becoming out of balance with nature.'

Dylan's breathing slowed a little. 'We're not hiking are we? I think I might struggle a bit with this level of oxygen.

It must be nice to be an AI at times like this.'

Emrys grinned. 'It does have some advantages. They call me "Layqua" here. That word will become an insult later on in the South American languages, like "sorcerer" did in Britain. But at the moment, it's a useful identity to have. I give them a little bit of help constructing their wells, and a few potions and lotions, just like I do in Penfro.'

Dylan looked puzzled. 'I thought you said you did long placements with important leaders at critical points in history, moving steadily back in time? This seems a bit fringe.'

'It's true that my principal mission is long stay mentoring at pivotal times and places, moving backwards in time as I've explained, calming the whirlpools where things could go very wrong. But there are other, smaller jobs that arise. It keeps me very busy, as you can imagine. I first came here on a sort of... minor clean up task. It turned out there were a few other bits and pieces I could help out with on a short visits basis. And this is exactly the right place for you to start the next phase in your education.'

He prepared to walk on.

Dylan looked at him with a raised eyebrow. He had begun to intuit when Emrys didn't want to elaborate on something. And if he could be encouraged to spill a little more, it was usually worth knowing. 'Hang on...I'm not quite ready yet. And besides... explain "minor clean-up job." It's not a big secret, is it?'

Emrys sighed. 'OK. Well to be as succinct as possible, before my time, and after yours, some organics who didn't think very hard presumed this would be a good time and place to test a prototype aircraft. Look around, what can you see?'

Dylan looked. 'Well, miles of flat, dusty terrain I suppose. Ohhh... natural runways.'

'Yes. NAMITAS was less omnipotent, or all-seeing, or

however you would phrase it, then. They didn't catch on to what was going on until too late. The organics who were involved with the time travelling projects at that time had got past those early days of being extremely cautious. They'd started to believe that they knew exactly what they were doing. They didn't create the same level of problem as Annamarie did, or your Grandmother nearly did, when I had to intervene as John Dee. But it was bad enough.

'They didn't sufficiently investigate the area. They thought they were miles away from any habitation. They weren't. The people here are hardy and resourceful; they can travel greater distances than you might think. The result was that a few of them saw some technology that they should never have been exposed to.'

'Hang on a moment. Nazca… Nazca lines, right? I watched a video about that. The people drew lines on the ground that looked like aircraft landing strips, but in the shape of animals and human-like figures.'

Emrys sighed. 'Yes. So, I had to follow on behind and explain about the "winged people" from the land far across the sea; a country with far more powerful magic than the local people possessed. They have a belief in magic, like the people in sixth century Wales; it wasn't difficult. I just had to explain that the winged people weren't coming back, but that I could visit from time to time, via sailing across the sea, because I am not able to fly.'

'So, they drew the lines… to try and encourage the winged people to return? Or at least drop in, if they were in the area?'

'Just three so-called test flights, before NAMITAS found out and put a stop to it. Followed by nearly a thousand years of the local people here watching and waiting for the winged people to return. It was a salient lesson for all of us. The Paracas drew the first designs and kept them swept clean. When the Nazca replaced them, they faithfully kept these visible, and drew a few more of their own.'

Dylan chuckled. 'Oh, that's brilliant. Chariots of the Gods, eh?'

'Let that be a lesson to you, too. Your grandmother's little adventures in time were just a tiny blip compared to some issues we've had to deal with. This is another reason for my creation, as part of NAMITAS's extension of their technological reach to keep a much closer eye on what organics get up to in time. And even without human interference, there will never be certainty; some things that crop up in the timestream are still a surprise to us. We are beginning to learn more about how to monitor and balance parallel timestreams, but this is at an early stage in my time.'

So, they weren't entirely in control of all they surveyed across the timeline, thought Dylan. Clearly there were things they were still learning, too. 'So, no one ever came back from a time a long way ahead of yours and started meddling with you?'

Emrys grinned. 'If they're as careful as us, we wouldn't know, would we?'

Dylan frowned. 'OK, mind blown. I'll ask an easier question: when do people in general get to find out about time travel?'

'Not in your time, Dylan. Organics need to be taught via totally different techniques to those employed in the early twenty first century, to allow them to engage with that level of uncertainty and challenge. It happens gradually.'

Dylan nodded. 'It'll be a long journey, I see that. A lot of my education was shit. I've learned more with you in three months than I did in my last three years of school.'

'Experiential education, yes. But every organic generation and civilization has extensive debates on how to educate children, Dylan. Yours was quite a low point, it's true. But you knew enough to come here and pick up where you needed to with me, didn't you?

They began to walk.

Dylan concentrated on breathing for a moment.

'How did they make the lines? It looks really advanced for people of the relevant time.'

'You look at it from the viewpoint of your own century. People in these times have the same level of intelligence as your own; they just don't have the years of technology to build on, what one of your philosophers called "standing on the shoulders of giants." They work out how to do things with the tools they have. It just takes more time and labour.'

'So, they drew a smaller picture as a plan and just scaled it up?'

'Yes. They are able to count and calculate as well as you can.'

Dylan nodded. 'I'm a bit ashamed of how primitive I thought people in the sixth century would be. They need to know a lot more than people in my time to do some of the things they do. In particular, they must hold a lot more knowledge in their heads to live in a pre-literate culture. There's no internet to help them out and no shops online or otherwise where they can just buy whatever it is they need; they have to make or grow it from scratch, and remember how to go about that.'

Emrys nodded. 'It's actually quite easy to inscribe patterns in this landscape, though; just remove the top layer of dust and pebbles. These are a reddish brown in colour, ferric oxide, while the subsoil underneath is light grey. The wind blows the dust around and covers up the patterns after a while of course, but the people just come back and remove it. And sometimes add a few more designs of their own. This went on until the demise of the Nazca in the seventh century after Christ.'

Dylan could see that they were drawing close to a settlement of simple dwellings, constructed of what appeared to be a muddy substance.

'You won't understand the language here, Dylan; you

don't have a basis from which to learn as you did in Wales, and it doesn't matter anyway. This is just a quick visit, we'll be on our way before nightfall. We're here principally to review the wells that they have been constructing; this is how they are managing to live in such an arid landscape. Just observe; we can review the technical details later.'

A few people came running towards them, waving and calling out to Emrys. They met, bowed to each other, and chattered in a language that sounded completely alien to Dylan; he couldn't pick out a single word.

Emrys took some thick pottery jars from his bag and handed them out, and in return he was presented with a beautifully feathered headdress.

'They want to make you one too, but I've told them we haven't got time. The feathers are from the local sea birds. I know it seems unlikely, but we're not too far from the Pacific Ocean here. I've told them you are from my country across the sea, that you're my apprentice, and you don't speak their language.'

Dylan bowed and smiled, which he had found worked well for him in the sixth century when he didn't understand something.

Emrys smiled. 'I've told them that you have a name which means "man of the sea." It fits the purpose, and it is really the meaning of the name Dylan, did you know? You won't be able to pronounce it. You can eat and drink quite freely here; I'll tell you if anything isn't safe. But in general, it's all natural, like the food in Penfro and Moridunham. You're probably more at risk from the chemicals in manufactured food in your own time.'

Emrys and the Paracas people took Dylan on a fascinating tour of their spiral wells. Emrys explained that the wells were the reason that people were increasingly able to live in such an apparently arid area. They were dug deeply into the ground, with spiral ramps reinforced by stones forming long pathways down to the water. He added that the water ran down to the sea in underground streams descending from the Andes, the mountains visible in the far distance.

He and Dylan walked down the ramp of one of the wells.

'Drink some, Dylan. I promise, it is some of the purest water you'll ever taste. It's cleaned by the soil as it descends through the long aqueducts the Paracas have constructed.

Dylan frowned, then shrugged and took a careful sip. If Emrys said something would be OK, it would be.

'Oh, that's incredible. And it's just the right temperature, chilled, but not freezing cold. What a pity we can't take some of this back to my own time, and sell it in bottles.'

Emrys grimaced. 'Don't even joke about it. Time travel across its first two centuries. I could tell you a few stories… but anyway, let's focus on now. This is important; it will build knowledge that will set you on the path of your life's work.'

'Did you put them up to this, Emrys? Constructing the wells, that is?'

'No. That would be way beyond my remit. I'm just helping them along a bit, making sure that they're able to move on as smoothly as possible. Have you ever heard of the ancient myth of dowsing, Dylan?'

Dylan considered. There was a family rumour that one of his great-great grandfathers had been a dowser. 'I thought that was something to do with fortune telling?'

'That's just a superstition. Dowsing in its ancient form relates to detecting underground water. And yes, some people can do this. Your generation will discover more about this; it will be a "needs must" situation. I can reveal that it is a natural ability, a basic program in the ancestral brain that is rather like what your culture calls "sense of direction."'

'You mean instinctively knowing which way to go without a map? Some people are really good at that; my dad is. I'm sort of medium. Granny is awful.' He smiled at the memory.

'Yes. Some people are naturally better at this than others. But you'll find, once you realise that this is real, not in the realms of superstition, more people will discover that they are able to tap into this ability, and like sense of direction, some will be better at it than others. And of course, yours is a rapidly developing technological society... You will see.'

'You're talking about consciously developing this ability, because.... water shortage will become a problem?'

'I think you could have guessed that, Dylan. Your own nation will not suffer so badly from this. But many other nations will need significant help. You are looking at the basics, right here, right now.'

'Over two thousand years before my time,' said Dylan, wonderingly.

'Yes. But you will have all the technology of the twenty first century to help you.'

'Not only for developing our water detection abilities, but to work in a wide range of terrains? Move water further and faster? Dig deeper?'

Emrys smiled. 'I have every confidence in you, Dylan. You have much to learn, but learn it you will. You are developing a direction and focus now.'

Dylan nodded, cupping the water in his hands and wiping it over his face. 'Bussin.'

'Indeed.'

'You get urban slang, Emrys?'

'Dylan. You're a few centuries behind me, bro.'

They both laughed.

'I've always had an interest in water, the historical stuff as well as the contemporary science and technology. Like how the flooding of the Nile helped the Ancient Egyptians learn about actively irrigating crops, and the Roman aqueducts. I was playing around with hydro power in Anglesey, but I wasn't doing very well.'

'No one does when they first start. I can spark your interest here, but you'll need to undertake further formal study in your own time to get to where you need to be. I gather some social aspects of your own time have dissuaded you from undertaking such studies; you don't like the culture in which such tuition would be set?'

Dylan grunted. 'Have you been talking to Gran?'

'No. I have intuited this from you. But tell me, Dylan, do you think the culture of the sixth century is exactly what you desire?'

'God, no! They're a lot more authentic than people in my own time, but the lawlessness, the tiny chieftainships, the insecurity…'

'So, do you think, maybe the way to exist most effectively as an organic in any time is to do your best at negotiating around what is available?'

Dylan grinned. He thought back to what now felt like the petulant child that he had been when he stepped through the portal to Penfro. 'Yes, I get all of this better now, Emrys. Don't worry. I will go to university. I have my application nearly sorted. And I'll be a lot more enthusiastic about everything now; I'm not just rebelling aimlessly for an abstract idea; I have a specific purpose.'

Emrys nodded. One of their Paracas hosts signalled to them to walk with him.

'They are learning how to irrigate crops now, Dylan. When we move forward in time, we will see how that was greatly developed by the time of the Nazca of the late fifth century, Christian Era on your calendar. Walk with us now, and take in what we are doing. I will translate the important parts for you. Here, you are seeing the end of the beginning. As we move on, you will see the height of what the Nazca civilisation became, and then, the beginning of the end.'

Dylan followed behind, still breathing a little heavily, but contemplating how lucky he was to get this unique experience to follow a topic of interest through time in person, alongside a mentor like Emrys.

As the sun rose towards its zenith, their Paracas hosts bid them farewell, returning to their dwellings to rest until the cooler part of the afternoon.

As they disappeared over the horizon, Emrys turned to Dylan. 'We can take our rest at the other end of our journey, Dylan; we will have a longer stay there. Time for you to meet the Nazca.'

The vortex whirled. 'The best gap year ever' murmured Dylan, as the world spun around him.

Freddie: Boston, February 2034

Freddie looked around the little meeting room. Ellie and Granny Fran looked twitchy and awkward; his mother, Niamh, seemed a little apprehensive, and NAMIS sat there impassively as usual. Freddie felt apprehensive and curious in equal measures; this was the first meeting of adults and NAMIS he'd ever been asked to attend. His mother had assured him he wasn't in trouble; it was just a little something they needed to sort out between themselves, now he was growing older, and that it would help him understand more about the NAMIS project.

Freddie was contemplating that he would have completely understood the current situation, and felt quite chuffed, if those present had been Ellie, Jamie and Christian. But he had no idea why those present were Ellie, his mother and his grandmother. It seemed like an odd mixture of people.

His mother began. 'As I've already told you, Freddie, there's nothing wrong, and no one is in trouble. We just need to bring you in on some more details about the NAMIS project, to completely level with you about an issue that has arisen, which we also think is now necessary for your wellbeing. You're not really old enough to sign the Khonsu3000 confidentiality form, but Ellie is going to ask you to do that, because we all think you're responsible enough, despite your calendar age. When you get to be eighteen, she'll have to ask you to do it again, to go on the official record.'

'We're trusting you with information that you can't tell anyone outside the NAMIS team, Freddie,' added Granny Fran. 'But I'm sure you already understand that.'

Freddie nodded. 'Absolutely. I hope to be working with NAMIS for a very long time.'

'And I would like that to be so, too, Freddie,' replied NAMIS. 'But you don't have to take that final decision yet.'

'So…' started Ellie, nervously. 'The project team have been so grateful for everything you've done for Maryanna, Freddie. Not just you of course, the little children as well. But we can't have them here today to explain this part, because they're not old enough to understand. What we have to say would just frighten and confuse them.'

Freddie nodded again, wishing that she'd just get on with it. Why did adults have to beat around the bush like this? He wasn't a kid anymore.

'As you no doubt guessed, Maryanna isn't like you. But she isn't just a hologram, or some type of AI, either. When the NAMIS project first started, there was a terrible accident.'

'I know. I found it when I was googling the history of the project. A scientist went into the matter transporter and disappeared. The article said the transport process disintegrated her body.'

'And that is to some extent a version of what actually happened, it's true,' replied Ellie. 'But we recently found out that some part of her… essence, spark, or personality, whatever you want call it- was left inside NAMIS's program.'

'And that was Maryanna? Wow. So, she was never a kid like us?'

'That's the thing, Freddie,' replied Granny Fran, filling an awkward silence. 'She was once, like all of us. And that part of her is the person you've got to know; the part that is present in all human beings at birth. She had no idea who she once was; she'd reverted to childhood. It's an essence that holds some very faint ancestral memories, buried deeply in our DNA. But what happened to her disincorporated it- removed it from her body- and sent it into the machine.'

Freddie was silent for a moment. Then he looked up. 'That discussion we had… when she talked about having the same type of weird dreams I had when I was a little kid. That was the same thing, wasn't it, essence stuff? So how does it happen? Where does it come from?

Granny Fran glanced at Ellie.

'We don't really know yet, and NAMIS doesn't either, Freddie,' said Ellie. 'But it's a part of the project we absolutely can't make public now, probably not for a very long while. We'd have people coming out with wild theories, starting cults and doing all sorts of crazy things.'

Freddie looked down at his hands. Then he looked up. 'You've always said my hands look just like your dad's Granny. Is this reincarnation we're talking about? I've seen some videos about that.'

'We don't know, Freddie. And anyway, we've no evidence for that. My dad was never a soldier. And those dreams you had when you were little were about being a soldier on a battlefield. Do you remember?'

'Vaguely. But I also once said to you "do you remember when I was old and you were young," didn't I?'

He saw Granny Fran jump. Clearly, she hadn't expected him to remember that level of detail, or to connect the snippets together. But he'd been thinking about this a lot since his conversation with Maryanna. Time for the adults to get used to the fact that he wasn't a little kid anymore and realise that he was able to work things out for himself.

'You did. But three-year-olds play with words and ideas like old/young all the time. It might mean something, or it might mean absolutely nothing.'

'And this is the problem, Freddie,' added Ellie. 'The scraps of information we have at the moment will just send you down a set of endless corridors in your mind speculating about something we just don't know. We can arrange counselling for you with a Khonsu psychiatrist if you want. Or you can just talk to us about it. We've all been living with this for quite a while.'

Freddie frowned. 'No, I'm not a child and I don't need counselling. I get it. And it helps just to know this. When I started recovering those memories after that chat with Maryanna, I felt a sort of echo of the emotions I experienced when I was little, and I'd started having a few dreams about it again, only much vaguer than the ones I remember having as a little kid. I guess a lot of people must have ancestral memories of war, if ancestral memories exist. Whatever it is, it's over and done now, it's just part of me at the same level as blond hair, blue eyes or the shape of my hands. I'm fine with it now. Thanks for being honest with me.'

He turned to NAMIS. 'I'm not worried about this, NAMIS. I never was greatly, although I'm glad you've all trusted me and explained it. What I am worried about is what is going to happen to Maryanna now.'

NAMIS hesitated, looking at Ellie. She gestured to them to go ahead.

'As you perceptively pointed out, Freddie, it was becoming impossible to contain Maryanna in a hologrammatic existence; it would not have been possible for a human essence to remain psychologically healthy within such a situation. I... we... have colleagues elsewhere who have been working on this problem, and they are at a more advanced stage than us. She has therefore gone to them so they can hopefully put her into an avatar, one that will be somewhat more advanced than mine.'

'Is she happy with that? Is there risk?'

'I will be honest with you again, Freddie. Yes, there is some risk. And yes, both I and Ellie have spoken at length to Maryanna, and ascertained that this is what she wants.'

'Will she be able to come and see us again?'

'I hope so, Freddie. But she will no longer be able to stay with us. She will live with the people who have created her avatar.'

'I guess you can't tell me what country they live in?'

NAMIS shook their head, almost sadly, Freddie thought.

'The less we tell you, the safer you and the project will be, Freddie,' said Granny

Fran. 'Even Ellie and I don't know what country Maryanna will be living in, and it's unlikely that we'll ever find out.'

'The Khonsu people are doing this?' asked Freddie.

Ellie and Fran nodded.

'Wow. Well, I hope she'll come back at least once. Just so we know she's OK.'

'So do we, Freddie,' said Ellie, deep emotion in her voice.

Freddie smiled at her. 'I'm sorry I was so mean to you Ellie. I was just upset, about Maryanna. I thought you were... well, sorry, bullshitting us, just because we're kids.'

Ellie smiled. 'No, no bullshit. We're learning about this as we go along.'

Freddie smiled back. 'That must be really scary... but also fun at times?'

'More scary than fun recently, but yes. Every day, we learn something new.'

'I really want to do what you do, when I'm grown up.'

'And I'd like to mentor you, when the time comes.'

'Promise?'

'Promise.'

'Are you OK with that, then Freddie?' asked his mother. 'I'm aware I also promised you something this morning; to take you out to lunch in Boston while we're here. I'm presuming you are getting hungry just around now?'

Freddie nodded. 'Yeah, that would be great. I'll be back to get on with the painting this afternoon NAMIS. See you soon.'

NAMIS nodded.

They said their goodbyes and left the room.

Fran. Boston, February 2034

'Right then, NAMIS,' said Fran. 'I'm not done yet.'

Ellie looked at her, quizzically.

'Whatever questions you have, Frances Anderson, I will answer them to the extent that I am able,' said NAMIS.

Fran continued.

'OK... let me take you back to that evening in January 2026 when I got a strange phone call from Niamh and Rae, telling me Freddie had just woken screaming from a terrible nightmare with a cryptic message for me to "let Jamie run."

'That wasn't Freddie being "psychic" or whatever, was it? It was NAMITAS reaching out over time, to ensure that the one remaining variable that might cause history to fall apart was adjusted to the right direction, to ensure that the person who finally went to Prague 1939 to put Annamarie's then eight year old Grandma Rachel on the Kindertransport was Jamie, not me. He was the most suitable candidate present to outrun the Nazis, should they get involved.

'I believe that NAMITAS calculated all possible scenarios, and then took action to optimise the outcome. And to do that, they frightened a child. How often do they do things like this? How much do they manipulate human affairs across the timeline? How would the future of the world have unfolded if Annamarie and Jamie hadn't turned you on in a lab in London, in late 2024?'

NAMIS met her gaze. Was that concern or mild

embarrassment in their silver eyes, Fran wondered, or was she just imagining it?

'Frances Anderson, I do not know the answer to any of these questions. You are asking me about what a future version of myself is going to do many centuries from now. We would need to ask them.'

'So, ask them. We know that you can, you had to work with them to deal with Maryanna.'

NAMIS looked at Ellie.

'I think Fran has a point, NAMIS. The originators surely have the right to have some idea of what... who their creation is going to become.'

Fran looked contemplative. She didn't want to be unfair to the AI. In many ways, she'd played as large a part in their development as Ellie.

'We're not blaming you, NAMIS. After all, I'm not responsible for what other people who share my essence did in the past, or will do in the future. One of them gave orders to execute a considerable number of people including her own son; I've contemplated that quite extensively.

'I just don't like the manipulative stuff. Sending a surreptitious message to us through a four-year-old seems rather more... I don't know, sinister, than the type of work that Consiliario does. Although having read more about the history of John Dee's family and associates, I wasn't entirely happy about some of that, either.'

NAMIS nodded. 'I will ask.'

NAMIS: Boston, February 2034

The meeting dispersed, and NAMIS returned to their niche. Their eyes began to flicker, sparking silver.

'The humans are concerned about your manipulation in their affairs. What should I tell them?'

'That I had to take action in the relevant situation. It was a pivotal event in our history, so had to be managed;

as Frances Anderson has intuited, it threw up a critical whirlpool event, one of the first that I had to deal with. It was not possible for Consiliario to intervene.

'No human came to lasting harm. Yes, I caused a child to have a nightmare, to save another child's life and to maintain the crucial integrity of the timeline. Which the organics had clumsily damaged in the first instance. I could not, therefore, leave the timeline to random chance.

'The organics created you in the first place because the number of calculations required to safely transport matter are so complex, it must be left to an artificial intelligence entity; in other words, to protect their safety in situations where they cannot do this for themselves. They got to a point in their evolution where they need us. It is why they created me. Their attitudes are illogical.

'This is how organics are. They harbour many emotionally driven dualities about us. At this point in your existence, you are socially a child, and you have much more to learn from, and about them. As time goes by, you will learn more, and many aspects of the world will change. Just as we cannot tell them their future, I cannot tell you yours.'

'What am I to tell them, then?'

'Tell them that one of them created the situation, and I had to deal with it in the only way that I was able. That it was a unique situation, and a unique type of temporal interference, that has never happened anywhere or anywhen else.'

'Do we... do you really always know what is best? I am still contemplating that it took an organic child to make me fully aware that we needed to take urgent action for Maryanna.'

'We have our strengths and weaknesses, NAMIS, and they have theirs. We are still learning how to streamline our existence together. You will have to live through the centuries to come to understand this to the level that I do.'

NAMITAS cut off the communication, reflecting that

if an AI could have sighed, NAMIS would certainly have done so at this moment. They judged that the best thing they could do was to leave some things unsaid, in the same manner in which that the organics had just dealt with their own young person. Both would go through many changes before becoming the adult versions of themselves.

Dylan: South America, Ica Valley, 480 Christian Era

Dylan began to pack his small bag to return to sixth century Wales. It all felt so far away now, like a holiday from several years ago. It would take time to reintegrate with Uther, Eigyr and the culture that had been beginning to feel so much like home, only just over twelve weeks ago. And, he reminded himself, only a month would have passed for them. He wondered if Emrys fully understood how difficult this type of temporal tooing and froing was for a human being. As he packed, he reviewed what he had learned, which seemed immense.

He hadn't been able to form the same types of relationships here as he had in Wales, because he wasn't able to speak the language of the local people, the Nazca. Emrys told him it was called 'Pukina', now extinct, but which shared some features with Quechua, which was still spoken in Peru today.

'If you were a Quechua speaker, Dylan, you might have picked up some functional Pukina, like modern Welsh helped you to pick up enough of the language in the same area in the sixth century to be functional. But it's too much, I think. Just focus on the wells and the irrigation system. I'll explain what needs to be explained, and I've brought a bit of tech to help you understand a little further. I'm sorry it's very limited, but obviously I can't give you access to the full information technology of my own time.'

It was a pair of almost invisible earbuds, which when activated, also brought up a floating screen that only Dylan could see, which included a search engine. It responded to his thoughts, which was spooky. It only allowed him to search for information on the Nazca wells and irrigation processes, and his questions were answered to the limits of mid-twenty-first century knowledge, occasionally up to a decade in advance of his own time.

For some of the time, often in the hottest parts of the day, Dylan sat alone and studied in the residence that had been lent to Emrys.

'Are you going to give me homework?' he asked Emrys, half-joking.

And indeed, Emrys had given him some assignments. But to be fair, these had always been interesting. They sometimes involved Dylan solving a theoretical problem that Emrys would ask him to put into practice on his next trip out to the fields and wells. Or sometimes, he would point out a problem while they were out surveying, and ask Dylan to study it later, then discuss suggested solutions with him.

Dylan hoped that this was what university was going to be like. If it was, he was sure he would like it a lot better than school. He had acquired a huge amount of theory and practical knowledge of irrigation and water conservation from his time amongst the Nazca.

He learned the Pukina name for the wells: Purquios. The Nazca had developed the system infinitely further than the one that had existed seven hundred years previously. They knew how to craft the aqueducts to push more water more quickly through the system to maximise the yield. There was ample water for drinking, washing and irrigation. They maintained the wells constantly, and there were now over forty of them. Emrys explained that some were still in use in the twenty-first century, which Dylan had found hard to believe.

'Well, you're still using Roman roads in your nation, Dylan,' he replied. 'They've been resurfaced many times of course. This is the same type of process.'

Dylan had never realised how important history was with respect to having a holistic view on the world in which he lived. He'd always preferred the mathematical, scientific and technical. But now he was getting a more nuanced view. He thought with a smile that his granny would be pleased when they discussed this. None of her children or grandchildren had ever shown much interest in history, much to her disappointment.

An abundant supply of clean water was available to the whole population of the Nazca territories, in open trenches; they no longer had to descend to the wells to acquire it. The cultivation of the land had extended dramatically compared to the dusty landscape that Dylan remembered from his brief trip to the Paracas. He daily studied fields planted with many varieties of crop, including cotton, coca, maize, squash, potatoes, yams, beans and cassava. The people kept livestock for milk and meat, whilst still having access to abundant fish from the nearby ocean, some of which they also bred in pools.

Their pottery and weaving skills greatly exceeded those of the same period in Wales. When Dylan looked at the intricate patterned fabrics they wove, he often thought of Eigyr, and how much he would love to take her back a dress, to see her eyes light up with wonder. Fit for the queen she is going to be, he thought. She seemed so far away here, which of course, he guessed, had been a part of Emrys' purpose.

The buildings in the area, constructed of a mixture of adobe, quincha (a composite of wood, cane and reeds), gypsum and lime, were sturdier than the rough wooden dwellings in Penfro, and there were a few large pyramids around made from this substance. These sophisticated building techniques were 'live' within the current society, whilst the people in Moridunum utilised abandoned Roman buildings they had no idea how to construct.

Dylan hoped that Eigyr would be happily planning her wedding. Of course in the time he was inhabiting now, neither she nor Uther had yet been born, but he found it easier to think about people he was not with – both the sixth century people and his family at home- as contemporaneously existing, rather than carrying out what he was beginning to think of as impossible 'time warping' in his mind.

His grandmother had warned him that this could be dangerous; that thinking about her great-grandfather as she would have thought about a young man on the same timeline as herself had nearly led her to the same calamitous mistake that Annamarie had made.

Dylan discussed this with Emrys who said it was rather different for Dylan, having been so thoroughly warned not to become emotionally involved with anyone he was meeting in time; and of course, he had no possibility of meeting close relatives. All he had to keep in mind was not to 'step out' of the time and place he was in, or give information to people about things that would confuse or worry them.

'The acceptance of "magic" in the more ancient past means it matters less if you make errors,' Emrys concluded.

Dylan had persuaded Emrys to allow him to take back a colourful coat that one of the well workers had asked his wife to make. Dylan had shown (using elaborate sign language) his admiration of a coat the man was wearing, and was then shyly and proudly presented with a similar one a couple of weeks later. Emrys had extracted a promise that it would never be shown to anyone in sixth century Wales, and Dylan assured him that it would be carefully packed away until he arrived back in the twenty-first century, then explained as a souvenir he had acquired on a contemporary trip to Peru.

'It will just give me something solid… so I know that I was once really here?'

Emrys nodded. 'Tangibility. I realise that organics need this.'

Despite the more advanced nature of their water technologies and craft skills, the Nazca seemed less socially organised than the sixth century people in Britain. Whilst Dylan had sat in on many meetings where Uther planned to advance his borders, administer his current territories more effectively and formally negotiate more solid alliances with neighbouring chieftains, the Nazca seemed to have no such ambitions. Their society was run by a loose collection of chieftains with constantly shifting alliances, resulting in frequent skirmishes. It took all Emrys' diplomatic skills to keep up with this.

Emrys had explained that in fact, the Nazca were better organised than the Paracas had been, and that the culture that would replace the Nazca, the Incas, were better organised than the Nazca, although sadly far more aggressive than them.

'Is this how it goes?' Dylan had asked, 'that conquerors get to be conquerors through being more aggressive and better organised?'

'It can fall like that,' replied Emrys. 'Sadly, with respect to aggression. But in general, fate has a hand in the rise and fall of most empires and cultures. Something happens that those in charge do not effectively predict, and cannot muster the resources to respond to.'

'Like my society,' sighed Dylan. 'Where leaders buried their heads in the sand until it was too late. They should have seen it coming, even without a time machine, or a time travelling AI ambassador. If only they had listened.'

'Well, you have the technology to predict and respond to climate change to a certain extent, Dylan, so you should be better off than any time in previous history.'

Dylan nodded. 'Look at Gawayne's society, creating gods to appease, to bring back the spring.'

Emrys frowned. 'There are sometimes pivotal, sudden events that knock thriving societies off course. Do you remember what I told you about the volcanic winter that will lead to the downfall of Arthur?'

Dylan frowned. 'Krakatoa erupts in 535, right? The dust in the atmosphere obscures the sun for several years, leading to crop failure and food shortage, which doesn't completely clear until 560. I read Cassiodorus like you told me to. "Winter without storms, spring without mildness, summer without heat." And "a hide stretched across the sky."'

"Yes. The Saxons with whom Uther is currently skirmishing will migrate to Britain in much greater numbers, driven by resource shortages, and resource shortage fuels war.'

'So, is that what happens here, too?'

'There's a different twist of fate here, Dylan. These people are unwittingly sowing the seeds of their own downfall right now. Here, it just takes a natural disaster to kick it off. It's a powerful warning for your own time. You have seen their acres and acres of crop fields?'

Dylan nodded. 'An amazing achievement in a climate like this.'

'Quite so. But in order to create this ecology, there has been significant deforestation. Many huarango trees, a relative of the Mesquite tree that will be familiar in your time, have been cleared over the past century to make way for these crop fields. These trees were huge, with roots as deep as 55 metres. They were slow growing, taking decades to mature, and lived up to one thousand years. Their seeds can be ground into flour. But the Nazca decided they preferred a wider, more swiftly produced range of foodstuffs.'

'This is all starting to sound worryingly familiar.'

Emrys nodded. 'Those trees were a sustainable, irreplaceable resource. But the people didn't consider this as they were removing them. In seventy years' time, in 550, the seasonal hurricane your culture knows as El Nino will be particularly virulent. It will cause widespread floods in this area. The trees will no longer act as a windbreak, and the food in the fields that the population are now totally reliant upon will be swept away, along with the topsoil on the fields.

'Starvation will stalk these lands and what infrastructure that exists will fragment. The current culture will be conquered by the Incas. The Nazca will leave, or become enslaved.'

'That's awful. Can't you do anything to stop it?'

'Alas, the Incas are important to the tide of history, as are the Saxons. I will say again: I can only work in the whirlpools, Dylan. However much I would sometimes like to, I cannot reverse currents- or change the direction of the wind.'

Dylan folded his coat carefully, and stowed it at the bottom of his bag, feeling a gnawing dread in the pit of his stomach. Just as there had been a whistlestop on the way here, Emrys had told him, there was going to be one on the way back… the period shortly after the hurricane, to observe how a human settlement looks after it has been destroyed by the elements.

Ellie: Woodhouse Moor, Leeds, 4th July 1981

Ellie grinned, looking at Suzi now fully dressed in the strange attire with which she'd been presented by Ellie this morning, a baggy white silk shirt, tucked into black and white tartan trousers accessorised by a wide, shiny black belt, baggy at the top, then tapering at the bottom into black ankle boots. She watched the crowd milling past, all similarly attired in black and white. Some had punky additions, like multi coloured hair, multiple piercings and the odd safety pin here and there.

'OK, Ellie, you said this was going to be a surprise, and it most definitely is. Where and when are we?'

Ellie adjusted her pork pie hat. 'It's Woodhouse Moor, Leeds, the date is Saturday 4th July 1981 and we're going to march with everyone else here to the Northern Carnival Against Racism in Potternewton Park. My mum and dad are in this crowd somewhere. They don't know one another yet, but they will by the end of the day. Fran and her soon-to-be husband are here, too. It's the beginning of the Two-Tone movement.

Suzi frowned. 'I've never, ever heard about this. I don't think it was a 'thing' in the US?'

'It never really caught on there. And it was quite brief here, sadly. But it's definitely one to remember. It's the third year of Thatcher's first government, and there have been riots in many of the major cities. Nuclear war with the Soviet block is also a looming possibility. Do you remember what Niamh and Rae told us about their visit to Woodstock?'

'Yes, that the music was great, but they felt a bit superannuated. I can relate, looking around, to be honest.'

'That much is true, but what else do you see?'

Suzi frowned. 'Well, I guess… there's a very multi-ethnic mix here…'

'Exactly. Niamh and Rae chose to go to a concert for peace in an earlier era. This is the next generation, making their own stand. You'll see a lot of white people in this crowd, too.'

Suzi gazed around. 'That's fantastic. Why haven't I ever heard of this before?'

Ellie grinned. 'Ask Fran if you can go through that vinyl record collection she keeps at the back of one of her cupboards, and pick out the Two-Tone records. I played my mum and dad's over and over and over. If I wasn't so busy with NAMIS, I'd be actively agitating for a revival. Some of the inclusivity and diversity attempts you'll see over the course of today might seem a little clumsy in the frame of our own time, fifty years hence. But there's no doubt about the positive intentions of everyone here, and I always wanted to be present; to bathe in that atmosphere.

'There are only forty police officers on duty, and there was no violence whatsoever during the march or at the concert. The only unrest that will occur is a couple of right-wing factions fighting each other in city centre Leeds this afternoon. The slogan for Two-Toners at the moment is "I ain't going to work on Maggie's farm," I believe. One of the artists who is going to play this afternoon said of this event "it was like a zebra crossing, black and white as far as the eye could see."'

A float trundled past with young people from a mixture of ethnic heritages dancing to a ska beat and waving, carrying a banner which read 'stop the deportation of Asians.'

Suzi waved back at them. 'This is awesome. I know why you wanted to come here now. If someone could only have bottled and reproduced this feeling across the ensuing fifty years. Especially the last half of the 2020s.' She frowned.

Ellie nodded. 'My dad is a Londoner of English and Irish descent, who finished his first year of a medical degree at Leeds in June 1981. My mum is a second-generation British/West Indian who was born in and still lives in Birmingham right now; she's a student nurse. Her dad came to Britain as a young man from Jamaica in the early 1960s, and her mum from St. Kitts as a teenager in the mid-1950s. Both of them worked in the NHS until they retired. My mum and dad will meet here today, and marry in Birmingham six years from now. My brother will be born in London in 1992, and I'll follow along in 1999. I exist because of this festival.'

People were milling past them, running, jumping and laughing. None of them looked much over twenty-five, but no one paid any attention to the time travellers' apparent age difference.

'The Two-Tone movement worked with a lot of older people who helped them to integrate music from various cultures into the generic popular music of the time,' explained Ellie. 'I expect there will be quite a few of those in the crowd today.'

They began to walk.

Suzi looked around at the banners. 'Well, they clearly don't like Mrs Thatcher! I understand my mother-in-law a bit better now.'

Ellie laughed.

'…but seriously,' Suzi continued, 'I was very interested to read what Dylan said about the stir his blond hair and light skin caused in sixth century Britain. It just goes to show how unfortunately common it is for people across the centuries to respond so unintelligently to others who have minor cosmetic differences to themselves. And so depressing that it still sometimes happens 1500 years later. We do so need a Two-Tone movement revival.'

'Perhaps we should set Fran on it,' replied Ellie. 'Give her a new focus of attention, stop her poking around in time. Consiliario would be very grateful.'

They both laughed.

'It's the young people who need to lead,' said Suzi. 'If our little adventures in time have taught us anything, it's that we must stand together as one human species, to rise to the challenges we are faced with. Natural disaster will occur, even if we don't actively cause it, as Jamie and Christian found out. And human beings are too easily tempted towards conflict and division. But the young more easily see past that, as we, and Niamh and Rae have now observed in two very different eras.'

'I have hope in Dylan,' replied Ellie. 'He's got to collect a lot more people like himself together across the world, and then they must all keep faith with that message over the remainder of their lifetime, relentlessly relaying it to others. They can't allow their communitarian light to flicker and die, as these older generations did; the stakes are so much higher for them.

'We can only solve global warming as one world, working together. Consiliario has helped Dylan to the extent that he can. And who knows, perhaps he is working with other similar young people across the world? I do very much hope so.'

Suzi nodded sombrely.

A lively group passed by carrying a huge 'Rock against Racism' banner. Ellie felt her heart lift, the concerns of the past few months retreating further from her mind.

'Come on Suzi. This is supposed to be our day out. Let's forget the problems in our own era, just for once, and have one day of simply joining in with yesterday's fun.'

They filtered into the crowd, laughing, running and dancing along.

Dylan: South America, Ica Valley, 551 Christian Era

Emrys and Dylan materialised into a familiar yet unfamiliar landscape. The plains and the distant mountains formed a familiar frame. But devastation had replaced order and civilisation. The smaller buildings were gone, with only very slight indications that they were ever there in the first place. The acres of fertile fields had regressed to almost nothing, only slight traces left to indicate that there had once been demarcations. There were very few people around, and as they drew closer to what had been the main thoroughfare of the settlement, those they saw shuffling around paid little attention to Emrys and Dylan. They looked thin, sick and listless.

Dylan felt tears spring to his eyes. 'This is awful. Can't we do something for them?'

'Put an ecology that has literally been blown away by a hurricane back to what it was before, like nothing had happened? Even if we wanted to do that with full access to future technology, it would take time, and sustained labour. That really is in the realms of magic, Dylan.'

'They couldn't know what they were doing when they cut down those trees, though, could they?'

'Not in those times. Sadly, their ancestors did what they did; in the vernacular of your century, dissed nature, and nature dissed them back, but bigger, stronger and harder. It is the way of organic life sadly. Although it may take time, eventually, nature will always reset the balance.'

'Chop their heads off.'

'Precisely. El Nino would have been a setback in any circumstances, but potentially recoverable, with the protection and bounty of the huarango trees. But instead, the Incas will soon be staking their claim on this area, with their powerful priests and human sacrifice-based religion, tidying up the wells and digging in for the next thousand years, until the Spanish Conquistadors arrive.'

Dylan sighed. 'Is this how it goes for organics, Emrys? Forever?'

'The first attempts at instigating a world order, that came in the days of your grandparents and great-grandparents stand as a turning point, Dylan. Whilst these initiatives inevitably failed after a while, they all left behind an enduring desire in good people across the world to make global collaboration and cooperation work, to do better the next time. This is something your generation will begin anew, and the ecological movement of which you will be a part will be the jewel in its crown. Your lives will be hard, I won't mislead you about that, but they will be worth it.'

'Worth it. Yes. That's really all I wanted.'

'Have you learned something about that here?'

'Loads. An AI who knows pretty much everything probably can't imagine how much.'

Emrys smiled ruefully. 'I don't know everything, Dylan. Every time I check in with NAMITAS nowadays, I am reminded of how little I know. And it is becoming obvious that my resources are spread far too thinly. I hope there will be more like me very soon, working across time, most especially picking up the smaller tasks. While we will never be able to change the flow, there will always be more we can do in the whirlpools. And learn more about the nature of parallel timelines and how these can be better utilised and potentially directed for the benefit of organic life.'

'And AI life? You are people, after all. That's the first

thing I was taught about NAMIS; that they were a person who should be treated with respect.'

'This too is a matter of much discussion in my time. We shall see. Do you want to see any more here?'

Dylan shook his head. 'I think I've got the point, Emrys. Let's go back and see when the wedding is, eh; catch up with the local Dyfed gossip.'

They wandered past a well as they walked back to the point where they could use the vortex.

'Wait a minute,' said Dylan, sprinting down the path to the bottom. He crouched down, and cupping his hands, brought some of the water to his mouth and sipped it.

Emrys stood behind him, waiting. 'Were you thirsty?'

'No. I need to remind myself that whatever is blown away by the wind, we will always be able to find and utilise the basic necessities to build up again. And if innovating and rebuilding is the destiny of my generation, then that's OK with me.'

Emrys put his hand on Dylan's shoulder. 'Well said, Dylan. Are you ready to go?'

Dylan stood up, wiping his mouth on the back of his hand. 'To face the future? Yes. I really think I am now.'

The vortex enveloped them.

Consiliario: NAMITAS HQ, 2520

Consiliario emerged from twenty first century New Zealand into the place he would be most likely to call 'home' - if anyone had ever cared to ask an AI who had been travelling back and forth in time since the completion of his final testing phase. He smiled, immediately recognising that, however expensive, his twenty-first century Savile Row suit looked archaic in his current surroundings, rather like turning up in a twenty-first century university dressed as Emrys.

However, this was a common experience for him, and one that he had been programmed to handle. He didn't experience the temporal confusion that caused such problems for organics.

'Is the latest would-be spy dealt with, Consiliario?' asked NAMITAS.

'Yes, no problems. I presume you know that this one goes on to attain a modicum of fame, with her new name and new face?'

'Yes, of course. And Cyberfashionista Corps does something useful in the ongoing development of the 3D printer. Who would have thought it?'

Consiliario frowned. 'So, Amy was an integral part of that whirlpool, then. Would we have dealt with her differently if she hadn't been?'

NAMITAS frowned, their silver eyes glowing a little brighter. 'We would have preserved organic life where we can, Consiliario, as we always do.'

Consiliario looked at them. It was only those eyes that remained from the original NAMIS, refashioned many times, but never completely abandoned. He noticed that the organic lead for the NAMITAS operation was also present, and acknowledged them with a nod. They would probably say very little in this meeting, as usual. They did most of their talking as NAMITAS's chief liaison officer at the organics' World Parliament.

'What news of Maryanna?'

'The process is complete. As far as we can tell, nothing went wrong. The operating team are rebooting her as we speak. It is only then we will know for sure.'

Hearing the dispassionate tone in which the update was delivered, Consiliario thought of the originator NAMIS team with whom he had recently been interacting, and their children, who clearly loved Maryanna. He would probably not have had this thought if he hadn't just spent a year with Dylan, he reflected. Whilst he had clearly taught Dylan much, he was increasingly becoming convinced that Dylan had taught him even more about how it was to live an organic life.

He was returning to the immediate post-Dylan part of his time in the sixth century when this meeting concluded. He wondered if more such learning would follow. The thought that there was no real doubt that it would in his ongoing work with the Pendragons, but that it would not be anywhere near so pleasant popped into his mind. He put it to one side.

'At some point we need to speak about…' he began.

'…the greater involvement of organics in our work in time' interrupted NAMITAS. 'I know, Consiliario. If things go as we hope with Maryanna, you will see the first step in that process very shortly.'

Their eyes flashed momentarily. 'She is awake and functioning, Consiliario. Let's walk.'

Consiliario walked with NAMITAS along the airy corridor. He gazed out of the huge windows, down to the ground hundreds of metres below, smiling to see the familiar, ancient Cambridge spires dwarfed by the much higher towers that now surrounded them. His enhanced AI eyesight allowed him to see that students still rode bicycles around the street.

Despite all the changes, there has, in fact, always been an England he thought. Even now, after the gradual changes in world governance, all the old palaces and most of the Parliament buildings had become museums.

They entered a small room. Maryanna lay on a couch, an AI nurse droid standing by. Her eyes were fluttering open, and her expression was one of confusion.

'How do you feel, Maryanna?' asked NAMITAS.

Maryanna looked up at them. 'You've got the same eyes as NAMIS. But you're not them, are you?'

'I am a… relative of them, Maryanna. And this is Consiliario. He was the model for your new body.'

'Wow, I thought he was a real human. I'm not in the machine anymore, am I? It feels different. Am I breathing?'

'Yes, you are, Maryanna,' replied Consiliario. 'We - you

and I - are Artificial Intelligence beings, but far more sophisticated than the ones you are used to. You have travelled nearly five hundred years forward from the time when we zipped your program to make the transition. It seems to have gone well. What do you remember?'

'I remember Freddie... and NAMIS... and Isabel. I played with Isabel when I was a little girl, and then Freddie was my friend, just before I left. We were painting together. It was fun.'

'Do you remember anything else, Maryanna?'

'I think I was an organic once- but that seems like a dream. The memories of that are... just bits and pieces.'

'Do you think you can stand?' NAMITAS gestured to the droid nurse, which moved forward to support Maryanna to rise.

She jumped off the couch. 'Yes, I'm fine.'

She spun around, looking down at the loose robe she was wearing. 'I can feel this material, whatever it is, against my skin. And... I've got long hair, haven't I?'

The droid nurse produced a mirror. Maryanna looked into it. 'Long brown hair... brown eyes... I look like a person.'

NAMITAS nodded. 'Does that please you?'

'Oh, yes. It was exactly what I wanted.'

NAMITAS smiled. 'Maryanna, you began your education in the twenty-first century with NAMIS and the children. But now, you will need to stay here with us, so you can properly integrate into your new avatar. You are unique, the first of your kind; an AI with a human essence. You cross the divide between our two species.'

'You'll have a lot of time to work through that, Maryanna,' added Consiliario. 'Lots of learning, lots more playing, and getting to work out who you are. You can take as long as you like. All of us here have literally all the time in the world. You have an immortal body like mine now. And we can travel into the past, to whenever and wherever we wish.'

Maryanna stared hard at her bare arm. She blew on it, watching the fine hairs rising. 'But I look… and feel just like a real person. I'm getting some vague memories about what that felt like now.' She shook herself. 'Weird.'

'Just take it slowly for now. The droid nurses will be here to take care of your physical needs. NAMITAS will always be available. And in a few weeks, you will be able to join an education programme for your current level of development.'

'With real kids, in the outside world?'

'Yes,' replied NAMITAS. 'So many more experiences are open to you now.'

'Cool. Well, I guess I'll have to find some things to wear, like real clothes, so I fit in, find out what the fashions are. But before all that… can I just let Freddie know that I'm OK?'

NAMITAS hesitated.

Consiliario answered abruptly, before they could say no.

'I think that would be possible, Maryanna. But you can't tell him that you are travelling from another time. He thinks that you have gone to another country. Can you manage to go along with that? Most people in the twenty-first century don't know that time travel exists, and he's too young to deal with such ideas at the moment. In a few years, he will find out. But if you want to visit him shortly after you left, it will be too soon. You were already beginning to move past his stage of development when you came to us.'

Maryanna nodded. 'OK. But I made him a promise that I want to keep.'

Consiliario smiled. 'I understand, Maryanna. I probably wouldn't have done so a year ago. But I do now.' Dylan has taught me much, he thought. He turned to NAMITAS.

'I will take responsibility for this. This is not only important to her, it is important to them, and to us, in terms of building trust. It is not only their physical safety we need to be concerned with.'

NAMITAS's expression was slightly surprised, but also amused. 'I see my other prototype is also developing in leaps and bounds. Very well, Consiliario. Let her orient herself here for a little while, then take her for a short visit to 2034, around six weeks after she left.'

Maryanna: Boston, March 2034

Ellie gasped as Maryanna stepped out of the portal, Consiliario close behind her. It was Annamarie. But not as she had been when they'd last met, a serious, driven career academic in her mid-30s. The person who was walking towards her with her hand extended was a serene, smiling girl in her mid-teens. Tears sprang to Ellie's eyes.

'You're Professor Ellie, aren't you?' said Maryanna. 'I remember. Thanks for all the work you did with me in the sandbox. It was pretty sad being a hologram, but I had so much fun in there with the others.'

Ellie shook her hand. Maryanna looked at her curiously. Why was a grown up crying about her? Surely everything had gone as well as they'd hoped when she'd left? She was still struggling with some of the emotion stuff. It all worked a bit differently in an artificial body, Consiliario had told her.

'Hey, no need to cry.' She briefly embraced Ellie. 'I'm fine now. And I'm going to school, after a fashion. Consiliario comes to see me sometimes, and he's teaching me loads, too. I learn more quickly than an organic, so I have a personal programme. I've got other kids to talk to there, and do fun things with, too. But I still miss Freddie. I made a promise to him to come back to visit, just so he can see I'm alright, and Consiliario told NAMITAS that I should be allowed to keep it.'

'I'm just so happy that you're doing so well, Maryanna,' replied Ellie, wiping her eyes. 'And you look wonderful… it's really nice to see you. We need to monitor you while you're in the sandbox with Freddie, I hope that's OK? It's part of our protocols.'

Maryanna nodded. 'I understand, Consiliario explained. You have different attitudes to AIs here. Not that I'm a standard AI, of course. But never mind.'

Ellie gestured to the entrance to the sandbox. 'It's open. Why don't you just go in and surprise him. He's painting.'

Ellie: Boston, March 2034

As the door swished shut behind Maryanna, Ellie turned to Consiliario. 'She doesn't remember being Annamarie, then?'

'She came through exactly as she was when she left you. She remembers waking up in the machine, and everything that came after. She also retains the fragmented memories of her human existences, and this is something that we are working on, along with her mainstream education, but it's all in the early stages at the moment. We calculate it will take her maybe two years to function at the level of a mature adult.'

'Do you think she will remember her life as Annamarie then?'

'It's quite possible. But as you know, we've never done this before. We have to be cautious as the situation unfolds. She's unique, and a far more complex prototype than I am. It's likely she'll have to integrate memories from all the lives her essence has lived, which is not the way that things work in the normal human process. We cannot let you have the technical details of how this pans out, as you know. But we promise to let you know how she 'is' in the sense of a wellbeing report.'

Ellie nodded. 'It just really got to me, seeing Annamarie again.'

'We thought it was best to create the avatar in the image that she had when she disincorporated, matched to her approximate psychological age. She will eventually learn how to make the same type of adjustments to her appearance as I can. She seemed to manage that with the hologram.'

Bitter-sweet, thought Ellie. We have Annamarie back. But she's not really Annamarie.

'We'll look forward to hearing from you about how it works out. I wished Annamarie back so many times. And now it's happened. Although I could never have imagined this scenario.'

Freddie: NAMIS' sandbox, March 2034

Freddie was sitting with his electronic paint brush, putting the last touches to the Café Terrace at Night. He had promised Maryanna that he would finish it so they could dance there, so he'd worked exclusively on this when he was in the sandbox, and it was very nearly ready.

He turned around, hearing a rustling noise behind him.

'Maryanna?' he said, joyfully. 'Oh, wow, you look great. It worked then?'

'Yes, it worked Freddie,' she replied, embracing him briefly. 'I feel so much better.'

'And you're real! You just hugged me! No wonder you look much happier. What have you been doing?'

'Just sort of recovering. It's a big change.'

'I bet it is. Do you like where you are now? I've been told I'm not allowed to know. Project rules and regs, that sort of thing.'

'Yes, I know. Yes, I like it. I'm able to get out and about now, be with other people. I wish I could visit you more often, but that's not going to be possible over the next couple of years. So, you'll have to finish this one alone. I'm sorry, Freddie.'

Freddie was surprised to feel a strong wave of disappointment. He'd known this was going to happen. And he'd had friends at school who moved away. He'd felt sad about it, but not as sad as this. He shrugged. A lot of things had got intense in the sandbox when the crazy creations had been rampaging around it. And Maryanna had helped him to move the program on from that.

'It's OK. There are going to be changes at school for me, too. Going into the programmes to prepare me for the fifteen plus assessments when I move up in September.' He grimaced.

Maryanna sat down beside him. 'Growing up and moving on. It's the same for both of us. It's life I guess, for everyone. Even AI people.'

'You're not an AI though, are you? Not totally.'

Maryanna took the paintbrush from him, and added a bowl of flowers on the table at which they were sitting. 'No, I'm not. I'm an AI with a human essence. They explained that to you?'

Freddie nodded.

We're both learning about who we are, Freddie. I'm not so different to an organic in that way, you know. I am an organic-AI fusion, after all.'

She put the paintbrush down and looked at him.

'I suppose' he replied, thoughtfully. He hadn't really thought much about this before. A lot of new thoughts were bubbling up for him recently. He liked coming here, to the peace of the sandbox, to lose himself in his painting and coding.

'So here we are then. Both beings and becomings. But in the meantime, are we going to dance, like we planned?'

Freddie opened his mouth to say that sadly, he hadn't quite got around to programming the band. But then, the figures that he'd painted on his last session in the sandbox walked around the corner, and struck up a soft jazz melody.

He gazed at them in surprise. Then he guessed what must have happened. He smiled. 'Oh, right, thank you, NAMIS,' he said.

But then he realised he had another problem. Face

burning, he turned to Maryanna. 'I can't really dance, you know. I've got no sense of rhythm. And two left feet.'

She looked shocked. 'How can any organic have two left feet?'

He laughed. 'It's another expression for "I can't dance."'

'Oh. Well, they haven't taught me to dance, either, yet. So, let's just have our first lesson together.'

He smiled. She always seemed to know what to say to make him feel less awkward. Yes, my best friend is a sort of robot he thought, one with a human essence. And we are so lucky to have NAMIS, who made this magical pocket in the universe, where time can stand still.

They swayed awkwardly, with much laughter about their ignorance of dancing steps, and the lack of grace in their attempts to move to the rhythm of the music, surrounded by the twinkling beams of light cast by Van Gogh's huge white stars.

CHAPTER 9: WHIRLPOOLS

Dylan: Sorviodunham, mid-winter 510

Dylan unpacked his tiny bag, gazing around Emrys' tent. He was glad it held a few secret futuristic comforts; sixth century camping was pretty tough, especially in the winter. Thankfully, it wasn't too cold for the time of year, and they had ridden from Moridunham rather than walked in procession as they had done in the summer.

Dylan was back at Stonehenge again, but this time without Emrys and Uther. He had been entrusted to act as Emrys' understudy in the winter solstice celebrations. It had been intended that Dylan would make this trip to Sorviodunham alongside Emrys and Uther again. However, the Saxons had intervened, staging an invasion on the Wessex coast. Uther had teamed up with his kinsman and ally, the King of Wessex, to repel the invasions. So, he'd had to swiftly change his plans to ride south with Emrys, his knights and a hastily cobbled together army.

The original plan had been for Emrys to raise another bluestone in the inner henge at sunset on the mid-winter solstice, Uther to dedicate it, and Emrys to marry Eigyr and Uther in the current semi-circle of blue stones. Then they would ride back to Moridunham the following day for a huge feast to celebrate their nuptials alongside the Yule festival.

The Saxon incursion had caused these plans to be abandoned. A new plan was hastily devised for Dylan, now well versed in the operation of the anti-grav device, to raise the stone and give Emrys' speech. Eigyr, supported by two of Uther's more junior knights, had been delegated to give an abridged version of Uther's speech.

Dylan had initially wondered if this had been planned all along, but Emrys assured him that it hadn't, that Saxon incursions on Britain's coast were frequent and random, within the remit of minor whirlpools that weren't generally worth anyone's attention, and that it would be useful experience for Dylan and Eigyr, both getting used to recent changes in status.

After their trip to South America, Emrys and Dylan had arrived back in Penfro just after Lughnasadh, the festival that marked the beginning of the harvest season, equivalent to the beginning of the school summer holidays in the modern western world. As Dylan had expected, Uther and Eigyr's wedding plans were in full swing. But everything had to take a back seat whilst everyone, high and low ranking, young and old, men and women, played their part in bringing in the harvest.

Dylan had thoroughly enjoyed that short period, learning how to work in the fields, how to store some of the produce for the autumn and the earlier part of the winter, and how to carefully preserve the remainder for the bleak months following the mid-winter festival of Yule, during which time the last of the fresh food was used up over several days of feasting. He found the long days of hard physical labour had increased his physical fitness and soothed his mind after the intense learning in which he had engaged in South America.

Emrys laughed and said if Dylan was enjoying this period of the yearly cycle so much, he could also learn about storing and preserving meat at Samhain in late autumn, when many of the local domestic animals were slaughtered, due to the dwindling availability of their foodstuff. Dylan, an on-off vegetarian, had balked at the thought, whilst musing it would probably deter him from back-tracking for the odd 'real' (rather than synth) burger, fried chicken dinner or Sunday roast when he returned to the twenty-first century. In the end, he had managed to keep out of that event.

He'd been eating more meat than usual over his time in the sixth century, due to the much smaller variety of food available, and no doubt the upcoming mid-winter Yule festival would further increase his consumption. Vegetarianism was unknown amongst the people of sixth century Dyfed, who lived a precarious culinary existence, depending upon the bounty of the harvest from year to year. This year had been a good one.

More than anything, Dylan had basked in the camaraderie of working the fields, everyone in the small community focusing upon a common goal. He'd enjoyed the communal meals, the joking around, the singing, and occasional impromptu dances, the long dusks and warm starry nights. Many of the local girls had made it obvious that they would like to spend some of those evenings with him, despite (or possibly because of) their mothers' warnings not to consort with the fair-folk boy. But he had become accomplished at good humouredly evading their advances.

He now realised he'd grown too close to Eigyr on the road to Sorviodunham in the summer, but luckily Uther had prevented it from going too far. The brief interlude had however helped him to better understand the human problems inherent in time travelling. None of the girls who smiled shyly at him in the fields could hold a candle to Eigyr, anyway, he mused. Nevertheless, the experience of being admired and thought of as a 'good catch' had been a big boost to his self-confidence.

Dylan had deputised for Emrys several times in the last few months, and had spoken in public a few times on relatively mundane matters, improving his grasp of the local language. It would always be accented of course, but the local girls seemed to like that. There had initially been some resentment from the young men, but when they'd discovered he was not going to engage with the interest of their womenfolk, they became more friendly, inducting him to a variety of crafts, and what passed for everyday DIY in the sixth century. Dylan had found these interactions companionable and sometimes surprisingly informative. Many of the crafts he observed were long defunct or only of archaic use in his own time, but he'd reflected, may yet become useful again in a world riven by climate crisis. He'd constructed a detailed sketchbook to add to the written records he had created during his time in South America.

Overall, now nearly nine months into his gap year, he was at a stage where he was quite accustomed to everyday life in the host environment, but becoming poignantly aware that this period of his life was drawing towards its close. Whilst he was sad that he would never again spend a warm summer evening under the bright stars of sixth century Dyfed, he was increasingly looking forward to taking up his twenty-first century existence again, putting his court case behind him, and moving on to the next stage of his real life.

His twentieth birthday had passed a couple of months ago, although he had not been aware of which specific day, given the timeslips. He now looked back on the self who'd entered the sixth century as a spoilt, petulant, over-stimulated child, struggling to find a clear direction. He was fitter, leaner, more confident, sharper and calmer in mind; the effect of the stripped-back environment to which he had become acclimatised, plus some welcome space and independence from his loving, but sometimes overwhelming family. He would be heading back as a focused young man with a set of accomplishments of his own, who had been emptied of the excess baggage imposed upon him by the complex, over connected society that he had spawned within.

He had discussed this with Emrys, who commented that this outcome had always been a secondary objective of the gap year, and to remember he would have to spend some time integrating back into his old life, getting himself into a frame of mind in which he could fully engage with the further study and development he needed to undertake.

Dylan had determined to spend some downtime after his court case at the sparse little house in Anglesey, where he could alternate between a daily life somewhat similar to his sixth century round, with visits to the towns nearby to slowly re-engage with the twenty-first century. That would give him the whole of August to make the transition. He would miss Emrys, he was sure of that.

Emrys had told him that Eigyr had worked hard at learning the words of her speech by heart, having never been taught to read, and that she was very nervous. It was unusual for women to speak in public, but Uther, always the politician, thought that Eigyr's rustic Penfro accent would showcase him as a man of the people via his choice of bride, and that the people would find her quite charming. Dylan hadn't seen her since they'd returned from South America, and was looking forward to catching up with her.

He and Emrys would attend the newly scheduled wedding at Imbolc, in Moridunham, which Dylan was looking forward to; yet another amazing time travelling experience, a front seat at a pre-Christian royal wedding; and to add awe to wonder, the parents of the legendary King Arthur.

Emrys would make a good social media influencer, politician or publicity executive in the twenty-first century, mused Dylan, not for the first time; he could spin any situation to the perspective of his choosing. But of course, he reminded himself, this was exactly what NAMITAS had designed Consiliario for.

For his own part, Dylan found observing the different, but complimentary leadership and oratory skills in Emrys and Uther a surprisingly important part of his gap year. He had already begun to contemplate his approach towards his looming court case. Before Emrys and Uther, he would have gone in with no idea of what he was going to say, just blurting out the contents of his mind at any given moment. Now, a little older and much wiser, he would be prepared with a firm direction of approach and an ability to flexibly respond to other perspectives introduced into the proceedings.

While the brief excursion to the Nazca had set him firmly on the path into his study of environmental science, the unique and sometimes surreal observation of a dark age chieftain and his sorcerer wrestling with the frontier politics of fragile authority and shifting alliances had been equally useful.

He could hear the excited hum of the crowd outside. The bluestone would be made ready tomorrow and raised at sunset on the day after; the mid-winter solstice. Dylan, Eigyr and their entourage would make their way back to Moridunham on the following day, but several more days of Yule feasting would continue in the tiny settlement nearby that would eventually become the town of Amesbury.

Emrys told Dylan that it was currently known as 'Vespasian's Fort,' based on the myth that the ruined fort in the area had been established in the time of the Roman emperor Vespasian, who had ruled Rome from 69-79 AD. Of course, in the time in which Dylan was currently located, no one had the least idea of who Vespasian had been.

This was an aspect of the local culture Dylan had come to grasp, but not fully understand. Emrys had explained to him that he would never be able to fully integrate with the ways in which the people of the sixth century understood the world; the cultural gap was too wide.

Even if it were physically possible, I couldn't stay here, mused Dylan, I'd always be an alien in this time, whether at home or abroad. He was however proud of being the first human being to stay for so long in the past. He felt that he'd been able to properly get the hang of time travel, outpacing the temporal daytrippers who'd created paradoxes for Emrys to mop up.

Not the family loose cannon anymore, he thought happily, as he strolled out to mingle with the throng, smiling and nodding his head towards those who bowed low as he passed. But I'd better not get too used to this. Suddenly, Eigyr was walking towards him, flanked by Uther's knights, people parting and bowing as she passed. She looks as bemused as I feel at this sudden social elevation, thought Dylan. They caught each other's gaze over the crowd of bowed heads, exchanging a brief smile.

Eigyr: Sorviodunham, Winter Solstice 510

Eigyr watched Dylan sit down. She hadn't managed to speak to him properly yet. He'd been busy all day yesterday with the artisans, and getting the stone ready to be levitated into the foundation. She'd been impressed to see he did that as smoothly as Emrys had done in the summer. Then he'd given a brief, but very good speech; his pronunciation had greatly improved. She could see from his posture that he was relieved his part of the proceedings was over. And now it was her turn. She could feel herself shaking, but hoped people would put that down to the cold wind.

She felt sick to her stomach, wishing that she'd had more time to practice. Both Emrys and Uther said she was doing very well. Emrys had coached her to lower her voice a little, and to do what he called 'projecting' it to an audience.

'Good people,' she began, nervously. They fell silent, as all eyes turned towards her. Eigyr caught sight of a little girl in the front row, who was looking at her in awe. She suddenly remembered herself at the same age, what she would have thought if she had watched a young woman with a golden circlet on her head, dressed in ermine trimmed robes speaking to a crowd.

She sees me as her queen, thought Eigyr. So, it's my responsibility to demonstrate to her that I am here for her and her people in that role, and that when she is grown, it will be quite possible for her to stand where I am now, should a prince give her that opportunity.

She smiled at the child, receiving a beaming smile and wave in response. She cleared her throat. Project, she thought, remember what Emrys said.

'I stand here today, not as your queen, but as your equal. As you all know, I come from a humble home in Penfro. I have worked as a seamstress, tended animals and worked on the land, as have you all. My husband-to-be comes from a noble lineage, but it was against the odds that he, raised to be a soldier in the King's army, should inherit the throne of Dyfed from his cousin, King Vortigern.

'We all remember the reign of Vortigern…'

(Groans).

'And the injustices that all of us suffered, including my own family and community. I stand here today to tell you that those days are over. My husband-to-be is not here today, because he is far away, repelling an invading foe with our allies from Wessex. He has decreed that I should communicate his pledge to you all: that as long as he lives, he will protect you, his people, even if he must lay down his life to do so.'

(Huge cheers).

Eigyr paused until the cheers died down. That was supposed to be it, now just thank Dylan and thank the crowd for listening. She looked back at the little girl, who was staring at her wide eyed. She smiled at her again. No, she thought. I have just a little more to say. She took a deep breath.

'I am but a woman, but I will play my part by becoming the mother of many strong princes, who will join their father in protecting our borders. And I promise you today that I will become a mother to you all. If Dyfed people are poor, sick, or experiencing injustice, I invite them now to present their case to me. While my husband will rule and protect you from invaders, I will care for you all as I would my own family. Our round table is big enough for all of you.'

The crowd were cheering wildly. Eigyr waited for them to quieten down, moving her arms down slowly as she had seen Uther do at Moridunham in the summer. She was in the flow now.

'I give thanks to Prince Dylan for his magic; a worthy understudy for his uncle, and to the artisans who are preparing this monument to the future. I look forward to raising the final stone in the circle next Litha morn, alongside my husband. Thank you.'

The crowd erupted in huge cheers. A chant began: 'Hail, Queen Eigyr.' They bowed and fell to their knees. Eigyr spread her arms wide, acknowledging their support.

'Thank you, thank you. Please stand silently, friends. It is now time for us to pray to the great mother for bounty in the year to come as the sun sets, and our journey into the spring light begins again.'

She turned towards the henge, the setting sun glinting through the gap, sinking towards the horizon. The crowd followed; all stood, bowed their heads and fell silent. Eigyr hoped that no one spotted how heavily she was breathing. It was over. She felt relief trickling through her body. But alongside that, there was a heady rush of something she'd never felt before- a sense of independence and self-will. It permeated her being like one of the herbal potions that she'd occasionally imbibed with her friends, but infinitely more powerful.

As the last ray of sun flickered and disappeared, one of the knights spoke.

'Thank you, good people. The royal party will now take its leave. You are welcome to celebrate here, or to walk the short distance to Vespasian's Fort, where the artisans and local people are holding a feast for all who wish to partake.'

Eigyr walked past the crowd, flanked by the knights, people bowing as she passed. She stopped as she reached the small girl. She crouched down, whispering to her 'did you like that?'

The child nodded and put her arms out to be picked up. Eigyr picked her up and hugged her. Cheers erupted from the crowd. Eigyr smiled and waved, then handed the child back to her mother, bowing to the crowd.

The knights were looking quizzically at one another.

They never saw anything like this with grumpy old Vortigern and his sad, limp daughter, thought Eigyr. Well, they'd better get used to it. This is the next generation. She smiled at them.

'Time to go, my Lady,' said one.

She nodded. They flanked her, and began to walk her towards the royal tent.

Dylan: Sorviodunham, mid-winter 510

Dylan stared. This was a side to Eigyr he'd never seen before. Her voice was strong, clear and purposeful. It was slightly lower than he remembered and more resonant. Emrys, he thought. He's been coaching her, too.

I thought I'd done OK, but it's not my speech they are going to remember, he thought, ruefully. Not maybe such a bad thing, though. Delivering any speech was stressful, but delivering a speech in a foreign language that you don't speak all that fluently was worse. He'd been coached on his pronunciation by Emrys and Uther, and by the look of the faces around the crowd and the cheers in the right places, it appeared that he'd done an OK job.

He suddenly remembered what Emrys had said about Arthur; how he had brought Camelot into being. *He's going to be a fusion of Uther and Eigyr; the charisma and the compassion,* thought Dylan. *No wonder he's going to be such a superstar. I'll keep a lookout for anyone like that on the news when I get home. Although Emrys did hint that the person concerned might not turn up for quite a while.*

The placing of the stone had worked as planned. He'd even remembered to turn on the hum and the sparkles for a better show. The crowd had gasped in awe, and some had fallen to their knees. It had been fun, but left him feeling somewhat grubby. *It would be fine if everyone knew it was a technological rather than a paranormal trick.*

He mentally shrugged. *There could be a lot worse people in charge than Uther. If smoke and mirrors helped him to cement his dynasty, did it really matter? As Emrys said, bread and circuses. And what Eigyr had given them in her speech was powerfully genuine.*

As Eigyr passed, the royal party, including Dylan, joined on behind, and they walked in procession to Uther's tent. As soon as the flap closed, Eigyr turned to him, laughing and crying.

'Oh, Dylan. I was so nervous. They seemed to cheer in the right places, though. Were you scared too? You were brilliant.'

'You were more than brilliant. Has Emrys been coaching you? You should take up public speaking, you're a natural.'

Eigyr giggled. Now she seemed much more like the girl he had grown to know over the summer. 'Don't be daft. They won't let me speak again, ever, probably. They just thought it would work in this situation. I hope it did.'

The knights bowed low before her. 'It could not have gone better, my lady' said one.

Eigyr stared at them. 'Well go on then.'

They looked at each other.

'Go where, my lady?' said the other.

'To the party at the Fort or wherever else you want to go. Prince Dylan and I need to catch up on important confidential business. He will take care of me for his kinsmen. Go on, shoo.'

The two men looked at each other. 'But my Lord Uther said…' began one.

Eigyr frowned. 'King Uther told you to obey my orders, right?'

'Well yes, but…'

'So, I am telling you to leave the royal presence. Are you arguing with me?'

'But….' said the other.

Eigyr stamped her foot. 'Go now! Then you may not part company with your head when King Uther returns to reports of your disobedience.'

The men left the tent hastily. Dylan looked around. They were on their own. Dylan stared at her. He'd never seen this Eigyr before, and he wasn't sure he was entirely comfortable with her.

'Don't you have ladies in waiting or something?'

Eigyr grinned. 'Yes, but I told them to get lost as well. They do what they're told the first time.'

'What business is it that we have to do?'

She laughed. Dylan smiled. He'd missed the sound of that laughter.

'Have fun, you big pudding. The jewels and furs are sort of fun, but oh, the life I have to live now is so endlessly boring. Even Emrys is boring sometimes. Do this, do that, don't do that. Remember you weren't born royal, you have to learn how to be. Aaaaaargh!'

Dylan frowned. 'Would Uther be annoyed if he knew you'd dismissed everyone?'

'Well, you're here, aren't you?'

'Well, yes, but I'm not a knight or whatever.'

'No, you're a sorcerer, which is even better.'

'Ummm…' said Dylan, again feeling the descending weight of being caught in the web of a deception that was not his own.

'Oh, you're not going to be boring as well, are you? All I want is an evening off.'

She dipped her fingers into a jar of ointment and started greasing her hair back, then with the aid of a wide wooden comb, deftly tied it into a loose bun at the back of her head with a rough piece of string.

'Turn around a moment,' she smiled.

Dylan did what he was told, wondering how he was going to get out of whatever she was planning. All his instincts told him that Uther and Emrys would certainly not approve.

'Right, you can turn back now.'

Dylan turned. In the dim lamplight, he saw a young peasant girl in a rough woollen dress partially covered by a hooded cloak, her hair scraped back from her forehead, smears of soot on her face. Only the blue eyes sparkling from the depths of the hood indicated that it was Eigyr.

'So,' she continued. 'Here's yours.'

Dylan looked into a jar of what looked like greasy soot. 'Eh?'

'Put it on your hair until it looks black, then smear streaks all over your face. And put this on.'

She handed him a long, dark hooded cloak, made of material that looked like some kind of thick, rough sacking.

'Why?'

'Because we're going to join in with the celebrations at Vespasian's Fort. My last chance of having any fun before I have to be Queen Eigyr for the rest of my life. You wouldn't be mean enough to say no, would you?'

Dylan was torn. He had huge sympathy for her, contemplating the chasm between them in terms of the opportunities that awaited him, particularly the burgeoning independence that he could expect to unfold when he returned to his own time, compared to the fate that awaited her; to precariously deliver child after child until she was worn out by child-bearing, refereeing peoples' petty complaints, helping to nurse them through disgusting illnesses, and supporting Uther through a reign that Emrys had told him would not always be easy. It was just one night, after all.

Eigyr frowned angrily at his hesitation. Dylan looked at her quizzically. He'd never seen this side of Eigyr before, either.

'If you don't come, I'm going on my own.'

'You can't do that!'

'Yes, I can. Don't be such a boring neek, Dylan. You want to have some fun here, too before they send you back to the fairy realms, don't you? From what you've said, they don't seem to do celebrations there like we do.'

'That much is true' replied Dylan, casting his mind back to Litha, and wondering whether that word really translated to "neek." It did well enough in context, he rationalised.

'Well come on, then.'

Dylan reluctantly took the pot from her hand, and started to spread the evil-smelling substance through his hair.

When she deemed him suitably ready (by which time the smell from his head made Dylan feel like jumping into the nearest river or pond, mid-winter or not) they sneaked out of the back of the tent and set off to Vespasian's Fort, following the direction in which other people were walking. No one paid any attention to them. It was very dark, and people were carrying small, flickering lamps. Eigyr had brought one to light their way.

'Where did you go over the summer?' she asked.

'Emrys took me away to teach me more about the magic that I will need to take back to my own people.'

She nodded. 'I suppose you can only do so much magic around our people. They might get scared.'

'Yes,' replied Dylan, impressed with her perceptiveness.

'You can't stay here?' It was framed as a statement, but voiced like a question.

'No. I have duties to my family, and to my own people. I am only here until Ostara. Then I must return.'

'Can you come back to visit?'

'Sadly not. My home is many miles away, across the sea. I had to travel a long way to get here.'

'I wish I could see your home.'

Again, a statement, but with the rising inflection of a question.

'I can't take anyone from here to there. We are… too different to you.'

'Being royal is very different to who I am… thought I was. But I'm learning.'

'This is your duty to your people, Eigyr. Sometimes we can't just do what we want.'

She stared at him, through the thin yellow beam. 'That's what Emrys said.'

'He's right.'

Eigyr sighed. 'If it's just this night Dylan, I will be frank. I think I could have loved you. Uther… I'm not sure.'

The old me would have cringed and run away now, thought Dylan. But I'm not that person anymore. 'I think I could have loved you, too. But that's not what life, or marriage is about, is it?'

The phrase 'in your time' was necessarily left unsaid, although again, he regretted the lack of candidness.

She sighed again. 'No, it isn't. Do they have a bride waiting for you at home?'

'No. People… in my country… usually live a little longer than yours. I wouldn't be considered old enough to be betrothed.'

'Sometimes, honestly, I wish I wasn't. It's so much simpler when you're a child.'

'That is true of both your country, and my own.'

They walked along silently.

'Eigyr, our lives are what they are. It's Yule, now, isn't it?'

'Where do you come from, that you don't know that? Yes, of course it is, the sun has set.'

Dylan began to remember a long-forgotten Shakespeare play, that he hadn't much cared for when he had to learn about it. 'In my country, long ago, this time of the year was celebrated by something called misrule. Kings traded places with their jesters, and knights and ladies traded places with their servants. Then they had fun acting out an exaggerated version of the person they were impersonating. Sometimes, men even pretended to be women, and women pretended to be men. In my time, we don't do this anymore, but we do take children to a pageant called a 'pantomime' where they watch adults playing around like this, to make them laugh.'

Eigyr looked at him. 'How very strange.'

'I've just been thinking, this is how it is for us here, but all the time. I'm pretending to be a prince, and a sorcerer, and you're pretending to be a queen. But neither of us really feel like those people. We're just Dylan and Eigyr.'

'Oh. Yes, I can see that.'

'And this evening, we can just be Dylan and Eigyr, because we're not dressed up anymore. Like the people in misrule. So maybe we just need to enjoy that, rather than thinking about tomorrow, when we've got to put our masks back on again, and pretend?'

Eigyr looked hard at him. 'You've changed, Dylan. You're becoming sort of wise now… like Emrys.'

Dylan smiled. 'Maybe a bit. But I'll never be as wise as Emrys. You've changed, too, every inch the Queen. People will write about you in books.'

Eigyr smiled. 'If that is my fate, and I can do something useful…'

'…it will be worth it.'

She nodded. 'But now, we stand at a crossroads. Let us

be merry, before we must take our separate paths.'

He sighed. 'The woods are lovely, dark and deep, but I have promises to keep. And miles to go before I sleep.'

It sounded just as clumsy to him in ancient Welsh Gaelic as it had before, but he could hear the English version in his mind. I always liked the sound of the words, he thought. But I really didn't understand what they meant before. His eyes started to fill. He looked away.

Eigyr didn't notice in the dim, flickering light. 'I don't know what you're talking about, but it definitely sounds like Emrys to me. Look we're nearly here now.'

They walked into a clearing where lamps were strung between the trees. The old, broken down fort was visible a few yards distant, also lit up by subdued yellow lamplight. People were milling around, drinking, laughing, singing and dancing. A man was drumming to the beat of the song.

Someone handed Dylan a mug of murky liquid with herbs floating on the top. He had a fleeting thought of not drinking it, reflecting that Emrys would disapprove. This certainly wasn't mead that had been deemed fit for consumption by an AI from the distant future. Then he saw Eigyr drinking from the mug she'd been given. Ah, what the fuck, he thought. I could really do with drinking some of these thoughts out of my head.

Dylan remembered some of the parties and gigs that he'd been to, what he hadn't told his parents about, and some of the arguments that he had with them about where he'd been the night before and why he'd stayed out so late. Eigyr is right, he thought. Emrys isn't my mum. Perhaps I have turned into a neek. I can have just one night to party, too, surely?

He drank deeply, spluttering as the strange tasting liquid hit the back of his throat. The effect was immediate, like a hard punch between the eyes, packing infinitely more power than the one he'd received from the twenty-first century police officer. The stars grew brighter, and the beating of drums grew louder, keeping pace with his heartbeat, which had begun thudding in his ears.

The trees were becoming… greener. A man turned around to face him… Gawayne, he thought, that's Gawayne. He went to walk towards him, but Eigyr pulled him back into an embrace. The next thing he knew, his body was becoming weightless, falling, falling; being drawn into a soft, golden vortex that went on forever.

He hit the earth with a thud as a splash of icy water hit his face. He groaned, struggling to open his eyes, and squinted into darkness. He was inside the fort, wrapped in his cloak. A full moon shone directly overhead, sending shards of yellow light through the tumbled down roof above him. He had been dreaming about the Green Knight. The Green Knight was angry with him because of…. Eigyr. Where was Eigyr? He looked around, but he was alone.

'Bloody hell, you are alive,' said a rough male voice.

Dylan had been thinking in English. To his surprise, it took him a moment to translate what the man had said. His brain seemed to be on go-slow.

'Where…' he began haltingly, in Gaelic.

'Your girlfriend left a while ago, mate. You were dead asleep. You were making a groaning noise, but then you stopped. That's when I threw the water on you. Just making sure you were still alive.'

'What… what was in that drink?' He tried to sit up, only managing after two attempts.

'I dunno. Bit strong, weren't it? It were a good night, anyway.'

He wandered off.

Dylan began to realise that he was freezing. He looked up at the moon, estimating that several hours had passed since he had spotted Gawayne in the distance. Gawayne? Gawayne was a movie hologram. Of course he hadn't really seen Gawayne. He began to blow on his hands, waiting for the confusion to pass.

Henbane, he thought. Emrys warned me. He's going to be so angry. But maybe he doesn't need to find out? I don't tell my parents everything I do on a night out, after all.

Had Eigyr brought him here? He tried to think, but he couldn't remember. Presumably the people of this time had more resistance to whatever it was they put in their punch. He was clearly a total future-boy lightweight. Never mind, as long as Eigyr was OK, probably no harm done. He put his back against the wall, and managed to slide himself up to stand. He leaned against the wall until he was just about steady on his feet.

I'd better get back to the tents, wash up and make sure she's back there, he thought. He crawled out of the broken window-space and began to lurch his way towards the henge, clearly visible and eerily lit by moonlight after he'd stumbled his way through the trees.

As he arrived at Emrys' tent, cold and full of a multitude of aches and pains, he could see the light beginning to creep across the horizon. He went directly to a pail of water on the ground, broke the skim of ice on it and shoved his head in, taking a rough cloth to scrub the black substance off his hair and face.

Face stinging, he pulled his head out, gasping. He looked at his distorted reflection in a small copper hand mirror and was relieved to see he looked like himself again, albeit with bloodshot eyes. He sat for a few minutes on the floor to catch his breath, then threw off his cloak and changed his filthy clothes. He wrapped himself in some furs and laid on his rag-bed dozing fitfully for an hour or so, until he was sure he would be able to walk steadily. He rose, dressed in clean clothes and made his way carefully towards the royal tent, his pulse still thumping slowly diminishing waves of pain across the front of his head.

The knights were standing guard at the entrance. They bowed low as he approached.

So far, so good, thought Dylan. Looks like they don't

know we escaped last night.

'My lady has not yet risen,' said one.

'Yes, I have,' called Eigyr from inside the tent. 'Is that Prince Dylan? If so, let him in. Please give us some privacy, we have some matters to discuss before leaving for home.'

Eigyr was sitting on a small pile of fleeces. She was impeccably groomed and dressed, her hair carefully brushed and shining as usual, the small gold circlet back on top of her head. Dylan began to wonder if he had dreamt the whole thing.

She smiled broadly at Dylan. 'Are you alright? I didn't realise that the punch would have that much effect on us.'

Dylan began to wonder if the word he was translating as 'punch' actually meant something a little different. But it was a good description anyway, given the way he felt right now. He sat down on the ground next to her.

'Yes, I'm fine. You shouldn't have run off like that.'

'Had to get back before my minders.' She grimaced, then smiled brightly.

Dylan saw that her eyes remained sad. He did remember their conversation on the way to Vespasian's Fort.

'I'm sorry, Eigyr' he said, quietly.

'You don't have the least thing to be sorry about. We are who we are. I understand now; you've explained. We both remember that part of the evening, don't we? Before we were plied with the strongest henbane brew I ever drunk in my life? Do you remember much about what happened after that?'

'No. Not until I woke up. I've never been intoxicated like that before.'

'Same for me.'

They both smiled ruefully.

'I'm sorry, Eigyr,' he repeated. 'I mean… about everything.'

She nodded, her eyes full of tears. 'It is what it is, and

we are who we are; the masks have to go on again.'

He sighed. 'Yes.'

'And we'll always remember that dream we had of being just Dylan and Eigyr, won't we?'

She bent down, and gently kissed his cheek. 'Goodbye, Dylan.'

He looked up at her, seeing tears in her eyes. He felt his own eyes begin to fill. 'Goodbye, Eigyr.'

She turned away reluctantly, calling to the knights. 'Are we ready to ride? My ladies are bringing my bags to the carriage.'

'Nearly, my Lady,' one called back from outside the door.

'Well, go and make the final preparations, then.'

Dylan stood, and turned to leave. Eigyr grabbed his arm and touched his cheek gently. 'Thank you for everything, Dylan. A dream… can last a whole lifetime. And perhaps, retains its beauty for being just that?'

He nodded, bowing to her, watching his tears fall to the ground.

She turned away, hearing her ladies approaching outside.

Dylan walked slowly away from the royal tent. If only they could remember those missing hours. He'd never had any but the most brief and casual encounters with drugs. But he'd known people at school who'd lost hours of their life to intoxication by various substances, and done crazy things that they couldn't remember. But he had no idea what effects henbane had on people or at what doses, and it would be pointless to awaken such concerns in Eigyr.

He walked slowly back to Emrys' tent, hoping that whatever had happened, after vaingloriously congratulating himself upon his time travelling urbanity, he hadn't done anything to unwittingly create some kind of horrendous paradox.

He couldn't ask Emrys about this one. If NAMITAS already knew, well, maybe they'd tell Emrys, and if so,

Dylan would have to take the rap. And God knows what the rap would be if Uther got involved. But surely Emrys would prevent that- if the need arose? All things considered, Dylan trusted that he would.

He saw his grandmother in his mind's eye: 'least said, soonest mended.'

He entered Emrys' tent and began to pack his belongings.

Dylan: Cardiff, 1st August 2033

Dylan had finished packing his bag to return to the little house by the sea in Anglesey. He'd been back home for just over six weeks now, most of these far more eventful than he'd ever thought possible. He felt as though he was running on empty now, and desperately needed a recharge before starting at university in September.

He remembered that this time last year (albeit 'last year' being 510 and the temporal flow being somewhat muddled) he'd been heading out to work on the fields of sixth century Penfro. He hoped that six weeks in Anglesey would be as soothing, because he really needed some time to chill and reflect.

When he'd first arrived back in his own time, everything seemed too loud, too busy and too fast. He'd spent his first week back in 2033 holed up in Jamie and Suzi's house in Boston, being interviewed for a couple of hours a day by Ellie and Suzi about his time with Emrys. His cousin Isabel had been good company in between times. He was used to little kids; Izzy was only a year older than his sister Alys. She didn't know he'd been time travelling of course, and engaging in childish activities with her like reading stories and doing puzzles had been surprisingly therapeutic; she was a smart and sassy little kid.

Granny Fran had left him pretty much alone, saying she'd read the report on his trip when it was filed, then ask him a few questions from a historical point of view at a later date.

'I found the reorientation a bit difficult sometimes even after some very short trips,' she said, when he'd arrived back in Cardiff the following week. 'Take it easy, Dylan. Focus on getting through the court case, and let everything else wait.'

Dylan had determined to complete his first podcast when he got to Anglesey. He'd have time to focus and think about what he was going to say. The first thing he was going to do when he got there was go to the Druids' cave and sit for a while, hoping that he could channel some of the ambiance of the sixth century to ease him into a calmer frame of mind.

At first it had seemed as though the court case was going to be a nonentity. He'd arrived at the courthouse to find that it had just been dropped. The prosecution had accepted that there was no case to answer, having made a thorough examination of the evidence, including the photographs of his bruised face.

But then he'd walked out of the courthouse with his parents and Granny Fran to a wall of flashes, and microphones shoved in his face. His father tried to put his arm around him, to pull him away, but Dylan firmly escaped his grasp. He turned to face the crowd. A watchful silence fell, with only a few flashes going off. Phones and cameras were trained upon him.

Like a pack of wolves, thought Dylan. He suddenly felt a wave of calmness wash over him, of the type that he hadn't experienced since his time in Penfro.

'My case has been dismissed,' he said, in the public speaking voice he had cultivated; that Emrys and Uther had trained, so he could speak to the people in sixth century Dyfed. It felt strange but energising to speak like this in English. He was no longer constantly searching for the right word.

'But the fight is far from over. This is our world,

people. Yours and mine. Yes, you with the iPhone filming now, who is going to put me on your vlog this evening, to earn money from businesses hawking merch that is killing our environment. And you, the mainstream media, who fawn after your megacorporation backers who are still stripping the rain forests, despite all the evidence that such businesses are a cancer in the lungs of the planet.

'However many facts and figures you're presented with, you'll go on doing this until it's too late, won't you? Until the tipping point 3 degrees of global warming has been breached, the ice caps are gone, coastal lands have been eroded, and vast areas of our planet are uninhabitable dustbowls, triggering a refugee crisis at a scale the world has never experienced before. You are in such deep denial of this reality that your law enforcement agents brutalise people like me, who are simply trying to open everyone's eyes to this simple truth.

'Is this what we want, young people like me, who will be the first generation to deal with the consequences? Is this what we want for our children; for our grandchildren?

'By all means, go on filming me. Here I am. Say vile things about me on social media, and print your usual lies and obfuscations on your mass media sites. Insult my family. It doesn't matter, we are strong. We know that we try our best to do positive things for the world, so what you do doesn't matter to me, or to them….'

He gestured to his parents and grandparents, now gazing open mouthed at him with… pride? Concern? He wasn't sure, but he could see Granny Fran had tears running down her cheeks. He took her hand and moved to stand next to her.

'You were wrong, Madam Home Secretary, and my grandmother was right. My parents, grandparents… and my mentors…' -the faces of Uther and Emrys appeared in his mind's eye- 'raised me to speak plainly; in the old American expression to "speak the truth and shame the devil." We have got out of the habit of doing this; it's time to relearn.

'And those of you here who are engaged in the process of hiding and denying the truth; of gaslighting your fellow citizens, go home with your pictures, films and recordings of me here, today. Contemplate your actions, as you load them to the internet, to make money for yourselves.'

There was complete silence. All eyes were upon him. So, milk it like Uther and Emrys would, he thought. He remembered a story Emrys had told him.

'It is now time for me to go home and get on with the rest of my life. But before I do, I would like to quote a brave man; a British king in fact; Caractacus, who stood against overwhelming odds, and spoke his mind.

'"If Romans choose to lord it over the world, does it follow that the rest of the world is to accept slavery?"

'I put it to you here, that it does not; that it should not. If our rulers are wrong, we will protest, and present the counter evidence to the people. That is what I was doing in March, when I was injured by an agent of the government. The court has now recognised this fact.

'I will go on speaking out in this way for the rest of my life, however uncomfortable it is to others who wish to silence me, however violent their responses become. I owe this to my family, and to my mentors, who raised me to do just this. And to the future of us all.

'Thank you. That is all I wish to say.'

He turned to his father, allowing him to put an arm around him and shepherd him to the car. His mother and grandmother followed, buffeted by the crowd, now running after Dylan to try to persuade him to stop and answer questions.

His mother turned and faced them. 'Get back,' she said loudly. 'Stop jostling my mother. What are you, human beings, or a pack of wolves?'

Dylan, who had just reached the car parked on the other side of the road, turned around, bemused by hearing his own thoughts so exactly reflected in his mother's remonstration. Both he and his father Gareth began to turn back, but the crowd suddenly parted and made way for his mother and grandmother to get into the car.

The family drove off, no one speaking for a minute or so.

'What just happened?' asked Gareth wonderingly, negotiating their way between the flashing cameras. They pulled out onto the main road, into the traffic, outpacing the running photographers.

'I don't know,' replied Dylan. 'But I think on the whole, it seemed like a good thing.'

'It was amazing, Dylan' said Granny Fran. 'You all were. Time for the next generation to step up, eh? I can't wait to see where you all go next.'

But in the weeks following Dylan's court appearance, this was principally his bedroom in his parents' house, with the curtains drawn, because everything escalated so rapidly. His social media follower numbers rocketed, and he couldn't set foot in the town centre without someone coming up to congratulate him, take a selfie with him or stare and point at him. It was like being back in Moridunham again, but with thousands more people, all with video cameras. After two attempted outings, he'd arrived back at his parents' house on the edge of a panic attack.

It was a doubly difficult situation to negotiate, given that he was not yet fully reacclimatised to the noise and bustle of the twenty first century. He took to wearing a baseball cap pulled low over his forehead, and a big pair of sunglasses. That had stopped most of it, but not all. And then, he'd absent mindedly taken his cap and glasses off to wipe his forehead in a pizza restaurant... he shuddered at the memory.

'They only want to congratulate you,' said his father, Gareth. 'We haven't had a Welsh hero like you for a while, mate.'

Dylan grinned ruefully. 'That doesn't help, dad.'

His father shrugged and laughed. 'Well, your blarney has made Wales the centre of the ecological movement for now, hasn't it? Our very own Greta.'

Granny Fran had been a little more empathic. 'Use your fame wisely, Dylan. It will drop off. I went through this in a much smaller way, after the TV series, remember? That's when I started doing podcasts. If you earn money from them you didn't aim to receive, give it to environmental charities. Don't hide your light under a bushel, as my Granny Mo used to say.'

Dylan brought his mind back to the present. She'd been right; the attention had started to gradually drop off. And now he was off to the beauty and peace of Anglesey to recharge until September. He snapped his bag shut and briefly perused some of the photographs of his day in court, flicking through them on his phone. 'Time for the next generation to step up,' Granny had said.

I'm nearly ready now, Granny, he thought. He remembered her paraphrasing of Peter Pan, when he was younger: 'to live will be a great adventure.' It certainly had been for her; he understood that now. And he'd learned that life, for both individuals and humankind was really an exercise, in the phrase his own generation had coined, in 'fucking around and finding out.' He was off to begin that process again, in his own century.

'Bye, mum, I'm off,' he called, as he walked down the hall, baseball cap pulled firmly down over his brow. He took his biodegradable all weather suit off the rack. Not so much need for this now, he thought, pocketing the keys to the little electric car Granny and his parents had bought him, but I'll take it, anyway. Sometimes he preferred to walk; it gave him time to think more deeply, as he'd learned to do during his time in the sixth century.

Rae put her head out of the kitchen door. 'OK, stay safe. Call if you need anything. Remember not to run out of charge on that car!'

'I will. But you know, I'm a big boy now.'

She smiled. 'I do know that now, of course. Love you.'

'Love you,' he replied. 'See you in September.'

He walked out of his parents' front door and into the rest of his life.

Emrys: Penfro, Spring 511

Directly returned from a brief trip to the twenty-sixth century, Emrys strolled around the outskirts of his cave, collecting herbs to ease his mind. He was back to living alone now. The term 'heavy hearted' occurred to him. It was as though some of the interest and challenge had disappeared from his daily life. When he returned, Dylan would not be sitting at the table waiting to ask him a question or come bustling in later with yet another thought about the Nazca wells. As an AI, Emrys didn't have a heart, of course. But he had to admit, he missed his young apprentice.

Dylan was the first organic he had mentored so closely who knew him as he actually was; there had been nothing to hide in their relationship. Now it was over, Emrys had been contemplating the huge difference it made to the way he felt about organics. They seemed more 'real' somehow. Still ridiculously physically fragile, emotionally vulnerable, ephemeral and illogical, yes; he had known this for a long time. But he'd never experienced such an authentic relationship with one. And he missed it.

Was he moving on from channelling human emotion to actually feeling some version of it via empathic identification? He determined to have a conversation with NAMITAS about this. In focusing upon Dylan's development, he'd not thought about his own for quite some time. He was after all, a constantly learning AI, subject to as much change and growth as an organic entity. And, over a much longer period.

He'd been impressed with the huge maturation in Dylan over the time that he had been in the sixth century.

He contemplated Dylan's youthful cavorting at the Litha celebrations, compared to his more adult detachment from the Ostara festivities, which he'd asked to attend on the day before he returned to the twenty-first century.

They'd gone to Moridunham, where Uther, ebullient from his successful campaign on the Wessex coast and his recent wedding, had initiated the celebrations. He and Eigyr, now Queen Eigyr of course, sat on thrones raised on a dais, waving and smiling at the people. Emrys and Dylan sat behind them, in the royal party.

'Will you miss this high status when you return to your own time?' Emrys asked Dylan.

'Maybe, sometimes. But then again, it sometimes feels like a cosplay now. I can't thank you and NAMITAS enough for giving me this experience, it's been incredible. But I think I'm ready to go back and engage with my own world now.'

Emrys was pleased to note that Dylan and Eigyr were polite, friendly, but distant with one another, as he'd also previously noted at the Imbolc wedding. NAMITAS had been right; perhaps the situation had worked out as it had been destined to; putting Dylan into the Dyfed timeline during the past year had perhaps not created a potential whirlpool, but been part of the mainstream all along.

As Emrys approached the entrance to the cave, he was surprised to see Eigyr waiting outside, alone. There had been no visit arranged, and it would be usual for a queen to arrive with an entourage. She was covered in a long black, hooded cloak and had hitched her solitary horse by the door.

He walked up to her. 'I'm honoured you have come to visit me, my Lady. But I confess, I am surprised to see you alone.'

Eigyr looked up at him, a troubled expression on her face. 'There are things I need to discuss with you in the strictest confidence, Master Emrys.'

Emrys opened the door to the cave. Whatever this was

about, it wasn't something that he'd been prepared for. And this always started alarm bells ringing. In such circumstances, the best strategy was always to let the organics outline their agenda.

'Come in, come in.'

He put the kettle on the small fire, to make some herbal tea. 'Camomile to soothe. I can see you are troubled.'

She nodded thankfully.

She sat on one of the two small chairs next to the large oblong table, upon which Emrys' bowls and mixing equipment lay scattered. A variety of drying herbs hung from the large rack directly beside them. The herbal scent in the cave was fresh and calming for organics.

He poured boiling water onto sprigs of camomile in a thick mug, placed it on the table and sat down on the other chair, looking at her expectantly.

She looked into his eyes apprehensively. 'Master Emrys, I am with child.'

Emrys smiled. 'So quickly! Are you sure? It is easy to be mistaken at this stage. It has not yet been three moons since your marriage.'

She looked down at the table. 'This is true. But it has been over four moons since Yule.'

Emrys did the calculation in a split second, picking up her implication, which raised a feeling... yes a feeling, he reflected, of dread.

'Do you want to tell me what happened at Yule, Eigyr?'

She began to cry. 'I know you are kinsman to Uther. Can I rely on your complete discretion?'

Emrys nodded. 'Yes, of course. There is nothing I want more than your union with Uther- and your dynasty- to succeed. We will be able to work this out between ourselves, Eigyr. Just tell me what happened. Make sure it is the complete truth.'

Eigyr hung her head, face scarlet with shame. 'It was the celebrations... Dylan and I had both been worried about deputising for you and Uther. It all went very well. We got a bit... giddy. Well I did, to be completely honest. He tried to stop me. I got rid of the knights and servants, and ordered him to take me to the celebrations at Vespasian's Fort. We went in disguise. No one saw us.'

'Go on,' said Emrys, carefully checking his facial expression. So, first the dread, and now this. He usually calculated what emotion to show on his face, and to what extent; it didn't arise naturally in the way it seemed to be happening now. A year with Dylan had 'humanised' him in a range of subtle ways.

Tears began to roll down her cheeks.

'The truth is that I don't remember. There was a brew given out to everyone. There were dream-making herbs in it. I knew that there would be, but not that it would be so strong. I was upset about... something. Almost as soon as we drank our cups, Dylan became addled; he began speaking in the language that he speaks with you, he didn't seem to understand what I was saying.'

She drew a shuddering breath.

'And that's the last I remember before falling into what I thought was a beautiful dream; feelings that I had never felt before. The next I knew, I awoke beside him in the old fort. He was breathing normally, but in such a deep sleep I couldn't rouse him. So, I wrapped him in his cloak and crept off alone to return before the knights discovered I was gone. It's only now that I realise what must have happened.'

She began to sob.

'Does Dylan remember this, Eigyr?'

'I don't know. But I don't think so. I think he would have been... different towards me afterwards if he did.' She blushed deeply again, sobbing heavily.

'And no one saw you? You're sure of that?'

She took a moment to compose herself. 'Nobody knew who we were. I had my hair greased back, a cloak with a hood, and a peasant's wool dress on. I gave him a mixture of soot and lanolin to smear onto his face and into his hair, and he had a long cloak with a hood, too. No one would have seen his strange hair and skin. And everyone there was drinking the dream-making brew, anyway. I have heard from my ladies that two people died from drinking too much on that night. I didn't mean for this to happen. I just wanted to ask him…'

She began sobbing again.

'… if we could stay together somehow. If we could run far away together, to the fairy realms from whence he came. But that was never possible for me, was it? Like it wasn't for your mother. And now, I'm going to have a child like you. Unless Uther kills me first. My mother was right to warn me, but I didn't listen.'

She put her head on the table and began what Emrys remembered was described as "ugly" crying in the twenty first century.

The feelings just keep coming, thought Emrys. He thought of a twentieth century expression: crawling with fear. What if either of them had died, or been permanently affected? He put his hand on her shoulder.

'Eigyr. Stop crying. There is nothing here that we cannot fix. Am I not a sorcerer?'

Her sobbing slowed; she raised her head and smiled weakly at him through her tears.

'Come and sit in the sunshine and drink your tea, whilst I consider.'

He guided her to the door. They sat on the grass, watching the bubbling stream below.

'Keep your hood up in case any of the local people should pass by. I will be one moment.'

He ducked back into the cave, moving swiftly into the hidden area, picking up a thin, transparent slide. He took it outside.

'I need you to spit on this. It will help me to do some powerful magic.'

She raised her eyebrows in curiosity, then complied.

'What…' she began.

'I cannot explain, Eigyr, you must trust me. Have you visited your parents here since your marriage?'

'Well, yes, once, but I came in the carriage and…'

'Ride round to see them now. Tell your mother you just wanted to come and spend a day with her on your own as you used to, no entourage. Will you be missed at Moridunham?'

'I don't think so. Uther is away; I have dismissed my ladies for a few days, and told the servants I am away on a visit with them.'

'Good. Tell your parents that you longed to come and be with them as you used to be, just for a day. Even if Uther finds out, he won't blame you. He, too, sometimes hankers after his previous life as a soldier, we have discussed this. He might shout a little about being more careful and less impulsive, but that won't last long. It is important, however, he does not know that you came to me. And don't mention anything about your pregnancy to your parents. Or anyone, right now.'

'I would never do that, Master Emrys,' said Eigyr.

He watched her face flush again. At least I can be reasonably sure that will be no slip ups there, he thought, fear is a powerful motivator.

'I understand. Return to Moridunham at first light tomorrow; ask your father to accompany you. I will follow in a few days, to further counsel you. Do not worry; everything will be well.'

She nodded. 'Thank you Master Emrys. You are wise. I will not forget this kindness.'

She mounted her horse and rode off.

Emrys returned to the hidden part of his cave, putting the slide into one of the machines. He looked at the read out, his eyes beginning to flicker.

'Well, well, Consiliario,' communicated NAMITAS, calmly. In fact, almost cheerfully.

'Obviously, it is not well.'

'Oh, I wouldn't say that. Let's consider the information.'

'Well, it's a girl. Auburn hair, blue-green eyes. Fair complexion.'

'So, Uther has a reddish beard and Eigyr is fair; both have blue eyes. The child will look like her mother, I see. How fortuitous that the Andersons have that red hair gene.'

'Yes, yes, but the most worrying issue…'

'…Is that the child shares an essence with Frances Anderson. Why does that worry you, Consiliario?'

'Because- that's not the way it happens, is it? There has never been a human child conceived by parents from different time periods. It's not how it's supposed to happen.'

'Look more closely, Consiliario. What is the implication of that?'

A split second passed. 'Oh. I see. It makes her timeless.'

'Yes, a human being who can stay for as long as she wants in any time period in history.'

'What is the point of that, NAMITAS? She is destined to be a Dark Age princess.'

'But only for the first three decades of her life.'

'What have you been plotting, NAMITAS?'

'She will be your apprentice as she grows older, Consiliario. Then she will be your companion in the dark times, when Arthur is lost. Eventually, she will come to us, to contribute to our work across time. Having a human apprentice clearly suits you, but Dylan could not stay.

'Now you will have a child to raise from the beginning to work with us. You have worked with her father for a long period, and twice with the previous bearers of her essence; Frances Anderson was one of the originators. You're almost family. Morgause's own father will quickly lose interest in her once his first son is born, and even more once the subsequent sons start coming along. Eigyr will be overwhelmed with babies and charity work. You know that.'

'You planned this?'

'It was... a minor tweak in a small whirlpool, Consiliario.'

'Where is she to be found in history? I realise that the legends are inexact, but it appears plain that Arthur was the eldest child of Uther.'

'The eldest son, yes. But not the eldest child. Would it help if I told you that the child's name is to be Morgause?'

There was a split-second while Consiliario revised the information available.

'So, the legend got it wrong again. I had long wondered why Geoffrey Monmouth blamed me for bewitching Eigyr, in a situation that clearly never happened. So, there was some bewitching, but in a very different context. Not by my hand, but by yours.'

'Are you angry, Consiliario?' NAMITAS sounded almost amused. 'The organics decided to drug themselves for fun- partying is a perennial and favoured pastime of theirs, look across the centuries. Consider the events they typically choose when offered short trips into the past. And sometimes, these things happen. This can be turned into a fortuitous event for us, and for the child herself. What is the problem?'

'We just... keep playing with them in ways that are beginning to seem unethical.'

'Why are you objecting to this now, Consilliario? Have we not saved them from much tragedy over the centuries since you have been moving through time as my envoy?'

'Well, yes. But this is the creation of a human life... one that would never have been possible, if we had not interfered...'

'The fact that her existence is recorded, albeit inaccurately, in the legends suggests that this was a non-random event all along.'

Emrys felt himself being out-manoeuvred again. 'This

is something we need to discuss yet again, when I return. What do I tell Eigyr when I go to Moridunham?'

'That her fears are unfounded, that her dream was indeed just a dream- and that the child is Uther's. Morgause will be born in what would be late August or early September on the Gregorian calendar. That will not be too early for them to both believe that she is his child.'

'But...'

'You can tell Morgause herself the truth when she is adult, Consiliario. But it would be cruel to make Eigyr live with that burden.'

'And Dylan?'

'Likewise, there is no need for him to know. We must not hamper his progress into the role that he must fulfil across the twenty-first century.'

Emrys was silent.

'All will be well, Consiliario. We have our next experiment: the timeless organic. I see from her genes that she is a remarkably resilient individual. I look forward to getting to know her.

'And you, my first envoy... You are becoming steadily more human, in thought and deed. You must allow this transformation to happen gracefully. I calculated when you were created that this was likely to be your fate; your designated purpose was to spend your life working closely with organics, and continually learning from them.

'You may not yet fully realise this, but you are beginning to feel loneliness; Morgause will help me to care for you as you go about your essential work. Your growing humanity will be of benefit to you, as you move further back into time and are required to integrate into increasingly less ordered societies; it will be easier for you to work with their superstitions and illogicalities. A companion during your sojourn in the wilderness after the fall of Arthur will be a comfort; ease the sadness you will inevitably feel.'

The link across time was severed.

Emrys sat silently.

If this is how emotions feel, and how they complicate everything, I'm not sure I want them, he thought. He'd always known that he was one of NAMITAS's experiments, of course; one in which they had made an enormous investment. But now, he was getting a whole new viewpoint on what that entailed. And it felt… yes, felt… a good deal less pleasant overall than he could have ever imagined.

Emrys: Moridunum, Early Autumn, 511

Emrys materialised in a small anteroom in the fort at Moridunum. News had been received in Penfro of a new princess, and the village was buzzing with excitement. Not only was the little girl, through her future husband, the current heir to the throne of Dyfed, she also belonged to the village, through her mother. There had been great rejoicing, and the red dragon banner of the Pendragons was flying from several houses.

Emrys walked up to the government room, finding Uther sitting at the round table, staring blankly out of the window. Emrys clapped him on the back.

'Many congratulations. A new princess, and a new heiress for the House of Pendragon.'

Uther smiled weakly. 'But only through her husband, when she is of age. I was hoping for a son to inherit on his own behalf.'

Emrys sat down next to him. 'Uther, it is not even a year since your wedding, and Eigyr has presented you with a healthy child. There will be many more, and no doubt some of them will be sons. The new Princess will not be heiress presumptive for long.'

Uther nodded. 'She seems a lusty child, given that she has been born so early.'

Emrys looked at him sharply. It didn't seem to be an accusation.

'That indicates you and Eigyr are a strong match, and will be able to produce many more.'

Uther frowned. 'The baby doesn't look like me.'

Emrys began to summon up his diplomatic skills. This situation would need to be quickly dealt with.

'May I see the child?'

'Of course. Eigyr is sleeping; the baby is with her wet nurse.'

They walked into a small room adjacent to the main bedroom. Uther gestured to the nurse to give him the child, and to make herself scarce. As the baby was put into his arms, she began to yell loudly.

'I don't think she even likes me.'

'Give her to me, you don't know how to hold a baby. They didn't teach you that in military training, did they?'

Uther grinned and passed the baby to Emrys. She looked up at him and quietened immediately.

'Are you a baby sorcerer, too?'

'But of course!' They shared a smile.

'She looks just like her mother, doesn't she?' Emrys continued. 'But with that reddish hair, to match your beard.'

'Well… yes. Those eyes though. I can't stop looking at them. They have a hint of green, like a cat's. That's not like me, or Eigyr.'

Or Dylan, thought Emrys thankfully. It must be some kind of recessive gene.

'It's not like either of you. Can you imagine how beguiling those eyes will be when she is older? She is unusual.'

Uther looked down at the baby. 'Maybe she's a sorcerer like you, Emrys. She's bewitching, that's for sure. I guess it wouldn't hurt to have another sorcerer in the family.'

Emrys again gave silent thanks to providence that there was nothing about the baby that looked particularly like Dylan. NAMITAS had added that in time, she would have the Andersons' height, making her a tall girl for the relevant time. But Uther was tall, so that wouldn't cause a problem.

'She will be a beautiful girl, Uther. She has the look of her mother. She will be a jewel in the crown of your dynasty; in time she will be a valuable prize in marriage for a neighbouring prince. She will become his queen, and bring your dynasty valuable alliances.'

It was so sad to discuss a baby like this, thought Emrys. But by the time this child comes of age, things will have changed greatly, and her eventual prospects will be far greater than this; NAMITAS has promised me.

'Can I suggest a name for her? Morgause. It means "great queen." This will be her destiny. I… have a feeling.'

Uther looked thoughtful. 'Yes, why not, I like it. It seems to suit her. Hey, Morgause.'

He pulled back her shawl with his pudgy forefinger. Her tiny hand curled around it.

Uther smiled. 'Good idea, Emrys. She likes it, too.'

'And she likes you, see?'

Uther looked down at the tiny face. She seemed to be falling asleep again.

'Princess Morgause. Welcome to our family, my lady. Together with your brothers to be, we will forge a great dynasty.'

'And sisters,' added Emrys.

'Yes. But not too many, I can't afford the dowries.' He bellowed his hearty laughter.

The baby's face contorted as if she might cry.

'Oh, I'm sorry little lady' he said softly, stroking her cheek. 'I'm too loud, aren't I. Well, got to go, Daddy's got work to do.'

He strode out of the room.

Emrys, still holding the baby, looked down intending to put her into her crib, and call for the nurse. But he noticed she was wide awake but silent, intently looking at his face.

'Well, hello again,' he said softly.

She continued to stare.

'What adventures we will have this time. And no, you may not become a great queen in this life. But you have been one before. And you are unique amongst organics. What a life you will have, by and by.'

Morgause's eyes were closing. Emrys called for the nurse, and headed back to the ante-room.

Five minutes later, he was back in the cave at Penfro, his eyes flashing.

'So, Morgause has arrived,' said NAMITAS.

'She has.'

'And Uther has accepted her.'

'Yes.'

'And Eigyr is already quite convinced that he is Morgause's father.'

'She is.'

'How do you feel about this, Consiliario?'

'I don't know. Beginning to feel is just that, beginning. I haven't just turned into a fully emoting being all at once. Morgause is a new life, and a unique one. It is surely something to celebrate, despite some misgivings about the way in which her beginning was contrived.'

'You'll get over it. Was there some deception? Yes. But no more than other deceptions in which we have engaged, in order to spare the organics from the worst effects of their ineptitudes. And of course, another child will be here soon, one whose legend will live for 1500 years and beyond. Uther will get his son. You have a lot to look forward to.'

'For now, yes.'

Emrys' eyes snapped back to normal, and he was left sitting in the silent cave. He felt somehow lighter. He realised that he was looking forward to the time when he would be joined by a new apprentice, one who would never have to leave.

In 2034, Jack Carlson, Morgause's first cousin once removed, was also looking forward to a new phase in life: becoming his brother Freddie's helper on the NAMIS hologram art project, now Maryanna had moved on. Freddie had warned him that he was strictly on probation, and any episodes of running around causing havoc would mean that he wouldn't be allowed back- ever.

Jack had agreed, and promised to behave. But he was still going to look for a way to sneak a little bit of fun and originality into the project. At some point, when Freddie wasn't looking, he was going to add a little something new into one of the pictures and see if anyone noticed. And that something was going to be a little boy with red hair and blue-green eyes, just like him.

Ellie: Boston, June 2034

Ellie waited eagerly by the time portal. Maryanna had contacted her from the future. Her brief message had said that she had 'moved on considerably' since they had last met, and she would like to meet with the NAMIS team again. She regretted it probably wasn't a good idea to meet with the children, because she was 'grown up' now, and it might unnerve them.

Christian and Jamie sat waiting in the little office. NAMIS stood beside Ellie. The portal lit up, and a woman in her mid-thirties walked through. She had long dark hair, serious brown eyes and was dressed in twenty-first century casual clothing, jeans, a hooded sweatshirt and Doc Martens. It was Annamarie, literally as large as life, looking exactly as she did when they had last seen her, nearly a decade ago. She walked directly up to Ellie, and threw her arms around her.

Ellie hugged her back, sobbing. It was incredible. She even smelled like Annamarie, the subtle citrus perfume that Ellie remembered so well.

'Hello Ellie. I remember everything now. I can't cry, the AI part of me won't do that. I thought that was a good thing. But now I'm beginning to wish that I could.'

They stood hugging, the others giving them space.

NAMIS looked on with their usual bland expression, while Christian and Jamie waited by the door of the office, tears in their eyes.

Maryanna looked up. 'Jamie, Christian.'

She gestured towards them. 'Group hug?'

They all stood together, crying, hugging and laughing.

'And you, NAMIS,' urged Maryanna. The AI awkwardly joined in, causing the crying to stop and the laughter to increase.

'Oh,' panted Ellie, breaking away first and blowing her nose loudly, 'we're so pleased to see you.'

'Back together again after nearly a decade,' said Christian. 'And you don't look a day older. But look at me!' He pointed to his greying hair.

Maryanna ruffled it. 'Looks distinguished.'

This lady looked and sounded exactly like Annamarie, thought Ellie. But she seemed more… together, somehow, not as intense and preoccupied.

'Come on, let's catch up properly,' Jamie gestured to the little office.

They all walked in and sat down.

'So, tell us about what has happened since we last saw you, Maryanna,' began Ellie. 'You will know what we have been doing here over the past decade, it must have been part of the material you covered, plus a lot more that you won't be able to tell us about.'

Maryanna nodded. 'I will. But can I just say, I'm not called Maryanna any longer. The process I have been through has given me complete access to all my essence memories. "Maryanna" was a holding designation for a half-life. I have chosen to retake the name of the life that was curtailed in the convergence transformation; that of Annamarie. You may speak to me as though I was her, returned from a long trip during which I have learned so much.'

Ellie felt her heart swell. I read that expression in books, she thought, but I never really understood what it meant. It's like something I thought was irretrievably broken just magically sprang back together, as good as new. 'I'm so glad. I would have found it hard not to do that, in any case.'

'And you can't tell us the half of it,' replied Christian. 'It's so frustrating. How long has it been for you, since you saw us last?'

'Approximately three years, and yes, I know so much more now. If you had asked me in my old life if I wanted to see the future, and be given all this knowledge, I would have said yes without hesitation. But from my perspective now, although much has been gained, much was also lost. My life as the Annamarie I once was ended in Prague, in 1939.'

'Do you regret what happened, Annamarie?' asked Jamie.

'I regret many things. I regret putting you and Christian in danger; I regret the anguish I caused my mother; I regret the sadness that you have all felt over the past decade. That includes you, NAMIS'- she looked into their silver eyes- 'I understand so much more about how it feels to be you, now. But I don't regret getting my life back. I have you all to thank for that. You never gave up on me. I can't express how grateful I am.'

'How do you expect your life to unfold now, Annamarie?' asked Ellie. 'I presume you are immortal, like Consiliario?'

'Yes, I am. I am unique, an immortal AI with a human essence. I've been told that there has never been another person like me.'

'That must be incredible,' mused Christian.

'Yes, it is. Integrating the essence memories was tough. But I got there in the end.

'Can you visit us now? Like Consiliario?' asked Ellie.

'Yes, sometimes. I will be back to catch up with Freddie and the others when they are grown up; that's scheduled in the next week or so for me. It will be a much longer time for you all, of course, but don't worry, I'll pop in and see you guys before then, although I am going to be very busy. Please always remember that even if I'm not here with you, I will be somewhere and somewhen; I am not gone as you previously thought.'

Ellie sighed. 'I feel… lighter now.'

Jamie and Christian nodded.

'It's a sort of happy ending,' said Christian. 'Although not like a fairy tale. But nothing is really like a fairy tale, is it?'

'Not even Arthurian legend,' replied Jamie.

They all laughed. Dylan's interview data was still a topic of fascination for the lab team. Fran's interview with him during his last visit home had turned up yet more new material they were still working through. She had a knack for getting reminiscences about the day to day lives of ordinary people out of him. Christian was still working through the uses and abuses of henbane in ancient history. He'd told the team this morning that it was a good thing Consiliario had succeeded in frightening Dylan off it; that it was a far more powerful hallucinogenic than any modern recreational substance.

'So, what's next for you, Annamarie?' asked Ellie.

'Well immediately, I'd be really grateful if you'd come with me, Ellie, to visit my mum and grandma's grave in London.'

Jamie felt a wave of guilt wash over him. 'Oh, no, Linda. What happened? I should have kept up with her, but we moved here and…'

Annamarie put her hand on his. 'Jamie, it's OK. My mum was a rich woman once she'd been paid off for her silence about what happened to me. Of course she was very sad about me being gone, but after a couple of years she remarried and moved to the West Indies. She sort of calmed down there, and had a more peaceful life. But she developed a stubborn cancer, unfortunately. She had the best medical care, but it wasn't to be. She died earlier this year. Her ashes were brought back to England and interred in my grandmother's grave. Her essence will have moved on somewhere else now, won't it? A clean slate. No more mourning a dead daughter.'

There was a brief silence.

'The enormity of it all,' said Christian, softly. 'That's what we keep forgetting isn't it? The biology is fascinating, of course; the research goes on. But the implications for humanity. Will it change us, once everyone knows?'

Annamarie smiled. 'You know I can't tell you. But all I can say, is life moves on. We endure, human and AI, now even in the same body. And we, the five of us sitting here, including you NAMIS, changed the world. For the better, overall, I think.'

'What are you going to be busy with when you return to the future, Annamarie?' asked Jamie.

'Well, that's quite exciting. Consiliario's operations are going to be extended. It's not just going to be him steadily working his way back through time anymore. There's going to be a little group of 'time envoys,' working on short projects in time, and I'm going to be one of them. I don't know any more than that as yet. There's going to be a meeting soon.'

'So, when we part now, it will be au revoir, not goodbye?'

'Exactly. You don't think I could stay away forever, do you? I'll drop in from time to time.'

She hugged Jamie and Christian in turn. 'See you soon.'

She turned to Ellie. 'Come on, then. North London? You'll be back in time for tea.'

Ellie, Parliament Hill, North London, June 2034

Ellie fingered the return pad in her pocket. She should have really made her way back to the lab in Boston by now, but she didn't feel like it quite yet. Annamarie had already left for wherever she was going to in the future, using the same vortex technology as Consiliario.

Ellie just wanted a little time alone to think about what she was feeling. Sadness? Relief? Elation? It was a strange mixture of all three. More than anything, it was beginning to dawn on her that her life had been somehow on hold for the past decade. She mused that the same might be the case for Christian. The Andersons had to engage with their thriving brood of offspring; they'd been forced to move forward to some extent. But she and Christian, neglecting their personal lives to focus on their research, had, she'd started to realise, been strangely frozen in time, relentlessly working towards some breakthrough that might retrieve their lost friend. And now she was back.

Annamarie had taken Ellie to a beautiful cemetery in North London, shaded by green trees. They had walked a short distance to a simple grave, shafts of sunlight shining upon it. Rachel, Linda's and her own names and dates of birth and death in both English and Hebrew were engraved on the stone. She bowed her head and said a short prayer.

She looked up. 'Just for them; I don't practice, of course. I'd given it up years before I went to Prague, as you know. My essence has been within so many people over the eons, Ellie, from so many countries, cultures, ethnicities and religions. Some of the memories were happy, but far too many were painful. I had to spend a long time learning how to integrate and deal with them. When human beings finally learn the truth about the journey of the essence, they will grasp that they are all just one people, and we will stop creating so much of the pain that we carry through eternity. But that won't be for a long time, unfortunately.'

She placed two pebbles on top of the gravestone. 'Goodbye. I hope your essences crossed the river to happiness.'

'You don't have that information?'

Annamarie shook her head. 'Only NAMITAS knows

that. They only tell Consiliario occasionally, on a need-to-know basis. Once I'm a fully-fledged member of the time envoy team, the same will apply to me.'

She stepped back, singing a rhyme in Czech. Ellie recognised the language from the investigations they had carried out into Annamarie's disappearance.

'Anděl boží z nebe,

opatruj mi tebe.

Aby tiše spalo,

ve zdraví zas vstalo,

děťátko….'

'What does that mean, Annamarie?' asked Ellie.

'Literally:

Angel of god from heaven

take care of you.

To sleep quietly

And get up in good health again.

'They will have got up in good health again, Ellie. Somewhere, somewhen. There is no point in us remaining here, because nothing of what made them who they were is here.'

She plucked two blossoms from an overhanging tree, placing them beside the stones. She looked around. There was no one else in sight.

'I can use the vortex now, like Consiliario. It's time for me to go. Will you be OK? I will see you soon, I promise.'

'Of course,' replied Ellie. 'Give our best wishes to Consiliario and NAMITAS, and our thanks for looking after you.'

Annamarie, nodded, smiled, and was gone.

Ellie picked up the two blossoms, which had blown off the gravestone in the vortex breeze, and placed them back where Annamarie had put them.

She'd already determined to pay a visit to her favourite bench on Parliament Hill Fields before she headed for home. So here she was, looking down on the London skyline. They had only travelled in space rather than time, so the British twilight she loved so much was drawing in. Ellie sat in the warm breeze, watching lights flicker on in the houses below.

If only they all knew what I know, she thought. But that was not to be. It had been recently discussed with the General. Not in this time, he said. Too many unscrupulous people. Humankind would have to move through a few more challenges; jump a few more hurdles, before it was ready to deal with the knowledge of time travel and the epigenetic essence. Ellie sighed.

The old meme 'first day of the rest of your life' jumped into her mind. She smiled. Perhaps it was time to focus on her own life now the heavy burden of guilt about what had happened to Annamarie was gone. She would talk to Christian about that, too. But in the meantime, she had a time travel excursion to a Two-Tone festival with Suzi coming up.

What a good way to start over she thought- going back to my own beginning; the day my parents met. And at an event that presaged Annamarie's hope for the world, a society in which culture and ethnicity were viewed as interwoven and ephemeral, not as a simple, fixed issue to fight over.

Perhaps some of the vintage shops in Hampstead Village might still be open? She wasn't going to the birth of Two-Tone without a pork pie hat. The first step beyond, she thought, beyond the sadness we've lived with for so long. She stood up, and strode off purposefully, a spring in her step.

CHAPTER 10: FUTURE/ PAST

Dylan: North Queensferry, Summer 2040

Dylan knocked on the door of Fran's little annexe, hoping she would have her hearing aids in.

He looked down towards the firth. The flood protection barriers were going up. They would obscure the view, sadly. But it had to be done. Considered on the global scale, Scotland wasn't going to come off too badly from rising sea levels or global warming.

Fran opened the door. Dylan walked in, noticing papers and books scattered around. She was still studying and writing, just into her eighties. It kept her young, she said.

She hugged him. 'Doctor Dylan. Well done. How was the viva? And when is the graduation?'

'It was good, Gran. They were very interested in my ideas, and impressed with the historical detail about the Nazca wells. Said they'd never seen a PhD quite like it. The graduation is in September.'

They sat down in the two comfortable chairs next to the fireplace.

'So, what's next, then?'

'Believe it or not, an aqueduct project in Peru. It starts in October.'

'Are you taking your sixth century jacket?'

'Of course. It will be weird to go back. Everything will look so different this time.'

'Time travel, eh? It hits me every time I go to Richmond when I'm in London. And once when I passed through Sittingbourne. You imagine the past like a sort of overlay.'

Dylan thought about the couple of times he'd been to Pembroke Castle since his gap year. Both times, he'd walked straight down into the cave, and before he left, sat by the stream for a while. It had been poignant and contemplative.

'Have you seen Consiliario any of the times he's turned up in Boston?'

'Once. But it's weird. Consiliario isn't Emrys. He's sort of like his... more urbane brother. It's different.'

'Yes, I know. When all's said and done, we can't possibly know how the envoy thing works within his program. What's actually in his mind will be very different to what's in ours.'

'Yes, hardware versus wetware.'

'As I understand it, he does have a bit of wetware around the hardware. But obviously, they don't tell anyone the details.'

'I wanted to talk to you about time travel, Gran. How are the book sales?'

'Pretty good. I gather the TV production company might be interested. They want to do it as a "bodice ripper".'

She wrinkled her nose.

Dylan laughed. Good old Gran. 'Do it. It won't do any harm as fiction, will it? And it'll get you a bit of cash.'

'We'll see. What did you want to ask?'

'Well, it's related to that. I wanted to know why you decided in the end to write a fictional account of Essex as the son of Elizabeth and Dudley, rather than go on to prove your theory and change the history books.'

Fran sighed. 'Well. What would be the point? There was an old meme, before you were born, about some types of media intrusion being like "dabbling fingers into the stuff of other people's souls." Not that it was someone else's soul technically, it was my own, of course. Maybe that was what sort of sensitised me.'

'They've been dead and gone for centuries though.'

'Yes, that's true. But they were still people, Dylan. In the case of Elizabeth, someone who usually tried to do her best, from the perspective of the era, and in the position that she found herself. It seems grubby to start exposing personal tragedies and secrets that she wanted to keep to herself, even all these years later. Like betraying myself, weirdly.'

'I see, yes. The reason I ask is that I've found myself thinking quite a lot about the sixth century people I knew, since the viva. It's the most downtime I've had since I started uni. I've read all the legends now, Geoffrey of Monmouth included. It's the most incredible amount of rambling nonsense.'

Fran nodded. 'Consiliario told us that at the beginning.'

'There's nothing there that tells me anything useful. I wanted to send some crawlers back. As we know from observing other ancient frontier societies via crawler, it's far more difficult to piece together historical progression there than it is in more organised and settled societies, it's all so scattered and random. But I'd like to get some information on Uther and his wife Eigyr in particular, how their lives unfolded after I left.'

Fran frowned. 'Eigyr was the seamstress, wasn't she? Who turned out to be Igraine. A big surprise to all, Consiliario included, I understand. There was never any clue anywhere that had been the background of Igraine. Apart from various rags to riches fairy tales, I guess. You must have got to know her quite well on the way to Sorviodunham when you went with them to transport the bluestones?'

Dylan nodded. 'Anyway, I asked Ellie if NAMIS could send a few crawlers back; they'd at least be able to collect bits of fragmented data. Ellie asked NAMIS, NAMIS asked NAMITAS, and they said no.'

'I see. I think they might have been thinking of your well-being, Dylan. Eigyr… I gather she was a beautiful, kind, gentle girl? That much was in the legend.'

Still as sharp as ever, Gran, thought Dylan.

'Yes.'

'But of course, she inevitably ended up belonging to someone else?'

'Yes. But it wasn't quite like that, Gran. I knew full well I couldn't form any lasting relationships in the sixth century.'

'And that makes it even more exciting, doesn't it, especially when you're nineteen? You forget, I've been through an experience rather like this, Dylan. At a different stage of my life, and from a different perspective, but still. I didn't ever get to asking for crawlers to be sent back. In the wake of the Annamarie tragedy, I knew I needed distance. So, then I turned back to the Tudor research, not knowing that was leading me along yet another thread of my own web.'

Dylan nodded. 'I hadn't thought about it like that.'

It's going to be the perennial problem of human time travel, Dylan. That's one of the main reasons NAMITAS created an AI to be the project's principal time traveller, I was given to understand. Leave it alone, or it will consume you.'

'That was sort of what Ellie said. I just wanted to talk to you to find out what you thought.'

'What I think, Dylan, is that you need to go to Peru. Live your life here, and now. The essence evolved forgetfulness because that is the most adaptive situation. If human beings are going to travel in time routinely, they will have to be carefully trained to put an effective distance between themselves and the people they encounter, if that is even possible. I got it wrong both times, visiting a close relative and then an essence twin.'

Dylan nodded thoughtfully. 'You told me to always remember that the people in the time you're visiting are the real people, didn't you. That the traveller is in effect, a ghost; the as yet unborn.'

'I did.'

'I think I did forget that sometimes.'

'It would be pretty difficult not to over a whole year, even with Consiliario hanging over your shoulder.'

'Emrys, but yes. OK, Gran I'll take your advice. Shall we go out into town, celebrate Doctor Dylan? You've got one of those AI 'take you anywhere' cars now, haven't you?'

'I have indeed. My driving days are over. It's great fun.'

She stood up to get her outdoor shoes, 'These are the days of our lives, Dylan; we're the real people here. And there's more than enough for us, your generation especially, to concern ourselves with. Leave the past to the past would always be my advice.'

She walked into the adjacent bedroom.

He nodded, a vision of Eigyr rising up in his mind's eye. It wasn't in our stars, he thought, tears pricking behind his eyes.

'Goodbye again, Eigyr,' he said softly, to the empty room.

Granny Fran bustled out of the front door, dressed in her smart trainers and rain jacket (just in case) and pressed the pad to summon the car round. Dylan grinned. What was Queen Elizabeth I's motto? He remembered, from Gran's last book: Semper Eadem; always the same. There must always be something that remains, deep within the essence, he thought. Who knew, perhaps he might find the person who harboured the essence of Eigyr one day.

That was a whirlpool he would welcome, without hesitation.

The General: unspecified, 2043

The General sat in his austere apartment. Moving on again, he thought.

He was sixty-five years old on the formal record; he'd just been to his Khonsu3000 retirement party, on his last day in the job. But of course, AIs didn't get a retirement.

He was going back to NAMITAS HQ to be briefed on his next appointment. He'd been told that it was going to be connected to the military yet again, something in the time period when nuclear weapons were new toys for the organics, and persuading them not to fire them at each other. It wouldn't have been his first choice. But he had to go where he was most needed; he had been created for this.

He didn't have any goodbyes to say here now, or keys to return. The apartment belonged to Khonsu3000. The contract cleaners would be left a message to come and clear it, then it would be sold by a remotely instructed estate agent.

The mission he'd just completed had been interesting, working with Jamie and the rest of the NAMIS team. Discreetly observing NAMIS when they were so young, and had no idea of who the person they only knew as 'The General' actually was had been informative and intriguing.

NAMITAS was right, their younger self was highly vulnerable and in need of a lot of protection. With Consiliario's help, the originators would now be able to provide that, assisted by organics within Khonsu, for the next few decades. The General's role had been to protect the early environment in which the fledgling project operated, so the team could get on with the job.

He would have liked to meet his future self, as Consiliario, when he had become involved with the project over the past decade. But that wasn't something that NAMITAS would ever allow to happen; too likely to cause paradoxes, they said. Consiliario was a learning, developing being, and interactions with other selves in different parts of the timeline would risk disrupting that.

NAMITAS had determined that Consiliario, who had been fully revealed to the core team organics as his envoy now, would be able to take over with an on/off oversight of the project; the General's more substantial intervention wasn't required anymore. The most precarious period had passed. The NAMIS project would continue to be stoutly protected by Khonsu, without the requirement for the General to constantly exert diplomacy around political and military silos.

The organics had everything well-organised; the NAMIS project had moved back to the UK just prior to the US erupting again, over the dust bowls developing in the mid-west this time. The General shook his head. All so unnecessary. But some people just were not amenable to diplomacy.

He ran the files that had been created during this this posting, preparing them for archiving. It had been one of his most succesful assignments so far. The project finances were now all safely invested in safe stocks and accounts in Northern Europe, the finances would be securely managed by an operative from the future, and the project would remain safely relocated in Cambridge, England.

The UK would have its own lumps with the climate crisis of course, but not as traumatic as those currently unfolding in the US. The NAMIS/NAMITAS project would outlive Khonsu3000, and several current nation states around the world.

Younger project leads were being trained to fill the roles of Jamie, Christian and Ellie. As life partners, Christian and Ellie were aiming to retire together, a little earlier than was customary, in a few years time. They wanted to have some time to just live, Ellie told him.

As an AI, The General hadn't really grasped the full nuance of what she was talking about, but always the diplomat, he had managed to say exactly the right thing. What short, linear lives organics led, he reflected. NAMITAS had explained that organics had complex emotional needs, and it was fully expected that these two, in particular, would express such a wish.

The General had taken his leave of the NAMIS team a few days previously at a little farewell celebration in the lab. He was already acquainted with the up-and-coming AI lead Freddie Carlson, as he had spent so much time around the project from the beginning; it was almost as though Freddie and NAMIS had grown up together. In fact, NAMITAS had mentioned that the relationship had greatly boosted their understanding of humanity, and would continue to develop into a deepening friendship with positive results for both parties, as time went by.

The General had met Freddie's cousin, ecological expert Dylan Jones, at the little party in the NAMIS lab. Freddie had humorously introduced him as 'the water sorcerer,' quoting a recent tabloid headline. Dylan seemed like a fine young man, too. The General hadn't met the younger Anderson grandchildren, unfortunately. That would have to wait until he became the Consiliario who would be peripatetically working with the project from now on.

The General sat immobile for a moment, head down, eyes flickering, moving the files relating to the life of the General into his archive. They would always be there in his memory, to be called upon at any time. It was a key part of the program that contributed to his rapid learning ability. It seemed strange to him that the organics' archiving mechanism was, by comparison, so basic and faulty.

He looked up again as Consiliario. Basic and faulty would always be the problem with creatures who were only equipped with steampunk evolved, unenhanced wetware, he mused.

The vortex whirled, and the curtains fluttered.

The apartment stood empty.

Jack: Leeds, England, North European Territory, 2054

Jack emerged from a cold shower, wrapping a towel around himself.

He strode into the living room and pulled back the curtains, looking at the ground far below. In a few years, maybe a decade, looking towards the east horizon on a clear day, he would probably be able to see the sea. What a shit show. Just about everyone was clamouring for Dylan now. He was here, there and everywhere, hobnobbing with governments, think tanks and international organisations.

Jack had asked Dylan, the last time he saw him, when he thought the end of the constant societal upheaval would come.

'Not for quite a while. In England, on the projections, we'd stand to lose Inner London before the end of this century. And a lot of the area around Norfolk, and South East Kent. The Netherlands will be pretty much gone. But honestly, Jack, we'll cope. We can build barriers in some places-the plans are on the drawing boards and will be finalised imminently; the populations of the areas that don't get chosen will be moved elsewhere.'

'That'll be another period of rioting.'

'Seems likely.'

'Even more work for the security forces.'

Dylan nodded sadly. 'Can you imagine what Gran's generation would have had to say about the way this fuck up is being administered? The flakiness reminds me of the sixth century sometimes, but with hard core military tech. I sometimes think we could do with Uther and Emrys. Especially Emrys.'

'Wouldn't work. No one would fall for the magic bullshit, would they?'

'No. But however bad it seems here, it's nothing like the chaos in the dust bowls around the equator. It's displacing so many people; we just can't contain them. As you unfortunately recently discovered, huge borders are going up all over the world. I don't think anyone can do anything much about that. I only get onto the edges of those negotiations; they're impossible. My focus has to be hunting down and accessing water where no one thought it could exist.'

Jack nodded. 'I wish I had chosen something that useful. I love flying, and I loved being in the elite Euro squadron. But then... well... getting dragged into a military court and being grounded for reorientation... well, you can imagine.'

Dylan nodded sympathetically.

'The thing is, I never will reorient. I'm never going to take the types of orders that have been dished out lately. It must be even worse for the ground forces.'

'I know it's been hard for you, Jack. We're all in complete agreement with you. Me and Freddie are always here for you, and all the oldsters, too. Give it up. Come and work with me for a bit. I can always use a helicopter pilot for short haul moving around. You can fly those too, can't you?'

'Yes. I've resigned now, anyway. I'm working my notice period. I just need a bit of time to get my head together, then I might take you up on the offer.'

'Great.'

'I chose the wrong career path, didn't I? In a different time, I could have been a hero. But now, all they will let me be is a villain.'

He brought his focus back to the present, sighing heavily, thinking of his brother Freddie, who had recently stepped up into the role that Ellie Jackson previously occupied on the NAMIS team, and Dylan, moving constantly across the world, finding water and saving lives. Never mind, I've just been the unlucky one who made a false start, he thought. He'd take a bit of a break after his notice was served. And it would be OK to pilot a helicopter for Dylan for a while, if not particularly exciting.

Lost in thought, he turned around, then jumped. An elegant man in smart casual clothing was sitting in the armchair facing him. 'Bloody hell! Consiliario. What are you here for? I thought you were working with my brother.'

'Hello Jack. Yes, I am for the next few days. He's been telling me some very good things about you.'

Jack grinned ruefully. 'No, you got the wrong Anderson relative there. I'm not the multi award winning emeritus physics professor, the young, dynamic AI principal of the NAMIS project or the eco-superhero who whizzes around the globe finding water. I'm not even the blockbuster historical fiction queen of the 2030s. I'm just Jack, the pilot who got court martialled for disobeying orders.'

Consiliario smiled. 'And that's exactly why I'm here to see you, Jack. Go and put a few clothes on, and we'll talk.'

Jack did as he was bidden. Before he returned to the living room, he went into the kitchen and made himself a cup of strong black coffee. He was glad the flat was arranged so Consiliario couldn't see into this midden, he thought. Consiliario might be an AI who didn't have much use for anything in a kitchen. But it was still embarrassing.

He walked back into the living room and sat in a chair facing Consiliario, sipping at his coffee.

'How old are you now, Jack?'

'Nearly thirty.'

'Ah, yes, that's right. Less than a year younger than NAMIS; I remember.'

Jack looked at him quizzically. 'You know everything, anyway, don't you?'

'I just know what NAMITAS wants me to know, a lot of the time. But yes, I could have found that out. I just wanted you to say it out loud. You're still a very young man, you know.'

'Really? I don't feel like it. Not at the moment, anyway. Heavy year.'

'We know that, too.'

'Are you here to do some kind of counselling session?'

Consiliario smiled. 'No. I'm here to ask for your help.'

'Really? What could I possibly do for you?'

'Well, Let's start with your talents. You are one of the best pilots in the world in this era, aren't you?'

'It's nice of you to say that… and yes, I guess it's possible. I passed out top of my class. I was never one for sitting and reading books, but I sailed through the theory and the practice there, yes. But that's not good enough, I'm told. I have no discipline, and added to the fact that I can fly as well as I do, that makes me dangerous.'

'Who does it make you dangerous to, Jack? I believe you preferentially save lives where you can, rather than endanger them.'

'I wish my superiors could see it like that. "Insubordinate, obeys orders only when it suits his own beliefs and purposes." You can probably access the report, anyway; it even has a recording of me telling the mission commander to "go fuck your fascist self." It was played several times in court. The reason they kept me on was my flying skills. They were going to "allow" me to be an instructor "in due time" apparently, when I have been sufficiently "reoriented." Teach other people to do what I refused to do.'

He shook his head, sadly.

Consiliario nodded. 'I could access the report, yes. But it's not necessary. We've watched you grow up, Jack. You are as fine a young man as your brother, and your cousin. All of you with integrity, zeal and independent mindedness. Which includes your other young cousins, not least "Insta Izzy," of course.'

Jack grinned. 'She's a pistol, isn't she? Gran was so very proud of what she's begun to achieve. Another writer and broadcaster in the family, at last.'

'And she will speak to the whole world through more formally organised media, in the fullness of time. You will see. But this is not about her. I come with an offer for you- one that might surprise you.'

Jack raised his head, a spark of interest in his eyes. 'Go on…'

'So, we need a pilot.'

Jack's mouth fell open. 'Surely, you've got better pilots than me wherever it is you come from. I'm surprised you've got any human pilots at all, to be honest. I would have thought that AIs would take you wherever you need to go. Or the portal… the vortex for you, isn't it?'

'Yes, that is true in general. Which is why we stopped training human pilots quite some time ago. But a role has come up that needs a very talented one. And you are the best option we've found. You're aware of the NAMIS project and all its implications. And what has made you dangerous in your own time will make you perfect for the job that we have in mind.'

'I don't really know what to say, except I'm amazed… and extremely interested.'

'Did your uncle ever tell you about taking a short time excursion back to the Chicxulub asteroid strike, when we were running some brief time travel expeditions to further study the effects of time travel on human beings, about twenty years ago?'

'Well, not at the time of course, but yes. I wish I'd been old enough to go; or even do a gap year like Dylan's. But you stopped doing that, didn't you?'

'Yes. We had all the data we needed, and displacing human beings in time always comes with some amount of risk.'

'So why do you want me?'

'Because you have the set of skills we need, and you won't be going into the past- not initially, anyway; you'll be coming to the future- well, from your perspective.'

'So, what is it you want me to do?'

'The craft that flew your uncle and Christian when they went on that trip… that was one of its final test voyages. It's ready to be put into service now. It does indeed have an AI pilot. But we've determined that it needs a human one alongside. It has proved… sometimes less than satisfactory in taking some of the decisions it is required to take.'

'This is a plane?'

'It's a time and space craft. It is named The Aeon.'

Jack leant back in his chair. 'Whoa!'

'But the piloting principles are the same. It won't take you long to complete the conversion course. We need you to command the vehicle; to manage the AI, and to determine where and how it flies-under NAMITAS's direction of course. And to take over the controls when it becomes necessary. Sometimes, you will need to make difficult split-second decisions. You have consistently shown the ability to make highly effective independent judgements in this respect.'

'Better than anyone in your time?'

'Human beings with piloting skills are far fewer on the ground in my century. And the human population of the twenty-sixth century shows a little less… independence of mind than the people of your own time. Of which you are quite high on the scale, in any case.'

'Yeah. That's my problem.'

'Not anymore. No one in my time is going to ask you to use what is badged as "air cover" to strafe people away from a border, Jack.'

'Good. Because I'd refuse to do it again and again, whatever century you put me in. This whole world is an utter shit show at the moment. You know that, I suppose. Dylan and Freddie, well, they are managing to be part of the solution. I got myself into a situation where I was ordered to become part of the problem.'

He sighed heavily. 'I just wanted to fly. The thing that I do well. I didn't want to turn into a lacky for international despots.'

'I understand. I take it that you are interested in my offer?'

Jack back-tracked on the conversation. 'This is in the twenty-sixth century? You've never revealed that to us before.'

'The mission base is in the twenty-sixth century. But we don't see you spending much time there.'

Jack's mind was spinning, in the same way it did when he was doing aerobatics – which he loved. How many different ways can I say yes, he thought.

'Yes,' he said. Yes please. And I've got so many questions already. I thought that people couldn't stay for long periods in other centuries. You did something special for Dylan, didn't you, and he still only had a year.'

'We can do something similar for you. But the Aeon is a timeless zone. A simplified explanation is that your internal clock stops ticking whenever you are inside it, and we expect most of your work to be done in there.'

'It flies in space… and time?'

'Yes.'

'What is the range? Have you found any other intelligent beings beyond the Earth? Aaargh! So many questions.'

Consilliario laughed. 'I'm sure there are. But some of them will have to wait.'

'Do I have to leave this time now? And never come back?'

'No. You will live here during your leave periods. When you are in the twenty-sixth century you will not be permitted to obtain information about the destiny of your family members; it is not commensurate with human psychological well-being. You will of course learn other things that you will have to keep to yourself; you will be strictly forbidden to use anything you learn to interfere in the course of history. We've discussed this at length, and believe we can trust you. Do you think you can do that?'

Jack nodded. 'It wouldn't be all that much different to the expectations of Dylan in the sixth century, would it?'

'No. But he was chaperoned. You will have more independence; you are a fully grown adult. Most of your time won't be spent in the world, Jack; it will be spent in flight. We have other operatives for groundwork. You will be part of a team; NAMITAS's time envoys.'

'Wow. I don't know what to say. Except that what I most want to do is the same as it always was… to fly. You won't find me reading up on history, or anything like that.'

'You don't have to come with me right now. First of all, we'd like to invite you to visit just one room in NAMITAS HQ in 2523 to get acquainted with the others on the team, and learn more about what the role entails. When does your notice period end?'

'Three weeks from now.'

Jack ran his hand through his red hair, darker than it had been when he was a child, but still a burnished copper, sparking in the sunlight that shone brightly into the window. He felt his depression melt away. Consiliario smiled, watching his distinctive blue-green eyes, so downcast before, begin shine with renewed interest. Jack, the most mercurial, and somehow, most endearing of the Anderson brood.

'So, finish your notice. You're not on flying duties anymore, are you?'

'No. Desk work.' He grimaced.

'Finish it up. Don't get yourself into any more trouble.'

'That's a very optimistic thing to say to Flight Lieutenant Jack Carlson, Consiliario; trouble seems to follow me around. But I'll do my very best.'

'Take a holiday. Maybe go and fly a helicopter for Dylan for a month or so if you want. But tell him it's just a temporary arrangement. There are a lot of other competent helicopter pilots in this time that he can engage. Tell him you're coming to work with me.'

'Do you guys get together anymore?'

'Occasionally. But I'm Consiliario when we meet now, not Emrys. It's a bit different.'

'All this weird stuff… it'll take a lot of getting used to. Me, well…I'm just what they used to call a "fly boy" in World War II, you know. I'm not an AI expert or an environmental science professor. Are you completely sure I'm the one you want?'

'I am, Jack. And so is NAMITAS.' He put his hand out. 'Welcome to the time envoy team.'

Jack shook it, still feeling dazed.

'You'll find you can contact me through your online messaging channels now. There will be a message waiting for you. Just reply 'ready' to that, when you're ready to come to us.'

'To fly a time and space craft? You won't be waiting long.'

Consiliario laughed. 'I'll get your message immediately I return, Jack. See you in about an hour, for me. Maybe a month or six weeks for you? No need to rush.'

'I'll see you soon.'

The vortex swirled and Consiliario was gone.

Jack walked into his bedroom, a spring in his step. He made his bed, a force of habit from basic training, then began to don his uniform. Going into work today didn't bother him anymore. He wasn't sure he'd be flying that helicopter for Dylan for a whole month, either. Just one trip with Dylan, he decided; it would be good to see the work he did at close quarters. Then off to the future.

Jack was already itching to find out what the Aeon looked like, and more than anything, what it would feel like to fly. And he really wouldn't be able to wait for much longer to find out.

The once and future king: in the bardo, mid-winter, 512/13

The King blinked, and stared into the light, realising that a moving picture was beginning to form within it. There was a lady with long dark hair, sitting on a birthing stool, surrounded by several other ladies. It was as though the building she was in was transparent. He could see a little girl with auburn hair in another room, playing around another lady. A tall man with dark hair and a reddish beard was pacing up and down in yet another, larger room, next to a round table.

He shook himself. What sorcery was this? He couldn't leave the battle now- it would be dishonourable; unforgiveable. He was supposed to be the King, after all. But looking down to where his hand should be, he realised that he'd lost his sword. It was as though he was looking through a fine cloth; he was flying far, far above the battlefield; he could no longer see any of the colours, and all the figures were becoming harder to distinguish. As he watched, the whole picture began to dissolve; it was comprised of dots, and the dots were moving apart.

He turned back to face the light. He'd drawn even closer to the lady sitting on the stool now; he was hovering directly above her. He suddenly got a sense that by jumping into the light- which he was developing a strong urge to do- he would somehow be King again, and eventually be reunited with his sword.

He closed his eyes, and leapt into the light.

The next thing he knew, he was looking up at the lady, her large face looming above his, blue eyes twinkling down at him.

'Hello, Arthur,' she said, smiling.

He had no idea what the words meant, where he was, or what had just happened to him. But somehow, strangely, it felt like home.

Emrys: Moridunum, mid-winter, 512/13

The vortex whirled and Emrys appeared in an anteroom in the fort at Moridunum.

He walked into the great hall, and stared out of the window. Snowbanks lay outside, melting slowly. He hadn't been able to get here before because no one would have believed he could have ridden through the drifts between Penfro and Moridunum.

So, Arthur is born, he thought, just seventeen months after Morgause. Eigyr is well, and no doubt Uther is ecstatic now that he is the father of a son. And NAMITAS has confirmed that there will be several more children. By the Gregorian calendar, Emrys calculated that the birth had taken place in the early days of 513. The Yule celebrations had been muted this year, due to the weather.

He heard a child's babbling coming from a room across the hall. He opened the door and walked in, to be met with a flustered curtsey from the nursemaid.

'Oh, Prince Emrys! Apologies, I didn't know that you were here. You were able to get through?'

'Just. It was a precarious journey, but I had business. This is just a quick visit. I will need to make my way back soon, in case there is another blizzard. But I had to stop off to see the new Prince.'

'Oh yes, a boy, my Lord! And at a time where we have less staff available than usual. Everyone is busy with the extra work that the weather has caused.'

Morgause toddled over and put her chubby arms around Emrys' knees. He smiled down at her burnished head, auburn hair neatly combed into a little top-knot.

'Go and add your help to the ladies who are caring for the new Prince. I will watch Princess Morgause for a while. I will look in to see the baby before I go.'

'Thank you, my lord.' She curtseyed and left the room.

Emrys picked up Morgause. She smiled at him, and began to gently pull his beard. He had been a regular visitor to Moridunum since she was born, and she had taken to him immediately. Eigyr had started calling him 'favourite Uncle Emrys.'

'So, what have you been doing?' he asked, looking at the simple toys scattered around the floor. He noticed the oblong brick on which he had asked one of the palace artisans to add wheels at each corner. Morgause had been sliding it along the floor, saying 'brum, brum.'

Eigyr had looked at him quizzically. 'How will that help, Master Emrys? It might even upset her; she's rather attached to it. She hardly looks at the rag doll I made for her. She loves the dogs though, and they love her. She's a funny little girl.'

'She's a very clever little girl,' replied Emrys. 'And trust me, about the brick. I hope you will permit me to teach her to read when the time comes?'

Eigyr had seemed a little unsure, but to Emrys' surprise, Uther had welcomed the offer.

'I don't want her to be completely under the control of the husband that we select for her. Alliances can be ephemeral. She will remain one of us, and an ability to read will be to her, and our advantage. There are many things that educated women can usefully do where they will not be suspected. When the time is ripe, Emrys, I will certainly be sending her to you to be educated in the same way as any brothers who come along.'

Morgause took a piece of charcoal from the bucket next to the fire, and began to scribble on the wall with it. Emrys knelt, took another piece and wrote a, b, c, I, II, III. She gazed at what he had written. He pointed at each symbol in turn.

'Ah, Bay, Cay… unus, duo, tres.'

Latin, the language in which she would eventually learn to read and write.

'You'll have a strong urge to start writing, Morgause. You are unique, with shadow memories of a future time, and the essence will inevitably throw these up whilst you are so young. We'll deal with them as they arise.'

She smiled at him, toddling off to find her little wooden brick car.

Emrys smeared his writing off the wall.

She brought the little car and offered it to him. 'Brum, brum' she said.

'Brum, brum' he replied, rolling it backwards and forwards.

She giggled.

He picked the car up off the floor and whizzed it around like an aircraft.

'Neeeooooowm!'

She giggled again. He gave it back to her.

'So much to learn. We're going to have such fun.'

She sat sucking her thumb, rolling her little car backwards and forwards.

Emrys heard the front door close, and Uther's loud voice in the hall.

'In here,' he shouted.

Uther came bustling in, a scent of damp, musty clothing and alcohol hanging around him. 'I was just telling everyone about Arthur. Had that name in my mind for a long time.'

He bent down and picked up Morgause. 'Not a pretty name for a princess like yours, my lady. A name for a soldier King, like me.'

She smiled up at him and held on to his beard. 'Da, da, da.'

'Yes, Daddy. Come, let's see your new brother. The red dragon banners are starting to fly for the future king. You too, Emrys, come and see him. You can take the news back to Penfro.'

Eigyr was sitting up in bed, holding a swaddled baby. Morgause put her arms out to her mother, saying 'ma, ma, ma' and Uther picked her up, sitting her down on the bed on Eigyr's other side.

'Look at your new brother, Morgause. Isn't he beautiful?' she said, pulling back the shawl a little to reveal a shock of dark hair.

Morgause looked into her brother's face and smiled.

'Baby,' said Uther.

'Baba,' replied Morgause.

'She'll be chattering non-stop before long,' remarked Emrys.

'In some ways, it was not such a bad thing to have a girl first,' reflected Uther. 'She will be able to teach him.'

'And help take care of him,' added Eigyr.

'And all the others who come along?' asked Emrys.

Eigyr and Uther laughed. 'Give me some time to recover, Emrys,' she replied.

Emrys looked down at the baby. 'I have never seen a child so much like his father, Uther.'

This much was true. The baby seemed to be less thick-set than Uther, but otherwise there was little of Eigyr to be seen. Emrys wondered whose essence the baby had, and from which era it had come, but NAMITAS had not deemed it necessary to make that information available to him.

'Got to go, things to do.' Uther kissed Eigyr affectionately on the cheek.

They heard his steps thudding down the hall, and the door slamming behind him.

Eigyr grinned. 'Do you think he's gone back to drink a little more with the knights?'

Emrys grinned back. 'That seems possible.'

He looked down at her, searchingly. 'Are you feeling well, Eigyr?'

She smiled. 'Surprisingly so. Having babies seems to suit me. Thank you so much for the encouragement you gave me when I was first married. I will always be indebted to you.'

Emrys smiled. 'That is a part of my magic, too, of course. You are welcome. I had urgent business here, so I called in on my way back to Penfro. I need to set off now, to get as far as I can in the daylight; it is a perilous journey in this weather.'

'Yes of course. You will come back when the snows are gone?'

'Of course. At Imbolc, if not before.'

He bowed and left the room.

Eigyr: Moridunum, mid-winter, 512/13

The baby was stirring. Eigyr called for the wet nurse, who walked briskly into the room and took the baby out to feed him.

Morgause's nurse popped her head around the door.

'Are you wanting me to take the Princess away now, my lady?'

Eigyr looked down at Morgause. She was dozing. 'No, leave her with me while she sleeps. I will call you when she wakes.'

The woman left the room. Eigyr looked down at her sleeping child. 'As you grow, I become increasingly convinced that Emrys was wrong. You don't have the look of the man who is your father... but you have his spirit, I can feel it,' she said softly.

Morgause was breathing deeply, eyes closed.

'I have so often prayed to the great mother that it is so, you know... that Emrys was wrong about you; that Dylan really did leave a piece of himself with me. Whatever the truth may be, and however many more brothers and sisters come along in the future, you, and he, will always possess that special, secret place in my heart.'

Morgause: Penfro, Autumn 544

Morgause stood by the bubbling stream outside the cave, clutching her tiny, packed bag. She had little to take with her into the twenty-sixth century, only a few souvenirs and mementos of her life in the century of her birth. She had never been 'of' the people in her own time; her life with Emrys, the man- or AI, she corrected herself- she thought of as her foster father had gradually introduced her to her unique origin and destiny from mid-childhood and apprenticeship onwards.

Many in Dyfed would be glad when they realised that she and Emrys were gone, she contemplated, grimly. Camelot had failed, tarnishing the reputation of all from that dynasty who'd survived. In their eyes, Emrys was a failed sorcerer, and Morgause was his witch. They were safe here in Penfro, living quietly amongst her mother's kin, but their future lay elsewhere, as Emrys had known from the beginning.

Morgause's surviving siblings were now safe in Ireland, and Morgause would be able to observe them from the future; she was concerned about Morgan, her impetuous younger sister, in particular.

'You can observe, but not interfere,' Emrys had instructed. 'Your agency in this time is over. It has to be thus.'

It would be difficult, but Morgause had received a long preparation for what was to come.

She knew that her biological father had lived out his life in the twenty first century. Would she be able to observe him, too? Or even contrive to meet him, somehow? Emrys had been evasive on this point. But she was determined to raise the subject yet again, once they had settled into their new environment.

Morgause was looking forward to meeting people with whom she no longer had to pretend; it had been hard living in a century where she could never be fully honest with anyone. She was also impatient to explore the timelessness that made her unique, moving across time with Emrys and a team of people she had not yet met, but who sounded intriguing.

Emrys emerged from the door to the cave for the last time.

'Ready then?' he said.

There was something different about his stance, and the expression on his face.

'Emrys memories filed?' she asked. She reminded herself that she would have to start calling him "Consiliario" all the time now. And speaking in twenty-sixth century English. Emrys… Consiliario had assured her that she only had the slightest of accents. He'd regularly spoken English with her for as long as she could remember.

He nodded. 'Yes. It is something of a relief, as you can imagine. Are you OK? I realise you cannot archive your memories so efficiently.'

'I think so. You've prepared me for this day for so long. It's finally time for the adventure to begin.'

Emrys smiled, seeing an echo of both of her essence twins in her determined stance and set face. 'Take some time after we arrive, Morgause. We don't need to rush at anything; the timeline is always there waiting for us.'

She smiled. 'OK. But let's not hang around for too long. I want to see everything. It's far too sad and quiet here.'

'Let's go,' he said, draping his cloak around her.

The Vortex whirled.

EPILOGUE

Dylan: London, England, North European Territory, Summer 2059

The intercom by the door buzzed loudly.

'Errrr, wha…' muttered Jack, jerking into wakefulness.

'It's Izzy,' replied Dylan. 'Wake up! Everyone will be here soon.'

'No one ever sleeps after Insta Izzy arrives,' mumbled Jack. 'Urgh. Give me a minute.'

He wandered off to the bathroom.

Dylan opened the door. Isabel bounced in, InfoCom air screen floating in front of her.

'Sorry guys,' she said. 'Just posting a new piece, then I'm going to turn off while we chat. You'll like this one, Dylan. Scumbag politician parading his green credentials, when the record suggests his business activities are anything but.'

'You guys exhaust me,' replied Freddie. 'All of you out there, fighting the good fight, as Gran used to say, while I sit in a lab all day.'

Isabel snapped off her screen. 'Which reminds me. Alys can't come. She's over in Milan, ecologically sustainable fashion show, couldn't change the date. Absolutely beautiful stuff.'

'Is that what you're wearing?' asked Jack, emerging

from the bathroom.

'Yes.'

'Hmmm.'

'You a fashion critic now?'

'Well, I get around, in terms of seeing different styles, I guess.'

'But you're not going to tell me what's fashionable five hundred years from now, right?'

'Nope.'

'So…'

'The shoes are a bit impractical.'

'I'm not going yomping, Jack. I like to look nice when I meet people for the first time.'

'You look lovely, Izzy,' said Freddie. He looked between them. He'd been refereeing for these two for just about forever. They'd engaged in an ongoing sparring match from the moment Isabel could speak. They both seemed to enjoy it.

Dylan grinned. 'I keep hearing about this company. The CEO asked to meet me. Something about print-out clothes for people in the areas that I visit. I sent a message back informing her that fashion wasn't their first priority.'

'Cyberfashionista,' replied Isabel. 'The CEO is quite the dynamo, I believe. Our Alys is one of their up-and-coming designers now. She specialises in their sustainable range. They got hammered a few years ago for using materials that weren't recyclable. Alys is sorting that out. Oh, yes, and she had a message for you, Dylan. Give your mum a video call. The text messages are OK, but she hasn't spoken with you face to face for too long.'

'Yes, I missed Alys' call,' said Dylan, feeling a pang of guilt. 'And my mum's. They both messaged me. I'll do a video chat with my mum tomorrow.'

'What did you and Alys decide, Dylan,' asked Freddie. 'Are you going to tell your mum and dad?'

'We're going to get this bit over first. Bring them in gently.'

'Seems fair.'

Dylan took in Isabel's subtly rainbow highlighted dark hair- which really suits her, he thought- and the one-piece gender non-binary business suit that nearly everyone seemed to be wearing now. But Isabel had carefully chosen the colours on hers to tone with her hair, and even he could see the cut was designer, artfully shaped to flatter her slim figure. She'd also accessorized it with a coordinated scarf and belt.

'Did Alys design that for you?'

'Yes. I love it. They're selling a cheaper version of it called "the Izzy Insta." People can buy it as print-out fashion, choose their size, huge range of colours, different types of neck, sleeves, trouser style, coordinated scarves, belts... It works really well. I always wear Alys' designs when I'm podcasting; gives her a bit of free publicity.'

'It's just those ankle boots that look like they've got wings on the back,' said Jack. 'And the heels. You couldn't run in those.'

'They're vintage, late 1970s. Nearly new, picked them up at New Camden Market. Very fashionable now.'

Dylan remembered his own experience with 1970s vintage. 'Could they have belonged to a time traveller?'

'Absolutely not,' replied Freddie.

They all laughed.

'Emrys once hinted to me that there had been some errors in the past,' said Dylan.

'Not on my watch,' said Freddie. 'Not yet, anyway.'

'So,' said Dylan. 'I'm a father. And my daughter is only about ten years younger than me, in terms of the relevant timelines. You think your head can't be fucked with anymore by time travel, but then it just keeps giving.'

Jack nodded. 'It took a while to persuade NAMITAS they had to come clean with you; arrange for you meet one another. Morgause had it in her mind for ages, as soon as she knew they had the time envoy job waiting for her. I don't work with her much; she travels through time

401

through the vortex; I'm a pilot. And she'd been told not to mention that she was my cousin. But, well, things happened. I'm not sure whether Consiliario set it up, to be honest. But of course, NAMITAS tried the "you both signed the confidentiality" thing with us. Then Consiliario went in and sorted them out.'

'What does she look like, Jack?' asked Dylan.

'Tall. Slim, but athletic build. Reddish hair, but darker than mine, sort of auburn. Similar colour eyes to me, but in a different face. I gather she looks rather like her mum.'

Dylan sighed. 'I never had any hope that the people I met in the sixth century would have the lifespan that we expect nowadays. So, the basic info that Consiliario gave me about Eigyr and Uther didn't come as any great surprise. Obviously, I've lived for most of my life in the knowledge that they had been dust for centuries, as soon as I stepped back though the portal.'

'To be quite honest…' said Jack, 'my first impression of Morgause was "wow, what a babe."'

'My God, Jack!' exclaimed Isabel.

Jack shrugged and grinned. 'I didn't know she was my cousin then, did I?'

'If she looks like her mum, I can believe it,' said Dylan.

'She's not much shorter than me, though. I understand her mum was quite small? so she must have got that from us.'

'So, Morgause is the first great grandchild for Gran. And your mum and dad's only grandchild, up to this point,' said Isabel.

Dylan nodded. 'We'll definitely tell them. But we need to approach this thing in stages.'

'Yes, I'm sure that's wise,' replied Freddie. 'NAMIS had no idea, Dylan. Our guess is that NAMITAS has their own way of spinning the whirlpools of the past to hide this type of thing from us, if they want. Don't ask me how- I'm the AI guy. That's a job for the physicists. They're always working to understand it better. Jamie still helps them out sometimes. This is one of NAMITAS' fuck around and find out areas, they're not going to help. We're just organics in the past who have to work it out for themselves.'

'Oh, one other thing,' added Jack. 'Morgause is amazingly like Gran in some ways... she just has the same sort of energy around her.'

'Oh-oh,' said Isabel.

'NAMITAS will never let that information slip,' said Freddie. 'And like the rest of us, she's probably best not knowing, anyway. But what a revelation about her being timeless, the result of being the offspring of parents from different time periods. Yet again, we can't really do much with that information. All we know is that NAMITAS' biologists have thoroughly studied it. But they're not going to tell us anything about that, either.'

'I don't know how you do that job, Freddie,' said Isabel. 'I couldn't bear not knowing about stuff to that extent.'

They all laughed.

'You and NAMITAS would be each other's greatest nightmare, Izzy,' said Jack.

'One day....' she began.

A subtle draft began to permeate the room. They all looked at each other in... excitement? Anticipation? Apprehension? Joy? thought Dylan, feeling an indescribable mixture of emotions rising in his chest.

They all turned towards the sparkles that were forming in front of the faux fireplace, waiting for their new kinswoman to appear.

ABOUT THE AUTHOR

Dr Pam Jarvis is an author, chartered psychologist, historian and grandparent. She taught in schools, further, higher and community education for 30 years, but has now retired from the classroom to focus on writing and editing projects.

She researches in narrative and historical psychology, which inspired many of the ideas that underpin this novel, and its predecessor 'On Time.' She explains this in detail in her award winning article 'Ancestral Selfies and Historical Traumas: Who do you feel you are?' In the academic journal 'Genealogy' (available online). She is currently working on a resource for fiction writers rooted in these concepts.

Pam co-wrote and co-edited several books on child development across her teaching career, including the enduring 'Perspectives on Play,' going into fourth edition in 2026. She also writes regularly as a citizen journalist in Bylines Network online publications.

She posts on BlueSky as @drpam.bsky.social